Unta

The Return of Jake Charm

For the Warren, Thank you, Matt Kreutz

By Matt Kreutz

Table of Contents

Author's Note

While the story in this book takes place in an actual small town of America, involving people, companies, businesses and events that may seem familiar, it is only a work of fiction. Any similarity to actual people, companies, or events from the real world is entirely coincidental.

In 1995, after Tim McVeigh and company blew up the Alfred P. Murrah Building in Oklahoma City, killing 168 men, women and children, I started researching Tim McVeigh. He grew up around the corner from me, went to the same school as I did and rode my bus for a while. Even though he was a few years older, we had a lot in common, mostly having to do with the fact that the years of our youth were spent at the same school being taught by the same fantastic teachers.

After the bombing in 1995, I went to our former teachers and friends that we had in common and took down story after story, all of which were filled with disbelief. Finding the origins of Tim McVeigh's madness in peaceful little Pendleton, NY was not going to happen. He was a student that teachers liked and a person about whom I could find no one who had anything bad to say. Knowing that no one wants to read a story about how a mass murderer led a normal childhood and was delightful, I set my notes aside and spent the next twenty-five years of my life looking for more clues in hopes of understanding all the things about the OKC bombing that didn't make sense. I discovered there are many who have vested interests in making sure I *never* understand the truth – that's the reason they put McVeigh to death so quickly. When was the last time someone on death row was put down only six years after the crime?

So, while this fast-paced fictional crime-thriller isn't about Tim McVeigh, it's about how the acted-upon venomous anger of one man from a small town can haunt those whom the mad man leaves behind for decades to come.

Again, this story is fiction. It is not intended to create sympathy for Tim McVeigh. I have no sympathy for Tim McVeigh or any of his fellow conspirators, including those who seek to kill the truth by any means necessary.

Please enjoy this book and thank you for reading.

Matt Kreutz

Chapter 1

On the last evening of my yearly one or two-day vacation from my life, I was closing up the family bar near last call. It hadn't always been a bar. Used to be a restaurant, until my twin brother took it over after Dad died. Mother was riddled with arthritis and a love for the sauce, so my brother Cash took over.

Cash and I were always close, but we were different. Looked exactly the same, but we were different. Even so, once a year, about six months after our birthday, we'd switch lives for a day or two. I'd play him, and he'd play me. A vacation away from life. It might sound stupid, but identical twins have been doing this since the beginning of man. Part of being in the club. Some secrets aren't for people without a twin, and this is one of them.

For my brother and me, it started out as a competition. As kids, we'd have five bucks that said, "You're the one that gets caught first." True to his name, Cash always claimed money talks. But those particular five bucks always stayed in our pockets. We never got caught. Our secret was never revealed. A part of me always wanted him to mess up though. Think about all the stories he and I could share if we'd finally ever gotten caught. Dad would've loved them. While it might have made mom sip her drink a little quicker, we'd have had dad cracking up for hours. Unfortunately, we never got to see that and still have to play this stupid game.

When I got married, it became kind of tricky at times, especially since the girl I married was the girl he dated most of the time I was in college. During those years, he was home taking care of the family restaurant that he'd later turn into a bar. They were broken up for a while before she and I started dating, but it was still a tricky thing. I trusted him though, more than anyone on the earth. He was my twin, and, until I'd gone off to college, we were inseparable.

This particular year's switched-lives vacation came six months after our thirty-eighth birthday. It was the beginning of 2011. Now, over the years, there was very often one of us who wanted to blow it off for one reason or another, but the other of us would always talk us out of it. Never missed a year. A point of pride. No matter what, we had to play this stupid game.

This year though, he was really insistent that we skip it, more so than ever. He wouldn't tell me why, so I put my foot down. No-the-freak-way was I giving up a chance to spend a couple of nights away from my wife Callie. I didn't care that he used to date her. I was sick of her coldness and was miserable in our marriage. We hadn't slept together in over a year, so I didn't worry a bit about his sharing the bed with her. She'd become so cold I probably should have left him an electric blanket. I'd actually met with a divorce lawyer but discovered divorce was too great a commitment to the giving up of all I'd worked for, so I decided to suffer – just not through my yearly vacation though. Maybe it *was* just half my stuff, as they say, but it's a lot more than that when you get right down to it. The lawyer never tells you that. Doesn't even put it in the fine print.

I loved being Cash, probably more than he did. He was always the favorite. I was the smart one academically. He was smart, but his grades weren't as good as mine. Probably would have been worse had I not helped him along and taken a few tests for him. But he was the hard worker. While I was studying, he was working in the restaurant, helping Dad keep the business afloat and developing his charismatic personality, which was needed to overcompensate for the personality of our mother. Her drunkenness was becoming more and more a problem.

So, it was nearing last call, and I was wiping down the bar when Jake Charm walked in. I hadn't seen Jake since high school. His last name was actually Chambliss, but everybody called him Jake Charm. I didn't like Jake Charm and was probably the only one who didn't, but he and Cash were tight. Cash was the quarterback. Jake and I were his wide receivers. It doesn't take a genius to figure out why Jake and I didn't get along, but I'll tell you anyway.

Cash was an amazing quarterback. Senior year, we lost only one game, and it was a game he had to sit out with a sprained ankle. He was magic when he threw the ball. A talent to behold. He could have played just about anywhere in the NCAA, but he didn't want to go to college. Just wanted to stay home and help our father. Me, I wanted to play in college. I was good, but I could have been a lot better – if I'd only gotten more of the throws. Cash liked throwing to Jake more though. I don't know why. He just did. I was just as good. Had I gotten more passes, I might've had some recruiters looking at me. It wasn't as if they weren't trying to talk Cash into leaving.

He'd say, "Check out Curt." That's me.

But they'd say, "No, it's you we want." The golden arm.

So, I didn't get to play in college. I could have tried to be a walk on, but I wanted to be wanted. I wanted them to be covering my college expenses. I was young and still a bit full of myself. Cash wasn't. He knew where he was needed, and he was completely humble enough to ask for nothing more than just to be needed, even though he was really wanted elsewhere. While I just wanted to be wanted, he was needed and wanted. Always the favorite.

Jake Charm, on the other hand, didn't need to be needed or wanted, but, like my brother, he was both and by everyone. He went into the Marines or the Army and was rumored to be Special Forces. That's the rumor anyway. He served in Iraq and then a whole bunch of other places that remain undisclosed, and then he disappeared. Word around the campfire was, he went AWOL, but no one really knew for sure and just about everyone was willing to forgive him. He'd served above and beyond, as far as anybody knew. His parents were gone and weren't able to update the record. So, if he had gone AWOL, there must have been an acceptable reason.

Nonetheless, I had to hide my dislike for him at the bar that night and remember I wasn't Curt Cutler. I was Cash Cutler, his actual friend. Now, I'm not a total jerk. I have my reasons for not liking the Pendleton, New York hero.

It was our last football game of senior year. It was the sectional championship game at Rich Stadium, the old name of the stadium where the Buffalo Bills play. With about a minute to go in the first half, we're up 14 to 10 against Olean High School. We're thirty-five yards from the end zone, and it's 3rd and four. I'm open and in the end zone with my arms up. Cash could have made the pass with his eyes closed. Instead, when Jake puts his arms up on the ten-yard line in three-man coverage, Cash throws it to him. With three men covering him and me completely open, he had no business looking for the ball. Cash threw it to him, it was intercepted, and the guy from Olean ran it back for a touchdown and the lead going into half.

I was pissed. Sure, I should have been pissed at my brother, but I took it out on Jake. As soon as Coach Sark left the locker room, I walked up to Jake, slammed his head up against the locker door and said, "What the hell's wrong with you? I was open in the end zone."

Sure, he could have just said, "Ask your brother," but he didn't. He punched me so hard my nose broke, and it was gushing blood. A circle had formed around us, but Cash came in to break us up. "Quit it now. We got to win this game, and I need you both."

He grabbed a towel and started wiping the blood off my lip, but, when he touched my nose, it hurt so badly I had to push him away. "I think my nose is broke."

"Suck it up, Nancy," Cash ordered, "No one's going to know about it 'til the game's over. You tell Coach, he's going to sit you both. I need you both. So, shut up."

He was right. I wanted to win the game just as much as he did, but I was hoping to shine. I knew there were a bunch of scouts there, and I wanted a call later. We got the blood to stop, but, for the whole second half, my game was shot. I couldn't run like normal. Every step was like getting punched in the face again. I got one pass, but Jake Charm got the rest. We *did* win the game, but I didn't have much at all to do with it. It was all Cash and Jake. Cash threw for nearly 400 yards and we won 35 to 20.

We never told the coach about our dustup, and eventually my nose stopped hurting. Maybe it wasn't broken. I don't know for sure, but that was my last game of football. Even though Jake and Cash were friends for the rest of the year, Jake and I barely spoke again.

Oh, by the way, even though Jake Charm could have had any girl in the school, even in the county for that matter, he dated Callie Olmstead for most of high school and maybe some of junior high. They were voted most likely to get married, have a bunch of kids and grow old together.

After Jake went off to war, the two people who missed him the most started dating — Cash, his quarterback, and Callie, his high school sweetheart. Cash probably would have stayed with her, but when he turned the restaurant into a bar after Dad died, he drank a little too much. He had his own bar, where he was the home-town hero serving up drinks to people always wanting to relive the good old days. She left him.

During that time period though, she used to occasionally call me at college and tell me all her problems. Maybe she thought I could help him, but I was at college and probably drinking just as much as my brother. What was I going to say? I promised more than once I'd have a talk with him. I did.

It'd start out, "Hey Cash, it's Curt."

"Thanks for telling me. I wasn't sure."

"Callie thinks you're drinking too much."

"I know that too."

"Okay, good," I'd say, and then we'd have a conversation like any of the millions we'd had growing up, sharing the giant attic that we turned into a two-man bedroom. We called it the barracks. It was an awesome place to grow up.

Jake Charm walked into my bar, and I hadn't seen him in about twenty years. I looked at him, and he looked at me. I didn't quite react though. See, I'd heard he was back in town, and while I hadn't yet seen him, that didn't mean Cash hadn't seen him. One of the things Cash and I learned from playing the stupid life-switch game is that people tell you everything you need to know if you just let them. Reacting too soon will cause you to make a mistake and lose your cover, but patience, masked as coolness, prevents you from making mistakes. Eventually, people will tell you everything you need to know. So, in addition to being a vacation from life, playing this game was also practice on how to go through life with the ability to know what to observe and how to interpret it.

He looked me in the eye a couple of times and then at the floor he was traversing. He'd come through the back door and had to veer around the pool table to get to the bar. There weren't that many people left in the bar. Pacho, the kitchen boy, had already gone. The kitchen was closed.

After swerving around the pool table and the row of tables that stood between it and the bar, he took off his green winter jacket, set it on an empty stool and then swung a leg over the center bar stool. He landed with the agility of a gymnast. It was nothing like I'd imagined, having heard all the stories about how he'd become some legendary Special Forces killer of America's enemies. No, he was smooth and agile like a ballet dancer and not all bulked up like I'd figured.

Even though it was winter, he was wearing a muscle shirt. He was ripped, but his muscles weren't huge. He was probably six-two and two hundred and five pounds. Just not a bit of fat on him. There were some tattoos on his arms, like a green military symbol and some others that seemed to have something to do with his service, but his forearms were more interesting. They were covered with orderly scar symbols. It wasn't like the random scars on a self-cutter. These scars were put there purposely, either with a knife or a brand.

I saw them and pretended not to notice, but he knew I had.

"What can I getcha?"

"Beer."

"What kind."

"Don't matter."

I gave him a Labatt's Blue after popping the top with my church key, as our dad used to call it. He took three swallows and set it down. "You Cash or Curt?" He hadn't yet seen Cash. Probably makes sense since Cash would've told me. The big question on my mind was whether he'd come back to reclaim my wife Callie. As part of me would be happy to give her back, no part of me would wish that curse upon anyone. She was no longer that sweet girl with which we'd all fallen in love.

"Which do you think?"

"You two haven't changed much, I see." He took two more casual swallows of his beer. "I think you should be Cash because you're in this bar, but something about you reminds me of Curt."

"What? You think I'm going to smash you upside the face?"

"Yeah, maybe." A big old smile broke out all over his face, and I couldn't help it — one broke out onto mine too. There went my cool. It wasn't the smile I had to give because I was pretending to be Cash. It was the smile I had for a kid whom I'd missed for a long time. At that moment, I realized I had thankfully grown out of holding onto my childish grudge.

10

I dried my hands on the white rag and walked around the bar to his side. I then picked him up in a bear hug and said, "Welcome home Jake. We missed you." I quickly realized I probably shouldn't have been speaking for my brother too, but it was too late.

He hugged me back, once I'd put him down, and said, "Yeah, I've missed you guys too." I knew he was talking about me and my brother. That's how it'd always been. We were one and the same to just about everyone but Jake Charm. Jake had apparently set that stuff from youth aside and seemingly forgiven me for attacking him at halftime way back when.

"How's your brother?"

"He's fine. He's good. The president of the bank. Pendleton Savings and Loan. PS and L."

"Pendleton's got a bank? What the heck's going on? I've been gone too long, brotha."

"You've been gone half your life, brother. Pendleton's actually got *two* banks. My brother's bank is in the middle of acquiring the other. What a can of worms that's become. He's miserable right now. Just miserable. The whole thing's a mess."

"I thought you said he was good."

"He is. He's just going through a tough time with this acquisition. He didn't even want it. The board of directors is making him do it, and it's getting a lot of pushback. Other than that, he's good." I realized I might have been saying too much about things Cash might not necessarily know. "You know he married Callie, right?"

"He married Callie? I thought for sure you'd have married her. You were together last I'd heard."

"We were, but I went and messed that all up. Once I'd opened this bar, it all went to hell. Drank too much and partied too much. Knowing Callie, you can figure out why she left me."

He smiled one of those fond-memory smiles, the kind that reminds you why we live. "Callie happy with Curt?"

"Yeah, I guess." Tough question. How do you answer that, knowing she wasn't but also knowing that Cash probably hadn't any idea of how unhappy she really was? Strategy. It's all a part of the game.

"Did you come back to reclaim Callie?"

"No, nah. I don't think so. It was just time," he said as if he wasn't quite sure why he was back. "Something was calling me back. Been a long time. Wanted to see what I'd missed."

11

"Makes sense," I said, even though it didn't. "I don't know if you know this, but some of the people around here used to say you went AWOL when you disappeared. And since your folks were already passed, there was no one to say any different. Just thought you ought to know."

"I didn't go AWOL. I was honorably discharged. I just didn't come right home, is all."

"You didn't come home, period. What are you talking about? You'd have been welcomed as a hero."

"Didn't need that," he said. "Just had some things to figure out is all. Did it in my own time."

"Where'd you go?"

"All over the world. I spent a lot of time in Africa and Europe, a little time in Asia. Just wandering."

"How'd you make a living?"

"There's always someone needing something done. For many of those things, I'm probably more qualified than most."

"Makes sense," I said.

Jake put a ten on the bar and said he'd have another beer. I looked at the clock and the rest of the bar. The last of the late stragglers had left through the front door. "It's after last call. Your money's no good here." I popped open another and set it down after wiping the condensation off the bar in front of him. "It's on the house."

He picked it up and pointed the open top at me while winking his eye. "You sure I'm not keeping you up, Cash?"

"No, I'm good. I haven't seen you in forever. I'm good as long as you are."

"Well, have a beer with me."

"I appreciate the invitation, but my stomach's been acting up. I need some Pepto-Bismol more than I need a beer. 'Sides, I have to get up early and meet my brother for breakfast." Loose lips sink ships. The real reason I wasn't going to drink is that it's harder to watch what you say when you've been drinking. Jake Charm had already come closer than ninety-nine-point-nine-nine-nine percent of the people ever get to figuring Cash and me out.

"No sweat," he said. "I'd like to see your brother too before I leave."

"Leave? You just got here. Where you going?"

12

"I don't know where I'm going or even when, but I know myself better than anyone, and I never stay anywhere beyond my welcome."

"You don't think you're welcome here?"

"I don't know, Cash. I just got here, and, like you said, they thought so little of me they'd think I'd go AWOL. There's more behind that than just a little gossip, I'm thinking. This isn't the first I'd heard about the AWOL rumors, of course."

"Yeah, I don't know. Just know that I never believed that bull. Benefit of knowing you, I guess." And I meant that sincerely.

"Thanks."

We sat for another hour and a half or so. He drank another three beers. We talked about the old days. Whether I was as tight with him as my brother or not, I was still there. I knew all the stories and enjoyed talking about them. The good old days in the local Starpoint bar. Starpoint is the name of our school.

Once he'd taken his last swig, he set his bottle on the bar with a thud. "That's it for me tonight. Thanks again, Cash. It's been a long time since I talked about the old times."

"You need a ride home? Where you staying?"

"I'm at my folks' house. Our neighbor's been taking care of it for me. Looks just like it did the day I left."

"You never even made it back for their funerals, did you?" His parents were killed in a head-on collision with a drunk driver.

"Wasn't even an option for me. I was in a deep-cover mission and eventually laid up in the hospital with a bloody bandage covering three bullets to the abdomen. I just couldn't make it."

"Well then, Jake, we're not done," I said. "I've got more questions for you. Three bullets to the abdomen. Make sure I see you again before you disappear."

"You got it. It's a promise." And I didn't doubt it for a second.

"You didn't answer the question though. Do you want a ride? I can put you on the back of my sled. It's cold out there."

It was January. After I'd locked the door, checked the kitchen appliances and turned out the lights, he followed me out the back door. There was more than an inch of snow covering the seat of my snowmobile.

Before he answered my question, he looked around and breathed in the fresh cold air. He grew a smile while taking in that cold air. I know the feeling. There's nothing

13

like the chill of winter air in the lungs. "No," he said, "I'm gonna hoof it. It's snowing, and I haven't seen much snow in a while. This is beautiful. I look forward to the walk."

"Suit yourself, Jake. Have a good walk."

I started up my sled and tied my hood up tight. I didn't have a helmet, so I needed the hood to keep me warm. He walked around the front and off to the east. He grew up about two and half miles away from us. I had about a mile to get to my folks' house, where Cash had been living since they died. It was all trails though. I could have driven the car over or the four-wheeler, but the snowmobile was my ride of choice when there's snow. Pure speed. I knew right then and there that there was little chance I was going straight home. To do what, fall asleep, only to wake up and go back to my real life with my miserable wife? Pshaw.

Chapter 2

I took the snowmobile for an hour ride before I got home. I went along a lot of the old trails and then to some of the trails in other areas. It was quiet. I was the only thing making noise.

Pendleton and the surrounding area is all old country New York. In the city, blocks are small, but here, the blocks between the roads are a mile or two by a couple of miles, sometimes many miles. There are houses and farms along the roads, but the center is uninhabited for the most part. Just woods and farm fields. Through those woods and around all those fields are trails for tractors, snowmobiles, four wheelers, and of course hunters. The woods are loaded with tree stands. Some metal that you'd buy at the store, many wooden and many left abandoned and unsafe. I can get from the restaurant to the family homestead through the trails without ever touching a road, but it's about a mile's worth of driving at the most direct route.

This night though, I drove for miles, even crossed some roads. I was trespassing in certain spots on a technical level, but I knew every farmer in the area. There's an understanding for the most part. It also helps keep the roads safer when guys would drink and drive through the fields rather than on the roads. If you're going to drink and drive, risk your own life and not everyone else's.

Chief Lyman Beck might try and get you if he thinks you're drunk and operating an off-road vehicle, but he wasn't going to catch you. That's for sure. His deputy Tyler Graveline grew up with us, and he saw the advantages in looking the other way sometimes. He played football with us but was a year younger. Good kid and isn't such a stickler for the strict adherence to the law as Chief Beck. Now don't get me wrong, Chief Lyman Beck is a good man. He and my father were friends, way back. Used to come over to the house for dinner and parties when we were young. He's just old school. Served in Vietnam and didn't take crap from anyone. And no favoritism. While that's good when you want justice, it's bad when you need leniency.

Back when we were kids, there were no police in Pendleton. Didn't need them. You might get a sheriff's deputy driving through, but that was it. There wasn't a lot of crime. People left their doors unlocked, the area was small, and everyone knew everyone.

15

The school was located in Pendleton. It was called Starpoint because it served five towns and, even so, the class sizes were small. It was considered a small school when it came to sports and, as a result, we played in the division with the other small rural schools, most of which were up along Lake Ontario. I think the towns were the towns of Lockport, Cambria, Wheatfield, Sanborn and of course Pendleton. The central school was the center hub in a star-like wheel with five towns at the points. Beyond those towns, you had the City of Lockport to the east, the City of Buffalo to the south on the other side of Amherst and Williamsville. To the southwest and west were the City of Kenmore, the City of Tonawanda, the City of North Tonawanda and the City of Niagara Falls. One of the "Seven Natural Wonders of the World" is in our Niagara County. To the north were just more rural towns and then Lake Ontario. It was a great place to grow up. You could get to any of those cities in two shakes of a pig's tail, but you didn't have to deal with the psychoses of those cities.

Then it started to change. Pendleton nearly doubled in population because people in those big cities wanted to escape. The parents would still work there, but they didn't want their kids growing up there. Who could blame them? Pendleton and the surrounding areas changed a bit. There were now houses along roads that had previously had farm fields right up to the road. Parts of the farm field were sold, and homes were built. Nice homes with small trees that had just been planted in strategic places by people with the big picture in mind. They weren't always going to be small trees.

The school grew so much they had to build a new high school on the old track and football field. They built new fields, of course. They then combined the old high school wing with the junior high wing to make the new junior high. Instead of playing sports against the small schools up along the lake, Starpoint played against the bigger schools in the Buffalo suburbs like Williamsville, Kenmore and Sweet Home. But the Starpoint teams were still great. I'd put a callous-handed farm boy up against a soft delicate-fingered city boy any day of the week.

Even still, we knew how to laugh at ourselves. We, the students of Starpoint, had nicknamed our school "The Starfarm." The school paper was called "Down on the Farm," and my brother named the bar "The Trough" to signify the trough from which farm animals drink. He had a mural on one wall showing a few cows wearing varsity jackets and standing up on two legs against a bar with beers in their hooves. It didn't look as absurd is it might sound. Although, one of the cows was wearing a Spartan helmet to honor our Spartan mascot. In order to sip from his beer, he had to lift the awkward helmet off his snout to see the beer he was drinking. A varsity-jacketed cow in a Spartan helmet drinking a beer – what's not to love?

Cash covered the walls with photos of the great Starpoint athletes over history, and even had a section to highlight the feats of the new kids. He did more to promote the athletic department than the members of the booster club. He tried to join them and sponsor them numerous times, but they rejected him because he ran the bar. Didn't want to promote alcohol and drinking. He understood though and didn't let it change his mind.

16

So, he sponsored a little league team. Glory days needed to be celebrated, and he had a lot of glory days.

It was about 5:30 AM when I parked the sled in the barn. Unfortunately, I smelled something burning and figured I'd try to remember to mention it to Cash later. Let *him* fix it. Imagine that though, something wrong with the snowmobile right when it's snowy enough to ride. What are the chances?

I called it a night and went into my brother's house. He'd set his bedroom up in my parents' master bedroom, leaving our old room, the barracks, as a dust-collecting memorial museum to our youth. I thought about checking it out but was too tired. I took a seat on the couch and started watching an old TV show on Nick at Night. I was asleep before it was over.

I woke up around 8:00 AM, all startled that I was late for work and not in the right place, but I wasn't. I remembered Cash was supposed to stop over about 9:00 AM, and we were going to switch our identities back. Just another fun year of switching it up without getting busted. Too easy. No five-dollar bill switching hands this year.

I went back to sleep. Meeting up with Jake had me up much later than normal. I was tired. I figured Cash would wake me up when he got here. But around 10:30 AM, I awoke again. Cash was an hour and a half late? That wasn't like him. This wasn't something we played around with. The goal was to never get caught. It was an obsession to both of us. Neither of us wanted to be the one that got busted. It would ruin the game forever once someone had realized what we'd been up to for the last thirty years.

Did my wife figure him out? I sure hope not. She was already crazy. How did a woman who was so amazingly sweet and wonderful turn into such a shrew? Maybe she thought Cash and I would be suitable replacements for her true love Jake Charm, and maybe we both failed miserably.

Then Jake freakin' Charm shows up just in the middle of this mess — what are the chances? The competitive side of me wanted Cash to be caught, but the rest of me didn't want to give up next year's opportunity to take a break from my life and my wife. That latter desire was much stronger than my desire to win a thirty-year-old five-dollar battle. Playing the game was better than winning it, like watching a movie you never want to end.

I waited another half hour and then called the house. No answer. Maybe they were outside. I called again in fifteen minutes and still no answer.

Maybe this was the year we got busted. I got in Cash's Chevy pickup and drove over to my house. My Trailblazer and my wife's car were both in the driveway, parked just like normal. Mine on the right and hers on the left. I just drove by. So, they were there.

I then drove over to the Convenient Store at Five Corners. Five Corners is the center of Pendleton where three streets intersect to make five corners — one road ends

17

at the intersection. My bank is located just off the southeast corner, next to the Star Pharm pharmacy, which is obviously run by another Starfarm graduate. The Convenient Store was on the northwest corner. I went there because they still had a pay phone. True, I could have used my cell phone, but I didn't want the caller ID to pick up too many calls from me. Callie might think something was up. No answer again.

As I was getting back into my truck, I saw Daren Flacks coming out of the store with some milk and a paper bag folded under his left arm.

He looked at my vehicle and then at me. "Hi Cash."

"Morning, Daren." He got into his car and took off. I did as well.

I took another pass by my house. Nothing was changed. I drove around the block and then pulled into my driveway. I parked behind Callie's car on the left and went through the small garage door. The big two-car garage door was closed. The cars would have been parked inside, but I had a project in the garage I hadn't finished yet. I hadn't moved all the sawhorses and tools.

The driveway had been shoveled recently, but there was still snow on it. Just not as much as on the two parked cars. Cash should have known I don't normally shovel the driveway until before I have to leave, unless we're getting a crap load of snow, in which case, I'd shovel it multiple times a day so it wouldn't get overly burdensome. Nonetheless, the driveway had been shoveled after the cars had been parked for a while. *No wonder you'd been caught. Little mistakes. Sucker. I'm about to be five bucks richer, Cash.*

I walked in through the small doorway to the garage, which led to the doorway into the kitchen. At first, I went to open it with my key, but I didn't have my keys. Cash had them. Good thing. I knocked like Cash would. Only strangers knocked on our front door.

I knocked again. No answer.

I knocked again.

And again.

Nothing. Not a peep.

I went out the back door of the garage to the back yard. Once on the porch, I knocked on the sliding glass door. No answer. Nothing inside looked amiss. I walked around the house and peered into the windows. The shades were down, but there's always a small sliver of view.

I saw nothing new. The bedroom was upstairs, so I couldn't see what was going on there. I went back into the garage and remembered I'd stashed a key in the nail and screw compartment box I had on one of my workbenches. It was hidden under an emptied box of finishing nails so it wouldn't be seen by someone rifling through all the little clear-plastic drawers.

I opened the kitchen door and wiped my feet as best I could on the rug in front of the door. There were actually water spots on the kitchen floor, probably when Cash had walked in after shoveling the driveway. They were partially dried because you could see a ring of salt left at the outer most reaches of the drying puddles. As the water dried, the spots got smaller. Cash must have wanted to get caught. Callie doesn't go for stuff like that, and he knew that. She's a clean freak compared to us. *There goes my yearly vacation, jerkwad.*

Callie's actual husband – me – hoping to preserve peace in my world, would have grabbed the mop from the closet and started to clean up the mess, but I didn't. If Callie walked into the kitchen to see Cash mopping her floor, my cover would be blown. When it came to keeping the bar clean, Cash knew what to do, but he wasn't married like me. Living alone and able to retire to his bachelor's castle at the end of the day, he was still impervious to the pleas and demands of women for his domestication. He'd never voluntarily mop a floor just to keep from having to hear my wife's complaining. But her real husband would. I couldn't risk it. I had to leave it and hear about it later.

As I walked through the kitchen, I said, "Helloooo. Hellooo? Anyone here? Curt? Callie? You guys here?"

Nothing.

As soon as I walked into the dining room, I saw little amiss. The wooden floor was covered with water like the kitchen. The table was cleared and dusted, other than the centerpiece. I looked into the living room area, which was just beyond the front-door entrance. The door was to the left, and the stairway was to the right. At the foot of the steps, I saw my baseball bat and a small puddle of blood that had dripped off the bottom step.

A shot of fear ripped through my body. I had beads of sweat forming on my forehead and my heart started pumping as if I'd just finished running a six-minute mile. When I picked up the bat, I saw it was speckled with dried blood, but I grabbed it for the security of knowing I'd have something to defend myself if necessary. I didn't have a gun on me. I looked up the stairs and saw Cash lying face down on the wooden stairway. He'd been shot, and his blood had made its way to the floor. He was wearing my flannel pajama pants and one of my t-shirts. That's how I'd be dressed if I wasn't in bed yet.

Did Callie shoot my brother? Why would Callie shoot my brother? Or was she shooting me? Did she want out of our marriage more than I did?

I stood there for a moment completely unable to move. Sure, I'd gone there to find out why Cash hadn't met up with me as per our prearranged plans, but this was no longer about avoiding being discovered. It wasn't a game anymore. My twin brother was lying dead in front of me, and it was like looking at my own dead body.

What if he's not dead?

I checked his pulse. "Cash, you still with me? Cash, I'm here." There was no pulse, and the blood on the bat was dried. Dried quicker than the water on the floor. He'd been there for a while.

My gosh, my brother's dead.

"Callie. Callie." I walked upstairs carefully. I did whatever I could to avoid walking in the blood. I got to the top of the stairs and quickly looked to the right to see that no one was in the bathroom. I turned to the left and walked towards the front of the house where the door to the master bedroom was on the right.

Callie wasn't on the bed, and the sheets were pulled back. Our bed was queen-sized with four lathe-turned wooden posts connected to a headboard and a footboard. The head of the bed was up against the far wall. Her dresser was to the left, and my dresser was on the other side. I walked to my side of the bed. Her body was face down on the floor, partially under the bed. There was a bullet hole in her head and a large puddle of blood soaked into the purple rug under her. It looked like she was hiding under the bed, but they pulled her out by her ankles. Her left arm was still under the bed. Apparently, they eventually pulled her by her right arm as well. It fell to her side after it had been dropped.

I was sweating. The fear of being killed had subsided because the killer or killers were gone, but I was sweating and shaking like never before. *What do I do? Fight or flight is kicking in, but there's nothing to fight, and where do I go?*

I knew well enough not to touch the crime scene, but I didn't have the first clue of how I was going to handle this. I stood there and contemplated my situation without disturbing the crime scene any more than I already had.

Who was being killed – Curt or Cash? Most likely me, Curt. Right?

When I report this, how do I explain that my brother Cash was killed with my wife and not be a suspect in the murder of my brother and my wife for apparently having an affair?

Do I admit that I'm really Curt and that we were playing a game?

If I do, that will mean I hadn't yet been assassinated and thus make me a target for death again.

What if I just report it as Cash discovering my brother Curt and sister-in-law Callie dead? Can I get away with it? At least then I'll be alive to figure out who did this and get justice for my brother and wife.

20

If I tell the truth that I'm really Curt, I will be the number-one suspect for sure. Can't do much investigation from the jail.

Is there a chance that Jake Charm did this after he walked home from the bar last night?

If they were murdering Curt and not Cash, why were they murdering me? This does not look like a robbery.

I looked around a little to see if anything was indeed stolen. Nothing seemed to have been touched.

I carefully made my way to my office on the other side of the stairway. It was the other room on the front of the house. My first step onto the dark hardwood creaked like normal. I made my way to the desk that faced the doorway. My desk was left as it was. I doubt Cash had even sat in it. I sat down and rolled over to the safe behind my desk. It seemed undisturbed, so I opened it. The papers were untouched, and so were the four stacks of cash. Each stack was $9,900 in hundreds. I grabbed two of them and put them in my coat pocket. Since only two people on the planet knew how much money was in there and one was dead, I figured I could get away with this without causing too much trouble for the investigation.

I closed the safe and then sat at my desk. My laptop was sitting right in front of me. It was closed. I went to open it but remembered that, if I did, there'd be record that I opened it as soon as I plugged in the password. That would be bad if I chose to remain as Cash. Even if I didn't, it would look bad because the investigators would wonder why I went on the computer before I called the police. Making me an even bigger suspect.

The best way to make sure they don't have a lot of questions for me is to make sure they have nothing to suspect. Which means I must tell them I'm Cash. Otherwise, I'll never get out of there. I'll be suspect number one, and the real killer or killers will get away. I sound like freakin' O. J. Simpson. This is not good. Understatement of the year, dingbat.

I grabbed the computer and the power cord, and I stashed it under my left arm. The stacks of cash were secure in my pocket. I walked out and made my way down the steps without disturbing the blood. I took a quick look at the rest of the house to make sure this wasn't some sort of burglary gone wrong but could find nothing missing.

In the garage, as I opened the door to the driveway, I realized my footprints were going to be in the snow, as well as my car prints. *That's who must have shoveled the driveway — the killer or killers.* They may have left snow tracks in the house, but they made their tracks outside disappear. I looked to where I kept my shovel, but it was gone. They didn't bother to bring it back. It was one of those big ergonomically correct plow shovels from the Home Depot. I had a snow blower, but unless there were huge drifts and blizzard-like amounts of snow, I just shoveled instead. Gave me a chance to get out of the house and breathe the fresh cold air.

21

Forget about the tracks. I'm the one that discovered the body, and I'm the one that will call it in. I'm just not doing it from the crime scene because I didn't want to disturb it. Sounds good, I guess.

I really just had to go and hide my computer and the stacks of cash. It's not as if I knew all of my brother's bank codes. I needed the cash to get me through for a while. The computer's mostly useless, but I did have an offshore account with money that couldn't be traced back to me. The info on that account – and this was probably a bad idea – was on that computer. The only problem, taking the computer makes it look like a potential burglary if they discover the computer missing. I then regretted not having wiped away the dust that might have fallen around the computer on the desk. There might not have been dust, but even a little would be noticed by the investigators. *Crap.*

Driving back to Cash's house, the pain of losing my wife and brother started dominating the adrenaline rush of figuring out how not to be blamed for a murder with which I had nothing to do. Writing this is like experiencing it again, and I'm baffled at how I didn't just break down and cry. I wanted to, but I hadn't cried since I was a kid. Cash and I were taught not to. Mom was allowed to cry, but we weren't. Our dad would say, "Quit crying or I'll give you something to cry about." After hearing it hundreds of times, we learned not to cry.

But I wanted to. And not just for Cash. For my wife. I know I had my problems with our marriage, but that had much more to do with her own hang-ups. Maybe depression. Probably. I couldn't fix it or control it. It frustrated me to no end. She wasn't willing to tell me what her problem was, or maybe just wasn't able to tell me. So, my life needed to be miserable, and she needed to make sure it was. That doesn't change the fact that I loved who she was. She was truly a special woman. I just preferred who she was before we were married. Maybe it *was* the marriage, and maybe it was my fault, but she really *was* amazing. Even though I thought about getting a divorce and decided against it, I did indeed decide against it and to dedicate my efforts to fixing the marriage. That was my choice. Not divorce.

Now she was dead, along with my twin brother. I mean, these are the two people I loved more than any others on the planet. Gone at once, and I was going to be the number one suspect. No way around it. To top it off, Cash was my contingent beneficiary for most of my accounts. Callie's sister was too, but Cash will inherit much of my money. While that is good if I stay as Cash, it's also another motive for murder.

I wanted to mourn. I wanted to break down and curse God for giving me something I didn't think I could handle, but I just didn't have time. I don't want to come off as a heartless guy. I'm not. I didn't even want to curse God. I was really praying for guidance. I just didn't know if I was getting any.

When I drove through Five Corners again, I remembered I made a phone call from the pay phone, even though I was carrying my cell phone. *That will have to be another*

22

reason I didn't call from the house. I didn't have my cell phone, which I have to remember to leave at home.

I drove past The Trough and decided to keep it closed today. People would understand later.

Before I got out of Cash's truck to go in the house, I covered the computer with a blanket I'd found in the back seat. After making sure no one was watching me, I made my way in. The house was a purplish-grey three-story with a big white porch that matched the trim on the garage that sat in front of the U-shaped driveway-slash-parking area situated between the house and the barn. It wasn't a working farm, but there was an old barn and a garage big enough for three cars.

Inside the house, I put my cell phone on the dining room table and went upstairs. Then I climbed the second flight of steps into the barracks. I hadn't been in our old bedroom in years. It was the attic, and it was the size of most the house, other than the add-on in the back. The floor was unfinished tongue and groove fir wood. The walls leaned inward and then up to the peak. When we were kids, our dad put insulation in them, ran some electricity and then covered the walls with knotty pine. There were windows on all four sides of the room. We, being kids who loved to play war, cops and robbers, or cowboys and Indians, called it the barracks. We were soldiers and mercenaries preparing for a life of war and adventure, and we could see our enemies coming from any direction. That's how God wanted it. All our friends loved sleeping over our house. It was built for the youthful mischief, and we lived up to our calling.

In addition to our dust-covered beds that were still there, there were numerous boxes. Cash was using the barracks as storage. Not a surprise.

I moved my bed off the wall and walked around to the corner of the room. When we were kids, we used a drill and a jig saw to cut through the tongue and groove of a few of the floorboards under my bed. It was my idea. We created a secret hiding spot that we used throughout our time in the barracks. Anything we didn't want our mother to know about went there – snacks, nudie mags, guns, bottles of liquor, a bag of weed, cigars, cigarettes and maybe a few other things. We were good kids, but we weren't angels. We were soldiers of fortune, and this was where we kept the spoils of our mercenary lives, the kind of lives our mother didn't want for us. She might have drunk too much in her later years, but she really was a good mama. We respected and loved her enough to make sure she didn't know all we were up to. It was out of love for our mama. A mercenary never tells the whole story. Some just can't handle the truth.

I used a key to lift the third board off the wall. I didn't think there'd be much there, other than a couple of forgotten trinkets from our childhood, but once I lifted all three boards, I discovered that Cash was up to something, probably no good. There were stacks and stacks of cash. *Living up to your name, I see.*

23

I didn't have time to count, but, in between the three floor joists, there were about eight piles of stacks of different denominations: mostly twenties, fifties and hundreds. Each of the eight piles were two stacks high, meaning there were up to about sixteen banded stacks of cash, each with about a hundred bills. I put my computer and charger over some of them, and then I put my twenty thousand dollars on top of my computer so as not to mix the monies up. The boards had just enough clearance. I lifted the bed back into place, careful enough again to lift from the bottom so as not to disturb the dust.

Crap, Cash, what are you up to? This must have been why you were so insistent we skip the switch game this year. Must not have wanted to answer the question I was sure to ask if I'd been curious enough to check our old secret hiding space. What if you were the real target and not me, Cash? If I report the murders as you, and you were the target, the assassin's bound to come back for me. Come on, Cash, help me out. What am I missing? I'm still talking to my dead brother.

Chapter 3

"Hodi... Hodi... Hodi..."

"Ignore him," the Tanzanian Pastor Gabriel said to the visiting American Jake Chambliss, as the pastor was comforting their host and his wife. Pastor Gabriel was a hundred-and-thirty-pound African minister to whom the missionaries from America would come to get coordinated and situated. That ended once they discovered he was so willing to proselytize to the Muslims. While missionaries wanted to spread the word, they also wanted to make it back home someday. Only standing five-four and sporting a dark African complexion textured with pockmarks and a few rogue white whiskers to match the color of his hair, this pastor walked as though he had an army of millions at the ready behind him. Unprepared for actual hand-to-hand combat himself, due to age, his faith gave him an air of invincibility.

Jake took it upon himself to reinforce that faith. Jake liked that Pastor Gabriel was still allowed to walk the earth and spread his immense wisdom and knowledge of the Gospel. He wore a black button-down shirt under his cross necklace and nice brown slacks that hid the dust that would collect on his regularly shined black shoes.

Their hosts had just lost their second child in a year. He'd succumbed to malaria. The first one was sucked into a drainage pipe during a heavy rain in the middle of Tanzania's rainy season. It was now June, and the dry season had begun. Instead of rain, the air was polluted with dust that would make the throat soar and the eyes redden.

"Hodi... Hodi... Hodi..." The gate knocker wasn't giving up. There was an obvious anxiousness in his voice.

Pastor Gabriel had been rolling some hot ugali in his right hand provided to him by his hosts. The left hand was the dirty hand. All eating and transactions must be done with the right hand because the left hand is used for going to the bathroom in a land where toilet paper is a luxury to those in the villages. Ugali is a paste made of pounded corn flour in boiling water. It's dipped in mchicha, which is like a spinach, or in meat if you're lucky. Its main purpose is the fill the belly and stave off hunger. The pastor dipped it in the mchicha, leaving the meat for his hosts who needed it more. He took a bite.

"Hodi... Hodi... Hodi... Pastor Gabriel, I really need to talk with you. Please, Hodi, please, please."

25

Whoever it was, it was rude to interrupt the pastor in the middle of consoling the bereaved. It was in times like this, when unfortunate villagers start to question the existence of God, that it was especially important for Pastor Gabriel to reinforce their faith with scriptures from the Bible. The amazing thing about Pastor Gabriel, at least in Jake's eyes, he didn't even need to open the Bible in his hands. It was as if he knew it by heart. Jake had met the pastor through some missionaries who would make sure the pastor was fully stocked and had what he needed. In exchange, they'd get informed about where their services were needed most. That was before they'd stopped coming as often or even at all. The missionaries were from the U.S., and Jake had been working security for them or whoever else needed it. He and the pastor really hit it off though, and he decided to stay with the pastor and his wife.

Gabriel said, "Can you go and help him?"

Jake dipped his ugali, took a bite and walked to the bamboo gate that walled off the center square of the U-shaped structure formed by the bereaved family's three mud huts.

"Hodi."

Jake opened the gate and said, "Marahaba." Marahaba was the term used to receive those who knock with the term "Hodi." Hodi was used as a verbal doorbell. There was no electricity on most bamboo doorways, so "hodi" is Swahili for "ding-dong," but not really. It's said with respect, which obviously implies that ugly Americans with their loud doorbells juiced up with a constant flow of electricity are just disrespectful. Jake recognized the elderly gentleman from church and from the Muslim cafes. He was a quiet understudy of Pastor Gabriel. Not quiet, as in secret. Quiet, as in he listened more than he talked. A lot more. Maybe it was in secret, but Jake was trained to see things. It wasn't a secret to him.

Seeing who it was, Jake said, "Shikamoo." That was the term used to greet elders with respect and reverence for their wealth of wisdom. Pastor Gabriel told him it was actually a term from back in the slave days. It was a term used by the slaves to greet their masters by saying "I am at your service" or "I am at your feet." That meaning had long been forgotten and replaced with more of a respectful meaning. It was more as if you were imitating Jesus when he washed the feet of his disciples before the Passover feast on the night in which he was betrayed. Not to be served but to serve, even those whom you know might betray you.

"Ali, Ali, they've taken Ali again." The elderly man was more agitated than Jake had ever seen him.

"Who took him?"

"The Muslim boys. Many Muslim boys. Five or six of them."

26

Jake looked to Pastor Gabriel for guidance. Without saying a word, the pastor waved his hand telling him to go and help Ali. Ali was a boy that helped out at the Muslim café. He'd get water and help the owner with whatever was necessary. The Muslim café was an outdoor pavilion with some benches under a straw-thatched roof. Mohamed, the owner, would make really strong coffee in a big black kettle, which he served in small cups to men who'd sit around and talk politics and religion while their wives worked in the fields. Unlike in America, in Tanzania, that's all they talked about. Politics and religion. And if you were a Muslim, your women worked.

Being braver than just about any man he'd ever met, Pastor Gabriel would visit the café at least three times a week. He liked to talk religion. While the Muslim men didn't admit to believing what he said and would crack jokes as his expense, they tolerated his company because he was so respectful. Maybe even enjoyed it. Most did anyway. Of course, he had his detractors. They'd occasionally express themselves with death threats, but Pastor Gabriel was fearless, almost recklessly so. So, Jake sort of felt it was his responsibility to make sure no one actually made good on those threats. He saw someone in need that seemed completely unaware that he even *was* in need, and Jake considered protecting Pastor Gabriel as an obligation.

Sometimes, Jake couldn't believe what Pastor Gabriel was telling these swarthy Muslim men, all hopped up on espresso-strength coffee. He'd bring the Bible and slap them in the face with what they saw as blasphemy against their religion. Jake knew the pastor was right, especially after seeing what he saw while at war in the Islamic world. Stuff that cannot be unseen and can only be described as looking Big Evil in its face with nothing more than the measly weapons supplied by the Big Government that the Big Evil considered the Great Satan.

Armed with nothing more than the Word of the God of the Jews and of the Christians, the same God these Muslim men considered to be Satan, Pastor Gabriel would regularly try to convince them that *they* were the ones who were actually worshipping Satan. It was not the preaching someone would give if he liked his throat uncut, but Pastor Gabriel's faith was as strong as the army of millions in front of which he walked.

He'd tell them about the prophecy of Daniel, that 1290 days after the daily sacrifices ended, there will be the Abomination of Desolation. In 583 BC, the daily sacrifices at the Temple Mount ended because the Jews, held in captivity by the Babylonian king Nebuchadnezzar II, were able to return to Israel. According to Genesis, the 1290 days were really prophetic years according to the prophetic calendar, where there are 360 days in a prophetic year. 360 divided by 365.24 days per calendar year is a multiplier of 0.9857. Multiplying that by 1290 prophetic years, he'd get 1271.5 calendar years. 1271.5 years after 583 BC would be 688 AD, and that was when the people of Allah began to build the Dome of the Rock on the Temple Mount where the second Temple was destroyed by the Romans in the first century. Then he'd talk about the forty-two months mentioned in Revelation, which is three-and-a-half years, or one-half of the seven-year tribulation. Forty-two months of thirty days is 1260 days. When translated into 1260 years, as had been done before, and added to 688 AD, he would come up with 1948, the year that Israel was reestablished. In brief, his point was that more than a thousand years before the birth of the Prophet Mohammed, Daniel had prophesied the return of the Jews to the Holy Land and the building of the Dome of the Rock, which Revelation had prophesied as put there by the Beast, though Daniel had prophesied that the Beast would be a kingdom. Then he'd go back to Revelation to prove that this beast of the kingdom was the kingdom of Islam and that the number of the Beast, 666, was actually the number of a man, and that man was Mohammed. Every day he'd come up with some new mathematical proof that the Bible was preparing for the rise of Islam for centuries before Mohammed, and he'd scold them for blindly worshipping the wrong god. He'd do the math in the dust with a small bamboo stick, and it would stay there until the wind erased it. He swore that math was the language of God and the only universal language.

Pastor Gabriel wasn't bringing a warm and fuzzy Christian message of love and that Jesus died for everybody's sins. He brought these Muslim men the Sword of Jesus. The Word of God. Jake realized he was Pastor Gabriel's witness. He let the pastor argue and make God's point, but he remained quiet. He was the army of one that the Muslims could see, but nowhere near enough in his own mind. For once in his life, Jake felt inadequate and liked it. The challenge this obligation presented made him feel needed.

Fortunately, Tanzania had a strong military. There wasn't a lot of war. These military guys were big, strong and completely unwilling to waste time on troublemakers. They'd break heads and ask questions later. However, there were indeed troublemakers, many who'd made their way south from South Sudan, Uganda, Rwanda and Burundi. For the most part though, the soldiers would let the pastor do his thing. Sometimes they'd cut him short if he was getting too close to a truth that was starting to inflame tensions around the peaceful coffee pot. Their job was to keep the peace and, not wanting to openly disrespect a man of the cloth, they'd use Jake as their interpreter. Some of the Tanzanian soldiers liked Jake and would often wonder out loud how Jake was crazy enough to stand by this man who was on his way to being put in the ground by unnatural means.

He could only tell them he had no need to make excuses for fulfilling an obligation.

"You could just go back to America. Why *your* obligation?"

"If not mine, then whose?"

They never had an answer to that question. Jake's selfless bravery only served to make him appear bigger in their eyes. He wasn't the missionary that came with words, books and food. His mission was one of deeds, and they appreciated that.

The old man led Jake to Ali, walking faster than he probably should have. Just another indication of the seriousness of the situation. First, they walked to the road along Lake Tanganyika. This lake was four hundred and fifty miles long by about thirty miles wide. The local fishermen were making their way out to the lake. At darkness, they'd light lanterns to bring the fish to their nets. The lake would be lit up at night with the many lanterns. It was beautiful. Jake loved to get his hands on the expensive and delicious Kuhe, but he was happy to settle for the sangara or even the degaa, anything to give the ugali some flavor. Nothing on the docks looked or sounded amiss. Just the sounds of wood banging and men talking.

The old man, whose name Jake couldn't recall, kept walking south and then suddenly turned left in between mud huts and into a large gathering of small huts. They passed several huts, veering left and right and left and right. Finally, the man pointed at an alleyway between larger buildings. He was done walking. Wouldn't say a thing, but just kept pointing with a look of horror on his face. Maybe the horror was inspired by the quiet.

Jake walked into the alleyway. He could smell trash and human waste. The sun was on the horizon and very little of its light was willing to venture into this godforsaken alleyway. Jake was starting to think he may have been lured away from the pastor. He kept going though. At the rear of the alley, right before it was blocked off by a wooden door, he saw light shimmering off the freshly spilled blood of Ali. They had killed him. Beating him was just for kicks. His belly was slit open, and his innards were hanging out. He had no breath.

Little Ali had been seeking out Pastor Gabriel's wisdom. He wanted to know more than just the math. He wanted to know about Jesus. Pastor Gabriel was low-key about this, and he had warned Ali many times he was going to get in trouble if he continued to seek him out. Ali kept coming though. He had brilliant questions for a child of his age, and the pastor had the answers.

Now, he was dead. A fury was building in Jake. It was the fury he'd spent years learning to tame. An old friend that can quickly become his enemy but moreso the enemy of his enemies. Woe be to his enemies once Jake's fury began to rise.

Jake took off his shirt and covered Ali's abdomen before he picked the boy up in his arms. The old man that had brought him was gone. Ali wasn't more than seventy pounds. Jake walked slowly back to where he'd left the pastor with a solemn scowl on his face. Others looked at him, but none offered a word or help. It was as if they'd all seen it coming and were afraid to take a position on any of it. They'd glance over and then quickly look away. Jake's shirt was covered with blood, but at least people were spared having to see what was under it. It was gruesome. Jake had to, at one point, put the boy down so that he could tuck the boy's innards back into his belly.

When he'd gotten back to where the pastor remained with their hosts, he opened the gate without knocking to immediately see more horror. Pastor Gabriel had been decapitated, and the husband and wife had been stabbed to death. The pastor's body had fallen to the ground, and his head was left sitting on his Bible splayed open upon the chair. A knife handle was coming out of the top of his skull. The Bible was soaked in blood.

Jake set the boy down and tied the goat away from the bodies. Its face was covered in blood.

The fury was no longer tamed. As if a switch in his head had been thrown, Jake Chambliss went from witness to soldier. Actions were dictated by instincts, while thoughts were for the civilized.

He ran shirtless through the village and back to the cement home where he stayed with the pastor and his wife. A brick wall with a metal gate surrounded the home. There was barbed wire above the wall, and shards of glass had been cemented into the top of the wall. He unlocked the gate and ran into the house to get his guns. There is a time for peace and a time for war. This was a time for war. There was no other way to satisfy this untamed fury. It would take an elephant tranquilizer to stop him, and that might not even be enough.

Before Jake ran into the house, he noticed a blanket left over the barbed wire atop the protective wall to the left. Following the muffled screams, he ran directly to the pastor's bedroom. There were three men in there with Pastor Gabriel's wife. Two were holding her arms, while a third was trying to rape her. Jake put the knife he'd grabbed off the table through the ear of the guy caught with his pants down and threw his body across the small room. The punctured head bounced off the wall. The other two came at him.

The guy on his right punched at him. Jake grabbed the guy's arm, brought him in and twisted his arm behind his back so hard he ripped it right out of the shoulder socket. The man's screams ended quickly after Jake lifted the man off the ground by yanking his neck back until the spinal cord had snapped. A death move he stole from Chuck Norris in the movie *The Octagon,* or maybe *Force of One.* He didn't have time to remember. He slammed the body to the cement floor for good measure. He wanted Satan to hear the sounds of hell being paid.

The other guy backed up after watching what happened to his friends. Jake walked after him to the rear corner of the room. With a look of horror, the man held his arms forward in hopes of keeping Jake at bay. No luck and no mercy for rapists. Jake grabbed the guy's hair, slammed his face on his lifted knee, and then twisted the guy's head until his neck snapped. Another twist, and he'd have ripped the guy's head right off his shoulders. But Jake was trying to control his fury. It's a multi-step process, but it was underway.

He went right to the pastor's wife. She hadn't moved. He pulled her skirt down and realized they'd stabbed her in the chest. He tried to wake her, but she wouldn't move. There was no pulse. They were trying to rape a dead woman.

It was still time for war.

30

In the kitchen, Jake grabbed some dried pork and put it in the mouths of each of the dead rapists. Let that be a lesson, let the rest of the Muslims learn that they have more than just their lives to give up. Yeah, it was offensive, but that was the point. No mercy for the wicked.

In the room where he'd been staying, he loaded his things into his backpack and put on his fatigues and a clean green shirt. His guns were loaded, and he put them in their appropriate places. He was armed to the teeth now. Finally, over some clean and dry socks, he laced up his combat boots. The mind was ready, and now the body was.

On his way out, he grabbed some food and stuffed it in the food pocket of his pack. Then, he went back into the pastor's bedroom. From the stand, he grabbed one of the pastor's Bibles. The one he used for private study when he was writing his sermons. He also grabbed his other cross necklace, made of turquoise and silver. He put those in the pocket for personal items.

Walking out of the pastor's home for the last time, he was breathing hard. With each breath, plumes of exhaled air would send the dust swirling around his nose. His fury was being converted into fuel.

***

Jake woke up covered in sweat and ready to battle whatever brought him out of his nightmare. He slowly realized he was alone in the room of his childhood. There was light sneaking in behind the blinds. It lit up the dust in the air of his dead parents' home. His home – the one he'd hoped he'd someday be able to live in again. The comfort of home wasn't enough though to let him escape the nightmares that regularly plagued his sleep. This was one of his three least favorites. It always had him thinking about Pastor Gabriel, the pastor's wife, and little Ali throughout the day, trying to figure out what he could have or should have done to prevent what happened.

Sure, his vengeance was swift and just as much a part of the nightmare as the deaths of his friends, but he'd been woken up before the vengeance part. Why this dream, he wondered, why? *Why now?*

As he sat up in bed with the blankets thrown to the side, he felt the cool morning air on his sweat-soaked skin. Anxiety rippled through his belly until his whole body was able to shake and shiver it off. It really was one of his least favorites – one of the dreams that almost invariably preceded a nightmarish day. While the body fuels the mind, the mind guides and prepares the body. Jake's mind did it with dreams that were seemingly unaltered portions of his life – there's nothing more nightmarish than real life. Sometimes life is so awful the mind doesn't even need to make up horrors.

Chapter 4

I knew I had to make that call before anyone else discovered my brother and my wife dead. There was obvious evidence I'd been at the house and that I had called the house earlier. I needed to be the one to report the murders. *But who am I?* While I ran through the list of reasons I'd been putting together in my head on whether I should call it in as Cash or Curt, I walked around Cash's house looking for clues. *Where did that money come from, Cash, and who are you hiding it from?*

I didn't find anything that stuck out, so I checked Cash's wallet in my back pocket. Standard stuff: bank card, credit card for the bar, another credit card, license and then I saw the gun permit. Nice. If I were going to be Curt, I'd have none of this.

I grabbed his .40 caliber Smith & Wesson from his night table. He loved this gun. It's what he carried behind the bar – gotta have protection. If someone was going to try and kill me because Cash was the target, I needed a gun. What kind of soldier of fortune dies without a fight? Not that I was any kind of soldier of fortune, but my competitive instincts kicked in automatically with Jake Charm in town. My whole life was about failing to outshine Jake Charm, at least the parts I hadn't gotten over, and if my wife were still alive, she'd tell you about it.

I checked the mag to make sure it was loaded. I knew I'd have to surrender this weapon at some point during my questioning, but I needed to have it on me, at least until then.

I went to the dining room to make the call and saw my cell phone on the table. I hid it in the cushions on the couch to have an excuse for not calling from the house as soon as I'd discovered the bodies. It would also serve as an excuse for having called from the Convenient Food Mart. The best way to get through the interrogation was to be prepared for the questions I knew I'd probably be asked. Criminals get caught because they don't think about stuff like this, but I wasn't a criminal. I had to be smarter.

I grabbed a cordless phone. It was dead, so I had to call from the base in the living room. *Who do I call?* Calling 911 is a bit impersonal. Who knows who I'd be talking to? At least I knew the number. Nah, I decided to call the local police department. At least I know the two cops. I found the number on the small Pendleton phone book cover.

I took a deep breath but realized I was way too composed for someone who'd just discovered the bodies of his twin brother and wife. *What am I supposed to sound like? How freakin' hard is it to get away with a crime you didn't commit? Should I be half crying? How about just slow and sad sounding? Yeah, that's it. I don't cry, and no one's seen me cry since I was a kid.*

As I was about to pick up the phone to make the call, it rang.

"Hello." I sounded really down. I really was, but I made sure I sounded that way.

"Hey, it's me, d'you just wake up?" It was Skylar Meade, the girl Cash had been dating for about a year. Way longer than I thought it'd last. She was at least ten years younger than he was and a whole lot less mature. She grew up in the city of Lockport and rented an apartment there. *The last person I want to talk to now.*

"No Skylar, I can't talk right now." I needed to get her off the phone without telling her why.

"You mad at me?" She said it as a question, but it was really an accusation.

"Nooo, not at all. I've got an emergency I have to deal with, and I just can't talk right now." *I've said too much. Crap.*

"What happened?"

"I can't get into it right now. I have to go."

"Where you going? You haven't been right lately. What's up? Who do you think *you* are? – Not telling *me* what's going on?"

"I just can't get into it now. I really *have* to go, Skylar."

"Are you cheating on me, Cash Cutler?"

I should have said yes and that I never want to see you again.   Hindsight's twenty-twenty.

"No, Skylar. I've got to deal with something, and I *really* have to go."

"You got a hoochie-mama over there right now?" Yeah, because my brother was all about the hoochie-mamas. How was I not supposed to laugh?

"No... gosh no." I should have said yes.

"Gosh no? Gosh no? Who the heck are you, Cash Cutler? I'm coming over there. You better not have a girl over there."

"I'm not going to be here, Skylar. I told you, I have to go."

"What, you taking her out to breakfast? Class act you are, Cash Cutler." *She must like saying my brother's name. My name now. Great. I'm Cash Cutler.*

"Yeah, I'll be at Ted's Pizza." It's the pizza shop on the southwest corner of five corners, across the road from the Convenient Food Mart.

"You better not be with that hoochie-mama. I'm gonna make a scene." *I'd expect nothing less.*

"I look forward to it, baby. I'll order you a calzone. I've got to go, though. I'll talk with you later." I hung up. I don't know if I was supposed to say, "I love you," but I didn't. The last thing I was looking for was a twenty-five-year-old girlfriend suffering a wicked case of jealousy. *What do you see in her, Cash? Other than that she's really hot? Never mind.*

I picked up the receiver again, took a deep breath, got back into my down, out and sad mood and dialed the number to the Pendleton Police Department. PPD. Pendleton's finest.

A gruff old man's voice, clearing the throat for a few seconds, said, "Beck." I was hoping to get Tyler.

"Is Tyler available?" I sounded really low and sad.

"Who's this?"

"It's Cash Cutler, Mr. Beck. I was hoping to talk with Tyler." I never grew out of calling him Mr. Beck. That's what my brother and I were told to call him back when we were kids and he was a cop with the Lockport Police Department.

"Is everything all right, son? Tyler's not here." The call waiting beeped. It was Skylar. I ignored it.

"No sir, it's not. I found my brother and his wife dead."

"My God, son. I'm sorry. Where are they? Where are you?"

"They're at Curt's house over on Fisk. I'm at my house on Aiken. I was there and came back over here to call you. Didn't want to disturb the crime scene."

"Crime scene?"

"Yes sir, they were murdered. It's a mess. I had to get out of there and didn't have my cell phone on me."

"You got the address handy?"

"457 Fisk."

"Stay where you are," he said.

34

"I can meet you over there and let you in. I have my brother's extra key."

"You sure, son?"

"Yeah. I'm sure. I want to be there. It's my brother... and my... sister-in-law." I almost said my wife.

"You might rethink that later, son, but I'm not going to stop you. I'll be there in ten." He hung up.

Sweat was dripping down my forehead, and my hand was shaking when I went to hang it up. The call was done. I planned to take a moment to gather my thoughts, but I wasn't given a moment. The phone rang just as it clicked. The call waiting. Crap. Like an idiot, I picked it up.

Skylar spoke as if our conversation had never ended, "Listen Cash, if you keep treating me like this, I'm not going to be around forever."

"Okay," I said. That's more like it. My natural male tendency was to fight for her, but Cash was dead. So was the relationship. My competitive side considered losing her a loss though.

"You're not even going to fight for me, Cash Cutler?"

"Listen Skylar, I told you. I have an emergency. I have to deal with something. I'm not cheating on you, there's no hoochie-mama, and I have to go." Back to trying to save the relationship, I guess. *Even though you're dead, Cash, I can't stop competing with you.*

"Are you sleeping with your brother's wife again? You told me that was over. Were you lying? Is that your emergency? Gotta convince your brother it wasn't *you* sleeping with his wife?"

I didn't have a quick answer to that one. But it got my mind working. "I gotta go. I gotta leave the house right now. I'm supposed to meet someone."

"Who? Your brother's wife?"

Before I could hang up on her, she slipped in one more accusation in the form of a question. "That's it, isn't it?"

Click and quiet...for ten seconds. Maybe two that felt like ten. Not sure. My cell phone started ringing in the cushions. I could hear its muffled ring, and I had to let it ring. It was part of my alibi. An alibi for a crime I didn't commit.

For the first time in about twenty-five years, I cried. *Why Cash?*

Chapter 5

It took me about ten minutes to get over to my "brother's house." Chief Lyman Beck was standing up against his patrol car. He must have been seventy by now. Some on the Town Council wanted him to retire, but he refused. Had enough loyalists to tell the others to stick it. They were talking about Pendleton, for gosh sake. The crime, when there was any, was high school kids playing mailbox baseball. There hadn't been a murder in Pendleton my whole life.

Chief Beck was in a black uniform, and he had on a black police hat with the ear flaps down. Standard issue, of course. You couldn't see any of his grey hair, but you could see his chubby reddened face. He looked shorter and heavier than in his younger years. Age can do that. Still had that sober look he always had. It didn't matter how little crime took place on his beat. He took it seriously. This was probably the most serious thing in his Pendleton career for sure.

"Hi Mr. Beck." Probably should have called him Chief, but just didn't know him that way.

"Hi Curt. I mean Cash. I'm sorry, I've always gotten you two mixed up." *Is he onto me? Was that a test?*

"Don't sweat it. People been doing that our whole lives." I made sure not to flinch when he called me Curt. No tells. I'd been developing that skill my whole life playing this stupid game with my brother. *You hear that, Cash? It's a stupid game. Sleeping with my wife. It explains a lot, doesn't it?*

"These footprints and car tracks yours, Cash?"

"Yes sir. I walked around the back of the house too. I saw no footprints back there, and this whole driveway had been shoveled clean before whoever did this left. My..." I almost said my shovel was missing, but quickly remembered I was Cash. "I'm figuring they had to have gone in through the garage door. There were water spots on the kitchen floor too. That's where they or he had to go in."

"What if it was a woman?"

Hunh. "I hadn't thought of that possibility. Once you see the crime scene, you'll understand." How would another woman pull my struggling wife out from under the bed

36

with one arm and put a bullet square in the back of her head with the other? Maybe a 'roided-up East German gymnast, but this was Pendleton. We don't even have a gymnastics team.

"What else can you tell me, son?"

Maybe too much if I keep talking. "I don't know right now. My mind isn't quite right. I just tried not to disturb the crime scene. Didn't even want to make a phone call from the house. That's why I went home first."

"Good. That's good thinking, Cash. You don't look good, though. You've been crying. Your face is all red."

"Yeah. Yeah." He caught me. I paused for a second to think. "I cried after I spoke with you. I put the phone down and just lost it sir. That's what took me so long."

"Don't worry about it, son. I ain't your father." I guess he knew my father's position on crying, and maybe he wasn't as stern as I'd always imagined. "Any man who loses his brother and sister-in-law in the same moment wouldn't be human if he didn't shed a tear."

"I guess. Once I made the call, everything I'd been keeping down that whole time just came up all at once."

"I get it, son. And didn't you date your brother's wife back when you were younger?" *This guy's good.*

"Yeah, for about three years." The last thing I wanted to do was let on I thought he was considering me a suspect. That whole thought needed to seem inconceivable. This town's so small, there are only two cops. Once they started trying to prove I committed the murders, they were no longer going to have time to be looking for the real killers. Look what happened to O.J.

"That must've made it even harder."

"No, that was a long time ago. I didn't think of Callie like that. She's my brother's wife, and nothing more. Should we go in, sir?" Change the subject. But those words were going to bite me once the chief discovered that Cash was having an affair with Callie.

"No, I'm waiting for Deputy Graveline. He's on his way. And you can't go in there. You'll have to wait out here until we secure the crime scene. We've got detectives and an ME coming from Lockport."

"Aren't you obligated to make sure there's no one in there alive and in need of medical attention?"

"Already checked, son. Coroner's on his way too, but I've already been in there. I don't have any question that they're dead. It's just not official yet."

I nodded my head as I processed this information. I was starting to regret my decision not to admit I was Curt. Add the fact that my fingerprints will be all over that house, there was no way they weren't going to try to pin this on Cash. Fear of being killed for being Curt still outweighed that regret though.

Then the chief changed the subject. "I hear Jake Charm's back in town, y'know... from wherever the heck he's been all these years."

"Yeah, he is. I saw him last night. Stopped in at the bar. We talked 'til three or four in the morning."

"Didn't he date Callie back in high school?"

"Right up until he joined the military."

"Then she started dating you?"

"Yep, his best friend."

"Huh, what are the odds?"

Tyler pulled in fast without his lights on. Probably not enough traffic to make the noise and draw attention. Pendleton's small, and sirens draw attention. He pulled up right behind my car. I was boxed in.

He was the muscle of Pendleton PD. Chief Lyman Beck was the brains and experience.

Tyler got out. He was stocky and ripped, spent a lot of time in the gym. Still about two inches shorter than I was, but I wouldn't think of messing with him. Trained to kill in seven languages. "Hi Cash. Sorry to hear the news. You called this in, right?" He shook my hand. Tyler was a good man. Always had been. Had a good family. I had nothing but admiration for him.

"Yeah. Curt was supposed to meet me for breakfast this morning. He never showed up and didn't answer the phone. I came over to check on him and discovered... yeah, well, you'll see."

"Well, let's go in, Chief. You stay out here, Cash. We can't have you walking around the crime scene."

"I get it. I'll be right here."

I stood in the cold for a while. The wind was the only noise. It whistled across the yard trying to draw up drifts around the house and in front of the garage door. Five minutes of quiet was followed by the arrival of the crime-scene squad. There were two

38

blue-and-whites, one ambulance, and two unmarked cars that arrived in the span of a few minutes. Unlike Tyler, these guys came with the sirens blaring. Big-city cops. All show, no couth. Little-city cops, really. Lockport's not really that big.

The paramedics brought out a couple of collapsible stretchers. The crime-scene squints had their science kits. The two detectives wore pants that didn't match their sport coats, but they did wear ties. They were dressed up, but not enough to suggest they didn't need a pay raise come salary renegotiation time. Every one of them looked at me with an air of suspicion, but not a one of them said a word to me. Tyler met them at the garage door. He let the squints, the detectives and the camera guy pass, but he put a hold on the stretchers. The guys with the stretchers waited inside the garage and out of the cold. I was alone again, but not for long.

Within five minutes, a blue Blazer pulled into the driveway. It backed out and parked on the opposite side of the road. It was at least ten years old. The wheel wells were rusted out, and it sounded a little like the muffler had a few too many rust holes.

A grumpy muffler was music to my ears compared to hearing the last voice on the planet that I'd wanted to hear, "Cash Cutler, I knew I'd find you here." Skylar Freakin' Meade was about to blow my alibi to smithereens. I put my finger to my mouth and then waved my hands downward so as to suggest that she shut her mouth. She was calling me from across the road like a classless drunk at last call, but she did look really pretty in the "I'm-still-only-twenty-something-and-not-looking-for-any-sort-of-commitment" kind of way.

She had long blonde hair with natural curls and expensive high lights. She was wearing tight faded jeans with expensive fringe-circled holes and white cowboy boots that matched her white leather jacket. Too good looking to have the sense to wear a hat in this cold, I knew she'd be looking for something to cover her head sometime soon. I had my hood and was pretty warm, but she'd trained herself to suffer much, so as not to mess up her hair. Lucky for me, there was enough snow on the ground that she had to struggle walking up the driveway in those smooth-soled high-heeled boots, so much so that she couldn't talk and walk at the same time. A part of me wanted her to fall. *Sorry, Cash.*

When she got close enough for me to catch her if she fell, she said, "What? Did your brother catch you? Call the police?" I wouldn't have lifted a finger to keep her from falling. I probably would have laughed.

"No Skylar, they're dead. They've been murdered."

She went white. Now, she was a fair-skinned girl, but all the anger-inspired blood in her face disappeared quicker than the drunks at clean-up time. Her face changed. It was up, and then it was down. She went from looking like she was ready to kill me to as if she just needed a hug.

"What are you talking about?" She tried to bring back her fierceness in hopes I was joking, but it wasn't there.

"They were shot. This is the emergency I had earlier. I wasn't joking, Skylar. I had to call it in to the police. I just didn't want to get into it on the phone."

"My God, Cash, I'm sorry." Her drama-queen fierceness was gone again for a second. "Wait, you didn't do this, did you?"

I looked at her like she'd just said the dumbest thing ever spoken by a human. I wasn't going to answer her.

"You don't think I did it, right?"

Again, dumbest thing ever, but I asked anyway, "Why would I think *you* did it, Skylar?"

"Cuz I said I'm gonna kill dat bitch." She didn't really say "cause" spelled "cuz," but that's what it sounded like.

I looked at her and studied her. She was serious. Suddenly, there was a reason to consider her a suspect too. "You said that a long time ago." I took a shot in the dark. I was obviously not there when she'd said it.

"No Cash, I said it the other day. This is your problem, Cash Cutler. You never listen to what I say. It's like I'm not even here sometimes."

"Sorry, Skylar. I'm just not thinking too straight right now. I remember. I just don't think that's what we should be talking about. You keep talking like that, they're going to think you did it."

"Well," she pleaded, "*you* don't think I did it, right? That's all I care about."

"No, baby, no. I know you didn't do it." It was then I realized I needed her close rather than as an enemy. If she started chirping about some love affair between Cash and Callie, there'd be just about nothing keeping me out of jail. So, I called her "baby."

"Awww, good," she said with a really, really happy smile. Her eyes sparkled. I still don't know how she did that. She grabbed my arm with both of hers and cuddled up next to me, rubbing her head into my shoulder. "Thanks, baby. I love it when you call me baby." She bent her head up to fish for a kiss. Within fifty feet of my dead wife and brother, I bent down to kiss my dead brother's girlfriend in order to keep her happy. She tasted like vanilla and strawberry. It was nice, but not in a natural way. Callie never tasted like that.

If there was one thing our dad taught us about women, call your honey "baby." That's what he called our mom. Lucky for me, Cash learned the same thing I did.

40

I put my arm around her to comfort her. "Hey, Skylar baby?" Being called baby is her apparent weakness.

"Yeah, baby?"

"Let's keep the thing about Callie and me quiet. It's just going to bring up a lot of questions and maybe cause the investigation to get sidetracked."

"Okay. You're right. I won't say a thing." She put her arm around me and hugged me. "I'm really sorry about your brother."

"Yeah, me too. About Callie, too."

She looked up at me with a lifted eye. I was about to blow this whole thing.

"Just not as much."

"That's right," she said as she got up on her tiptoes to kiss me. She stuck her tongue in my mouth this time and still tasted like vanilla and strawberry. "I'm gonna take care of you, Cash Cutler. You're mine, all mine." She hugged me again. One of those pull me in close, hold me tight for a few seconds and then let me go hugs, but without taking her arms off me. "I'm cold. Can we go inside?"

"No. It's a crime scene. We have to stay out here. They said so."

"Can we sit in your car then, 'til they come out and get you?"

"Sure."

Once the heat was pumping out warm air again, Skylar backed away from the vents and settled into the seat. She turned her body to face me and put her head back against the passenger window.

"What do you think happened, Cash? D'you think your brother was into something bad?"

"I don't know, Skylar. I've been trying to figure it out all morning. I can't come up with anything or anyone who'd want to kill them," *that I'd tell you about.*

It was true. I didn't really have any definitive idea of what happened, but the hunches I had weren't about to be shared with the girl that could rat me out for having an affair with my brother's wife. I had to keep her happy so she wouldn't put Chief Beck on to my scent, and I had to keep her convinced that I was indeed Cash. Thank God I was wearing his deodorant and cologne. *What a freaking mess, Cash. What were you up to?*

I was quiet and trying to figure this out, as you'd expect. Skylar wouldn't stop looking at me. It was like she saw me in a whole different light, and I was hoping and praying it wasn't because she might have thought I wasn't Cash. But my brother always could be broody at times. This would probably be one of those times. She might just have been happy though that her worst fears weren't true: that I was cheating on her with Callie. *How messed up is that?* Her boyfriend's brother is dead, along with his wife, and she's happier that it's that, instead of discovering her boyfriend had been cheating on her again. Love can be a messed-up thing, not that I was sure that's what it was. I never got the idea from my brother that he was actually in love with Skylar. Just got the feeling she was the girl he liked spending his downtime with. Nothing more. He wasn't the commitment type. He was committed to his bar. That was his first love. Skylar was a hobby.

Maybe that's what Skylar thought too, and when I called her baby after her discovering this wasn't Cash cheating on her again, maybe she was getting excited about being a bigger part of Cash's life. I couldn't be sure. I didn't know too much about how Cash had treated her when no one was around. If I think about it, it probably wasn't that good, considering he might still have been sleeping with my wife. *Why Cash, why my wife?*

That's probably what screwed up our marriage. I had no idea whatsoever that they were sleeping around behind my back. Maybe her depression was a result of Cash and not me. Must have felt she married the wrong Cutler boy. Cash was always the favorite. More fun, riskier, more dangerous, always happy-go-lucky Cash. I was the cerebral one with the goals and the plans. Cash was the fun one. He was the quarterback with the golden arm, while I was only his second favorite target. If I were a girl that had the choice of Cash or me, I'd choose him too.

"Do you think we're in trouble too, Cash?"

"No." *I'm not sure.* "You think we're in trouble, Skylar?"

"I don't know. There's just a lot of crazy things that go on in that bar of yours."

"Like what?" *Now I'm getting somewhere.*

"Don't play dumb with me, Cash Cutler. You know all about it. You know, with Pacho and all his friends."

"Yeah, well that doesn't have anything to do with me." I didn't know what the heck she was talking about.

"Don't be naïve, baby. It has everything to do with you. You don't accept that deal, it's going to piss off a lot of people. Powerful people." *What deal?*

"D'you think I should accept the deal? I want your honest opinion."

Oh man, she just lit up. "Really? You want *my* opinion? Who are you, Cash Cutler?"

"I don't know any more. If this were a Dear Abby letter, I'd sign it 'Befuddled in Pendleton.'"

42

"Who's Abby?" *The girl's young. My brother likes 'em young.*

"No one. It's just an old advice column. I'm asking for your advice, baby. I really could use it right now."

"Okay, baby. I like this. Should you accept the deal? I know you love that bar... but it's a lot of money. It's a *lot* of money, Cash. You could get yourself another bar and still have a big old pile of cash, Cash." She smiled at me. Thought she was clever. "We could roll around on it naked. Wouldn't you like to do that just one time? I'd be the stripper, and you'd make it rain. Mmmm." She reached over and purred as she kissed me and rubbed my crotch.

"Look solemn, girl." *Who am I? John Wayne?* "If they're watching us, you look a little too happy to be sitting here. Don't forget that two people are dead."

"Sorry, baby. You just got me all horny. I'll try and control it...'til later, of course." *Of course.*

"So, you think I should take the deal, huh? But that bar used to be the family restaurant. It's part of my family. I'm the only one left now."

"You've got me." She went sad and meek for a moment, as if the meek shall inherit *all* the love of the one and only Cash Cutler.

"Yeah, I know. I mean in my family. My brother and both my parents are gone now." I paused for a thought. "So, what if I don't take the deal? Will you still like me?"

"Right now, Cash, I've never liked you more. I was starting to doubt you, but I shouldn't have. I can't wait until we're alone. No, take that back. You can't wait until we're alone."

"Control it, baby. We're probably under observation right now. This is serious. We're both going to be suspects, and we have to work together on this."

"Anything for you," she said as she pretended to wipe tears from her dry eyes.

"So, what if I don't take the deal? What happens?"

"I think you're going to piss off a lot of people. That's what. If you want to do that, okay, I'll stand by you, but there's going to be a lot of people really pissed off."

"Why do you think they want it so bad?" *Surely an answer I should have known, but why not?*

"Money laundering, duh, just like we've been doing all along. Except they want to cut us out by paying you off for the bar. Better than killing us off, right?" *Who is this girl, Cash? With one question she goes from vacuous horny trophy girlfriend to my partner in crime. So, I'm a criminal now, with your trophy girlfriend, Cash?*

"Do you think they had something to do with this here?" I asked.

"Like, they're sending a message? Sign on the dotted line, or more people will die, see?" She pursed her lips in thought while her tongue moved from up against her left cheek to up against her right and then back again. "I sure hope not, Cash. The last people I'd want after me were Pacho's friends. They're monsters, but you know that."

Tyler came out the garage door. He peeled off some rubber gloves, put them in a plastic bag, sealed it and wiped his brow. After a few deep breaths to get the smell of death out of his lungs, he walked over to my window. I remember having to do that when I got out of there. It wasn't rot. It's just that collusion of smells that comes out when the body can no longer hold it all in. I started to get out, but he told me not to. I rolled down the window.

"Stay warm, Cash." He shook his head again. "I'm really sorry about what's happened. I haven't seen anything like this since my rookie year in Lockport."

"Did you find any clues?"

"Uhh, no. It was clean. There will be fingerprints galore, and blood samples to check. But they won't get to those for a few days. Barring the holy grail of DNA evidence, if you didn't do it, it looks like a professional hit."

"You think I did it, Tyler?"

"No, I don't, but don't tell him I told you, but you're atop Chief's suspect list. He's just doing his job. Don't take it personal."

"Figured I would be there. I was just telling Skylar as much. You and Skylar met?"

"No, hi, Skylar," he said.

"Tyler used to play football with me and Curt. Back in the day."

"Back in the day," Tyler repeated with a bit of nostalgia in his cadence.

"Nice to meet you," Skylar said.

"Anyone else on that list?" I asked.

"Yeah. Jake Charm. Our boy's back in town. You know that, right?"

"Yeah," I said, "I spent a couple of hours with him at the bar last night. I told the chief that earlier."

"That's right. He *did* mention that. How's he doing?"

"I can't tell," I said, "He's been all around the world though. Said something was calling him home."

44

"Wonder if it was this. Everyone at Starpoint thought he and Callie would end up married. What are the chances?" *Yeah, as if I haven't heard that same question for years: what are the chances she'd end up with you? I could never get out from under the shadow of Jake Charm.*

"Yeah, that's what the chief said."

Tyler then turned serious cop and asked, "Do you think he had something to do with it?"

I didn't hesitate. "No, not a chance. I was with him 'til three or four in the morning, and then he walked home."

"He walked home? It was cold last night. Snowing too."

"Yeah, I know. I offered him a ride on my sled. But he wanted to walk home. Said he hadn't been in the snow in a long time. Wanted the fresh air."

"Okay, I get it. Which way'd he walk?"

"East."

"Towards here, right?"

"Yeah, but no, he had nothing to do with it, I'm sure. He was going to his parents' old house. Someone's been taking care of it."

"That's not far from here."

"True," I admitted. He was just doing his job though.

"So, you're absolutely sure he isn't capable of doing this?" Cops love to ask the same question multiple ways. See if they can get you to slip up.

"Tyler, I think he's capable of killing everyone in this town in one night. He's a total badass Rambo-like killing machine. But he didn't have any bitterness in him. He was peaceful. In total control. He was really nice. I can't wait to see him again. Seriously. If you get to see him, you'll see."

"Oh, that's great," Tyler snapped out of cop mode and was back in Tyler mode. "That's great to hear. I can't wait to see him too." He caught himself for a second and looked at me seriously again. "I didn't mean to be insensitive. We're going to have a lot to deal with here for the next few days. I'm just happy to rule out the chief's suspicions."

"I get it. I understand, Tyler. You gotta do your job. I'm going to do whatever's necessary to help solve these murders." *Just like O.J., right?*

"Don't get me wrong, though. Chief's still going to be all up your butt the next few days. Jake's butt too, I'm sure. He's old school. Solved a lot of these cases in the

45

past, and he's always going to look at those closest to the murdered first. That's you, my man."

"I know."

"All right Cash, listen. They're going to be bringing the bodies out in a couple of minutes. You don't want to be here for that. Go home and get some rest. We'll be in touch. I'll move my car right now. Again, I'm sorry for your loss. Nice meeting you, Skylar."

"Thanks, Tyler. Tell your folks I said hello."

"I will."

He got into his car and moved it over a space and parked behind the Chief's car. As I was backing up, Tyler yelled for me to stop. Chief Beck came waddling out of the garage and over towards my car.

"Hi, Mr. Beck. Tyler said I should get out of your hair."

"He's right, son. I just wanted to tell you I'm sorry for your loss-- oh, who's this?"

"This is my girlfriend Skylar. She came over to comfort me."

"Oh, well, nice to meet you, Skylar. Did I say that right? You young people with your slick names." *Your name is Lyman, Mr. Beck.*

"Yes. Nice to meet you too." Skylar was being delightful.

"Listen son, like I said, I'm really sorry about all this. We're going to find who did this. I promise."

"Thank you, sir."

"Go get some rest, son." He was testing me again. Not saying I blamed him. Just an interesting way to check me out.

I rolled up my window and backed out. More snow had accumulated on the driveway. When I pulled out onto the road, I pulled up next to Skylar's Blazer and stopped. Moment of truth. *How do I get rid of her without getting rid of her?*

"Here you go," I said.

"Where we going?" *I wasn't getting rid of her.*

"I just figured I'd go back to my place and go to sleep. I'm exhausted."

"All right," she said, "but if you think you're exhausted now, check back with me later when I'm done with you." She rubbed her crotch to make her point.

46

"I'm serious, Skylar. I'm really not sure I want company right now."

"Okay, Cash. You want me to just sit there and be quiet, I will, but I'm not leaving you alone tonight, Cash Cutler. Not gonna happen."

"Okay, fine." I just wanted this discussion, whatever it was, to end. The police officers investigating me were watching my every move. I had to give in and hope she'd never figure out I wasn't Cash.

"Good," she smiled and reached over to kiss me on the cheek before getting out.

She followed me home.

She was my number one suspect. How'd she get to Curt's house so quickly after telling me she was going to check Ted's Pizza and then to Curt's house? She had been to Curt's house a couple of times in the last year, but Cash had driven her there both times. So, she technically did know where to go, but how did she know I'd be there? It's one thing to accuse Cash of getting in trouble with Curt over Callie, but it's a whole other thing to actually believe it might be true. I figured those accusations were just trial balloons to see how I reacted on the phone. What in our earlier conversation convinced her that I'd be over at Curt's? I mentioned nothing of the deaths. To give her the benefit of the doubt, maybe she just decided to drive by there on her way to Five Corners and then to Cash's house. That was hopefully what happened. If she really was that jealous though, maybe she did do it.

Chapter 6

Walking up the steps to the family homestead felt different this time. Sure, I'd grown up here, but with Curt and Callie officially gone, this was my home now. There was no going back to the Fisk Road house.

I got out of my truck as soon as I'd parked between the house and the barn. Skylar pulled in right next to me, having followed closely. I went right up the steps before even acknowledging her. I was pretty low, but I wanted to make sure she knew that. I didn't want her to think I had any interest in her. I was serious when I told her I wasn't up for company. At the same time, I wasn't about to start a fight about the whole thing. A fight might lead to a breakup, and a breakup would have her telling the interrogators about the affair. I was between a rock and a hard place made of diamond.

That in mind though, I did think it might be a good idea to keep her close and figure out if it was indeed Skylar that killed my brother and my wife. I just needed to make sure I kept a balance between my wants and needs. I wanted her to leave me alone, but I needed her to feel comfortable enough to tell me what she knew, whether it was a lot or just a little.

I unlocked the door without having even looked at her, but she was right behind me. I walked in, kicked the snow off my shoes and went to the living room. I dropped my coat on the couch. It had my gun in the inside pocket. I wanted the gun close to me, but I didn't want her to know I was packing.

She dropped a pink bag of overnight clothes and her purse on the dining room table before following me into the living room. As soon as my coat was on the couch, she was hugging me in a comforting way. She didn't say a word, but I let her hug me, reluctantly resting my arm on her lower back. It made her hug me ever harder. It lasted at least a minute, but it felt like a half hour. Weird and uncomfortable. I wasn't used to such warmth. Callie had been cold for a while. Probably saving all her warmth for Cash — he always was the favorite.

"I'm really sorry about your brother, Cash. I know what he meant to you."

"What about Callie?" I asked. If I were Cash, sleeping with my brother's wife, why would someone get the idea that my brother meant a lot to me?

"I hate her. She's a tramp... I'm sorry she's dead, but I'm only kinda sorry. I hate what she was doing to you..." She saw me raise my eyebrows in surprise. "I'm sorry, I'll stop talking now. I'm going to get a shower and then I'll fix you something to eat. You must be starving."

She kissed me on the cheek, grabbed her bag and purse and went upstairs as if she lived with me. If she did do it, she really wasn't worried about saying anything that might tip me off, that was for sure. Maybe that was part of her genius. Avoid suspicion with pure honesty drenched with lies.

I sat down next to my coat and turned on the TV for some background noise so I could think. It was the second half of the one o'clock football game. It wasn't the Bills. They didn't make it to the playoffs.

In addition to the interrogators, I obviously had to deal with Pacho the kitchen boy and all his friends. I had no idea how long they were going to let me play stupid before they'd concluded I was either disrespecting them enough to be shot or wasn't really Cash. They obviously had to be considered suspects as well, but why in the heck would they go after Curt - me? – and Callie? How would these murders facilitate the business transaction? Are money launderers that stupid? The dumbest thing criminals can do is attract the attention of police. Murder is a big attention getter. Maybe I was giving the criminals in my brother's life a little too much credit, but it just seemed a little too unlikely they could be that stupid.

A breaking news session in the middle of a commercial break highlighted the murder of the bank president of a small Pendleton bank in the middle of acquiring another small Pendleton bank. The news stations were all out of Buffalo, so they must have just gotten news vans to my old house where the murders had taken place. There was still one cop car there, but the police and ambulances from Lockport were gone. There was still one of the unmarked cars, probably belonged to the detectives. There was crime-scene tape stuck to the doors, and Chief Lyman Beck was holding all his cards close to the vest. He gave the newsgirl pumping him for information and hunches absolutely nothing. Instead, he focused on how this was the first homicide in Pendleton in decades and how he was personally saddened by the deaths of Curt and Callie, having known and watched them grow up.

Then the news lady asked a question out of nowhere, the kind of question that reminds you of why journalists are so despised by regular people. "That's all well and good, but Chief Beck, can you comment on the common knowledge that Curt Cutler has a twin brother who was still in love with Curt's wife Callie, going back to when they were kids?"

The chief went white and sunburned the newsgirl's face with the hot anger in the look he gave her. Get her, Chief, melt her like a snowflake. He looked like he wanted to drop kick her back into Erie County, but he held it together. "I can't comment on rumors. Two people are dead, and there will be an investigation. That's all I've got to say right now."

A small gaggle of reporters from the other stations then sent a barrage of questions at him as he walked away from them and back into the garage beyond the crime-scene tape. Then I heard another curious unanswered question coming from the gaggle: "Does this have anything to do with return of Jake Charm?" The reporter didn't even know Jake's real name. She used his nickname.

Who the heck told the newsgirl that Curt had a twin brother who lusted after his wife? Was there some sort of inert Pendleton gossip oracle the newsgirl could consult on her way to the crime scene? It must be inert most of the time. How often do these Buffalo newsgirls ever need to come to Pendleton? Who's putting a dossier of gossip together on everyone, just in case something interesting happens that needs to sound a little more interesting for the sake of the newsgirls' audience?

Is it Skylar? Am I in the same house as the news gossip? Nah, can't be Skylar. What kind of mindless resentment could outweigh the asininity of spreading rumors that turn you into a murder suspect along with the guy you can't keep your hands off? Someone else is talking to the media. The only reason they'd be doing this is to turn attention away from them. Find out the source. Whoever it was knew about the murders before the news hit the fan.

The regular programming resumed. It was the New England and Kansas City. As a Bills fan, I was rooting for Kansas City. But it didn't matter. The Bills were done. I just hate New England.

After a while, Skylar came down the stairs with a quiet grace. Nothing like the sound I'd make banging my shoes on the wooden steps. She walked into the room with a sympathetic look on her face, but she was dressed in nothing but lacy underwear and bra. They were both off white and probably matching. Didn't have the time to determine that. Her body was model-like. Whether her underwear matched her bra didn't seem important at the moment.

She looked at me as if she were completely oblivious and unaware that she was in nothing but her skivvies. If she actually knew I wasn't Cash, she sure seemed to want to make sure I saw what my brother saw in her. It was working. *Why?*

"You forget to bring your clothes?" I sprinkled a little hard-to-get on a plate full of indifference.

"No," she said completely dismissing my indifference, "it's really warm in the house. Didn't feel like wearing them. But I do want to cuddle up next to you."

"It's a free country."

50

"No, it's not." She grabbed the couch blanket off the chair on the other side of the end table, moved my coat over, and plopped down next to me with a blanket covering her parts.

I did my best to remain indifferent, but it was hard. She reached over for my coat. "What do you have in your coat that's so heavy?" By the time she'd finished the question, she'd already brought out my gun.

Instead of being afraid of it, she checked the chamber to make sure it was clear after making sure the safety was on. "Just wanted to make sure you're being safe." Without asking why I was packing, she put it back in my pocket and pushed the coat to the other end of the couch. Then she put her right arm across my belly to hug me while she lay her head on my chest to get a good view of the TV.

It was one of those old cathode-ray tubular deals. It was black and modern, not one of those old wooden console TVs, but it was no big old flat TV. My brother never did have a taste for the accoutrements of life. He'd be happy living in the wilderness if they'd let him. One of the things I loved about him.

"The Patriots are getting their butts kicked.

"Good," she said, "I hate the Patriots."

I smiled at her. It was actually a sincere smile.

"Cool," she said and sent a return smile with that eye sparkle thing she can do. She rubbed her head into my chest in search of comfort and watched the game. By the time she was set, my right arm was around her and laying against her side, and my hand was on her bare belly. It was smooth and warm, a little wet with moisture from the shower. I'd been married to a woman who'd had no interest in me for too long to be totally indifferent.

I was saved by the doorbell. It rang and then there was a knock on the hardwood door.

"Who could that be?" she asked.

"No idea," I said. "Want me to go and get your clothes?"

"No, baby. I'll just stay in the blanket. They won't stay long. Probably just want to give condolences."

Yeah, but what does that say about me, that on the day my brother was murdered, I have a mostly naked girl on my couch? I'm no longer Curt. I'm Cash. The favorite one always gets away with things that most people don't. I hoped.

Before I opened the door, I looked back into the living room where her body was fully wrapped. She looked happy. Her cheeks were red with warmth. But no shame. It baffled me.

As I opened the door, I could hear the seal break and the whistle of the snow-drift wind. The cold hits you quick as it beats back the warmth in the house. Jake Charm stood on the other side of the screen door.

"Come on in, Jake."

He stomped his boots and shook the snow off his body on the porch before he stepped in. Took off his hood, wiped his upper lip and shook his head in disbelief. As if he were fighting back his tears, he said, "I'm sorry, brother." He shook my hand as he walked onto the rug in front of the door. "I'd hug you right now, but I'm covered in snow."

"I know, Jake. Thanks for coming."

Skylar called in from the couch, "Who is it, Cash?"

"It's our old friend Jake Chambliss. He just got back in town. Jake, this is my girlfriend Skylar."

"Jake Charm!" she said, "I've been dying to meet you, Jake. Cash's told me all about you."

Under his breath and so only I could hear, Jake said, "You've told me nothing of her though." Raised his eyebrows to scold me.

"Didn't come up, I guess."

He flashed me a smirk only I was supposed to see. "Nice to meet you, Skylar."

"I'd come out there, but I'm not wearing any clothes." *Like I said, no shame.*

"That's all right, Skylar. I won't be long. I just wanted to talk with Cash for a bit."

"Well, if you want, I can put some clothes on and make you some lunch."

"I don't want to put you two out."

"Don't sweat it," Skylar insisted, "after what happened today, you guys have a lot to talk about. Go out to the barn and have at it. I'll make you both a meal. Call you in when it's ready."

"Thank you, Skylar. We can do that." I really did want to talk with him in private more than she could have possibly known.

"Okay," Jake said, "I've got no place to be."

I walked into the living room to grab my coat. When I reached down to kiss her puckered lips demanding my attention, she whispered, "Don't worry, baby. I'll take my clothes off again as soon as he leaves." *She was impervious to my indifference.*

Chapter 7

The coat's heft reminded me I had my gun in the pocket. Skylar put it in the wrong pocket. I like it in the left inside pocket because I'm right-handed. Whatever, I didn't think I'd need it with Jake. I didn't believe for a second that Jake was the murderer.

Walking across the parking area in front of the garage on the way to the barn, I noticed the winds had picked up since earlier. Jake said, "I see you're packing heat."

"Always."

"Huh. In Pendleton?"

"I close a bar and walk out with cash... at night. Don't do *that* without a gun."

"Makes sense. Skylar's nice."

"Yeah."

"Young."

"Yep."

"Good for you."

"Yep?" I said it with a question. Don't know why.

"No?"

"No, no. Didn't mean it like that. She's great."

I opened the small door on the left side of the barn. I didn't feel like moving the ice and snow in order to move the sliding door in the center. Water would drip from the icicles on the gutter above and turn the snow into a chunk of ice. The small door had a lock, but it probably hadn't been used in a long time.

My dad's workshop was on the left side of the barn. Workbench space went the length of the left side of the barn and then for about ten feet on the back side. We walked in and moved over to the right. There were stairs to the second floor, along the wall facing the house, in between the small door and the sliding door. There were two snowmobiles, two four wheelers, a tractor, some empty cow stalls and two generations' worth of collected junk to keep the dust off the floor. The stalls hadn't been inhabited for decades, I imagine.

"You know I didn't do this," Jake said, as he dusted off the seat of a raised stool up against the steps and sat down.

"Yeah, of course. Never even crossed my mind. I was with you last night." I climbed up on the four-wheeler that I ride. It was parked facing where he was sitting.

"Not after I left," he reminded me.

"You know *I* didn't do it, right?"

"Yeah," he said, "but Callie told me that you were in trouble. You *and* your brother."

"Curt was in trouble? Didn't know that."

"You too."

"Me? Nothing I can't handle. But I didn't know about Curt's trouble. What'd she say it was?"

"She didn't give me details. Just said that both of you needed my help."

"How'd she get a hold of you?" I asked in disbelief.

"She called the recruiter, the recruiter happened to know someone who knew how to contact me."

"What she say about the trouble?"

"Nothing. I'm telling you the truth. No details. But she said, please, please, please come home. Three pleases."

"That's a lot. I see why you came."

"Yeah," he said, "It's hard to resist one, let alone three. Callie was always really polite."

"She was. But three pleases. Surprised you weren't here last week."

"I only got the message two days ago."

"Oh," I said. "Those were some powerful pleases."

He smiled. "Never could resist Callie."

"You did when she tried to talk you out of joining the military."

55

"No," he said, "she broke up with me after graduation. I was destroyed. I wanted to marry her. Was ready to do the right thing. Scared her off. *That's* when I left."

"And never came back. What did you mean, do the right thing?"

"She was pregnant."

"Oh," *she never told me that*, "she never told me that."

"Why would she? She was devastated. Didn't want her parents to know." *I could see why. They're traditional folks.*

"What happened?" I asked.

"How do you *not* know this? You dated her for years after I left."

"She never told me any of this. Not a thing about being pregnant."

"She had an abortion. I begged her not to. Like I said, I was going to marry her. She did it anyway. Worst day of my life, and then she broke up with me. And that's when I left."

"And never came back," I said again.

"Never had a reason to. My folks were gone."

"I get it."

"Doubt you do," he said as he reached over and picked up an old football from the steps. He hit it a couple of times. The dust rose up into the light coming from the dust-covered bulb above his head. "Needs air." He threw it at me.

I had to reach up into the air to catch it. I threw it back. Hit him in the chest. The golden arm had to be accurate. He threw it back and made me reach to my right in order to catch it. But I couldn't without falling off the four-wheeler. It landed on the other side of the barn after bouncing off the rear sliding door that was used to let the cows out into the pasture. I climbed off the four-wheeler and walked around the tractor to get the ball. I threw the ball a little harder this time. He had to reach to his right but couldn't get it this time. He got off the stool and walked around to the front of the steps to pick up the ball. "You're a little rusty, old man."

"Probably. Just a little, though. I've been drinking milk." He smiled at the reminder of the Dairy Farmer Cartel's commercial campaign from our youth. The gist was, you can pick on me now, but I'm drinking milk, so I'm going to be huge and payback is coming, bully. Then the pink belts in charge of raising up the millennial snowflakes put the kibosh on that campaign. Something about drinking milk and growing bigger so you can get revenge on the bullies of your youth was nothing more than bullying the bully, which is still bullying. Moral lesson for America's youth: get your pink belt in sissy fighting and take the bullying like a weakling. And don't drink milk. It'll make you phlegmy and force you to get asthma.

We threw the Tom Brady-approved football back and forth for a while. Neither of us spoke. It was a lot easier throwing with accuracy while standing up.

"Come on," he said after catching the ball. He headed out the door. "I'm going long."

I followed him into the tundra. It was a little cold in the barn, but it was single digits at best, maybe a little negative, out in the wind. He threw it at me as he was walking out a little sideways. I had to work to catch it in the wind, but nothing I was too old to do. He ran out into the open snow-covered grass behind the garage. I threw it out his way, aiming for about three yards further. He didn't get to it though. The wind was blowing the ball past him and a little to the right. He threw it back, and it almost got to me. The wind was strong.

"Let's see what you got old boy," he had to yell over the raging of the wind.

I threw a Hail Mary. Put a really nice arc on the ball. He only had to run a little bit to catch it. We went back and forth a few more times. He came in and started calling off patterns. He ran a post, an out, a slant and then a go. He caught every ball. Just like the old days, except we were old.

He came in finally from the long go route, breathing pretty hard and admitted, "I'm getting old." He opened the barn door, and we both took our seats again. *We're no longer kids.*

Once he sat down, he inhaled hard in order to catch his breath again. He just looked at me, and I waited until he could breathe again. He broke the silence first.

"Were you going to tell me you weren't Cash?"

My face started to sweat. Freezing to sweating bullets in half a second.

"You guys still playing that game I see." Wasn't even a question.

"What game?"

"The one where you switch lives every year? Why do you think your brother always threw me more balls? I busted him." He started smiling as if he just realized he'd gotten away with the biggest ruse ever.

A smile betrayed my poker face. A secret from my youth had finally been revealed. I wasn't about to call him stupid. "So, you caught him? He never told me that. Didn't want to admit defeat. Good ole Cash."

"Nah, it wasn't anything he did. It was you. You were playing quarterback during practice. You and Cash throw differently. Cash was the golden arm. He threw like a

57

magician. You throw like a regular guy. That's how I knew you weren't Cash. When he threw, he always kept his arm up in the air as he watched the ball fly, unless of course he was about to get knocked down. You don't. You just bring your arm down. The golden arm acted as though he could control the ball even after he'd throw it. You, you throw it, and you're done."

"Huh," I said. "I always resented him for throwing more balls to you."

"Yeah, I know. I remember that last game."

"Like it happened yesterday," I said.

"You know it."

"So, you told him you knew he wasn't the one throwing to you, huh?"

"He begged me not to tell anyone, so I said I wouldn't if he always threw me more balls than you. You were better, but I wanted the balls."

"I always thought you were better than me."

"Yeah, because I got all the catches. Simple as that, Curt."

"Shhh, don't call me that, ever. Please, please, and please." Three pleases.

He smiled. "So, what happened?"

"We were playing the game," I said, "just like we have every year since we were kids. Haven't missed a year, and never got caught."

"Well, as far as you knew."

"Guess so. This year, he really didn't want to do it. But that's not new. Some years I was the one that didn't want to do it. Every time, we figured out a way to do it. Move it around, cut the time, whatever. We've never missed a year. So, I wasn't about to let that end. We switched for the weekend. I get to work the bar, and he doesn't have to worry about my job at the bank. And then someone killed them."

"You're not going to tell Chief Beck you're not Cash?"

"Are you kidding me? That would make me a prime suspect."

"You're already a suspect."

"True, but if someone was trying to kill Curt for whatever reason, if they find out I'm Curt, they're going to come for me."

"Good point," he said.

58

"I need to figure out who's behind this. Mr. Beck. Chief Beck's going to be looking at you and me. You know the media mentioned your return, right?"

"Yeah. I heard it on the radio. We're both suspects."

"I feel like O.J.," I said.

"Why, 'cause you did it?"

"No, because if I don't find the real killers, everyone will think I did."

He laughed. "You were good, but you weren't anywhere near as good as O.J. in his old days."

"Who was?"

"Good point," he said.

We got quiet. I was kind of happy he was in my boat, or even that anyone was. *If neither of us can be proven guilty, we're innocent until proven guilty. That gives me time to figure out why this happened.*

"What about Skylar? Does she know?"

"No, not that I can tell. If she does know, she's up to something. I just can't figure her out yet."

"Do you think she could have done this?"

"I honestly don't know," I said. "If what she's told me is true, then she'll be a suspect for sure. At the same time though, if it's true, there'd be no reason whatsoever to bring it up if she didn't want to be a suspect."

"What's that?"

"When I didn't have time to talk to her today, she said I'd been weird lately. Which is probably true because I'm Curt. She accused me of having an affair with Callie again. I just couldn't talk with her because I was trying to figure out how to call in the murders. Then, she showed up at the crime scene. My house. Sure, it's only a little out of the way to Cash's house from hers and maybe she was just driving by to make sure I wasn't there, but you know, what the heck?"

"This is getting complicated."

"Yeah, exactly. If she were guilty, she wouldn't have brought up her motivation, unless she actually wanted to get busted or maybe just throw everyone off her scent. Other than that, she's been amazing. The girl of every man's dreams."

"At least your brother wasn't gay."

"I thought about that. If he were, we'd have stopped this game immediately."

He laughed.

"You and Skylar..." he nodded his head like he didn't want to say what he was asking, "...you know?"

"No, not yet, thank God. But I don't know how much longer I can keep that from happening. She's nothing like Callie."

"What do you mean?" he asked, maybe for personal reasons.

"Callie's been cold for a while now. Real cold. Like we're not even married, you know?"

"Think it was Cash?"

"Maybe. I just found out about that this morning. I don't know what's what. All I know is, if someone was trying to kill Curt, they think it's done. If they find out it's not, they're coming for me. It's better I get to them before they figure that out."

"Man on a mission."

"It's not like I have a job at the bank anymore. I've got time."

"Well, I do too, brother," he said. "The girl of my dreams was killed and so was my best friend. I'm in. We're going find out who did this."

"I do appreciate that, Jake. You have no idea. Thing is, we got to make sure Chief Beck doesn't think we're colluding. Tyler might be all right with it, but Beck is by the book. Tyler knows us."

"No, hold off on Tyler too," he said, "We don't want to compromise him. We shouldn't make him choose between us and his job. This is between you and me. The other thing is, we can't be talking on the phones. That can all get subpoenaed."

"Should we get some burners?"

"Hold off on that too. You've got Skylar all up in your business. If you can't trust her yet, neither can I."

"All right. How do we communicate?"

"Probably in person. You, they might be watching you. So, you have to do what you always do. Me, they have no idea where I'll be at any moment, and I can lose them in two shakes of a lamb's tail."

"You got a four-wheeler or a sled over there?"

"Yeah. I've got an old Yamaha. Just needs a tune-up."

60

"Good," I said. "When I close up the bar, I take the back trails from the bar to my house here. You know where the Bull Creek Bridge is?"

"Same place as when we were kids?"

"Yep. It's been reinforced since then, but yeah. Just east of the creek, there's a clearing on the other side of the hedge rows. There's a trail going north off the trail to the bridge, about a hundred feet east of the bridge. Take the trail to the clearing and park behind the deer stand on the left. I'll be there about 2:40am any night the bar's open. Not tonight though. The bar will be closed in honor of Curt and Callie. Meet me there tomorrow night. 2:40."

"Sounds good," he said.

"In the meantime," I said, "watch the news at 6 tonight on channel 3. Get the name of the girl that brought up Cash having a thing for Callie and see if you can figure out who brought your name up. Find out who their sources are. That'll be key. You're probably a lot better trained at making people talk when they don't want to."

"I've got some skills," he said with a smug look.

"I figured you'd be good at that. I'm going to talk with some of the bank's board members. This may have something to do with the acquisition they have me working on – had me working on. Now I'm Cash, just the dead CEO's twin brother trying to figure out why my brother was killed. There's a lot of people that don't want this merger to go through and, since it's early in the process, I have no idea why. Actually, I do, but I have no idea why some of the board members don't want it to go through. I'm going to talk with the three board members that don't want this merger. Something weird's going on. Then, if I have to, I'll get in touch with the board members of the other bank. From what I hear, most of them are *really* against the merger. I just figured it was because they'd be off the board, but maybe there's something more to it."

"You sound like you knew I'd be a part of this."

"No, those are just the first two places I plan to look. I've been going over it in my head all day. I just figured if you were going to help, I'd put you to work finding out who the newsgirl's source was."

"Makes sense," he said.

"Tomorrow night at the bar, I'll feel out Pacho, and try and figure out what kind of trouble Cash was in. I don't have any idea why Callie knew about that and I didn't. If they really were having an affair, they were really good at hiding it, but it would explain Callie's seeming depression. Maybe she was depressed because she wanted..." *a baby and couldn't get pregnant* "...I don't know. Never mind that. We'll get to that if necessary. Right now, I just want to find out who did this, so I have something to say come interrogation time. I know what kind of questions they're going to ask, but I have to give them something to think about, so they'll proceed with the investigation that doesn't involve making me or you look good for it."

"How are you going to explain why your fingerprints are all over the bedroom?"

"That's a big one," I said. "I imagine I'm going to have to admit to having an affair. It's already out there. Just say I took a keen interest in my brother's stuff. Something like that. Hope it flies."

"What about Skylar? How will she take it?"

"Haven't a clue. But I figure she's bound to figure out I'm not Cash at some point. I just hope she can keep a secret."

"You are in a fine mess. That's for sure."

"Aren't you glad you came home for it?"

"Can't answer that. When Callie sent me the message, I didn't know what to make of it. Wish I'd come home under better circumstances a long time ago."

Skylar knocked and then opened the door. "I hope I'm not interrupting anything."

"No baby, come on in."

She smiled at me. A powerful smile. Almost as potent as the smile she gave me while sitting next to me in her underwear. She had me in way over my head. I could see Jake watch me and see it too. He knew.

She closed the door and shook off the snow. "It's getting blizzardy out there. I've made you guys some sandwiches, and I'll have chicken noodle soup done in about five minutes. It's in the pressure cooker. It's going to be good. I promise."

"I don't doubt it for a second," I said. Figured I'd throw her some confidence. She was in the middle of trying to make a good impression on my old high school buddy. "You up for a good meal, Jake?"

"Absolutely," he said without hesitation.

"Then follow me, boys."

She opened the door, and the sounds of the wind kicked up harder. It *was* blizzardy as she'd mentioned. She wasn't at all exaggerating. For a moment, there was such a big whiteout that I could barely see the house as we walked past the garage. Sure, it's a good hundred and fifty feet, but the house might as well have disappeared a couple of times.

62

Chapter 8

As Skylar was releasing the valve to the pressure cooker, she said, "Have a seat, you two. I'm just finishing this up." It was a nice programmable pressure cooker that sits on the counter and doesn't need a stove. The steam was shooting up at the ceiling in front of the cupboard. Skylar opened the fridge and pulled out a plate of intricately constructed sandwiches on hard rolls. There was turkey, ham, cheese, lettuce and tomato. She grabbed a bottle of Italian dressing and some mustard and placed them on the table that was already set with three plates, three glasses, three soup bowls and silverware. It was nice. Way more than I expected.

"That soup smells like we're in heaven," Jake said. "You have no idea how long it's been since I've had a bowl of homemade chicken noodle soup."

As she placed some already boiled egg noodles in each of our bowls with some tongs, she said, "There's nothing like my pressure-cooked soups. Cash likes them so much he actually bought a pressure cooker. I have one at home, but this is for here."

"Where'd you get all the ingredients, Skylar?" I asked.

"Snuck them in the other day. I was planning on making you a nice Sunday dinner. It's not like you ever look in the bottom drawers much. He's always eatin' at the bar. I'm always tellin' him it's not healthy."

"Well thank you, Skylar."

"You're welcome, baby. I thought we'd celebrate the news I have, but that was before what happened today, of course. I'll just save that for a better time."

Oh man, Cash. What have you gotten me into? She's got news.

She grabbed the three bowls, ladled soup into them and set them down. Jake's, mine, and then her own. Grabbed a box of oyster crackers and sat down. And then she prayed for a blessing on the food and that we'd be successful in bringing the killer or killers to justice. Didn't see that one coming.

I tried the soup and burnt my tongue. Blew on it for a few seconds, and it was amazing.

But Jake beat me to the compliment. "This is amazing, Skylar. All of it. You've got a keeper, Cash."

"Thank you, Jake," she said, "Sometimes I don't think he knows that. Hear that, Cash? I'm a keeper."

"You keep making soup like this baby, I'll never let you go. I'll burn down cities for you." I don't know where that last part came from, but the soup was really good. The kind that makes you lose your mind. She rubbed my knee with her socked foot under the table and winked at me.

"So, Jake," Skylar changed the subject, "I'm really sorry for your losses today. I know both Curt and Callie meant a lot to you, especially Callie. Cash and I are in total shock. Life doesn't prepare us for anything like this. So, let me apologize right now if I do something or say something wrong. I just don't know what I'm supposed to be doing today. I'm still at a loss." She paused and shook her head. "Listen to me, I'm just rambling. I'm sorry."

"Thank you, Skylar, for the kind words. I don't know how I'm supposed to act today either. You're forgiven ahead of time."

"All right then," she said, "forgive me for asking this right now, but I have to know. Was Cash as good as he says he was?" She smiled at me and touched my knee again. "You can tell me the truth."

"In all honesty," Jake created some suspense, "if I'm absolutely honest with you... and you're not going to leave him if I tell you the truth, right?"

"No, wouldn't think of it. I just want to hear it from you, you know, the myth and the legend of Cash's childhood. You know he always talks highly of you. So, tell me. Was he as good as he says he was?"

"Honestly, Skylar, he was probably better. Cash had the golden arm. Best in three counties, maybe four. Probably could have played anywhere in the NCAA, maybe even the NFL, but he wanted to stay home and take care of the family business. Don't ever doubt him when he tells you he was *good*. He was the best."

That was Jake reminding me who my brother was. Maybe even his way of saying, hold off on judging Cash for what Skylar told me had happened. Cash really was good. I always say he was the favorite, but he earned that. I was the selfish one. Aside from his drinking years after our parents died, he was the selfless one. It really was nice to have Jake in on my secret. For once, since the discovery of my dead brother, I didn't feel absolutely alone.

"Wow," Skylar said, "that is not what I expected to hear. Must mean I'm gonna be a football mama." She blew on her spoonful of soup as if she'd said nothing out of the ordinary.

"What do you mean?" Jake asked innocently.

"What did you just say?" I asked more directly.

"Cash Cutler..."

"Yes?"

"I'm pregnant. We're pregnant." Her face lit up, her cheeks got blushed, and I knew right then and there I was supposed to embrace this as if it was the best news ever. Cash was serious about this girl. My doubts dissolved in the glow of Skylar's face.

So, I smiled back at her. I could sense Jake breathing a sigh of relief. He saw it too.

Skylar expected nothing less. Didn't even flinch when I smiled. Just smiled back before saying, "We're having a baby, Cash. I know, it's an awful time to tell you, but I've been dying to tell you, and you've just disappeared the last few days, and I figured, with how we've lost Curt and Callie today, this might help a little. We're having a baby, Cash." Then she turned to Jake. "And Jake, even though you've already forgiven me for saying or doing something wrong today, I'm sorry, and I expected to tell him when we were alone, but now just seemed to be the perfect time."

"You're forgiven. This really is great news. I'm happy for the both of you, and you're right, it does make me feel a little better after all that's happened today. However, I am going to finish this soup and take another of these delicious sandwiches to go. You guys deserve to be alone."

"Don't be silly, Jake," Skylar said. "Stay and watch the game."

"I appreciate the hospitality more than you can imagine, but you two need some time alone." He had a glowing smile. I'm sure it was for my predicament, but it seemed to answer a question both of us had. He put on his coat and blizzard gear, grabbed a sandwich, wrapped it in a few napkins, stashed it in one of his glove pockets and put on his boots.

"You need a ride, Jake?"

"No, I'll walk."

"Want to borrow one of those four-wheelers?"

He thought about that, probably thinking this would save him the time and stress of giving the one at his parents' house a tune-up – that's what I was thinking too. The last thing he wanted to do was find he need a part on a Sunday. Hebeler's, the ATV and motorcycle shop at Five Corners was closed on Sunday. "Yeah, okay, sure. That'd be fine."

"Take the camo one. Key's in it." The camo one was the one I, as Curt, normally rode. I imagine that's the one that Skylar rode as well. The red Honda was Cash's – bigger, faster, stronger.

"Thanks, brother. Skylar, it's been a pleasure. Thank you for this amazing meal, and congratulations to the two of you. We sure can use a little good news." He gave her a quick hug and one last congratulations.

"Thanks, Jake. See you soon."

"You bet." He let himself out.

Looks like I'm going to be your baby's daddy, Cash. Who'd a thunk it?

Chapter 9

Once the sound of the four-wheeler disappeared in the distance, Skylar took off her clothes and climbed onto my lap to hug me, right at the dinner table. It was kind of the hottest thing that had ever happened to me. Callie was the girl next door muddling through depression and a desire to make me disappear. Skylar not only wanted me there, she wanted me to be happy while I was. Now, I'm not trying to bad-mouth my dead wife. I get it. She was suffering from depression. I didn't know if the depression might have been caused because she had cheated on me or if she had cheated on me because she was depressed. That was something I hoped I'd eventually discover. Or maybe it was because she couldn't get pregnant. She was apparently hiding the secret that she'd killed her baby when she was younger, and now she couldn't get another. Wow. What I didn't know about my own wife boggles the mind. Callie and Skylar were just totally different. While Callie took me for granted, Skylar wasn't doing that at all.

I could tell you I resisted the naked Skylar or felt bad about not resisting, but none of that would be true. I did, however, feel bad about not feeling bad – not even a distinction without a difference. Maybe I was being dishonest in not telling her that the man to whom she was giving all this love was actually dead. I did feel bad about that, but I couldn't give up my cover. It was too dangerous. Rejecting her after she had told me about the baby might have destroyed her. Had to take one for the team. That's what I told myself anyway. Like I said, I *am* the selfish one.

We ended up in the living room butt naked, wrapped in the blanket and watching the second game. I suggested going upstairs, but she was having none of it. She wanted the game on in the background. I'm not kidding. Eat your heart out, gentlemen: Cash Cutler was living like a rock star, and I was living as Cash Cutler.

In those moments, I stopped judging him for dating a younger girl in a relationship that Callie and I had agreed was going nowhere. There was a lot more to it than either of us had realized. Or maybe just more than I had realized. Callie might have had a better understanding and was just jealous. I couldn't be sure. Was Callie actually depressed because Cash like Skylar more than he like Callie? *You've got me living in a soap opera Cash.*

"Cash," Skylar said in a sweet voice with her arms around me, "I'm glad you didn't react badly to finding out about our baby."

"Why would I?"

She looked at me as if I were from Mars. "Because Cash, you said you didn't want children. Didn't think it would be a good idea to be working in a bar late at night and have children. Remember? Said you were never gonna have any."

"Yeah, I remember. Maybe that was just me not wanting you to get your hopes up."

"But they *are,* Cash. They always have been. I don't know what it is about you. I just can't get enough." Overkill with the love.

"Yeah, I know." I said it like I was just joking around.

She play slapped me. "What do you mean you know?"

"Just joking with you, baby."

"We're having a baby, Cash."

"I know. What should we name it?" I asked.

"Not an it, Cash. Him or her. The baby is a him or a her."

I smiled. "What should we name a him or a her?"

She said without hesitating, "If it's a boy, Curt."

"If *it's* a boy?" I said.

"You got me," she smiled, "If *our baby* is a boy, we'll name him Curt."

"And if she's a girl?" I asked.

"Not Callie."

"Of course not," I said.

"What do you mean, of course not?"

"I mean we won't name her Callie. How about Kelly?"

"No, sounds too much like Callie."

"Didn't think about that one," I said.

We did several more rounds of "how about…" Not one name we came up with was good enough for Cash's daughter. Skylar slept over that night. My first night with Skylar.

Chapter 10

Jake Chambliss' hope that sleeping in his childhood bed might give him the comfort needed to escape his demons was all in vain. He awoke that Monday morning just on time at 4:00am, drenched in the sweat to which he'd become accustomed. His reaction to the nightmares.

Back in Africa, he did at one point get his hands on some tribal tea. Definitely not FDA approved. It helped with the demons, just not the sweat. It was Africa though. Nothing helps with the sweat when you're out in the bush.

He looked at himself in the mirror above the toilet while he was taking care of his morning business. His long hair and beard were both gone, leaving a brown buzz cut and years of scars covering his chiseled face that could be seen for the first time in a long while. A reexamination of himself in the bathroom mirror of his childhood. He looked like he'd been domesticated after years on the run, but he felt just as wild as ever. Maybe even more so now that he was back in civilization. No longer anonymous and willingly putting himself in a spotlight with "I dare you" written across his forehead.

It was a risk. He knew it was. But Callie used three pleases. There's no kidding himself. He hoped she'd come to her senses. He'd never gotten over his first and only love. Nor the death of their child. He blamed her for a while but then learned to forgive. That ability came with age and wisdom, especially the wisdom that comes with exposure to so many vile killers, marauders and monsters.

Luckily though, most killers and monsters aren't anywhere near as persistent or as ambitious as the rogue crew of FBI agents from the Clinton era that have made it their life's goal to erase Jake Chambliss off the face of the planet, along with all he knew, which they wanted to remain hidden. The reputations and the honors of many, going right up to former FBI Director Louis Freeh himself and even President Clinton and Attorney General Janet Reno, depended on burying Jake's secrets. They all wanted Jake Chambliss dead, gone and forgotten, and they had a squad of former FBI agents on the permanent off-the-books payroll to make it happen.

Even though Jake knew that few would ever even believe him if he ratted, the Clinton crew didn't like loose ends. Jake was a permanent target, and he knew they'd be here soon. His name had been on the TV. Just a matter of time before scout agents

Simon and Dillard were here to verify the Jake Chambliss sighting before they'd call in the big guns.

Forget that for now. The newsgirl Ainsley Reed lived in Amherst, right off the Millersport Highway. While her address was unlisted, not everyone in the government hated him. One phone call, and he had everything he needed to know about the girl with the inside information, including photos to see what she looked like. She was pretty, but newsgirls and guys with targets on their heads don't mix. Newsgirls can't be trusted to keep secrets, since it's their job to divulge secrets. This was going to be tricky.

Jake grabbed a cup of coffee and a breakfast sandwich on his way through Five Corners at the Convenient Food Mart. He parked on the south side of the building, out of sight of the camera pointed at the gas pumps. Probably didn't matter though. There were surely cameras inside the store.

The bread on the sandwich was stale, but the coffee was all right. Bitter swill, the way he liked it. He drove south on Campbell Boulevard and crossed Tonawanda Creek as he left Niagara County and entered Erie County. A few miles later, he passed a house that some guy had been working on since he was a kid. The guy had been turning it into a wooden castle with intricate little Japanese-style woodwork designs all over the property. He'd made much progress in the last twenty years.

A few miles later, he took a left on Dodge Road. Her house was down another mile or so on the left. It was a small white ranch with a sidewalk from the driveway to her front door. The blinds in the front windows were all closed. Her blue Prius was parked in front of the small one-door garage. Strange she didn't park it in the garage in such cold weather.

He drove past her house and turned into a small parking lot next to a pizza joint about five houses down. The parking lot was separated from the pizza joint by a wooden privacy fence that ended at the sidewalk. The dumpsters were in between the fence and the restaurant. He parked in the spot closest to the sidewalk and put his head back. He was facing her house and had just enough angle to see it around the fence. He'd wait until she would leave towards Campbell Boulevard to go to work at her office in Buffalo. It was 4:45 am.

To remain as inconspicuous as possible, he turned the engine off. It got cold quickly. The wind didn't waste any time. It immediately started to build a drift around his car. Stay too long, and he was going to be trapped. That's the way the snow-belt winds of Buffalo like it. If people can move, the winds aren't doing their job. Having spent so much time away from Buffalo and in much warmer climates for most of that time, one would think him crazy for enjoying the cold, but he did. It reminded him of his youth and his freedom. Roaming the world as a wanted man with a target on his back made it impossible for him to indulge his yearning to be a winter-loving Buffalonian. Not that Pendleton was really Buffalo, but it was in Buffalo's Snow Belt. An outskirt on the outskirts of the suburbs of Buffalo. The cold was nice.

At 6:20 am, Ainsley Reed came out of her house all bundled up in a grey hooded coat to shovel the driveway behind her car. It was mostly a drift that had formed along the sides and around the back of her car. The rest of the driveway had about three inches of powder snow that she easily pushed to the sides after taking care of the drift. When she pulled out, she did indeed go towards Campbell Boulevard. Luckily, he waited for her to get some distance before he pulled out. After driving past only a few houses, she stopped, pulled over and got out to shake the ice off her windshield wipers. Then she used her gloved hand to wipe the snow off the rear window, which had come off her roof. After shaking the snow off her coat and gloves, she got in, put on her left signal, rolled down her icy window to wipe the snow and ice off her driver side mirror and then pulled out into the traffic-free road. Diligent.

Jake backed up and pulled out of the pizza joint after Ainsley had gotten another twenty to thirty seconds head start. In considering his next move, he was already regretting not having approached her while she was in her driveway. Waiting until she got to the TV station meant all kinds of cameras and security guards. He had to speak with her before that, but he had to do it without scaring the crap out of her.

He followed her back onto Campbell Boulevard, going south past the North Campus of the University of Buffalo, then down to merge onto Bailey. She then turned right onto Main Street at the South Campus. Her station was less than a mile up. Time was running out, but the sun hadn't yet risen. It wasn't even 7 am.

Ainsley then pulled into a gas station on a side street with a Dunkin' Donuts inside. Perfect. She got out and went inside.

Once inside, he pulled in and parked to her left. The windows in the store did not come over to where he was parked. He parked in front of a white cinderblock wall behind a four-quarter tire pump. He tried to roll his passenger-side window down, but it was still frozen stuck. He got out and calmly walked around the car to wipe the ice off the window. Then he finished walking around the car to get in. She was still getting her coffee and just about to pay for it.

He got in his car and rolled the passenger window down.

Ainsley had beeped the car unlocked before she'd even stepped off the curb, taking quick small steps in struggling not to slip while holding her coffee and a bag of food in her gloved hand. She opened the door, put her purse and food on her seat and her coffee in the holder. She grabbed the snow brush to do a little needed window touch up. When it snows in Buffalo, it doesn't stop accumulating.

Once she'd closed her door to keep the snow out, Jake said, "Ainsley Reed?"

"Yes."

"Can I talk with you for a second?"

She came over to his window and squinted in. "About what?"

"The murders of Curt and Callie Cutler."

"What about them? That's an old story. My manager already had us drop coverage. Said it was cut and dry."

"It only happened yesterday, Ainsley, and that's what they want you to think."

"Who are you?" she finally asked.

"I'm Jake Chambliss. I went to school with them all. Callie was my high school girlfriend, and Curt's brother Cash was my best friend. Seriously, can we talk?"

"We *are* talking."

"I mean in private. Will you get in my car?"

"I don't know you, and you're one of the suspects. You and your friend Cash. Story's over as far as anyone's concerned. I'm not going to get in the car with you. You nuts? I can call the cops though. You can have a talk with them. That what you want?" Trying to get into her car to get away, she grabbed her purse and put her food bag on the passenger seat.

"One second, Ainsley. Think about this. Within an hour of the murders being reported to the police, you had information insinuating that Cash was having an affair with Callie and that I was in town for the first time in two decades. If Cash and I weren't your source, why would you have that information so quickly? How'd you even know about the murders so quickly, anyways? It's Pendleton."

Ainsley squinted as if she was looking up into her brain for an answer.

"Who was your source, Ainsley? And why did they know so much so quickly?"

"I can't tell you that," she said. Standard boilerplate nonsense. *I'll never reveal my sources.*

"Can't tell me what? Why he or she knew so much, or who he or she is?"

"I can't tell you any of that."

"All right, then. What if your source is in grave danger? What if, by not telling me who they are, you might be endangering their lives?"

She stared at him. "I'm listening."

"Get in then."

"I'm not getting in there with you."

72

"Okay. Go to your car, get your purse, take out the pepper spray, take off the top and get in with it pointing at my face. I don't want to have this conversation out where random people can hear it. I'm not going to hurt you."

She looked at Jake with a smile. "How'd you know I have pepper spray?"

"Because you drive a Prius, work in TV and aren't married. You hate guns, but you've taken several girls'-night-out self-defense courses with your girlfriends. Every one of those courses told you to disable the predator by taking out his eyes, either with your thumb, finger or pepper spray. The classes probably even came with complementary canisters of pepper spray. I bet you have three of them."

She smiled again but not without a follow-up question. "What does me being single have to do with it?"

"I didn't say you were single. You did. I said you weren't married. Not the same."

"Okay, what does it matter that I'm not married?"

"In your line of work, you come into contact with a lot of dirt bags. Your husband would make you carry a gun. If he didn't, it'd only be because he's having an affair with some guy on the DL and didn't care if you get killed."

"What's with you?" she asked as she got in after putting her pepper spray back in her purse. "You're funny. Roll up the window, would you? It's freezing."

She took off her hood. She had red hair in a bob that she easily fixed with a couple of quick combs of her fingers. Not a lot of freckles on her fair skin though, just some redness from the cold. She was pretty in the nice-girl-next-door kind of way. The kind of pretty of a good girl who isn't the flashy type in miniskirts, tight shirts and red lipstick.

"Will you tell me who your source is or how you got that information so quickly? Please." Jake emphasized please.

"Polite too. No, though, I can't. How do I know you're Jake Chambliss? Got any ID?"

"Nothing that wasn't expired a couple of decades ago. Don't even have it on me."

"What are you talking about? You *are* nuts," she said.

"No," I said, "I've been working undercover for two decades. I don't have the luxury of traveling around as Jake Chambliss. All my documents are in a different name."

"What name?"

"Can't tell you that either. Not only would it put you in danger, it would put me in danger too. I've already told you way more than I should."

"Well then, Mr. Mysterious, if I'm not going to give you the information you seek, why are you still talking to me?"

"Because I don't want to see you get killed. Or your source."

"Are you going to kill me?"

"No, I'm going to protect you. This isn't some robbery gone bad or some love-triangle-murder situation. This is much bigger than you can even imagine. Why do you think your boss really wants to wrap up the story? 'Cause nobody cares about the people of Pendleton?"

"No," she said, "I don't know."

"Look, I got a hundred bucks that says he's your source, and that means he's in trouble. The only reason he wants this story shut down is to cover up what really happened. Planting information about me and Cash is to pin the murders on someone else."

"You're full of crap," she said as she gathered her things to get out.

"Am I really? Do I owe you a hundred bucks?"

She stopped and looked at him again nervously.

"Do you like your manager?"

"Yes," she said. "Why should I believe you? You can't even prove you're Jake Chambliss. What are they trying to cover up? Why are you here?"

"Now you're doing your job, Ainsley. Asking questions. Finding the truth. Good." Jake said it with a smile and a wink. It was his unpatented, but never duplicated, lady-killer smile and wink. He only used it to get information though. His love for Callie had never died.

She was not spellbound though. "Answer the questions, or I leave." Starting to remember what her job was.

"All right, Ainsley. But if I tell you all this, you can't run with it yet. There's no way to solve this crime if the perpetrators know we're after them. This might be the biggest story of your career. Agreed?"

"That's a lot of buildup, buddy. This better be good."

"There's nothing good about this," Jake said. "Two people are dead. And more are going to be dead if we're not careful."

"We're not careful?" She emphasized the word "we're," as if she wanted to keep herself independent.

"Yeah, we're. Look, once you know this, you're a part of it." At this point, Jake really was just making stuff up. He really didn't know much more than bits and pieces, but those bits and pieces were big enough to paint up a big conspiracy that might help throw the dogs off his scent for a while. He already knew that Louis Freeh's big dogs would be here soon enough. Their flight was probably landing in Buffalo some time that day.

"All right then, answer the questions."

"Three days ago, I got a message from one of my buddies still in the military that Callie wanted me to come home. Callie is the only girl I've ever loved. I'd do anything for her, and this was the first time she'd contacted me since I left."

"Why'd you leave if you love her so much?"

"She broke up with me after high school. I wanted to get married, and she broke up with me. I was destroyed, so I joined the military. Did some intelligence work. But there's people who want to kill me, so I have to travel in secret."

"Who wants to kill you?" She was sympathetic. Her antagonistic stance was melting.

"Can't tell you, but don't worry about that for now," Jake said. He could tell he was sucking her in.

"Well, if they want to kill you, aren't they going to want to kill me?"

"Yes." Jake saw Ainsley's face redden with a rush of warm blood as her heart started pumping a little harder. "That's why you can't talk about what I'm about to tell you. Not yet anyway."

"I'm a journalist," she said.

"Yes, but sometimes the big story takes time to unfold. You want the big story, right?"

"Sure, who doesn't?"

"Well, I have to find out who told your manager about the affair and me being back in town."

"I don't know," she said, "I really don't know. While I was being driven to Pendleton, he called and told me what questions to ask."

"Did any of the other news organizations have any of this information?"

"No," she said, "just me."

"That's good." Jake quickly reached into his inner coat.

"What are you doing?" Ainsley jumped back into defensive mode.

"Just grabbing my phone."

"Slow. You probably got a gun in there."

"Of course I do, but if I wanted you dead, I'd have killed you while you were shoveling your driveway."

"You watched me shovel my driveway?"

"Yes," Jake said, as he pulled up a gallery of photos on his phone. He punched open the hidden folder with his index finger and opened up the photo of Agent Dillard.

"You stalked me?"

"No, I waited for the right moment to ask for your help. You're giving it to me, Ainsley. Thank you. I do appreciate it. I'm not going to hurt you. You have to trust me."

"My dad said never trust a guy who says trust me."

"Your dad's a wise man."

"He's dead."

"Sorry. Have you seen this guy?"

Ainsley took the phone in her hand and looked at the photo closely. "Maybe, why?"

Jake flicked the screen to the next photo. "What about this guy?"

"He was with the first guy."

"When?" Jake demanded with a new urgency in his voice.

"They came in to see my manager Saturday after the six o'clock news. I saw them going into my manager's office after they'd finished taping. Who are they?"

"That's Agent Simon, and the first one was Agent Dillard. They used to be with the FBI, but they still pretend to be. They're rogue, and they're trying to kill me."

"Why are rogue FBI agents trying to kill you, Jake?" Ainsley was losing her ability to keep a straight face.

"Never mind that for now, this changes everything."

"You think these guys killed the Cutlers?"

"No," Jake said, "I don't know. I didn't think they'd get here until today. Why did they get here on Saturday, even before the murders, and tell your manager about me and Cash? Until this bit of information, I didn't think the murders had anything to do with me or these guys."

"What's going on, Jake? Who did you suspect?"

"Well, when Callie got me the message, she begged me to come home because both Cash and Curt were in trouble."

"What kind of trouble?"

"Not sure, but I have some sort of idea. You promise to keep this quiet for now, right?"

"Of course," she said, "the big story. Takes time. Got it."

"Exactly, the big story. This is what I know. Curt was the CEO of the Pendleton bank. One of the banks. His bank was in the middle of trying to acquire the other Pendleton bank. A lot of people didn't want that to happen. I don't know why though. Cash was being pressured to sell the family bar to some Mexicans. Again, don't know why. Maybe as a front. The big question is, why did Simon and Dillard meet with your manager, even before the murders?"

"This is a big story," she said, "kind of exciting. Either that, or you're full of crap." Ainsley then accidentally giggled like a schoolgirl without meaning to break her professional demeanor.

"Careful, Ainsley," Jake warned, "these men aren't to be trifled with. If you see them, walk away, slowly though. Don't draw attention to yourself. Get out of the building and drive away. Don't come back until you know for fact they're gone. Even if it means losing your job. If they're watching us, they already know you know too much."

"Are they watching us?" She looked around.

"No. But they might be. So be careful. Here, take my number, but put it under the name Steve or something. Don't use my real name."

She entered his number in her phone and then gave him hers.

"Jake," she said without the journalist's hard nose for news, "why do these guys want to kill you, and why should I protect you from them?"

He thought about it for about ten seconds. She just stared at him with the politeness of patience. So, he decided to try and buy her trust with the potential of another big story. "That's an even bigger story than this big story."

She lit up. "How could it be?"

"You remember the Oklahoma City Bombing?"

"Of course," she said, "from when I was younger. What about it?"

"Well, Cash, Curt, Callie and I went to school with Tim McVeigh. He was older, though."

"Oh my gosh," she covered her mouth in awe. "That's right. I'd forgotten about that. He went to school right here, didn't he?"

"Yeah, he grew up around the corner from me."

"My gosh, did you have something to do with it?"

"No," Jake said, shaking his head as if he found the question offensive. "I was in intelligence when it happened. I know about the cover up."

"What cover up?"

"One of the biggest cover ups of American history but forget that for now. We've got to deal with the Cutler murders first."

"You talking about John Doe Number Two?"

"Yes," Jake said, "exactly. You're a smart journalist."

"Thanks, but you're not John Doe Number Two, right?"

"No, I captured him after the bombing and interrogated him in a safe house."

"Where?"

"Wouldn't be a safe house if the news media knew where it was, now would it?"

"No. So, what happened?"

"I've never told anyone about this. I haven't even been back in America since it happened." Jake was feeling a little vulnerable, but he wanted it out just in case he was about to be disappeared by these two agents.

"I won't tell anyone," Ainsley said. "Don't even know if I'll believe you."

"All right, that's fine. Don't worry about it."

"No, sorry about that. Tell me."

"Listen, I'm only telling you this because there's a chance I don't make it through this. If I don't, it's those two agents. Sam Simon and Bob Dillard. Remember those names, but don't write them down. If we make it through this, I'll tell you everything later, but you have to keep this stuff to yourself until I tell you otherwise. Let me control the dissemination of the news. I want to figure out who killed Curt and Callie just as much as Cash."

"Okay, deal," she promised without hesitation.

"I had John Doe Number Two for three days of sleep deprivation and all sorts of fun with terrorists that the government loves to call torture."

"John Doe Number Two was a terrorist?"

"Yeah, he was an Iraqi Republican Guard. That's the cover up. The Oklahoma City Bombing's connection to terrorism."

"My gosh, what happened?"

"Simon and Dillard were charged with picking up John Doe Number Two to take him into custody and get the information that we'd gotten out of him. They came in, and it was only me and my buddy Josh. Simon put two in Josh, one in the head and one in his chest. He went down and died immediately. Dillard wasn't as good a shot. The one to my head just skimmed my skull. Right here." He took off his hat and showed her the scar on the right side of his head under the short hair of his buzz cut. "The other shot missed my heart. I played dead, and they took our prisoner. Made him disappear, the FBI then denied the existence of John Doe Number Two, and they facilitated the biggest cover up in American history. McVeigh and Terry Nichols were just patsies in the rise of the Islamic movement, most likely with the help and approval of the FBI and those in the government looking to make money off wars. You know what happened later, and you can see why there are some very important people that want to hide their role in covering up the connection. Could have prevented 9/11 if it weren't for the cover up."

"My gosh. This can't be true."

"Good, you keep thinking that. Let me focus on the Cutlers. But if I die, you're the only one that knows why."

"Why me, Jake Charm?"

"Jake Charm?" he chuckled.

"That's what they called you, right?"

"Long time ago, they did. Long time ago."

"Why me then?" she wanted to know.

"Other than Cash and his girlfriend, I don't know anyone else anymore. Cash's got enough problems. Mine don't amount to a hill of beans compared to his."

"They're trying to kill you." She said it with an un-journalistic bit of concern in her voice.

79

"Yeah, but we've been playing this game for twenty-some odd years. They might be trying to take out Cash as well, but he doesn't even know they're coming. At least I know what to expect. So, yeah, Cash has more problems he doesn't even know about. On top of that, he's going to be a suspect in the murders. And the Mexicans might use these murders as leverage over him. I'm a little more concerned about his problems right now. Mine are just a side adventure."

"You really *are* something, Jake Charm."

"That's what they tell me. But for now, forget we had this conversation. Go to work, see what you can dig up, but be careful. Call me if you need me. Otherwise, I'll call you later."

"Okay."

Ainsley fumbled around putting on her gloves, zipping up her purse and getting her keys ready.

"You'll probably have to scrape your car again." Jake's windshield was already opaque with snow. "Careful out there, it's probably cold."

"Oh dang," she said as she looked at her car. "I'll see you, Jake Charm. You be careful too."

She closed his door, got into her car, and did a quick dusting with windshield wipers and by rolling down the windows. She pulled out.

Jake considered his next move. He had time to kill before meeting with Cash after last call. He wanted to find Simon and Dillard before they found him.

Chapter 11

For the first time in Ainsley Reed's career, she felt special. She had something no one else had. She was the keeper of the secret that formed the foundation of the biggest story her local news station's had, maybe ever. She was walking with an involuntary swagger.

She also kind of really liked this Jake Charm guy. He'd been pining away for the same girl for twenty years with a broken heart. Gets called back home to help her but then discovers she's been murdered before he'd even gotten a chance to see her. It was all so romantic.

Seriously, she thought, this isn't just a big news story. It's a novel in the making. A love story with action, intrigue, betrayal, conspiracy... and a gorgeous hunk whose number was in her phone just aching to be used. It was moments like this that made her happy she was a heterosexual. Of course, she'd never say that out loud – she'd be lucky if she were only out of a job and not spontaneously combusted.

As she walked down the hallway to her office, she looked through the windows that separate the hallway from the studio where the anchors read the news stories that she and her fellow grunts put together every day. Their job was easy, but it was the glamorous job. As much as she despised them for getting all the credit for the work she does, she wanted their job. She wanted some other grunt to be despising her for her cushy job of reading the news in between long bagel and doughnut breaks. This was the story that might get her there. An award-winning story, but she had to play it right. Something about the whole thing stunk. Why?

The hallway that led her past her dream job ended at the break room outside the bullpen. It was empty, but the bullpen wasn't. Sam, the weather guy, saw her first. He was a skinny blond kid, fresh out of grad school with a bunch of meteorology degrees, a face for newspapers and a sophomoric crudeness that was chauvinistically inappropriate in any professional setting. He did the work that makes the weatherman on the TV a prophet. As soon as he saw Ainsley, he said, "Woooo, look at you. You get laid last night, Ainsley? You're sporting that sleepless night glow. What's his name? Or *her* name?" He winked twice.

"Shut up, Sam. I got a really good night's sleep last night." Others were starting to pay attention to the daily battle of wits.

"Yeah, I get it," he said, "you spent a lot of time in bed, but what's his name?"

Sheila, a rookie news girl, said, "Oh, no he didn't!" as if she were auditioning to be on the Jerry Springer Show.

"Grow up, Sam," Ainsley said, "Maybe it *was* a she. Wouldn't you like to know?"

"Feisty too. Good *morning*, Ainsley. Like it. Cap wants to see you. Wipe that glow off your face."

Cap was the station manager, the guy who'd met with the two "rogue" FBI agents – Jake's description – and the guy who'd fed her the information about the affair and the return of Jake Charm. The chill before the moment of truth ripped through her body. Or maybe it was the thrill of thinking about Jake Charm again. She thought he was gorgeous. Either way her face was feeling the rush of blood.

"What's he want?" she asked.

"He wants to know what that guy did to put such a smile on your face." He laughed at his own crudity.

"Clever Sam. How's that working for you?"

"What?"

"Pretending you're clever?" she said.

"Not working as well as the guy that gave you that smile, that's for sure. Wooo."

"I think it stopped snowing, Sam. Go verify it and try to find someone who cares."

"Good burn, Ainsley," Sam complimented her with sarcasm.

Ignoring him, she knocked on Cap's door.

"Come in," he yelled. He always talked like he was angry. Too little time, too many stories. "Hurry up. Close the door. I don't want anyone out there to know I'm giving you this story." That meant it was another crappy story. Yay. Try to buy her in with the anticipation of something interesting and then the letdown.

She opened the door, squeezed through and closed it.

"Have a seat," he said, "No, stay standing. Look it, you gotta get over to the Buffalo Zoo. Something's going on."

82

"What's that?" She pretended to be intrigued. She had to be on his good side with what she was about to propose.

"I don't know. Some animal died or they got some new animal from China. Zoo's barely open in the freakin' winter, but they think this is really important. Probably trying to get everyone ready for the spring. Whatever, it's a big story, and I want my best girl on it. By the way, where've you been?"

Ainsley saw her opening. "I'm working on something big, Cap."

"No, you're working on the zoo story. That's big. If it's a dead tiger, you got to get over there before they cart away the corpse. Get some close-ups. Pet the freakin' thing if you can."

"No problem, Cap," she said, as if she were happy to be a part of the team, "but I've got another story I'm working on too. You're going to love this one. It has to do with the Cutler murders."

"The Cutler murders? What's that?" As if he'd actually forgotten.

"The murders in Pendleton from yesterday. You know, the husband and wife found…"

"Nah," he cut her off, "Reed, that story's done. Not even interesting. It was the brother and the old boyfriend. Cut and dried. When they solve the case, we'll report it. I'll let you do it. Promise."

"Cap," Ainsley pleaded, "there's more to this story. I'm talking Mexican cartels forcing the one brother into selling the family business for money laundering, and the dead brother in the middle of merging the two banks in Pendleton when just about no one wants the banks to merge for some reason. That smells rotten, big time."

Cap's face looked like a billboard of incredulity. There was a little sweat on his upper lip. He took a few seconds to absorb what she'd said, thus making her feel like she was crazy, and then shook his head, "No. Stay away from that story. It's a dead end. Who's been filling your head with this nonsense? It's Pendleton. Nothing interesting has happened in Pendleton ever. Stay off this story."

"What about Tim McVeigh? He was from Pendleton."

"This got to do with Tim McVeigh?"

Ainsley was on the hot seat. How do you use McVeigh to get the go-ahead without giving up your source? And what if Cap knew more about Jake Chambliss than she'd thought? "Maybe, Cap. I'm not sure, but there's a lot more to this than the old boyfriend and the brother. I don't think either of them did it."

"My gut tells me different," he said. "It's a non-story."

83

"Well Cap, where did you get that information about the affair and the old boyfriend? Why do you think you had that information before the murders were even reported?"

"What are you suggesting, Reed?" He looked furious, but he wasn't ready to blow. Cap was doing everything he could to keep from blowing just to maintain a sense of dignity.

"I think your source was the two FBI agents that came in here on Saturday, even before the murders."

"Someone's putting a bunch of crazy ideas in your head. Those guys are old friends. I was in the service with one of them, and they were in town. Just wanted to stop by and say hello."

"Then where'd you get that info, and do we even know if Cash was actually having an affair with his twin brother's wife? How sure are you on this? It just sounds like someone's trying to misdirect attention. Don't you see that Cap?"

"No, Reed. What I see is a young reporter who needs to get over to the zoo and get that story before the dead animal's gone. I want footage. Get me that story by eleven. I want it on the noon o'clock news. You mess this up, you'll be doing stories on children that do nice things for old ladies, or something even more soul-killing."

"Okay Cap, but I'm taking the afternoon off..." She left and shut the door before he could say anything.

But she heard him through the doors, "You stay away from the Cutler murders. I'm telling you, Reed. Stay away."

He made her even more interested in the story. He was either in on it, or he was under the thumb of someone that had a lot to hide. She figured it was the latter – didn't think for a second that he was actually in on it.

Chapter 12

I was awakened with three knocks at the door on Monday morning. The clock said it was 8:10, and the warmth of the woman next to me reminded me I wasn't next to my wife. That was a bad joke, and luckily, no one heard it. Forgive me, I was in a dark mood. Yes, I felt bad about being next to this beautiful woman, but I had to keep my cover.

Another knock meant it was important. Skylar moaned but didn't wake up. I got out of bed and looked out the window. There was cop car parked in front of my garage. I couldn't see who was knocking though. The porch was right below the bedroom window. I was hoping it'd be Tyler, but I figured it was Chief Lyman Beck. *Great.*

I lifted the window. It was one of those weighted windows that use pulleys, weights and friction to keep them from slamming down. Most of them are so old they slam anyway if you don't prop them up. "Hold on a minute. Gotta get dressed."

I heard some footsteps on the porch. Chief Beck waddled down the steps and looked up with his arm over his forehead. He looked like he was trying to block the sun that hadn't yet risen, but it was probably just to keep the snow off his glasses. "Take your time, son."

"Good morning, Mr. Beck. I'll be right down."

I closed the window and put on a pair of my brother's jeans and a T-shirt – a faded grey and black three-quarter-sleeved Journey concert T-shirt with holes in the armpits from the 1980s. A classic. I remembered going to the show at the old Aud in Buffalo, but Cash still had the shirt.

Skylar'd woken up and rolled over with a smile slowly forming on her morning face. "What's going on, baby?"

"Chief Beck wants to talk to me. I'm probably going in to get interrogated. Just hang here, get some sleep, but don't come down now. Let me deal with this."

"Okay. Hurry back. This bed's freezing without you."

I bent over to kiss her on her cheek, "Thanks. Be back ASAP."

85

I shut the door on my way out. I had my socks in my hands.

"Come on in, Chief."

He shook the snow off himself on the porch and took the step over the threshold. The screen door squeaked shut behind him. "This place doesn't look much different than before your folks left us."

"Haven't changed it much," I said.

"I'm really sorry to bother you this morning, but I've got some questions for you."

"I figured you would. Just didn't figure you'd be here so early."

"That's right, you work late," he said.

"I didn't even open the bar last night."

"I'm really sorry for your loss."

"Thanks, Mr. Beck. I appreciate that. You want to squeeze me here, or do you want to take me downtown?" I sat down on the couch and started putting on my socks and boots that I'd left on the living room floor.

"Unfortunately, I gotta take you downtown, son," he chuckled at the thought of downtown Pendleton. "Want to give you a heads-up though. The feds want to talk to you."

"The feds?"

"Couple of guys from the FBI."

"What's the FBI want with me?"

"Not you. Chambliss. They're after your buddy Jake."

"They think Jake did this?" I asked as if the thought was absolutely crazy, which it was.

"I don't know for sure. These are the same two pricks that were here back when McVeigh blew up that building down in Oklahoma. Had me rounding up any brown kids they found in the Starpoint yearbooks."

"Back then, there couldn't have been more than two or three."

"That's about right," he said, "they were looking for John Doe Number Two, the guy they thought helped McVeigh. They made me round up a kid from Colombia and an Asian kid. What a waste of time."

86

"I remember John Doe Number Two."

"Their efforts went nowhere though. All had alibis."

"Was there even a Pendleton PD back then?"

"No, I was in Lockport at the time."

I put on my coat and opened the fridge. Took a swig of OJ and grabbed one of the uneaten sandwiches from the day before. "You mind if I eat something on the way?"

"Not at all."

"Want me to follow you?"

"No, just ride in the front seat." Serious enough I had to be driven to the station but not serious enough I had to put me in the back seat. Better than I thought it'd be.

He continued to ride through the U-shaped driveway, exiting through the driveway closer to the house after entering the one closer to the barn. No backing up necessary. He'd parked behind Cash's truck and Skylar's car. They were still facing the three-car garage. Neither of us felt like lifting a door and parking them inside. The driveway hadn't yet been plowed. Cash would normally do it with the tractor, but I hadn't bothered with it. The chief's tires spun a bit to get going through the four to five inches of light snow still in the driveway. Wasn't a problem though. Cops don't drive cars without power. He got up on the road after a little fishtailing.

"So, the feds want to talk to me?"

"Yep. The feds."

"Who do you think did this, Mr. Beck?"

"It's really too early to say. Lab results aren't in, but all signs point to you, son. Or Jake. I just can't figure out why either of you'd kill Callie too."

"Is this part of my questioning?" I asked.

"Yes. Once we get to the station, the feds are taking over. They wanted to come to your house, but I talked them out of it. Said you were an old family friend. So yeah, I'm looking for an excuse not to hold you. The best so far is I just can't figure out why you did it. Hope that means you didn't."

"I didn't. I was at the bar until 4 or 4:30. I went home and went to sleep."

"Got anybody who can corroborate that story?"

"Yeah, Jake. I told you yesterday. He and I were at the bar late, catching up."

"No one else was there?"

87

"No, just us two."

"That's a problem, Cash. Jake's the second suspect. I'm not telling you something you haven't figured out."

"Let me ask you something, Mr. Beck. Do you really think Jake or I did this? You've known us all our lives."

"I don't know anything about Jake since he left. You, I don't know what to think. All the evidence we got so far points to you. Were you having an affair with your brother's wife?"

"No. That's just something the newsgirl said. I don't know where she got that information... Think about it. Why would she even have that information unless someone was trying to frame me?"

I noticed he was driving slowly. Nowhere near as fast as he would be normally and not because of the snow.

"Who do you think is trying to frame you?"

"I have no idea," I said, "We're, I'm trying to figure that out."

"Who's we?" he asked without skipping a beat.

"Me and Skylar."

"You mean you and Jake?"

"Yeah, me and Jake and Skylar." I didn't have the ability to lie to him. Didn't want to. Figured if the feds were going to turn the screws on Jake, we needed someone in our corner. *What had Jake done? Must be why he disappeared for so long.*

"You admit you've been in contact with Jake?"

"Yes sir."

"Don't tell the feds that."

"You're telling me to lie to the FBI?"

"Yes. At least for now. I want to talk to Jake before they do. Something about these guys stinks. I didn't like them in the '90s and I don't like them now. You can tell them you were with him the night of the murders, but not since then. Hold off on that. They get that piece of information, it means more trouble for you than you can imagine."

We were a quarter mile from the police station. He was still creeping slower than normal.

"One more thing," he said. "Were you having an affair with your brother's wife?"

88

"No. Not so much an affair, but a friendship. We were friends. Always have been. I used to talk with her here and there. She was going through depression. So yes, I was at their house more than once while my brother was at work. I'd come over for lunch, and we'd talk." I was just making stuff up. Wanted to account for the fact that my – meaning Curt's – fingerprints were all over the place, but he probably didn't know that yet. "So, that might be construed as an affair, but it wasn't. Callie was my brother's wife, and she was my friend. I had no reason whatsoever to kill either of them."

"How did that news lady come up with information about an affair?"

"I don't know. Someone's trying to frame me."

"Why? Look, I'm running out of time. The feds are about to get their hands on you."

A part of me wanted to tell him all I knew, but I was too afraid that others might end up dead if I did. "I don't know. Not yet."

"What do you mean, not yet? Don't hold out on me." He acted like he was looking out for me.

"I just mean, I don't know yet."

"Let me ask you one more thing?" He was pulling into the station. There was a rental car parked in the lot. Tyler's car wasn't there.

"Okay."

"When the lab results come back, am I going to find your prints in their house?"

"Sure, like I said, Callie and I used to talk. During that time, I'd snoop." I had to account for the fact that my fingerprints would be found everywhere. I just had to hope Cash's would be too.

"What do you mean, snoop?"

"This is weird, Mr. Beck, but Curt and I are twins. For the first half of our lives, we spent just about every minute not in the bathroom with each other. Curt and I are close, always have been. While Callie was talking, I was looking at his stuff. I touched it and examined it. I'm closer to Curt than any other human on the planet. I look at his stuff."

"You know he's no longer with us, right?"

"Yes sir. But I'm still having a conversation with him in my head. The same conversation I've been having with him our whole lives, whether he was there or not. He used to do it too. I can't explain it. I told you it was weird, but he's the other part of me."

He parked but didn't turn off the engine. "Are you saying that you are talking with your brother in your head?"

"No sir. That would make me crazy. What I'm saying is that the conversation in my head is with Curt. I know how he thinks, and, when making decisions or observations, I run it by him...figuratively, not literally. I told you this was weird. I don't know why I'm trying to explain it. Look, Mr. Beck, I miss my brother." I almost lost it and cried, for real. Stopped myself. "Even though he's gone, he's still in my head. Maybe it's a twin thing, but there's just not a thing I don't know about my brother."

"Then why would someone want to kill him?"

I just answered without thinking. I had a problem lying to Mr. Beck, and he sounded like he was on my side. "The bank merger he was doing. A lot of people didn't want it to go through. I don't know why, and he didn't either. He didn't even want to do it. The board was making him."

"Now we're getting someplace. Was this bank merger public knowledge? I don't know anything about it."

"I don't think it is, sir. That's why I was hesitant to mention it. I'm not supposed to know anything about it. Pendleton Savings and Loan is trying to buy out First Iroquois Trust."

"The Indian bank?"

"Yeah. I think they like to call it the Native American Bank though. Not that I care."

"Doesn't matter what they want you to call it, I wouldn't put a cent in that bank," he said with absolute disgust.

"Why? What's wrong with the bank?"

"It's casino money, son. The Indians are running all the casinos in the state, and the government looks the other way. They're doing whatever they want because the government has no control over the Indian Nation's sovereignty. Land's not taxed, and they make their own banking rules. State gets a piece of the action but lets them do whatever they want. Trouble all around. Do me a favor. Don't mention this to the feds either. They don't give a crap about who killed your brother and Callie. They just want Jake. I may think your story about touching your brother's stuff is weird, but this other stuff is something to look at. Let's go."

He turned the engine off, and we walked through an inch of new snow on the sidewalk. The snow was steady and unceasing. The Pendleton Police Department building was small. forty feet by forty feet, if that. It was right out on Campbell Boulevard, south

90

of Five Corners, in front of the park. The door was on the right side, and there weren't any windows, other than on the door.

We entered into the receptionist's room. There were a bunch of chairs, a TV that was off and an empty receptionist's desk. He unlocked the blue door that led into the main room. There were a couple of desks in the center, an office with no walls for the chief to the left, two one-bed holding cells to the right and a kitchen in the back next to the interrogation room.

Two guys were working their cell phones at the desks in the center of the room. They simultaneously looked up from their screens when I came in.

"Did you find Chambliss?" the one with the scraggly hair asked. He had grey and blond hair. His face was fattened with age, and his chin had dropped. He did not have the typical fed tightness about him. Probably one of those guys you can't fire because he's the brother-in-law of some senator.

"No," Chief Beck said. "This is Cash Cutler. He's Curt Cutler's brother."

"I'm Special Agent Bob Dillard, and this is Special Agent Sam Simon. We'd like to ask you some questions."

Agent Simon had a short haircut much cleaner than Dillard's. His hair was salt and pepper, but he was thinner in the belly and the face. However, he had too much muscle for the suit he was wearing. He was the kind of guy that needed suits custom made in order to make room for his chest, arms and legs. His suit was not custom made; probably bought it off the rack at the Marshall's outlet. As a bank president in my former life who had to get his suits custom tailored to account for my arms and chest, I did not envy the guy for having to wear that suit. Eating dinner in that suit would be like a Tyrannosaurus Rex doing pushups, God forbid you get served a tough steak and a dull knife.

"About who killed my brother?" I asked as if Chief Beck hadn't told me a thing about these guys. "And his wife?"

"Maybe. We're not sure yet. But maybe. Would you join us in the conference room for some privacy? Have a seat."

It was the interrogation room, and they wanted privacy from Chief Beck. What a load. "Sure." They closed the door on me after I walked in.

Chapter 13

Around 8:30, Skylar grabbed Cash's extra key to the house. Didn't want to leave it unlocked, but she would if she had to. She left a note on the table. Said she had to run some errands, get some clothes from her house, pick up her check and explain why she was taking the day off work. Most of her note was true, but she left out the most important thing she had to do.

She took Aiken Road north to Lockport Road and took that to just before Transit, where she took a left and avoided all the business traffic in Lockport. She took the shortcut over to Summit that turned into Lincoln, which she took up to Pine Street and stopped into her apartment. Her thirteen-year-old Blazer rattled the whole way and did a little too much slipping here and there. She needed new tires, but she really needed a new car. Working at Tops Grocery Mart for twenty-nine hours a week wasn't going to get her that though. Helping out at Cash's bar once in a while gave her a little extra cash, but she had bigger things to worry about.

Did the people who were holding her mother just kill Cash's brother to get Cash to sell his bar? Or did they just kill Cash because they were sick of him? Yeah, she knew she had just spent the night with Curt. Curt was much too nice to be Cash. Cash would have flipped out when he found out she was pregnant. That guy did everything he could to make sure she never got pregnant. Curt acted like a guy who was actually in love with the woman who was bearing his baby. It's not like she didn't know Curt and Callie were having trouble getting pregnant. By looks, Skylar couldn't tell the twins apart, but with the way they treated her, it was day and night.

Skylar really was pregnant though. Cash, unlike Curt, couldn't keep himself from scoring. He'd slipped one past the goalie, as he always called it. She'd laugh at his crudeness but wished it weren't at her expense. Made her feel small, and that reminded her of why she was really with him. Not a happy thought.

She still wasn't sure how she was going to play this though. She definitely had to make up her mind before she got to the Indian reservation to visit her mom. Mr. Nighthorse would accompany her mother on their once-a-week visit. Her mother Shelly had a huge gambling problem – like a lot of people once they started letting the Indians open casinos everywhere. It was the red man's revenge. That's what some called it. White man got the red man hooked on the alcohol but comforted him with smallpox-infected blankets. The red man got the white man hooked on gambling and then provided loan sharks and pawn shops to make sure being broke wasn't an excuse to quit gambling. What comes around goes around. That's how they justified it anyway.

Skylar's mother Shelly had gambled away everything. She was sleeping in her car down the street from the casino until she lost that too. Then she got even further into debt with the loan sharks. The loan sharks are the cousins of the guys who run the casino and the Mexicans, she suspected. Of course, no one technically owns the casinos but the tribes, but that's bunk. The Indians on the reservation are just as poor as normal. The money never makes it to the people as was promised, but the state doesn't care. It gets its piece and looks the other way. Indians get away with murder. Literally, sometimes.

Shelly had been working off her debt to the loan sharks for over a year. It's like they knew she'd get into so much debt that they let her destroy herself. It wasn't even about getting the money back. They already had it. The casino stakes the loan sharks, and the money just goes back to the casino because the addicted gambler doesn't have the ability to spend it anywhere else. What a racket. It wasn't about making money at this point. It was about scoring debt slaves.

They had Shelly working on the hotel cleaning staff with the illegal Mexicans at the Grand Island Hotel and Casino, even though she ran up her debts in Niagara Falls. They had her on a bracelet that went off any time she'd leave the casino without being accompanied by that jerk Nighthorse. If she said anything or complained, Skylar was going to be killed. Simple as that.

The Indians were getting away with enslaving her mother, but it wasn't really slavery. They were paying her. It was peanuts though, especially because they charged her for the room she occupied and for all the food she'd eat. She wasn't allowed to do her own shopping or cooking. No leaving the casino, and Skylar wasn't allowed to see her at the casino. No chance of a scene that nobody wants to see.

Skylar didn't have to be a math genius to figure out the math wasn't working, and they didn't deny it. Shelly owed over $100,000 at 30% interest – supposedly a cut rate for a preferred client. She was making ten dollars an hour for seventy hours a week, but they charged her fifty a night and fifteen for food per day. Not so bad, but after costs, she was only making $35 a day. The interest on the loan was over $82 a day. It was growing even more because the amount she owed was growing faster than she could make it go down. If Shelly complained, Skylar was dead, and if Skylar complained, Shelly was going to take a suicide swim in the Niagara River over the Falls. Nighthorse promised that the police would never get to her mother before her mother would make it over the falls. The cops were on their payroll.

They did say Shelly could make much more as a sex slave, but Shelly wanted nothing to do with that. They called it being a high-class escort, but Shelly and Skylar knew what it really was. Shelly had Skylar, and Skylar was willing to do anything to make that hundred-thousand-dollar miracle happen, except be the sex slave they really wanted.

She saw no way to beat them. That's why she offered to help. They made her get close to Cash in order to get him to sell the bar. She wasn't sure why they wanted that specific bar, but she figured it was to do the money laundering. It was one of the two bars within a stone's throw of their bank, the First Iroquois Trust. Most of the land in Pendleton was residential, and it wasn't about to get rezoned, not without a posse of townspeople wielding pitchforks and torches.

They wanted Cash's bar, but he was holding out. Either way, they already had him running money for them. Sure, he'd get a piece of the action, but that just made it harder and harder for him to get them out of his business. She had no idea what he'd do with the money though. She'd love to get her hands on it, so she could buy her mother's freedom. Get her out of there and leave New York for good. Cash had no idea about her mother though. She wasn't allowed to say anything without getting killed.

That in mind, how was she going to play this? Did they mean to kill Curt or Cash? She didn't know. If she told them they killed Cash by accident, it might mean they would kill Curt to finish the job. Take out Curt, and that's the last chance she'd have to complete her obligation to the tribe. However, maybe they'd smile upon her loyalty for telling them the truth. Nah, they're a bunch of cold-hearted bastards who treat their own people worse than dogs. Look at the reservation. Everyone still lives in fifty-year-old trailers, and no one has a pot to piss in. The banks won't lend to people that live on the reservation because the land is owned by the tribe. When the bank can't repossess the home, what reason would they have to lend? Maybe that's why they started up their own bank, but that money's still not making the reservation any better. Nothing changes there. It's always squalor.

Her friend was a teacher at Niagara Wheatfield, the school across from the reservation, and she told Skylar some of the most heart-breaking stories about kids on the reservation. In the winter, one kid had to skip about ten minutes of his last class every day to go to the bathroom because he didn't want to do it in the outhouse behind the makeshift shack he lived in. There was no heat in the outhouse, and that's not even the worst story.

She saw no way out of her situation. She had to keep working Curt as if he were Cash, and she had to get him to sell the bar. It was the only way to save her mother. Assuming they wouldn't welch on the deal. That wouldn't surprise her – was it impossible for the Indians to Indian-give a deal? Didn't matter though. She had to assume they wouldn't. Otherwise, her mother was going for a swim.

Skylar got to her apartment and parked on the street because the driveway was still covered with snow. She grabbed her overnight bag and ran in. What a dump. The whole building was falling apart. It used to be a beautiful building, but put a slum lord in charge of upkeep, and you have a building that should probably be condemned. There was a giant crack in her kitchen floor. One side of the crack was an inch lower than the other. The fridge was leaking, and the water that made it past the wad of paper towels was getting soaked up by the particle board in the crack that split up the floor. The drop-down ceiling was loaded with water spots, but this was all she had.

She went to her bedroom and dumped her dirty clothes on the bed. Then she took a bunch of clothes from her dresser and reloaded up the overnight bag. She was going to make the move. Curt wasn't anywhere near as distant and hesitant about her as Cash. She was moving in and capitalizing on his time of need. She had clothes for about five nights, maybe six, depending on her need of socks. It was cold though. So maybe five, but Cash had socks. Curt wouldn't mind. She was sure of it. Curt's been underappreciated for too long now. He had no idea what's about to hit him. She actually kind of liked him, especially compared to his brother. He was just as gorgeous as Cash but a whole lot more human and less self-absorbed. Full-court-press time.

On her way out, she stopped in the bathroom where she wiped her nose and checked her face. For no makeup, she was looking good. She brushed her teeth and put the toothbrush back in her bag. Then she grabbed her razor and some body wash. Full-court press.

After locking the door, she took Pine to Walnut and that to Route 31, which she drove about twenty miles out to the gas station and smoke shop at the entrance to the Indian reservation. More pumps than any gas station around and lines to get to them. Tax-free gas, tax-free cigarettes and tax-free Indian dream catchers, moccasins, artwork, jewelry, pottery and whatever else they can get made in China. Sure, some of the stuff may say *assembled* in Canada or in the USA, but that's after it was *made* in China. Skylar researched it and couldn't believe what she discovered. People had their eyes so closed.

The state contended that letting the Indians run the casinos would be good for the Indians, but that was a big lie. It just created jobs and money streams for everyone except the Indians who needed it the most. On the outside it looks good, and all those who support it can declare themselves saints for supporting something good for the needy. Cure for the white liberal guilt.

Skylar saw the dark underbelly that lurked right behind the wooden door in the back of the store that she had to walk through, once passing through the makeshift tobacco, liquor and Indian outlet. Skylar parked in the parking lot for the café and diner that was in the back of the store. She meandered her way through the store and then through the diner. The whole room was brown. Brown wooden paneled walls, brown tile floors, brown ceiling, brown counter and brown tables. The walls were covered with New Age Indian artwork full of Indian spirits, perfectly arranged star patterns and animals willing to bow to the will of the Indians. The New Agers called the American Indian the "noble savage," but she couldn't think of that without scoffing. There was nothing noble about the savage that was in charge of her mother.

The restrooms were in the back on the left, and she had to go to the brown door on the right, just left of the doorway into the kitchen behind the long diner counter that went along the right side of the dining room. Like normal, the door was locked. She knocked, and a kitchen guy manning the griddle behind the counter told her to hold on. He flipped about four separate piles of hash browns and plated some eggs. He booked to the back through the kitchen doorway and then came back. "Less than a minute," he told her. He was back to rolling his sausages and flipping his hash browns in no time.

The door finally opened, and no one in the room even bothered to notice her walking into the belly of the beast. They probably had no idea though. Money breeds greed, and greed breeds the need for more money. The beast must feed.

She entered the room just like any other Monday. The door closed automatically behind her with a click, and the sounds of the outside world disappeared. She was in the employee dining room, but all the doors were shut.

Nighthorse was sitting at the table in front of her. He had his hands crossed. There was a stern look on his face though. His ponytail must have been pulled back too tight. His pockmarked face didn't move. He was wearing his black vest and a bolo tie with a picture of an Indian in a headdress. Probably bought it in the same store she just walked through. Her mother was standing in the back of the room next to another younger Indian with a ponytail. He was wearing a monster truck T-shirt and some ripped jeans with a red bandana serving as his belt. He almost looked more Mexican than Indian, but who could know? A lot of the Mexicans were Indians originally.

Shelly was in her street clothes and not her work uniform. She looked like Skylar but older. They never let her out of the hotel in her uniform. Someone might figure them out. She looked sadder than normal.

"You all right, Mom?"

Shelly shrugged her shoulders and shook her head with her lips squished shut. Not a peep was allowed to come out of her. The young thug next to her smiled at her obedience and shrugged as well.

Nighthorse broke the silence. "She's fine. Take her in the back."

The thug opened the door and led her into the back. She could hear the kitchen noises for a moment, but the room was silent again the second the door closed.

"Sit," he ordered.

Skylar took the seat across from Nighthorse at the picnic table. Sat down with her head held high, pretending she didn't fear him. She looked right into his eyes and refused to give up eye contact.

"I'm sorry about your boyfriend's brother and his wife," Nighthorse said.

"Did you kill them?" She wasn't into beating around the bush.

"No."

"How can I believe you?"

"You don't have to," he said, "but we didn't do it."

"What about the Mexicans? They do it?"

Nighthorse was just as measured. "Why would they do it? They're in business with Cash. How does that benefit them? We wanted to make sure *you* didn't do it."

"Of course, I didn't do it. I don't want to kill anyone."

"How are talks going with Cash and the bar then? The Mexicans really want to get this done, and we'd like nothing more than to reunite you with your mother."

"Is she all right?"

"Yeah, she's fine. You'll be able to talk with her next week, but no one is happy that Curt Cutler's been killed. This complicates things greatly."

"How? You got what you want. With Curt dead, the bank merger's probably dead too."

"A dead bank president is not a good way to kill a bank merger. No one wants investigators looking into the bank deal. We need to get this murder investigation wrapped up quickly."

"How's that happening? You don't even know who did it."

"And that's a problem," he said. "Get your boyfriend to sell, and you and your mother can get out of here. Same deal. I'll tell her you love her. See you next week."

Nighthorse got up and left. Skylar was alone in the quiet for a moment. The tears started, and she left.

Chapter 14

After his meeting with Ainsley the newsgirl, Jake Chambliss knew the feds would be watching his house. He wanted to see if they'd be watching Cash's house too. After seeing no one, he parked in the entrance to a lane back into some fields. In the summer, it would be used for tractors to get back to the fields. It was a little snowy, but not enough to worry about. He backed in. His rear end was a full foot and a half lower than his front end. That might cause a problem. Worry about it later.

He got there between 7:50 and 8:00 am. He wasn't sure how accurate the clock on his neighbor's car was. His neighbor Stanley was an old guy who'd been taking care of his parents' house for him. He'd been sending Stanley and his wife money over the years. Stanley didn't drive much and was more than happy to let Jake borrow his Caprice. "Drive it all you want, Jake. Not a problem." Stanley took care of his bedridden wife Gloria but didn't need to drive much other than to get the essentials.

Jake was situated a little to the southwest of Cash's house. He could see the trees blocking the view of the house and anyone who came or left. Both Cash's truck and Skylar's Blazer were still parked in the driveway. Jake had no idea of what to expect, but he figured something would happen. Just had a hunch.

A little after 8:00 am or so, he saw a cop car pull into the driveway closest to the barn. Time to ask Cash some questions, he figured. No big deal. Cash knew they'd be coming. A little while later, the car left with Cash in the passenger's seat. Pendleton was big-time now with their own police department to butt heads with the sheriff's department. He wasn't around to know why that happened, but he was sure it had something to do with money flowing into someone's political coffers. Maybe it had to do with Pendleton growing so much with people moving in from Erie County, all the while Pendleton was just the peaceful drive-through town between the urban centers of Lockport and the North Tonawanda/Niagara Falls area. In essence, the sheriffs weren't giving Pendleton enough attention, and the people voted themselves their own protection – of course, only after the guys getting the money in their coffers convinced them to do so. Follow the money, he thought. It's the modern political way.

Jake's time in Africa made him even more cynical. At least in Africa, the corruption is a part of the process. In America, people hide it because it's supposed to be illegal. The problem comes when they're willing to kill in order to keep it hidden.

Jake was now interested in Skylar. With Cash gone, what would she do? Twenty minutes later, she pulled out of the driveway closest to the house. Her wheels were sliding a bit, but she made it. Drove right past him without seeing him ducking below the steering wheel. Go time.

Jake's wheels spun at first, so he backed up into the lane a bit. By the time was almost level, the snow he was pushing was over the bumper. He put it in drive and just hit the gas a little. The new tires on his neighbor's rusty old Caprice Classic still had some good grip. Not a problem, he drove right up the hill and onto the road this time. He followed her to Lockport Road and into Lockport. While she was in her apartment, he waited for her up by High Street. She was too focused to notice anything more than twenty feet away. She was on a mission, and the bag she took into her apartment came out twice as fat. Her go bag?

He followed her out of Lockport going west on route 31. When coming down the hill, just west of Campbell Boulevard, he almost tooted the horn when passing Mr. Olick's house – a habit from when he was in high school. Mr. Olick, the American History and Economics teacher was everybody's favorite teacher, and in the old days, one was likely to see the white-haired teacher running his daily six or seven miles in the fields, but Jake wasn't even sure he was still alive and didn't hit the horn out of fear of drawing Skylar's attention. Didn't keep him from cracking a smile at the thought of the unforgettable Mr. Olick though.

After she pulled into the Indian reservation and didn't drive right up to the pump, he tried to remember if she smoked. Was sure she didn't. He drove in and went right for the gas pumps as she parked on the right side of the store and diner before she entered the store through the front door. After he filled up, he drove around the back of the building and parked about eight spaces to her right. There was brown door in the back, probably a kitchen door to get rid of the trash and bring in products, and there was the door she'd used in the front. He was back far enough that he didn't have a direct view into the window of the store. Behind the store, where the diner was, the building was made of brown cinderblock walls.

He brought out his phone and pretended he was using it so as not to look conspicuous, especially if, for some reason, she left through the back door. Didn't think it was likely but had to have a way to hide his face from her if she did. People loved their cell phones these days. Called them smartphones in the U.S. But it wasn't much different in Africa. They had them too. Even starving people in Africa have cell phones and internet access. They're more likely to have a cell phone paid for by the American taxpayer than they are to have plate of food. Follow the money. The Christians help with food, but the U.S. government spends more energy and money on making sure the women of Africa have access to an abortion than to a plate of food. Killing an African is cheaper than feeding him. But there's nothing like a cell phone to help you look inconspicuous.

Five minutes later, a Skylar look-alike did come out the back door. She was walking in front of a ponytailed Indian kid who had a tight grip on her right arm. As she got closer though, Jake realized she was too old to be Skylar. Looked just like her though. Their bodies and their hair were remarkably similar. Weirder still, the ponytail put her in the front seat of the almost perfectly shining black Cadillac two cars to his right. The salt must have been washed off within the ride over. Nice car. The ponytail closed her door and got in the back seat. They just sat there.

Jake didn't have a good view of the ponytail, but he could see the blonde lady through the front windows of the car parked between them. She held her head down with her fingers on her forehead. It looked like she was trying to keep the tears out of her eyes, but he wasn't sure. Knowing the other guy couldn't see him so well, he looked directly at her in hopes of getting her attention. She noticed him for a second but pretended not to. After a moment of head shaking and forehead wiping, she stole another look at him. Jake nodded to her, but she turned away from him without acknowledging him. Maybe that was her acknowledgment. After taking a few photos of her, Jake went back to pretending to be on his phone, but his eyes were turned her way. He wanted a direct shot of her face.

The brown door in the back opened again, and a big ponytailed Indian came out. He was in a long leather brown suede coat. It was unbuttoned in the front, and Jake could see the bolo tie and a black vest. This guy was the power. He got into the front seat of the Caddy and touched the back of the blonde lady's hair, kind of gently. She flicked his hand away. He put the car in reverse and pulled out. They drove behind Jake and then behind Skylar's car.

Skylar came out the front, just as they were nearing the road. She lifted her middle finger and thrust it at him right before the Caddy turned right towards Niagara Falls. It was her quick burst of rebellion, hopefully noticed by no one other than Jake. Skylar got in her car and started crying. Her head was resting on the steering wheel when Jake pulled out and went around the back of the building and then up to the road to catch up to the Caddy with the ponytails and the blonde woman. He'd catch up with Skylar later.

He swung around the main building and noticed some large buildings in the back that helped to hide the view of the entrance to the reservation. It had been built up a lot since he was a kid, but still had the ironic patina of squalor that helped to hide the hundreds of millions that the casinos were bringing in. The reservation didn't suddenly look like the five-star hotels that helped fund the growing empires of the connected few. It still looked the same. They didn't even pave the ground. He was driving over gravel – cheap gravel, the kind that kicks up and dings your ride when not covered by snow and ice. There was cement around the gas pumps, but the rest was gravel with water-filled potholes layered with broken ice. There was so much traffic the snow didn't have a chance to stick.

The Cadillac was up about eight to ten cars, actually driving the speed limit. The cars in front of Jake seemed anxious to get around the slow driver. They were easy to catch. Jake blended in with the impatient people behind the slow poke in the really clean Caddy.

Eventually, he drove under the Route 190 overpass and took a left to take it south. As soon as they'd turned, the cars ahead sped up. Jake stayed at the speed limit. Didn't need to look suspicious. Just a guy on a joy ride in a big old Caprice Classic. Happens to be going the same way as the Indians and their white girl. Nothing to see here, look at something else.

They continued to drive the speed limit through the outskirts of Niagara Falls and then La Salle. Jake had to go even slower than the speed limit in order to keep cars between them, but it wasn't working. Cars were passing Jake on the left and then then the Caddy. Jake went even slower. Now he looked suspicious, but at least he was a ways back. By the time they got to the toll bridge to get onto Grand Island, other cars had filled the gap. Traffic slowed while going over the bridge so that those on the Grand Island side could pay the toll. A dollar now. Used to be fifty cents.

Grand Island is an island in the middle of the Niagara River, which flows around either side of it before it goes over Niagara Falls. Unlike its name suggests, the island is actually small but big enough to be its own community. They have a school system and everything that goes with a small town, but, other than by boat, there's only two ways to get off the island. Both are bridges on the 190. The other bridge goes south into Kenmore, Tonawanda or Buffalo, depending on which way you head.

They drove past the old Fantasy Island theme park. Jake used to go there when he was a kid. He only remembered the Wild West shootout and the Devil's Hole ride. It spun really fast so that you stuck to the wall due to centrifugal force. Then the floor would disappear, and there was nothing to keep you from falling into the black Devil's Hole but the centrifugal force. Scary as hell when you're a kid, and that's why they called it the Devil's Hole.

For someone who might be in the potential business of crime, Grand Island didn't seem like the ideal situation. It's a small community with few spots to hide and only two ways to escape when in the middle of a chase. How hard would it be to lock down the whole island with the help of the Coast Guard in the river and cops at either bridge? The only way any of it makes sense is they're either on the up and up or they've got law enforcement in their pockets. Money talks. Grand Island's probably bending over any which way, in order to keep the casino there and bring in all the money.

After about four signs getting you ready to exit for the Longhouse Casino, the Caddy then signaled to get off at the Whitehaven exit. Jake didn't have to be a genius to figure out where they were going. He had to slow down and then pull over. He couldn't afford being seen exiting right behind them. He pulled over and pretended to be looking at his phone. Up ahead, the Caddy turned right instead of towards Fantasy Island, which was snow-covered and closed. Jake got back on the road and took the exit ramp to the bottom where he waited a moment before he turned to watch what they were doing. They drove up past one intersection and then took a left into what looked to be a private driveway. The road looked rural with trees and fields making up most of the landscape. Not many signs of commercial life.

Jake took the right, just as they disappeared behind the leafless trees blocking view of the driveway. He followed the Longhouse Casino sign at the corner telling him to turn right. This one was just a sign with words. The ones he passed on the 190 had a woman in a skimpy seductive outfit pointing the way with her free hand that wasn't holding a full house with aces high.

Jake drove right to the casino, which was just another third of mile down the road on the right. He was driving through mostly farmland, but there was some commercial property in the direct vicinity of the giant Longhouse Casino and Indian Heritage Resort Spectacular. There was a gas station, a First Iroquois Trust bank and a Turkey Feather's Gun and Pawn Shop.

Another First Iroquois Trust branch? Jake had no idea there were more branches and wondered how the one-branch Pendleton Savings and Loan figured to purchase the multi-branch First Iroquois. How many branches were there? A clue.

Out front, in the center of the giant parking lot, they had a life-sized longhouse that people could walk through and get the experience of life in New York before civilization fixed things up. Nothing like a longhouse with neon lights pointing to the entrance as if it were a freak show up in Niagara Falls on Ontario's Lundy Lane. The only thing is, this longhouse came with an air conditioner sticking out of the faux thatch roof. Can't have casino goers getting all sweaty in the summer. Gotta get 'em ready to feel good about losing their money to the Indians who used to live like animals. Because of the white man, of course.

Another five rows of cars behind it, and the casino goer was entering Chief Water Bear's reimagining of Las Vegas run by Indians rather than the Italians and Jews. A little fake nature thrown in to temper the lust and glitz that the Vegas mafias use to dazzle us before they take our money.

Jake parked in one of the rows in front of the longhouse with a view of the Caddy's driveway. Wasn't a great view, but it was enough to see them coming. He busted out his phone and pretended to be at work.

A few minutes passed before the Caddy came out of the driveway, already having turned around. It took a left out of the driveway and drove right to the casino. It was following an old blue Sentra with a muffler hanging on for dear life. A buildup of black smoke and a thunderous gurgle would accompany each gear shift. Both turned into the first casino driveway. The Sentra slowed to figure out where to park, but the Caddy had no patience. It passed the muffler-needing gambler as if he were a pus-covered leper offering free full-body massages.

The Caddy went right to the back-parking lot. The big ponytailed driver in the suede coat hadn't bothered to notice Jake. He was more interested in getting around the smoky Sentra. Weird, since he didn't seem to be in hurry to get anywhere quickly earlier.

The hotel and casino were huge. Jake counted twenty-five stories, but that was just the hotel part. The three-storied casino and wonderland's footprint was four times the area of the hotel. There was no way Jake could catch up to them on foot. He started up the old Caprice Classic and drove around to the back. Nice and slow. Just a guy looking for a better parking spot. Even this early in the day, the parking lot was about full. Either with overnight guests or people that just don't have time to waste before they get to deliver their money to the casino. As he pulled back there, he passed a little driveway to the left that was separate from the rear parking lot. There were a bunch of cars there as well. Not bad for a Monday morning. The Caddy was parked in a small row of cars to the left of the driveway. All the cars were nice. Must be the executive parking. Next to it were some stairs up to a loading dock. Trucks trying to reach that dock would back in from the center of the parking lot.

Jake parked in the rear and watched as only the driver and the blonde lady got out of the vehicle and entered from the loading dock. The muscled little ponytail in the back must have gotten out at the last stop. Probably back to playing video games and doing bong hits. America doesn't make its youth like it used to.

Instead of taking the rear entrance to the right, he walked up the loading dock steps. They were metal steps with holes connected to a cement loading pad. He walked the loading pad back to the door with a window, but it was locked. He didn't see anyone. The hallway had beige walls and a beige floor with lights that helped it all look just a little beiger. He checked the aluminum door that he passed. There was a lift handle on the ground. Doubting it'd be left unlocked, he reached down and lifted. The door lifted right up. It was the entrance to the warehouse. The forklifts and golf carts were parked in this room, but the actual warehouse was on the other side of the other big door, which was closed. The lights to the room were out, but the light from the beige hall gave him enough to see. He let the door down and opened the door to the beige hall. No one was there to say he couldn't.

The elevator was at the end of the hall to the left. There were some empty offices on the right with locked doors, and there was a brown door at the end of the hall that probably led into the casino. He looked at the elevator pad. The thirteen was partially rubbed off, but the rest of the floors weren't used nearly as much. Lucky thirteen. That's the button he pushed.

The elevator opened up in a hallway that looked like most hotels, except the lighting was dim. He walked around the corner and saw an office setup right in the middle of the hallway. The lady at the desk asked, "Can I help you, sir? You've just used the service elevator."

"Oh, sorry about that. I think I'm lost," Jake said in his best puzzled tourist voice.

"No problem, sir. What are you looking for?"

"I was looking for Bob."

"Bob?"

"Yeah, they said to ask Bob on the thirteenth floor for a job. I'm looking to work in service."

"Well," she said, nice as can be, "I don't know a Bob, but, if you want a job, you need to speak with the people at the front desk. They can help you best."

"Why'd they tell me to come to the thirteenth floor?"

"I'm not sure."

"What is the thirteenth floor for?" Jake asked.

"It's where the live-in staff stay."

"You mean I can live here?" Jake feigned excitement at the possibility.

"If you qualify, I guess."

"What do I have to do to qualify?"

"Well, normally, it's for people that live in another country and don't have a place to live when they come here to work. That, and for people that come from other states to work seasonally."

"Oh, okay. Can I take a look around, see if this is what I want?"

"Umm, we don't normally allow people to walk around unaccompanied, and I...I need to stay at this desk. I don't have anyone else that can help you."

"Okay then," Jake said just as innocently as can be, "I'm just gonna be a couple of minutes." He started walking up the hallway.

The lady at the desk panicked without acting. "Wait a minute, sir, you can't be up here. I'll have to call security."

"Will they give me a tour?" he asked without looking back at her.

"Well, no. They'll escort you off the premises."

"Don't call them then. I'll just be a minute."

"All right, just be quick please."

"You got it, ma'am. Thank you very much for all your help. I will be sure to tell your superiors how helpful you've been." He kept walking down the hallway to her right, hoping to get out of her sight. Do a little door knocking.

"Please hurry back, sir."

The hallway was completely empty. Doors to the left and doors to the right, but no one in the hall.

Eventually, a skinny brunette with wavy hair below her shoulders opened the door and headed right towards Jake. She was barefoot and in nothing but her bra and underwear. It was nice bra and underwear. The sexy kind. She was sexy. Had a model's face and a body to match. Took a moment before she noticed him.

"Woo, you scared me," she said.

"You should look where you're going."

"Cover me in syrup and lick me till I'm raw. I agree. Look at you, cowboy. You the new guy?"

"Maybe," Jake said. "I'm just checking out my living arrangements. You clean rooms, young lady?"

"I ain't no housekeeper. I'm room service," she looked at him with a smile that was made wet by a lascivious sweep of her tongue, "for the special guests. I hope you're a special guest."

"I'm just visiting at this point, ma'am. I don't think I'm a special guest. Let me ask you something though." He opened up the photo gallery on his phone.

"You want my phone number?" She looked ready to give it.

"No. I want to know if you've seen this woman."

"Let me see." She sidled up next to him to get a good view. She touched his forearm to lift the phone. "I don't have my glasses on." She smelled really good and wanted to make sure he knew it. "Yeah, I know her. She's in housekeeping. Lives down there." She pointed in the direction he was heading. "Third to the last door on the right."

"Thank you so much. You've been a big help. Is there anything I can do?"

"Yeah," she said without thinking longer than a nanosecond, "you can call me."

"Call you what?"

"On the phone, dummy." She grabbed his phone and put her number in it and hit dial so she could get his number. Then she added herself to his contacts. "They call me Samantha. You'll find me bewitching." He didn't mind for a second having a phone number of a person that might help him in the future. Even if she was a prostitute.

"Okay, thanks. Don't tell anyone you saw me up here."

"Your secret's safe with me, cowboy. Call me anytime. I have to go and get my schedule before Lucy goes on break."

"Don't tell Lucy I'm still here. Tell her I went down the other elevator if she asks."

"She'll never believe it. There's only one elevator to this floor, the one you came up. Hotel guests skip right over this floor."

"That's pretty smart."

"Yeah, they thought of everything. Listen, honey. I gotta go. Call me."

"I might," Jake said. But not for the reason she was hoping.

He knocked on the third to the last door on the right. He had to knock a second time before he got a "Hold on a second."

The lady from the Indian reservation opened the door. Her eyes were red from crying, and she was still wearing the same clothes from the morning. "Can I help you? How'd you get on this floor?"

"I'm a friend of Skylar's."

"Oh my God," she stuck her head out the door to make sure no one else was in the hall, "get in here. Quick." She yanked him in and shut the door. It was hotel room that looked like it was lived in. It only had one bed, but it had all the things that come in a normal hotel room. "What are you doing here? You're gonna get us killed. Get yourself killed. Me killed, Skylar killed, all of us...killed. Why are you here?"

"I saw you at the reservation this morning. You look like you need help."

"No, I need you to get out of here before they catch you."

"They got cameras up here?" he asked.

"No. They don't want anyone to see what goes on up here."

"What is it?"

"It's the place where they keep the slaves, the prostitutes, the sex slaves, the illegal alien indentured servants."

106

"You a slave?"

"Yes, to the loan sharks, and Skylar gets killed if I get out of line. So, you've got to go."

"Why wasn't there security? How'd I get up here so easily?"

"I don't know, there's normally two security guards that sit with Lucy, but you've got to go."

"What's your name?"

"I'm Shelly. I'm Skylar's mom."

"You want to leave with me?" Jake asked, "I can get us out of here."

"You're crazy. You'll be lucky to get yourself out alive. They see you with me, they'll kill us all. I can't go. Skylar'd never be safe."

"Okay, but I'm gonna get you out of here. I promise."

"Who are you?"

"Better that you don't know just yet, Shelly, but I'm a friend, and I'm going to get this straightened out."

"Not till Cash sells the bar you won't. Now that his brother's dead, fat chance that happens."

"You know about the murders?"

"Yeah, the boss is pissed."

"He didn't have anything to do with it?"

"No, but he's pissed. I don't know everything, but things are scary right now. You've got to get out of here."

Jake's phone started buzzing in his coat. "Who's calling me? Nobody has this number?" It was Samantha. "Oh." He hit the green button, "Yes?"

"Cowboy, you gotta get out of here. Lucy just called security. I have no idea why they weren't there, but if you don't want your lady friend to get in trouble, make sure they don't see you coming out of her room. You're welcome and call me. I'm serious, cowboy."

"Gotta go," Jake said, "Security's coming."

Shelly opened the door to make sure they weren't in the hall yet. "Go."

"I'll be back," he said as he booked out. He was to the middle of the hallway before two giant tuxedoed brown guys with short black hair turned the corner. They looked more Mexican than Indian. Professional muscle. Look intimidating, but totally untrained. Jake wasn't worried about them for a second.

"About time you guys get up here," he said as they clod-hopped their way down the hall trying to intimidate them with their size. "I got lost. You know there's no elevator down there. Thank God you're here. I'm looking for a bathroom. Those tuxedo's make you guys look classy."

They both grabbed him by the arms. "Come with us."

"Let go of me. You guys aren't classy." Jake shook them off a little, but they grabbed him harder. A few doors opened to let some peaking eyes get a glimpse of the commotion, but Jake didn't have the ability to see who.

"I'm going to tell you one more time," Jake said, "get your hands off me."

They had no idea who they were dealing with. They tried to pick Jake off the ground by his arm so they could carry him.

Jake lifted his legs up and to the left. He got his right leg behind the neck of the guy on his left and put his left knee into the guy's neck. As he squeezed, he used his weight to bring the guy down. The other guy let his right arm go. The guy on the left was bent over coughing, trying to reestablish an air passage to his lungs. While the guy to his right was fumbling to get his gun freed from its holster, Jake grabbed the choking guy by the hair and smashed his head into the side of his knee. Then into the door trim on the wall. The guy was out. Not dead, just out.

He turned around, and the other guy was in a stance pointing his gun. "Freeze, homes."

"'Freeze, homes?' They teach you that in Security Guard 101? Use Mexican lingo to scare the gringo?" Jake was mocking him. Even though he had fifty pounds on Jake, the guy looked scared.

"Don't move."

"That's not as intimidating as 'freeze, homes.' Let me ask you something." He didn't wait for the security guy to answer. "Do your bosses want you to shoot me and bring the police up onto the thirteenth floor? You gonna kill me in front of all these people?" The guy looked around, and a few of the peepers closed their doors.

His gun started shaking more. "Don't come any closer."

"Your forehead is bleeding." It wasn't, but Jake figured he'd divert the guy's attention.

The guy took his left hand off the gun to check for blood, and Jake simultaneously hit the gun with his left hand and the guy's forearm with his right. Jake was fast. The arm went to the guy's right, and the gun went left. In a split second, the gun was in Jake's right hand and pointed at the security guard with his hand on his unbloodied forehead. "Oh, maybe I was wrong. Must have been the lighting. It's kind of dark up here."

The guy lifted his hands. Jake smashed him across the forehead with the butt of the gun. Then he hit him for good measure on the back of the neck. Needed to make sure the guy was out. Pressured for time, he found the guy's key ring. And then an extra magazine. Why'd a security guard need an extra mag? Jake needed a gun, so this was good as any. He'd indicated to Cash he was packing, but he wasn't. You don't get to fly around the world with your guns unless you're important, and Jake had no idea where his father's gun stash had gone. Couldn't find any in the house. Jake grabbed the other guy's gun too, as well as his key ring. Keys to the casino aren't a bad thing to have.

Jake ran around the corner, and just as soon as he had, Lucy saw him and ducked behind her desk. "Thanks Lucy, for all your help. See you later."

"You're welcome," she said from under her desk. Her voice was somewhat mumbled.

He pushed the down button on the elevator. The wait. Crap. He stood back and pointed his two guns at the elevator doors while he looked for a stairway. No stairs? One elevator? What kind of fire trap was this? A secret fire trap.

The down light blinked, and the elevator beeped as the doors opened. There were two more security guards inside. They must have been laughing at a joke, but their smiles disappeared quickly when they saw Jake ready to put holes in their heads.

"Drop your guns slowly. Then get out of the elevator."

Neither said a word as they unclipped their Glocks – must be standard issue – and set them on the floor in the elevator. The elevator doors tried to close, and Jake stepped forward and stuck his foot into the doorway to force them to open again. The guy on the left turned his side a little, thinking Jake was about to shoot him. After backing up, Jake jerked his head to the right to tell them to exit and walk over towards Lucy. They inched their way over. These guys had short hair too, but they were white as far as he could tell.

Without taking his guns off these guys, Jake backed his way onto the elevator and pushed the ground floor button with the tip of his gun. The elevator doors closed, and Jake breathed a sigh of relief. He had four new guns. Nice.

He put the two on the floor in his pockets and checked the two in his hands. Only one had a bullet chambered. He chambered the other one and backed against the wall, keeping the guns pointed at the doors.

The doors opened with two more security guards in tuxes pointing ARs at him.

Jake said, "Nice guns. Those for me? I'll add them to the collection your buddies gave me." With his Glocks pointed squarely at their foreheads, he said, "Set those down nicely. I don't want them scratched. Those are nice."

In unison, they said, "Drop your guns."

"Jinx," Jake said, "you owe each other a Coke. Listen, don't end up like your buddies upstairs. They're not going to be able to work for a while, especially the first two. Just drop your guns, and I'll only beat you up little bit. You won't get fired for surrendering, and I won't put you in a coma like the guys upstairs."

"Drop your guns, funny guy. I'm gonna count to three. One--"

"Listen. Take my deal," Jake said, "even in a casino, best deal you'll get." Now, Jake didn't want to shoot anyone. He just wanted to beat the crap out of these guys and walk away with their guns. Run away with their guns. No time for walking.

"Two..." the guy offered.

Well, it's not like these Indians are going to bring in the police, Jake concluded, not with what they got going on upstairs. Jake finished the countdown for them and saw the look of surprised mixed with fear on both their faces right before he put a bullet in each of their foreheads. While he shot two guns, he pulled the triggers at the same second. One loud sound that would hopefully be muffled enough by the elevator to be ignored by the regular folks in the casino.

He pulled them into the elevator by their feet. He left their heads in between the doors so the doors wouldn't close and the two goons he didn't comatize would be stuck upstairs without an elevator. He grabbed their ARs. Two Bushmaster M4s. He thought about wrapping them in his jacket but thought better. He wasn't going through the parking lot.

He left through the small door with the ARs slung over his back and his hand on the Glocks in his jacket pockets. Instead of going back to the car he'd driven in, he walked behind the executives' cars up to the road that led back to the rear parking lot. There were woods and fields on the other side of that road. He'd find it much easier to get away that way than walking back into a parking lot on camera to let them know what kind of car he was driving.

They could follow his footprints in the snow, but they shouldn't. If they hadn't figured that out though, it would serve them right. Jake was pissed. Really pissed. He was all measured until those two jerks with ARs put him in what he assessed to be a kill-or-be-killed situation. He hated that. He was almost in full-blown war-machine mode, and he was really pissed at the two dead guys who'd put him here.

110

Being able to get into war-machine mode is great when you're at war, but Jake was in civilization. There's a reason the government has the Posse Comitatus Act to keep the military guys from being sicced on Americans. It's just not fair. It's something he'd thought a lot about, ever since the Oklahoma City Bombing. The militarily-trained kid he went to school with blew up a federal building to supposedly get revenge on the federal government for waiving the Posse Comitatus Act in order to send the military in to kill all the people at Waco, including the children. At least that was the official statement for what motivated Tim McVeigh. Jake knew a lot more though, and he was a marked man because of that knowledge.

Jake was fifty yards into the woods when he started hearing the yelling of the guys chasing him. Fools, he thought, coming at him so noisy-like. Stay home and live. His hot breath steamed like that of a bull in the cool morning. He was a machine again. It's these types of events that necessitate putting thought on hold and letting instinct take over. But he tried. He promised himself not to kill them, or at least try not to.

He saw a boulder next to a thick black walnut tree about twenty feet further. He ran up and put the boulder between him and his pursuers. Mice frittering into the slaughter. Jake slowed his breathing to a quiet nothingness. He stood still and let his ears make him aware of every sound in the woods. A bit like hunting, but not really. He was the prey, as far as they knew. When hunting, the prey rarely comes to you on purpose. These fools were offering themselves to the predator.

There were four men in black. Maybe the tuxedos, but they were wearing winter coats. One of the center guys was following Jake's foot trail, while the rest were spread out. They all had guns at the ready.

He was going to take out the guy to his right first. He was rounding the area to the right, and he would be the first to have an angle with which he could see Jake. Jake moved from behind the boulder to behind the walnut tree. He meant to shoot him in the right shoulder, but the bullet went straight through the guy's forehead. He was dead before he'd hit the ground. Jake's instinct overrode his desire.

Jake quickly got back behind the boulder. The other three were shooting back, but nothing good enough to take him out. They were just going full semi-automatic, but bullets don't go through boulders. Pure amateurs. Random shots with no direction or thought behind those shots.

Once the shots slowed, Jake said, "It sounds like you're convinced you'll never run out of bullets." They didn't respond with anything but clicks of changing magazines.

As soon as all the shooting halted, Jake popped his head out between the boulder and the walnut tree. He took three shots in about two or three seconds. All three of the still-standing men were falling like dead elms in a hurricane. So much for shots that only wound. Whatever. He'd warned the two in the elevator. Take the deal and live.

Chapter 15

Once I'd entered the police headquarters with Chief Beck, the two FBI agents told me to have a seat in a small room. They closed the door to have a pow-wow with the Chief. The interrogation room had no windows, but it did have a camera pointed at me as I sat at the table. There was a bar on the table to cuff the perp, but they didn't cuff me. Small favors. Just told me to have a seat.

Maybe they were going to sweat me for a few hours. Get me hot, hungry and thirsty. Make me beg for sustenance and only give it to me if I answered the questions the way they wanted them answered. At least I thought.

Instead, the door opened, and the two feds came in. One took a seat across from me and the other stood by the doorway. The camera was right over his head.

The chubby blond guy that sat across from me said, "I'm Agent Dillard. This is Agent Simon." They'd already introduced themselves when I came in, but whatever. He'd taken his coat off and was sporting a coffee stain on his white shirt. His tie was loose around his neck. Even still, it wasn't long enough to make it to his belt buckle after having to traverse the roundness of his belly.

"Nice to meet you. I'm Cash Cutler."

"Yes, we know," said Dillard, as if I'd spoken before I was supposed to. "D'you kill your brother?"

"No," I didn't pretend to get all offended. I knew they needed to ask that question. I just had no idea why the feds were here.

"D'you have anything to do with it," Dillard said.

"'Course not," I said, "I was hoping you had some ideas. S'why I thought I was here."

Agent Simon snapped, "Don't get lippy, buddy. Where's Jake Chambliss?"

"I don't know."

"You been in touch with him?"

112

"Not since the night of the murders."

"Was that before or after you two killed the Cutlers?" The muscled Simon took over a little more aggressively.

"Is that the end of good cop?" I asked with an offended smirk. I probably shouldn't have said that.

"Answer the question," Simon snapped as if he'd finally gotten me to where he wanted me.

"If we both killed the Cutlers, wouldn't that mean it was during, and not before or after? What kind of question's that?"

"Well, did you plan it, or did this just happen spontaneously?" Good cop Dillard chimed in to bolster his moronic buddy.

Bad cop Simon finished the round of questions. "You guys have too many beers catching up and decide to go and kill that slutty ex-girlfriend you shared… and the guy who took her from you?"

He knew how to get under my skin. "Don't call my" – I paused before I almost called her my wife – "brother's wife a slut. You know nothing about that woman. Nothing."

"So, it's true?"

"What?"

"You were having an affair?"

"No. We weren't. She was my sister-in-law. We were friends. She confided in me. That's it. But we were close. We've been close since high school." I was working really hard to control my thoughts and my anger. My love for Callie was coming back though. It was the kind of love that got us married. Not the kind that held it together in the tough times. The real stuff. I had to watch it. Focus.

"Since high school. Back when she was dating your buddy Jake Chambliss. Were you having an affair with her then, too?" I could see Simon was trying to provoke me into anger. I had to control it.

"No."

"But you were having an affair with her when she was married to your brother?"

"Again, no. I was not having an affair with her when she was dating Jake in school. I was not having an affair with her when she was married to my brother. But I've always been close to her since grammar school. We've been friends since like first grade. She and I dated for a few years, it didn't work, and that was it. Nothing more. We were better at being friends. I had nothing to do with killing my brother or his wife. I loved them more than anybody. They're my family."

They thought for a second. Checking me out. Looking for tells. I became self-conscious about how I was involuntarily squinting at them, waiting for their reaction. They just observed. Sweating me out. I don't know if this was good or not, but I decided to take control of the situation. Maybe not successfully though. I just had to make sure I wasn't acting guilty. I had to somehow prove to them I wasn't.

"I gotta tell you guys, so far, you aren't giving me much confidence. I don't think you guys have any idea how to find the killer of Curt and Callie."

"How do you know it was just one killer?" Simon was quick. Must have learned that skill at Quantico.

"Or killers. Might be more. Either way, you don't seem to be on the right trail, sitting here wasting time with me."

"So, you don' mind if we take a look around your house? Take a look at your guns?" Good cop Dillard was back.

"How do you know I have guns?"

"Everybody has guns out here. It's the freakin' hinterland."

"Then, of course I don't mind." I don't know what got into me, but I did it on the spur of the moment. Maybe just to prove how incompetent these guys were. As I grabbed the gun in my pocket, took out the magazine and put it on the table, I said, "But you ain't gonna find this gun at my house."

Both of them fumbled around for their guns like they hadn't had to in years. By the time they had their guns on me, I'd had the clip, the gun and the un-chambered shell on the table and my hands in the air. I was unarmed, and they were on camera looking like total fools. They let an armed perp into the interrogation room. It was priceless. I knew these jerks didn't give a crap about who killed Curt and Callie. They just wanted Jake, and that made them my enemies.

Now they were shaking in fear. They had their guns pointed at me like amateurs. "How'd you get that in here?"

"Did you ask me for it before you brought me in here?" I asked.

They didn't answer. Probably didn't want to incriminate themselves on camera.

Good cop Dillard pulled out a pen and moved the gun over to his side of the table. He opened the drawer on the table and pulled out three plastic evidence bags and put each piece of evidence in its own bag. "We'll take care of this for you."

114

"I figured you would. That's why I gave it to you. Sorry about the misunderstanding. I didn't know I was a perp until you started treating me like one. Figured when I came down here, you'd be asking me questions about who might have done this. My bad."

Dillard asked me to stand up. He patted me down. Took out my keys, my wallet, a pocketknife, a small wad of cash, my gloves. "You always carry a gun?"

"Yes sir. I run a bar, and I take a bag of cash out of the bar every night. You better believe I carry a gun."

"Makes sense."

"Right now, especially," I continued. Probably shouldn't have.

"Why right now?"

"Because Curt and Callie just got killed. How do I know they ain't coming after me next?"

"Who's they?" Dillard asked.

I'd said too much. "Whoever did this."

"Who do you think that is? You said yourself, if we were doing our jobs, we'd find out why someone would want to do this."

I stayed quiet.

"The more you clam up, boy, the more you're looking good for this." Good cop Dillard called me boy. Turning bad?

"Far as I can tell," I said, "you guys are here to get Jake."

"He tell you that?"

"No, but Jake shows up for the first time in twenty some odd years, and the feds show up right after. Doesn't take a genius."

"Yeah," Dillard interrupted, "but don't forget what happened in between."

"Nah," I said, "that's just incidental. Small town murders don't hit the fed's radar. You guys were set in motion by Jake's being in the country. I'm not buying this you're-here-to-help-solve-the-murder crap."

"You saying we're full of crap?" Simon let a blood vessel pop out on his forehead while his face went voluntarily red. Good intimidation tactics for sure.

"No," I said, "I'm just telling you you're barking up the wrong tree if you think Jake did this. There's not a bad bone in Jake's body. I've known him as long as I've known Callie."

"That's where you're wrong, boy. You know nothing about Jake Chambliss over the last twenty-some-odd years. Those are your own words."

"Yeah, maybe, but I know he didn't do it."

"How?"

"He was with me at the bar until like 4 or 4:30 in the morning. He didn't just come from killing anyone, and he wasn't on his way to kill anyone when he left."

"How do you know what he was doing?"

"Well, he didn't have a car. Whoever killed Curt and Callie had a car."

"How do you know?"

"They shoveled the driveway to get rid of all the footprints and the tire tracks. Then they took the shovel."

"What shovel?" Simon asked.

"Shouldn't Chief Beck be in here for this… since he's the one that's going to have to solve this case?"

"He's watching," Dillard said.

"All right. Good. My brother is obsessive about his tools. They all have a place, and they get back to that place as soon as he's done. He's much more ordered than I am. He keeps his snow shovel on the double hook between the small garage door and the big one. It was gone, and the driveway had been shoveled in the middle of the night. It still had snow, but not nearly as high as what was on my driveway just from the night before. It was snowing all night that night."

"You a cop?" Dillard said.

"No, but when I'm walking out of a murder scene that I'd just discovered, I knew I needed to find clues. First clue I looked for was footprints in the snow. They were gone. Why? They were shoveled, and the shovel is gone. If it was still there, there might have been fingerprints. I checked. It was gone. Find the shovel, find the killers. It was a yellow ergonomically correct shovel, and my brother wrote Cutler on the back of it in black permanent marker. Killer or killers."

"What else did you notice?"

"The water left on the kitchen floor. They dragged in some snow. Curt must have heard noise and come down to investigate. They shot my brother while he was trying to protect his wife. Then they executed Callie while she was hiding under the bed. They shot her execution style. This wasn't some burglary gone bad."

"What, are you a psychologist?"

"No," I said. "Just can't get the images out of my head."

"You seem to think there was more than one killer."

"Kinda do."

"Why?"

"Too much to get done and get out of there without leaving evidence. The way I see it, there was one or two in the house, probably two, while there was one shoveling the snow on the driveway. You can't shovel someone's driveway and think they're not going to wake up, so the guy or guys on the inside had to wait until the driveway was clear, but they had to make sure Curt and Callie didn't wake up and call the cops on the dumbasses shoveling their driveway. It had to be shoveled before the murders. What killer shoots guns and then sticks around a crime scene until the driveway's shoveled? Don't make sense. So, I'm thinking at least three people."

"Sounds like you put some thought into this."

"Yeah, of course. How could I not?"

"Why do you think two in the house?"

"A lot of water on the kitchen floor, and Callie is strong. Was strong. She wasn't some dainty little princess. Whoever pulled her out from under the bed by her feet needed two hands to do it. It wasn't the shooter. Both feet were out from under the bed. If the killer was only pulling on her one foot, her other would still be underneath doing all it could to pull her back under."

"Good work, detective." It was the first smile I'd seen on Simon's face. "I've seen the crime photos. I think you might be right. That's why we thought Jake had help doing this."

"Jake didn't do this," I said.

"Jake's a bad guy. He's a killer. He's killed many."

"Of course, he was. He was in the military. So, what. He didn't kill Curt and Callie. He loved Callie more than anything. He might have had problems with Curt in high school, but that's all water under the bridge."

"What do you mean?"

117

"I was the quarterback, and they were my two receivers. Curt always felt I passed to Jake more."

"Did you?"

"Maybe. Probably. But so, what? It's a long time ago. It's forgotten. It was a problem Curt had with Jake, not the other way around. It had nothing to do with these murders."

"What did? You were telling us you had some idea of who might have wanted to kill them."

"Look," I said, "I have a couple of ideas, but I need to check them out myself. I can't have a bunch of cops sniffing around where they don't belong. Everybody'll clam up, sure as crap."

"You go in there snooping around on your own, you're gonna get yourself killed," Dillard said with actual concern.

"That's more likely now that you've taken my gun," I said.

"You'll get that back once it's gone through ballistics and you're proven innocent," Dillard said.

"Aren't I presumed innocent until proven guilty?"

They both laughed.

"Yeah, maybe in the eyes of the court," Dillard said.

Simon completed his statement. "It's our job to protect America *from* the courts."

"I guess that makes you America's finest," I said with a smirk.

"Something like that. So, tell us where to look if it's not you and Jake."

I thought about it while they watched me. I was fairly sure it had to do with the bank. I didn't know enough about why the Mexicans wanted the bar, but I didn't really want it. The bar was Cash's excursion into business. So, if there was a way out of the bar business that involved a chunk of change in Cash's pocket, why not explore that before destroying the opportunity by putting cops up the would-be bar-buyers' butts? Regarding the bank merger though, I really wanted to get to the board members before the cops spooked them into silence. The question was, if I turned these feds, who only wanted Jake, onto the merger, would they even be strategic enough to get on the right trail in time? – No.

"Listen, son," good cop Dillard had gone from calling me boy to calling me son, "we know that Callie sent Jake a message telling him you and your brother were in

118

trouble. We intercepted the message. That's why we're here. I'm being honest with you. How about letting me in on what's going on?" Couldn't argue with that too well.

"All right," I said. "Curt was the president of the local bank here. This isn't public information. It's still on the down low. His bank was in the middle of acquiring First Iroquois Trust. Some people don't want this merger to go through. Apparently, someone's willing to kill people in order to kill the deal. I just don't know who."

"First Iroquois Trust, you said? Who runs that? – The Pilgrims?" Dillard looked at Simon and laughed, but the joke went over Simon's head.

"Apparently," I said, "it's the Native Americans that run all the casinos in New York State. But, like I said, I don't know yet. It's what I aim to find out."

"You're crazy, son," Dillard was giving me advice now.

"Why?"

"You're talking about snooping around in the business affairs of really, really, really rich Indians who, I promise you, will do anything to keep you from their secrets. No wonder your brother's dead."

"What are you saying?" I raised my voice a little more than I should have.

"We're saying," Simon said, "if the Indians killed your brother, they're probably gonna get away with it."

"Again, what are you saying?"

"Nothing we can do. It's out of our jurisdiction."

"We're talking murder here. Doesn't that make it your jurisdiction?"

"No," Simon said. "Remember the recession?"

"Yeah."

"The state governments needed money, they made deals with the Indian reservations. The deals were made in the darkness of night without campfires. The Indians get to put casinos on land the state gives them. It becomes Indian sovereign land. In exchange for a piece of the action, which somehow isn't a tax, the states stay out of Indian affairs. That was the deal."

"Who would make that kind of deal? That's nuts," I said.

"Your governor did. The state gets money from the Indians, and the Indians get a stay-out-of-jail-forever card."

"All the Indians?"

119

"No, just the ones that keep the money flowing to the state. Jails are loaded with the little Indians."

"So," I said, "What are you guys gonna do about this? Now that you know?"

"Nothing. Can't. We're just going to find Jake and bring him to justice."

"You kidding me? Why am I here?"

"To help us find Jake Chambliss." Dillard smiled at me as if he'd only realized just then how naïve I was. Felt like he was calling me "silly."

"Can I go then?"

"Sure. But here are our numbers." They handed me their cards. "If you see Jake, you need to tell us right away, or you'll be charged for aiding and abetting a wanted fugitive."

I put their cards in my pocket in a way that was meant to show them I didn't want to, put on my coat, hat and gloves, and I left the interrogation room as soon as Agent Simon opened the door. Chief Beck was in his office watching the interrogation from the computer on his desk. He got up with an apologetic look of helplessness on his face. I guess being Chief of the Pendleton Police Department really was a ceremonial job created for the benefit of whoever gets the grifted tax dollars and the big pensions.

"You want a ride, son?" I guess he didn't want to be totally helpless.

"No, Chief. I'm gonna walk. I need some fresh air. I can't believe what I just heard."

"Sorry, Cash... sorry."

I walked through the door and would have loved to have slammed it, but it was on one of those pressurized systems that make it impossible to close the door faster than it takes to let out all the air. Serves them right.

Chapter 16

Jake started running again. He put as many trees between him and the men he'd just killed as he could. There were some old trails through the woods, but none had been tended to in a while. People probably weren't hunting on the property now that there was a big ole' Indian casino right there.

Jake ran about another quarter mile towards the house where the Caddy had stopped to drop off the ponytailed kid in the backseat. He slowed as he neared the road and waited to make sure no cars were coming. He sprinted across the road and into the woods next to the farm.

He walked through the smaller patch of woods and saw he was coming upon a farmhouse with a bunch of barns and some vehicles. Also, a silo. Must have been an actual farm at one point. He decided he would take the black Dodge Ram pickup. It was shiny and trimmed out in chrome. The other vehicles weren't as nice. One was a tractor. It was too slow.

He walked across the lawn and then the driveway up to the grey house with white trim. The grey was old cedar siding that needed a paint job, and the white paint barely remained on the weathered trim wood left porous and cracked after years of minimal protection from the weather. All the blinds were drawn over the smoky film-covered windows. As he walked up the steps, he heard the sound of thunder and shooting inside. It was the artificial sounds of war coming through a speaker system with a powerful subwoofer shaking the foundation of the whole house. Video games. Must be playing some shooting game. This was going to be easy.

With an AR slung over each of his shoulders, he opened the screen door and knocked on the window of the grey wooden door with one of his Glocks. His taps were loud and rattling; the window was loose inside the frame. They didn't hear him over the sounds from the game. He waited another few seconds until the sounds had simmered and tapped again. The game was put on pause, and someone yelled something in Spanish. He tapped it again three more times, just because.

More Spanish. Jake couldn't tell what he said though.

The yellowed curtain that prevented him from seeing into the house was moved to the side with a gun. They guy from earlier in the morning looked at him, using his raised eyebrows to ask why in the heck Jake was making him pause his game.

"What do you want, esse?" Mexican. Not another Indian.

"I ain't your esse. I'm your gringo. I need the keys to the truck," Jake told him as he turned the knob and slammed the door into the kid. The window shattered on his face. He was bleeding.

"Sorry about that."

His buddy in the next room said something as he got up and pointed his gun at the doorway. As soon as he saw the other guy's gun, Jake pulled the door closed, holding the guy from earlier to the door by his gun hand through the broken window. The guy actually shot from the other room, but the kid who opened the door was the one who took the bullet. With friends like that...

The kid screamed in Jake's ear, so Jake grabbed his gun and slammed it upside his bloody head. "Don't yell in my ear."

Through the broken window, he pushed the kid into the dinner table inside the doorway and slipped his gun inside the broken window. Jake said, "You shot your buddy," as he took two quick shots at the kid in the next room. He was gone. "Quit bleeding. Look what you're doing to the rug. You're gonna lose the security deposit."

He grabbed the ponytail from earlier that morning by his monster truck shirt. Gravedigger. How appropriate. The kid had a bullet in his ribs and a bleeding face. "Give me the keys to the truck. Who else is here?"

The kid spit at him. Jake smashed him again with his gun. "Quit that. I don't want your blood on me. How many more?"

The Mexican kid, who looked like he could have been Indian, swore at him and spit again.

"You're not helping yourself." Jake smacked him again and took the keys from the kid's front pocket. He clicked the buttons on the Dodge key fob until the truck chirped. "Thanks for the ride. Now I've got some questions."

The kid coughed involuntarily and then spit out the words, "gringo" and "puta" and maybe a couple of other mumbled words with a loogie of blood, saliva and lung butter that slid down his lower lip. He hiccupped so hard his belly and chest lifted, and then his eyes closed as if he'd fallen asleep.

"You dead?" Jake slapped his face around to wake him up. Looking at the exit wound, he realized he took a shot to the lungs. "A lot a good you are."

Jake wanted to take a quick run through the house, but he knew he had to get off Grand Island soon. He didn't expect them to call the cops, but they'd surely set out after him again once they realized all their men were dead. He stepped into the living room and saw they were playing Call of Duty. The game was paused, but the screen was moving. There was a hallway to the left and a stairway to the second floor.

He opened the door to the steps. They were painted black, and they were steep. The house was old. He stuck his head in the hallway to the left and heard a muffled scream. Opening the first door, he saw a woman in a dark room. She had a gag over her mouth. It prevented him from hearing what she was saying. She lifted the blanket to show him her hands were tied. A hostage. She was a tiny young lady. Not more than ninety pounds. Brown skin and long straight hair.

Jake lifted her gag and realized that her bound hands were tied to a bar bolted to the wall. As he was untying her, he asked her to stop screaming with his finger to his lips. "Are there more people here?"

She shook her head. "S'only me."

"You speak English?"

"Poquito."

"Good. Mi tambien." Jake did take Spanish in high school but had forgotten much of it. Miss Carballo taught it. Nice lady but crazy at times, especially if she didn't like you. Luckily, she liked him. Maybe this was why he sat through four years of her class? He untied the woman and said, "Vamanos."

She stood up and was in her underwear and a T-shirt and bare feet.

"You have clothes? Shoes?"

She shook her head three times real fast with a guilty look on her face like he was going to punish her or smack her across the face with a gun because she had no shoes. Captivity messes with the head.

"Wrap yourself in the blanket. It's cold. Mas frio."

When they got to the kitchen, he picked her up, so she didn't have to walk over the glass and through the snow. He carried her right to the passenger side of the truck. Too much snow. He put his two ARs in the back seat of the truck and then ran around the front, got in and started it. It was a Hemi. It roared.

"Get down. We've got company."

A dark sedan pulled into the driveway coming from the direction of the casino. Reinforcements or a fetch-it boy coming to get reinforcements. If the two video-gamer Bobbsey boys were their idea of reinforcements, this gang was in trouble.

Jake drove up on them quickly with the ferocious roar of an overworked first gear and lowered his window to see what they wanted. The Hemi purred its rumble, and Jake's smokey breath of the bull returned with the cold.

It was the two tuxedoed muscle heads he mercifully didn't kill on the thirteenth floor. "I see you've come back for more." The driver looked up and went white. Must have seen all his dead and comatose buddies. He tried to get his gun out but wasn't quick enough. Probably got caught on some rogue hem in his cheap tuxedo pocket.

Jake took out his front and rear tires with two shots and was spewing rooster tails of snow and rocks before the guy was ready to shoot. By the time they got out of the car and started shooting, Jake was on the road and heading for the I90. *Probably should have killed them*, he thought as he drove under the overpass and took the entrance ramp. He was still fighting his inner war machine's rage.

Once on the road, he tried to stay the speed limit as best he could while making sure he wasn't being followed by some overly aggressive goon in the rearview mirror. The last thing he needed was to get pulled over with all these guns. Then he remembered: ARs aren't well liked by the state of New York, and he had to pass by the toll booths. Probably didn't have to pay the toll to get off the island, but he didn't want someone high up to get a look at what he had on his back seat.

He couldn't think of the words in Spanish, and he didn't want to stop.

"Cubre los fuegos."

"Que?"

He pointed to the guns, and used his hands illustrate covering.

"No entiendo."

He shook the corner of her blanket and pointed at the guns. "Cubre."

She finally understood but was then sitting in his front seat in her underwear. Crap. He turned up the fan on the heat, reached back, moved the blanket, grabbed a gun, put it between her legs with the muzzle pointing down, did the same with the other gun and then grabbed the blanket. "Cover yourself."

She did right before they came up on the bridge. There was no toll this time, but traffic slowed. The vehicles coming onto Grand Island to the left were coming through the toll booth. The bridge goes up an incline at an almost twenty-five-degree angle before it goes down at the same angle. It makes room for big ships to get under it in the middle of the Niagara River. Jake couldn't stop looking into the rearview mirror for tails. He couldn't believe they'd let him get away so easily. What was that about?

It was 11:30. He didn't expect to be calling Ainsley this early, but he needed someone to take this girl off his hands. He dialed her number.

124

"This is Ainsley Reed."

"It's Jake."

"Jake?"

"Yes, Jake. What are you doing?"

"I'm driving into Pendleton as we speak. Just crossed the bridge. Why?"

"I need your help."

"What do you mean?"

"I've got a girl here who was a hostage. She don't speak English. She speaks Spanish. I know a little, but not enough, and she's not saying much. She has no clothes, and I need to get her help."

"You can't be serious," she said.

"Serious as a bullet to the head. This is getting big, nasty and horrendous quickly."

"My boss won't let me touch the story," she said.

"He's already compromised. He's smart."

"What do you mean?"

"You know what I mean."

"You mean those agents?"

"I don't know what you're talking about," Jake said to keep her safe. It probably didn't matter. There's little chance she'd be bugged quite yet. There's no way they'd know he'd spoken with her.

"Simon and Dillard."

"Never heard those names before," he continued to build his case for plausible deniability anyway.

"Oh yeah," Ainsley said, "me neither. Just so you know though, they're retired. Haven't been agents since right after 911."

"Figures," Jake said.

"What do you mean?"

"I told you I'd tell you everything later. Suffice it to say, Oklahoma City was a precursor to 911. I'm not the only one who knows it, but I *am* the only one alive who had John Doe Number Two in custody."

"You told me that."

"I know. But that's why they want me dead."

"What are you getting me into, Jake Charm?"

"Nothing. You're the one driving yourself to Pendleton without your boss's permission. If you want out, I won't stop you. Turn around and forget you ever met me."

"Not a chance. You're kind of unforgettable."

"Well, you'll have to eventually. Once these murders are solved, I'm gone. I can't stay around here."

"What if your name is cleared?"

"The only way it'll ever be cleared is if I'm dead, gone and forgotten, and my secrets get buried with me. So seriously, Ainsley, if you want to turn back now, I won't hold it against you."

"Not a chance. Let me talk to the girl. I know Spanish."

Jake put the phone to her ear, and they spoke for a few minutes. He kept driving with an eye on the mirror.

When the girl gave him back the phone, Ainsley said, "Jake, you're a hero."

"What are you talking about?"

"Those guys you killed were raping her over and over."

"I didn't kill them. They killed each other. She was in the room though. No way she coulda known that."

"Whatever, Jake. She was brought up from Mexico with a bunch of others. She'd been in that house for days, maybe a week."

"Were they looking for a ransom?"

"She didn't say. I didn't get the idea that she had anyone who'd pay a ransom."

"Sex slave?"

"I think so," Ainsley said. "Where'd you find her and how?"

"Can't say yet.".

126

"What do you mean, you can't say yet? This is slavery."

"Look. I've got to go back. There are some other slaves there too. If word gets out about what's going on there, they're all going to be killed. Sent for a swim over the Niagara Falls."

"You found her in Niagara Falls?"

"Yeah, sure. It doesn't matter right now. I need you to stay focused on the Cutler murders. But first, I need you to take this girl and get her some help. Make sure she says nothing about where she's been though. Not yet. Give me 'til tomorrow."

"What are you going to do? You're not going in there by yourself, are you?"

"Don't worry about that. I'm a trained professional."

"A trained professional, huh? Where do you want me to meet you?"

"Where are you?"

"Just turned onto Beach Ridge."

"Where you heading?"

"Cash Cutler's house. See if he'll talk to me."

"Hold off on talking to him. Skylar too."

"I didn't hear you, you broke up," she said.

"Skylar too. Hold off on talking to them. Meet me in the rear parking lot of Cash's bar. If someone else is there though, get the heck out right away. Head towards Cash's. Act like you were just pulling in to turn around. And call me right away."

"He's only got the one bar, right?"

"Yeah, just the one, and I assume you know where it is."

"Of course," she said, "See you there, Jake Charm."

"Be there soon, Ainsley Reed."

This girl had no idea what she was getting herself into, Jake thought.

He looked at the girl next to him shivering and cowering in the blanket. "We're getting you ayuda." Help. "Ayuda por ti."

She smiled.

Chapter 17

It was cold, and it was still snowing. I was walking on the left shoulder of Campbell Boulevard towards Five Corners from the police department. One of those little small-town vanity programs. It's not like the sheriffs don't drive through. Pendleton had to have its own police department in order to accommodate the huge influx of people trying to get away from Buffalo and the suburbs. Interlopers that just don't understand the freedom of small-town living. Gotta bring their better learnin' and need for a hands-on government to make sure we yokels don't go astray. Pendleton will never be like it used to be.

Each step required more energy than normal because of the inch or so of slush on the shoulder. The salt on the road puts the snow in, what the scientists probably don't call, a semi-solid-slash-semi-liquid state. As soon as I'd get to the ball of my foot, my entire weight was focused on that little part of my foot, and it would break through the more solid portion of the slushy layer. My foot would drop down to the road and slip a bit as I slung my other leg forward. Not the ideal walking circumstances. By the time I'd turned onto Beach Ridge, right before the Convenient Food Mart, I'd broken a sweat. I should have taken Chief Beck's offer of a ride. Whatever, the exercise wasn't bad. I needed to clear my head anyway.

What I really needed was a gun. They took the one I had. I knew that Cash kept two others in the bar, and I wasn't about to ask the chief if he'd stop at the bar and let me pick up another gun.

I entered the bar through the back door. First, I checked the safe in the office. I had to walk through the kitchen to get there. It was there, along with a few piles of cash to fill the registers. Just like normal. I didn't touch it. Ready to go in case someone's telling me to open the safe and give them the money. "The only good robber is a holy robber." It's what my dad used to say. Since he was really old school, that meant full of bullet holes. Not like he expected there to be many church-going robbers. He was funny sometimes. Most of the time, without even trying. That's why he was funny. He came from a different generation. Man's got no time to be funny in his generation. So, that he was funny, it was a little extra special.

The two guns Cash kept in the bar were the same two guns our dad kept there when it was a restaurant. He kept the other one in a special receded shelf he built under

128

the bar behind where he kept the vodkas. I had to move three bottles, reach up under the bar to the left, over the wall that protected the shelf and then down to get the little .38 Special snub-nosed revolver. Our dad loved this gun. Easy to hide but always ready to go.

But it wasn't there. Every pore on my body started sweating in fear. There's no way Cash would have moved this gun, and no one, other than me, knew about it. It was the best hiding spot ever. The two of us built it after he'd had the bar put in. He wanted my help figuring out where to put it.

I was a little freaked out at that moment. I started moving bottles around, I looked under the sink, above the sink, under the beer gutters, behind the keg lines, under the taps, behind the refrigerators, under the cash register, in the drawer. It was nowhere. *Cash, guide me to the gun. Come on Cash. I need you.*

Cash was no help, and just as I was about to give up and get my dad's other .38 Special in the safe, someone opened the back door. I heard the bells on the door chime while I was down looking under the sink for the third time.

I should have locked the door. "We're closed," I said, "We'll be open after four."

"You're not closed for us." He said it in a Mexican accent. He spoke every word without pause in between words. "The boss wants us to deliver a message." He pronounced it like "deleever ay may-sayge."

As I stood up to look at who might have killed my brother, he finished, "With condolences. You know, for your losses."

I looked at these two guys walking through the pool table area towards the bar. I'd never seen them before. Both were big and built, but slightly chubby. As they walked, their shoulders swayed front to back, like they were wading through the air. Both had short black hair. Neither wore a hat or a hood, but they wore matching brown jackets over nice button-down shirts and blue jeans. Not twins, but they looked enough alike they could have been brothers.

"Thanks," I said.

"For what?"

"The condolences."

"Oh, yeah. Neither of us know what those are, but he said you would."

I nodded my head slowly, sizing them up. Should have grabbed the gun in the safe. "Who said I would?"

"You know who. Señor Ortega, the guy you're selling the bar to."

129

"What I thought. Just wanted to make sure. What's the message?"

He put his hands up and said, "I'm just gettin' the envelope. Inside my coat." I nodded as he slowly unzipped and reached into his jacket. He gave me a tan envelope with designs around the border and a cactus in the lower left corner. The word "Cash" was written in the center of the envelope. It was sealed so the couriers didn't mess with it.

I opened the envelope and pulled out a piece of stationary that matched the envelope in color and design. It had the number 500,000 crossed out, and below that, the number 250,000 was written in. "What's this?" I demanded. I had an idea but wanted to hear it from them.

"It's the new deal. Señor Ortega said you'd understand."

"Understand what? We have no deal, and the land alone's worth twice that. This is commercial property in a town that doesn't rezone." I looked at it again to make sure I wasn't missing anything. "Is that in cash?" I asked. I'm not sure why.

"No. The money will be delivered to the account they set up for you at the bank."

"My brother's bank?"

"No. FIT."

"First Iroquois?"

"Of course. That's Señor Ortega's bank. You know all this. I know you do."

"Yeah, I guess. Things have been a bit crazy the last two days. So, two hundred and fifty thousand, huh?" I just wanted to hear it said.

"This is all he said. Fire sale. He said, someone's trying to frame you for your brother's murder, and you know, you're going to need money to defend yourself soon. Fire sale."

"What do you mean someone's trying to frame me? Did Ortega do this?"

"That's Señor Ortega to you. Don't ever call him Ortega to his face. Señor Ortega."

"Never mind that," I said. "Is he trying to frame me for murder?" I was getting pissed.

"Señor Ortega is a prominent businessman. He doesn't get involved with crime. So, no, he's not trying to frame you for murder. He doesn't even think you did it. Knows you didn't."

"Then why's he say I'm being framed?" I asked.

"Your brother had big enemies. The kind that get away with murder. You're number one suspect. Señor Ortega just put two and two together. He good at math. S'why he got so much. We know you just came from first round of questioning. They let you go so you can cover up tracks. They catch you then. That's how they do it. Always how they do it."

What if they're right? The gun's missing.

"Tell him no deal. The land is worth twice that number." I wasn't going to be pushed into selling because my brother was dead. That would make me look even guiltier.

"Señor Ortega said if you don't sign paper, deal get worse when heat get hotter. His words. He promises heat get hotter."

"Is that a threat?"

"Señor Ortega is brilliant businessman. Don't need threats. He's giving you 'til tonight. We'll be back. Offer goes down at midnight."

They turned and left. The guy chewing gum didn't say a word the whole time. Only the one guy spoke, and he went out the door first. As soon as they'd gone, I locked the door and got the gun from the safe.

The only good thing about the possibility that someone was trying to frame me was that, if they used the snub nose to do the murders, my fingerprints weren't on it. I hadn't touched it since we were kids. They'd only find Cash's fingerprints, and those would match the dead body. A little foil in the plan.

It was nearing noon and I needed to get home, to get some food and a shower before I opened the bar. This was going to be interesting to see who was going to be coming at me, besides all the people coming to give me condolences, of course.

Chapter 18

Once I had my coat, hat and gloves on, I peeked out the back door to make sure they were gone. The wind was whistling through the doorway blowing a dust of snow onto my once dry floor. I locked up. I wasn't going to take the shortcut through the fields. The snow was eight to twelve inches deep in places, and it was just too hard to walk through. I was going to take the long way home on the road. Beach Ridge veers southwest, and then I have to backtrack north on Aiken to get home. The shortcut's about sixty-five percent of the trip. Maybe less.

As I was walking up front, I noticed two more sets of tire tracks in the parking lot. In addition to the car the Mexicans came in, there were two cars that turned around in the rear parking lot. Those guys must have had two carloads of protection. What the heck? Three cars to muscle me?

Unfortunately for me, the shoulder on Beach Ridge is just a little gravel next to a ditch. There wasn't much space for me to walk, and I had to keep looking for cars coming my way as the wind blew the snow in my eyes. I had to look up while my eyes were tilted lower. Snow was collecting on my eyelashes.

A few cars passed going slow on the slippery road, like normal humans. Then a big black pickup came at me from around the curve a lot faster than was safe. I didn't see who was driving. It slammed on the breaks when whomever it was saw me and skidded to a stop about thirty feet past me. It started backing up towards me. Great. Just what I needed. More of Cash's friends and acquaintances.

He opened the window and said, "Get in." It was Jake. Nice.

"You're a sight for sore eyes."

"You better believe it," he said. "Hurry up, it's cold."

As I was climbing up into the truck with its raised suspension and chrome foot rails, I noticed the two ARs in the back seat. "Nice semi-automatic persuaders. Rob a gun store?"

"No. They're mine. Here, you want a Glock?" He pulled one out of his pocket while he steered with his left hand. "These are nice. Got four of 'em. You can

132

have two if you want. Or give one to Skylar. I don't care. They probably took your gun this morning."

"Who?"

"The cops. The feds. You just came from interrogation, right?"

"No secrets in this town, are there?" I asked without expecting an answer.

"Why'd you say that? I was just stating the obvious. You're walking back after Tyler or the chief woke you up and brought you in."

"I guess the Mexicans knew I was in interrogation, too."

"What Mexicans?"

"Three carloads of Mexicans came to tell me about the new deal for the bar. Lowered the offer by fifty percent. Said I'm being framed and that I'll need the money now more than before. For defense lawyers."

"If it makes you feel better, I only saw one car. The other tracks at the bar were me and Ainsley."

"Who's Ainsley?"

"Ainsley Reed. The TV newsgirl. She's my new friend. Our new friend. I told her to meet me behind the bar, but if there was a car there, I told her to turn around and get the heck out of there. Fast. I went in, saw the car and her tracks and followed her to your house. I gave her the Mexican sex slave that I saved from earlier."

"What the hell you talking about? Mexican sex slave? Thought you didn't want to meet until after last call."

"No time for that, brother. Things are getting crazy and dangerous quick. Real quick."

"What? You talking about the feds trying to find you?"

"Well, that too, but they're nothing compared to what's coming at *you*. You met the feds, huh? Simon and Dillard?"

"Yeah. How'd you know?"

"Ainsley told me. They've been chasing me since '95."

"Is that why you never came home?"

"Partly. Forget that for now. We gotta get Skylar and stash her someplace safe. She's in trouble. Big trouble."

133

"Hold up," I said, "just stop for a second."

He slowed the truck.

"I don't mean the truck." He resumed speed. "Mexican sex slave? ARs? Glocks for everyone? Feds chasing you since '95? Skylar's in trouble? What is going on?"

"Skylar's mom is a debt slave at the Indian casino on Grand Island. That's the reason Skylar was sent to get you to sell the bar. If she does, they'll free her mother. I think that's how it works. She didn't have time to tell me everything. But I've got the phone number of one the prostitutes that lives right down the hall from her. I'm going to use her to bust out Shelly, but we have to make sure Skylar's safe first."

I stared at him and thought he'd lost his mind. He took his eyes off the road to look at me and said, "I get it. Sounds crazy, but if you want the Mexicans to leave you alone, we just gotta bust Shelly out, but we can't do that until Skylar's safe. Shelly won't come. Cares more about her daughter than her own life...I respect that."

"Oh." *Was Skylar's relationship with Cash a total sham?* "Jake, do you think Skylar was only with my brother to save her mother?"

"I don't know. You ask that question like you're falling for her...are you falling for her?" A thought-inspired smile broke out on his pursed lips.

"No. Just can't tell, is all."

"You slept with her! You dog. Your dead brother's girlfriend? Day after your wife was killed? Oh, man. You're a dog. I'm so glad I came home for this. This is turning into so much fun." He had a big old smile on his face. The kind he used to have in the huddle when we were utterly tearing up our opponent's defense. Then he remembered himself. "I don't mean I'm glad they're dead. You know that. And honestly, this isn't really fun at all. So, don't take any of that excitement as serious. It's just, you slept with your dead brother's girlfriend." And his devious smile came back. He couldn't help but shake his head.

"Yeah. I know." I wasn't having as much fun though. I didn't have the ability to smile, that's for sure. He pulled into my driveway on the barn side. "Park by the barn," I said, "there's a lot of tracks in the driveway."

"Yeah," he said, "I met Ainsley here just a bit ago. Pulled up right there, and I gave her the Mexican girl. She's going to take her to a hospital. I can't do that."

"Yeah, but what's that over there?" I pointed to some footprints coming out of the house at the foot of the porch steps up to the driveway. "You guys didn't go in the house, did you?"

"No, we didn't. Let's check it out."

134

"Hold on a second," I said. He pulled back from the door he was about to exit and turned back to look at me. "Regarding Skylar, I didn't have a choice."

"I know that, I was just busting your chops. You're still a dog though."

We opened the doors and got out and walked to the right of the car tracks. There were about four or five sets of tracks. Skylar's car was parked, but she'd backed out, left and then parked it again once she'd gotten back. It was still ticking, so she'd just parked it.

Her tiny footprints lay a trail to and from the car, but the ones from the car were much fresher. Then, from the porch to the tire tracks near the porch, there were two sets of men's footprints to and from the house. There was a partial set of Skylar's footprints.

While Jake was mulling over the footprint story, I said, "Someone's taken her. They carried her to the car, set her down here, see those two, no, three prints, and put her in the car."

"Probably right," Jake said after some further thought. "Are we sure she didn't walk in their footprints to keep snow off her shoes? Maybe she wasn't being carried. Maybe she went voluntarily."

"Let me get some photos before you get too close." I took close-ups of the tire tracks, the footprints and a wider shot of how the footprints were scattered.

We looked for her print inside some of the men's prints, but no. They were carrying her. There was no way she could traverse the twelve feet from the base of the steps to where the car was parked. Impossible.

"Yeah, they were definitely carrying her," he concluded. "Call her."

"Already am." It rang four times and went to voice mail. I hung up. "Hey, when you met your new friend Ainsley here, was Skylar's car here?"

"No, just yours."

"That means they took her right after you left, which means she pulled in after you left, and they pulled in right after her."

"Check the door."

"It's locked."

"She never even made it into the house. If they knocked and took her, the door would still be unlocked. Probably even left open."

"The door locks automatically," I said.

135

"Oh, never mind." He followed the tracks to the road. "They turned right. Make sure she's not in the house."

While he got in the truck and pulled it up, I ran through the house real quick. She was gone.

I jumped in the truck, and we left through the driveway we'd come in. He was flying. The roads were slow, but he had four-wheel drive and big tires with a lot of traction.

"You think it's the Mexicans that just visited you?"

"I don't know. They said their boss Ortega was a businessman. Legeetameete beesinissman," I said.

"Who kidnaps your girlfriend's mother? Yeah, real legitimate."

"You said she's with the Indians, though."

"Yeah, but the Mexicans and the Indians are together. I saved that Mexican girl from a couple of bong-hit Mexican video gamers down the road from the casino."

"How'd you know to go there?"

"It's where the Indian with Skylar's mother dropped him off on the way to taking Shelly back to the casino."

"Why'd the Indian have Skylar's mother?"

"Took her to the diner on the reservation to meet with Skylar. I was following Skylar until I followed the Indian and the Mexican with the mother, who I first thought was Skylar. Skylar looks just like her mom."

"What happened to Skylar?"

"I don't know. She was crying in her car at the reservation when I left. Figured it had to do with the meeting with her mother. Couldn't follow both of them."

Jake stopped short of the Mapleton Road intersection and put the hazards on. "Get those pictures of the tire tracks up." He meant on my phone.

We got out and looked at all the tire tracks in the thick snow at the end of Aiken. Mapleton is a bigger road with a lot more traffic than Aiken. The snowplows leave a lot of snow at the end of the road when plowing Mapleton and ignoring Aiken. We found the tracks. They turned left. They were the freshest on the road, in fact. We weren't far behind.

"Heading to Niagara Falls or maybe even Grand Island," Jake said. "Vamanos. That's Mexican for let's go."

"Thanks, Miss Carballo."

"Or Mrs. Bernstein."

"Yeah, I liked her too."

Mapleton was salted and plowed. Jake was driving fast. When we passed our school, he slowed and noticed the new high school that was built on the old football field. The school expanded because of the huge influx of people from Buffalo and the suburbs. "Look at a that," he said, "school's huge."

"Yeah, it's nice too."

"Here." He handed me his cell phone. "Call Ainsley."

"What do I say?"

"Find out what the girl told her."

I selected Ainsley's number from Jake's list of recent calls.

"Jake?" Ainsley answered.

"No, this is Cash Cutler."

"Is Jake all right?"

I covered the phone mic and whispered over to Jake with a smile. "She likes you."

"Yeah, I know. Just find out what she knows. Quit wasting time."

I uncovered the mic. "Yeah, Jake's fine. He's right here. He's driving."

"Where's he going?"

"I don't know. Skylar's been kidnapped. We're…"

Jake cut in, "Don't tell her that." He smacked my arm.

"I already did."

"Take it back."

"You already did what?" Ainsley asked.

"Nothing. We just want to know if the girl told you anything."

"Did you say someone's been kidnapped?" Ainsley ignored my question.

"Maybe. We're not sure. Forget that for now. Did the girl tell you anything?"

"Who is this? How do I know you're Cash Cutler?"

I held the phone up to Jake's face. "Tell her it's ok to talk with me."

"It's Jake. That's Cash. You can tell him anything."

I pulled the phone back. "We good?" I asked her.

"She's in with the doctor right now. I'm sticking around to make sure she gets help once they let her out. She has no clothes, shoes, ID, money, nothing."

"That's good. You know, that you're helping her. She tell you anything?"

"She was supposed to have a job, a nice job, but those brutes, and there's more than two. There's a bunch. They come in and out, but there's always someone there. Those brutes have been keeping her for a while." At this point, Ainsley's voice went to a whisper, "They were raping her. Like, all of them."

"That's sick. Anything else?" I felt bad about my lack of time for sympathy, but time was a luxury and luxuries are for people who didn't just lose their wife and brother. And now brother's girlfriend.

"They've been giving her pills. Makes her sleep a lot."

"Any names?"

"She mentioned Conchita Garcia."

"A woman? Another sex slave?"

"No. I don't think so. I think she's the one that brought her here. Promised her a job," she said.

I turned to Jake. "Jake, did she mention Conchita Garcia? Ever hear that name?"

"No."

"Did she mention anybody else?" I asked Ainsley.

"No, she didn't say much. I think she's in shock, maybe still drugged. I can't tell."

I saw the lights in the side view mirror before I heard the siren.

"Oh crap, I gotta go. Getting pulled over."

"Tell Jake to call--"

I hung up. Jake pulled over quickly and got out of the truck with his hands up. He walked back towards the cop.

138

Thank God, it was Tyler Graveline. We all played football together. As I got out, I saw Tyler pull his gun and get behind his door for cover. "Stop right there, Jake. You're under arrest."

"I don't have time for this, Tyler.'

"Shut up. Stop right there. I don't have a choice. I gotta take you in."

Jake kept his hands up. I stood right behind my open door with a view of Tyler over the truck bed. I said, "Tyler, they kidnapped Skylar. My girlfriend. We don't have time for this right now. That's why we're speeding."

He didn't budge. His gun was on Jake. "Who kidnapped Skylar?"

"We don't know for sure. We're chasing them right now," Jake said. "You're letting them get away."

"There's an APB out on you, Jake. I gotta call this in."

"Yeah, I know. I won't hold that against you. But those feds, Simon and Dillard, are retired. They're not agents. They're full of crap. Check it out yourself. I'm innocent, and those guys have been trying to kill me since '95. Remember Timmy McVeigh?"

"Yeah."

We all used to play hockey with him out on the ice in the winters. We'd get driven to the iced pond, but Timmy McVeigh would walk through the fields with his skates in one hand and his stick in the other. It was a miserable walk. Walking through unleveled fields of snow-covered tractor ruts. I felt bad for the kid. His dad was always working. No mom. We had rides. He walked.

"Those guys are in charge of the cover-up," Jake said.

"What cover-up?"

"The one they get away with if they kill me. Look Tyler, I'll tell you all about it later. You gotta call it in, go ahead. I'm going. You want to shoot me, at least they won't be getting credit for it. Get in, Cash."

Jake turned his back on Tyler and the gun pointed at him, got in the truck, slammed it into gear with a perturbed look in his eyes and shot snow and pebbles at Tyler as he climbed back onto the road.

"You're freakin' nuts," I said.

"No. He wasn't gonna shoot me."

"How do you know?"

"I've had a lot of guns pointed at me."

"How do you know who's gonna shoot?"

"People shoot for two reasons. Fear they're going to be killed if they don't or fear that someone else is going to kill them if they don't. Of course, there's the psychos, but Tyler isn't psychotic. If I pulled a gun on Tyler, I think he would've shot me. I'm not stupid. He only had a gun on me in case what those feds said was true. You told him it wasn't."

"But I'm a suspect in a murder investigation."

"Yeah, but, unless they have evidence or a weapon, they've got nothing on you. I doubt Tyler thinks you did it."

That reminded me of my discovery that my dad's gun was no longer under the bar. I'd completely forgotten about it. I got a body-glow dose of that anxiety that starts in the belly and ends in every sweat gland on my body. I was in the middle of chasing down kidnappers, and not feeling anxious, but the thought of the missing gun got me nervous. There was something comfortable about riding shotgun with Jake Charm. The dude was trained to win, and I was just happy being along for the ride. Happy he was calling the shots.

"I forgot to tell you," I said, "when I was at the bar, I discovered the gun under the bar was gone. Same gun my father kept under the cash register in the restaurant. An old .38 Special. A snubby one."

"Not a great gun for long distance. I can see why he kept it under the register."

"His least favorite gun but his favorite too," I said, "Small and always there. Even still, it could be the gun that was used at the murders. Both my brother and Callie were shot at close range. No aiming necessary. Just point and shoot."

"Does it have your prints on it?"

"Just Cash's. I haven't touched that gun in decades. I'm sure my brother's cleaned it fifty times since."

"Don't worry about it then. If that's the gun they used, they'll think it was Curt's. Just say you haven't seen it since you were a kid."

"Hope you're right."

"What kinda car were the Mexicans driving?"

"A silver one," I said, "maybe grey. It was an old sedan with rounded edges. Like a Monte Carlo from the years they weren't cool."

"When was that?"

"Late '90s maybe. Muscle cars for the family man with kids. What a joke."

140

"Heh. Thank God I wasn't in the States for that. America really did go soft after the Berlin Wall came down. Keep an eye out for that car."

"You think it was the Mexicans?" I asked.

"They were right there. Timeline fits. Maybe they got real lucky with timing, but it fits. It's not like we don't know the Indians are working with Mexicans."

"But," I said, "these guys said Ortega was a legeetameete beesinissman."

"That's how they said it?"

"Almost exactly."

"I think that's code for gangster." Jake looked in the rearview mirror again. "You know your buddy Tyler's following us. No lights, but he's right behind us."

"He's your buddy too."

"He pulled a gun on me."

"There's that."

"I'm joking," Jake said, "I know he was just doing his job."

"What you think he's doing now?"

"I don't know. Think he's out of his jurisdiction though." We'd already crossed over Shawnee Road a while back. I think we were in Wheatfield by now.

"It's not like the Wheatfield PD are going to show up," I joked.

"Wait, Wheatfield's got a police department?"

"No, just kidding." Wheatfield was more podunk than Pendleton.

Jake sped up and passed three cars. Tyler stayed right on our tail. We couldn't shake him.

When we got to the 190 entrance so we could get to Grand Island, Jake drove right past it.

"Where you going?" I asked.

"I'm going to go up a bit and turn around. Give up for now. I can't tip our hat to Tyler. We can't have that casino crawling with cops. They'll kill Shelly, maybe Skylar and who knows how many other people before the cops ever even figure out where the thirteenth floor is."

"It's between the twelfth and fourteenth."

"Nah. There's only one entrance to the floor. I looked all over for another. The only entrance is the back-supply elevator used by the service workers. The cops will try and use the regular elevators, see that everything's fine and walk away."

"Why don't you just tell them about the thirteenth floor?" I asked without thinking.

"Because I just killed six, seven, I don't know, eight people over there, depending on who you ask. I give them that info, they find all the bodies, they put me in jail, the fake feds get me, take me away, and I disappear forever. All the while, Shelly and Skylar disappear as well. And I don't mean on vacation."

I took some time before I responded. "We're screwed."

He laughed. "Not yet we're not." He pulled into a gas station and hooked the pump up to the truck. "Got any cash?"

"How much?"

"Go give 'em a twenty. I'll talk to Tyler."

As I was coming back, Tyler walked up on Jake with a smile. He'd been sitting in his car looking at the computer screen. "You always were a crazy SOB, Jake."

"That's what they say. Sorry about that back there."

"Can I take you in now?"

"Not yet. This is what I need you to do. For your own sake, find out for yourself. Agents Sam Simon and Bob Dillard are retired. That's Sam Simon and Bob Dillard. These guys are working off the books, trust me."

"I just did. Chief Beck doesn't like them either. So, I'm listenin'."

"I know this can be bad for you," Jake said, "but this is important. Thanks for trusting me on that. I need you to be at Cash's bar tonight, in plain clothes, from around 10:30 until at least midnight or so. Some people will be visiting Cash about the deal they made. If they have Skylar, we might find out about it then. Wear a hat. Make sure you don't look like a cop. Do you know the name Conchita Garcia?"

"I've heard it."

"You know who she is?"

"She's in charge of undocumented workers. She's like a union leader that the farmers go to when they want cheap labor. She supplies the fake documents and the workers. The farmers get away with it, and she gets a piece of the action."

"If you know all this is going on, why haven't you arrested her?" I asked.

"I want to keep my job, that's why. She's got bigger connections than any police officer out there. Arresting her would destroy me. Cheap labor is big money. They buy the politicians of both parties. They're all bought and paid for." Tyler shook his head and lifted his hands in acceptance of corruption as the reality he was forced to live with.

"So, America's become just like Africa," Jake said, "part of the third world now, huh?"

"You have no idea how corrupt things are around here. It goes all the way up to the governor's office." Now we were getting somewhere.

"What does?"

"The drug money. The husband of one of the governor's main advisors is a federal attorney here in Buffalo. Every time the cops make a bust at one of their bars in NT, Tonawanda, Wheatfield, Niagara Falls, money from the drug dealers' attorneys goes right to the attorney in the form of campaign donations, all just under $10,000 – don't ask me how that's legal – and the next day, come hell or high water, these guys walk. I've followed the money and checked the dates." He looked at the gas pump. "You can start pumping, Jake. Cash gave the guy the money."

"Oh thanks, forgot about it." Jake started pumping. "Who owns all these bars?"

"Mostly all Italian kids. They're all related, and their fathers are all a part of the Niagara Falls mob. What's left of it."

"Where are the drugs coming from?" I asked.

"That's the big question. Every time we get one of these guys in, they clam up for a day or two, and then they're sprung. Like clockwork. I've been following this for years, secretly kinda. I mark down the days and then look at the campaign donation filings. I've got it all journaled. It's like clockwork. It's this attorney. I'm sure of it. Federal attorney. Appointed by President Obama."

"Nothing you can do about this?" Jake asked.

"Nah, like I said, I'm just a small-town cop whose whole department would get shut down in a nanosecond if the wrong people got wind of what I was up to."

"What's this attorney's name?" I asked.

"It doesn't matter. He's untouchable."

"Maybe," Jake said, "but what if this is all connected? If there aren't a lot of mob wars, it's because they're all working together. Think about it. If they all have a guy

143

giving them the get-outta-jail-free card, all their businesses remain much more profitable if they don't draw attention to themselves."

Tyler said, "Sounds good, but I think you're giving them much more credit than they deserve. I mean these guys are animals. All of them."

"Yeah, but what if he's the guy?" Jake said. "Don't you think we should have the opportunity to check him out?"

"The guy is powerful. I can't have this coming back on me. Keep my name out of it." Tyler was nervous about this guy.

"Absolutely. We have no desire whatsoever to see you lose your job. Promise."

"His name's Bennett Glazebrook. He's out of Buffalo. Let me know what you find. I gotta go though," Tyler said, "I can't be caught hanging out with a wanted fugitive."

"I get it. Go up 31. We'll go back on Lockport Road. I want to see if there's anything we might have missed chasing the guys who took Skylar."

"You sure she's been taken?"

"Pretty sure. Either that or she don't want to be found. I don't think they'll kill her though. They haven't gotten what they want."

"The bar?" Tyler asked.

"Yep."

"But they're Mexicans? Not Italians?" he asked.

"Pretty sure. Unless they're working on behalf of the Italians, but how many Italians let the Mexicans do their business deals?"

"Not many," Tyler said, "that's for sure. This might be the Mexicans moving in on the Italians' turf."

"That's what I was thinking," Jake said. "What if the Italians are moving the drugs that the Mexicans are bringing and now the Mexicans want to cut them out? Get their own distribution system going?"

"All hell's gonna break loose, that's what. I'll see you tonight."

"See you then."

Tyler took off.

Chapter 19

Jake pulled away from the pumps and up to the far side of the store, as if he were about to go shopping. He called Samantha on speed dial and put her on speaker.

"Hey cowboy," Samantha was trying to be flirty, but she was hushed. "Never thought I'd be hearing from you again. Looks like you really pissed off all the right people."

"You in trouble?"

"Not yet, but that girl you met is. They got two guards down there. We're all locked down. No one gets onto this floor, and no one gets off."

"What about the elevator?"

"Shut down and out of order. They're cleaning it. Guards everywhere, but it's up here. Not downstairs. No way to get up here."

"What else?"

"Nothing, honey. I'm laying low. Not leaving my room. Unless they make me. Wish you were here though. We'd be having some serious fun, cowboy."

"We'll have to save that for another time."

"Promise?"

"No. But listen, our friend has been kidnapped. We think it has something to do with Shelly down the hall. Shelly's daughter."

"She your girlfriend?"

"No. My buddy's. She's pregnant."

"He as cute as you?" Couldn't stop flirting. As they say in sales, ABC, Always Be Closing.

"Probably not. I need you to focus though. If they bring her up on the floor, I need you to call me."

"Sure thing. I'll call you anyway."

"Yeah, I know. This is important. I don't think they're ready to kill her yet."

"Kill her? What are you getting me into?"

"Nothing. I'm getting you out if you want. You're already in it, and you know it. Lay low, but if they bring her up, I need to know."

"So, you're gonna be my hero, cowboy?" She said it as if she didn't believe it and was still just roleplaying.

"Yeah, sure. Unless you want to stay a slave."

She changed. In a snap, she was a real person. Must have been the word slave. "You have no idea what's going on – do you?" The flirty voice was gone, and she was all business.

"What do you mean?" Jake didn't flinch.

"There's no getting out of here. I leave, there's not a place on the earth they won't go to kill me. Even if you were here to save me, I wouldn't go. I have family, and they know where my family is. If they have Skylar, she's either dead or she'll be doing what I do. Maybe not here but somewhere. Just as soon as they get rid of the baby, probably even before. There's no happy ending to this, cowboy. You might as well ride off into the sunset right now. Save yourself. Quit wasting your time."

"How'd you know her name is Skylar? She there?"

"I'm friends with Shelly. She's like a mother to me. Skylar's everything she lives for. Wish I had a mother that loved me like that."

"Wish you did too, Samantha." A natural sadness hummed through Jake's voice. "Don't give up just yet. The elevator can't stay up there forever. I'll see you soon, Samantha."

"You're really optimistic, cowboy. Believe it when I see you."

"Just let me know if you see Skylar."

"Sure thing, sweetie."

Jake hung up, jammed the truck into reverse and got us out of there.

I called Skylar again. It went right to voicemail. "Voicemail again. We going to the casino?"

"No," Jake said, "I'm going to the casino. You're going to talk with some of those board members of yours and then get that bar opened. Go about life like nothing's wrong. When they want us to know about Skylar, they'll let us know. In the meantime, don't sell the bar. I'll be there watching from the fields behind the bar tonight. Tyler will be on the inside. Slip him my phone number so he can keep me apprised. Tell him text only."

"What are you going to do at the casino?" I didn't want him to put Skylar in jeopardy.

"I don't know yet. I might do a little gambling."

"You nuts? They know what you look like."

"They won't do a dang thing about it if I'm in the casino, in the public part. Bad for business."

"What about your girlfriend, what's her name? Samantha?"

"You think she likes me?" Jake mimicked the excitement of a junior high girl.

"No. But I think she wants you to think she does."

"You think she's using me? Aww, man. You don't think I have a chance. With a prostitute? Thanks, buddy. For the vote of confidence."

"No sweat. I'm gonna see if I can find out about this Conchita chick."

I hit the speed dial for "Pacho the kitchen boy." That's how my brother Cash had it on his phone. I didn't find a number for Conchita Garcia. Her nickname probably would have been "the Coyote Lady."

"Hey Pacho."

"Who deess?"

"It's Cash."

"Oh, ey boss man. Yo name didn't come up."

"That's all right," I said, "I want to open the bar at four today."

"Oh, okay. I be dere. By da way, I am really sorry about yo' brother. I can't imagine."

"Thanks, Pacho. Hey, do you know how I can get a hold of Conchita Garcia?" I asked the question with the assumption he'd know something about her, rather than sound like an idiot who'd forgotten that I'd done business with the woman. Just in case Cash got Pacho through her. I was running blind on this one.

"Why, cuz I'm Mexican?"

147

"I didn't mean it like that." He put me on immediate defense. There's always a fine line when dealing with minorities that work for you. I deal with it at the bank. Used to anyway. Can you be familiar and ignore the fact that they're minorities, or do you have to suffer the scorn when they take offense at your treating them as if they're no different, even though they *are* minorities? There's no handbook on this. When it comes to friends who are minorities, it's easy. If they actually think you should treat them differently because they're minorities, they aren't your friends – avoid them. At some point or another, you'll do something or say something that will make them play some minority card on you and screw you in the process. A friend that can't be trusted isn't a friend but a liability. Simple as that. But when someone works for you, it's a whole big thing with tons of yapping lawyers on a leash just fifty feet away aching to get at you so they can rip out your lungs and feed your carcass to pigs after they've taken your business, livelihood, honor and social acceptability. When it's up to them, you'll have to change your name and move to another state if you ever want to work again. That's why so many businessmen and CEOs seem like a bunch of gutless wussies. They have to be. They all have boards loaded with beta males married to liberal harpy do-gooders who are always looking for another reason not to put out. "Fire that bigoted CEO and hire a woman, or you'll never get any of this again" – famous last words of woman in aa once healthy marriage.

"I know, boss man. I's just kiddin'."

"Pacho, my brother and his wife just died. You think it's all right to kid with me?" Thought I'd turn it right back on him. I decided I needed to treat him as if he were no different than anyone else. He has a problem with that, who cares? – I'll sell the bar, and he can work for criminals.

"Oh, boss man. I'm sorry. I didn't mean it like that."

"Yeah, I know, I was just kidding right back."

"Oh man, you got me on that one. But I really am sorry about your brother and his wife." He put a little emphasis on the wife part. Must have realized he'd forgotten her in the first apology.

"That's all right, Pacho. I appreciate it. Back to Conchita."

"Yeah, of course. She's a beach." He pronounced it like "beach," but I'm sure he meant something else. Jake was flying down Lockport Road, passing everyone that needed passing, which meant everyone he came upon.

"You know how to get a hold of her?"

"Hell's no, boss man. She da last person I'd ever call. My cousin Linda Chavez came here on Conchita's bus. Turned her out, got her hooked on heroin. My cousin was useless in lesssin' a month. Dead in six. My cousin thought she was gonna be picking apples up by the lake. Conchita keeled my cousin."

148

"I'm sorry to hear that, Pacho."

"Gracias, thanks."

"No problemo." Dead end. What the heck? "Hey Pacho, what about the guys that want to buy the bar?"

"Yeah, they know how to get a hold of her."

"She work for them?"

"More like they work under her. She got seniority. 'Sides, her cousin is one of the top Zetas back home."

"Cartel?"

"Sí, cartel. All of those guys are cartel. That's why you're selling them the bar. You loco?"

"You think I should sell it to them?"

"I don't think you got a choice. If they give you money for the bar, take it and run. Be thankful you still have your life."

"Huh... What about you? You want to work for them if they take over the bar?"

"No, boss man. I like working for you, but if they make me work for them, I not gonna say no."

"I appreciate that, Pacho."

"I like being your Pacho the kitchen boy. You get another bar, I'll do whatever I can to work for you."

"Sure thing... Pacho, do you think these guys that want to buy the bar might have killed my brother and his wife?"

"Uh, I don't know. I don't think so. Not their style."

"What do you mean?"

"If they did it, the bodies'd be hanging from a bridge. They don't leave bodies in the house where they kill dem. First, they torture dem for a while, then they keel dem, and then they put dem on display. They take pride in their work. Whoever killed your brother and hees wife don't wanna get caught. Not showy enough."

"You're talking about the same guys that want to buy the bar?"

"Sí. These guys are all business."

149

"They're coming tonight to the bar. Said I need to sign by midnight."

"You gotta sign den. If you ain't, let me go home early. Please. I don't want to be dere."

"I don't know what I'm gonna do yet." I said. "Listen. Just close the kitchen at ten and take off. There's no need for you to get involved."

"I *am* involved. I'm your kitchen boy. You really should take the deal."

"You sound like you're working for them."

"No, boss man. I just don't want to see you get killed by these guys. They don't take no for an answer. They're not from America. They don't live by your rules."

"I'll consider that. See you at four."

"Hasta luego."

"Hasta luego."

I hung up and said to Jake, "They're cartel."

"Yeah, I heard. Kind of suspected."

"You suspected?"

"Yeah, the whole thing's got that kind of feel."

"Can't say I disagree."

Chapter 20

Jake dropped Cash off at the house. Cash had some people to talk to in the next couple of hours before he opened the bar. It was still snowing. Probably three-quarters of an inch of the fluffy stuff an hour.

Jake had to drive a bit slow on Aiken. They plowed it a couple of times a day, but not often and not with a lot of salt. That was reserved for the main roads, like Mapleton. Once on Mapleton, he was back to speeding. He had one big question: how do you have a thirteenth floor that no one can get to? Was there another way onto the thirteenth floor that wasn't the service elevator? That was two big questions. Jake's a bit more complicated than most would think.

He was back on Grand Island in record time. The Guinness World Record people were trying to get a hold of him, but he didn't have time for that nonsense. He slowed down a bit as he drove by the house where he let a couple of video gamers go stiff. He couldn't tell much from the road. The car with the two flat tires had been moved up closer to the house. There were footprints in the snow. Older footprints from earlier, filled in with fluffy snow, looked like rounded indentations in the snow. Only shallow foot-shaped indentations were left to tell the story. He wasn't about to revisit the place yet. He wanted to get into the casino without them knowing he was on the way.

First, he wanted to drive through the parking lots and look for the old curvy grey sedan. If it *was* there, maybe see if they'd left any clues. Kidnappers looking to get their prize to safety are often careless about their breadcrumbs.

He drove right to the rear parking lot and slowed before the executive driveway to the loading dock. The vehicles from earlier were still there, and there was indeed a curvy grey sedan. Not having the ability to make the turn, he went into the rear parking lot, did a lap, came back and entered the executive driveway. Parked right next to the sedan.

There was nothing in the front or back seats that looked interesting. Some Burger King wrappers and unfinished drinks in the cup holders. He smashed the driver's side window.

Who puts an alarm on a rusted out old beater from fifteen years ago? Pulled the lever to open the trunk, all the while keeping an eye on the doorway to the loading dock. No one interested yet. Car alarms go off all the time though. People don't even check on them normally. They only serve to quicken the thief into getting his business done.

Jake Chambliss is the luckiest guy in the world sometimes.

Skylar was in the trunk.

Her hands and feet weren't even tied, and she didn't have gag. They'd knocked her out cold. Must have been inside trying to figure out what to do with her.

Jake tried to wake her, but she could barely even moan, let alone carry on a conversation. Jake pulled her out with his hands in her armpits. She offered a few more moans. He held her with his right arm around her lower back as he opened the passenger-side door of the truck. He heaved her up into the seat. She was light. He then put the seat back all the way down so her head wouldn't be showing in the windows.

The answers to his two big questions would have to wait. He needed to get Skylar back to safety. Shelly would have to wait as well. Samantha too. He'd been back in the country only a few days, and he had more obligations to women than at any other time in his life. Weird.

Just as he was walking around the truck to get in, even though the horn alarm was still tooting, he figured, what the hell. He grabbed his knife and slashed the rear tire on the grey sedan. He noticed it was a Monte Carlo when he slammed the trunk shut. He then stabbed a tire on the next two cars as quickly as possible. After the third car, a guy with a gun appeared at the glass window door. He was just a shadow that killed some of the orange light behind him before he opened the door and cursed in Jake's direction. The curse was followed by a gun shot. But not more than one. It's not smart to be shooting at the bosses' cars. Underlings don't always realize it until it's too late. They get blamed for losing the girl, and then they get blamed for the flat tires and the bullets in the expensive vehicles. If the boss has a habit of fixing his unwanted help with a set of cement galoshes to see if that makes you go over Niagara Falls quicker,, it's best not to put bullets into his leather interior.

So, instead of shooting back at the guy, Jake put some bullets through the windows of the cars. Made sure he punctured the seats in the finer vehicles. His gunshots kept the guy inside the building and did some damage as well. He put a bullet in the tire of the fourth car as well. It was the Cadillac from the morning. Only one vehicle was left with four working tires on the ground, and it was the forklift.

He ran behind the cars with random shots to keep the guy uneasy and got back to the truck. He'd kept it running, so he just had to get in, jam it in reverse and get the heck out of there. Before he did, he put himself up against the hood of the truck and waited for the guy to stick his head up again. Might as well have been playing Whack-a-Mole over at the Fantasy Island amusement park. A little patience and quiet coaxed the moron to stick his head up, and that was the last thing this guy would do voluntarily. The glass shattered and the wall behind him was turned into a blood-splattered Jackson Pollack. Jake wanted to call it *Sunburst Blood on Orange*, but he didn't have time to sign his work. He had to go..

By the time he'd gotten to the front parking lot, he'd hit forty-five. He held his head down in case they had shooters waiting for him, but they weren't that anxious to destroy their business with a casino shootout. Kind of smart, were it not the fact that they'd just let Jake Chambliss live again. This is why it always pays to do research on your adversaries before you start a war. This was the second time in one day they'd flicked Jake's switch to go time. Might as well have started a land war with Russia in the winter. But he was still in control of the war machine that rumbled inside.

The unconscious Skylar lying next to him was his priority. Laying waste to the fiends behind him would have to wait. As he turned out of the parking lot, the war machine growled a vow of return to conquer only he was able to hear.

Chapter 21

Ainsley was growing anxious at the hospital in Lockport. It was the quickest place to take the Luce, the Mexican girl. At least that's what Ainsley thought her name was. Wasn't sure, but she thought Luce was short for Lucy. The girl pronounced it "Loose." Ainsley Reed was on the verge of busting out the biggest story of her career, and she was stuck making sure no one discovered the truth about this slave girl before Jake Charm had a chance to save more lives. A hero's sidekick?

Jake Charm...what was it about him? If he failed to come through with the story of her dreams, she was out of a job. Even still, she'd do just about anything for him. She kept asking herself, what's that all about? Cap had called her twice. She'd ignored both calls but listened to the messages. He was telling her to stay away from the Cutler murders by yelling and swearing and threatening her job. But how do you drop everything, turn around and go back to doing news stories about an upcoming exhibit at the Buffalo Zoo when you've got a Mexican slave girl getting treatment for being drugged and brutally raped multiple times every day for who knows how long?

The whole Buffalo Zoo story was about getting approval to borrow a koala bear from some zoo in Australia. They didn't even have the bear yet. Just some photos. They could have emailed the photos, but instead, Ainsley had to go to the zoo, go through a briefing and then look at some photos in the hands of the guy that heads up the bear exhibit. There was no dead tiger to pet before it was incinerated. Just a boring local interest story.

Yet, she was here with Luce, and the doctors weren't telling her anything. She knocked on the window to ask a few times, but they were tight lipped. Just kept telling her she had to wait. Cap was about to blow a gasket, and she wanted more than anything to call Jake. Partly to get reassurance he was all right, but more so to find out he wasn't welching on his deal. She needed this story. It didn't matter that she told Cap she was taking the afternoon off. He knew exactly what she was up to. Probably had a trace on her phone. Being at Lockport Hospital screamed Cutler murders. Lockport makes the news in Buffalo nearly as little as Pendleton and mainly just for human interest stories or high school sports. She was in trouble.

She feared that fact even more when the two big, suited guys came into the emergency room looking for answers. They were the same two she saw talking to Cap two days earlier. One was chubby with messy hair, and the other was muscly with a buzz cut. They looked right at her with a message of "don't move, we know who you are, and we'll get right to you." Ainsley's heart started pumping thunderously.

While they were waiting to talk with the nurse at the window, she texted Jake. "Those agents just walked in here."

Twenty seconds later, her phone rang. It was Jake. He told her to say, "Hi boss" and act like she was having a pleasant conversation with her boss.

"Hi boss," she said.

"You need to get out of there right now. Stand up and walk out like you're looking for privacy. Say hold on a second, I'm not getting good reception."

"Hold on a second, I'm not getting good reception."

"Ainsley Reed," the chubby agent said, "Wait a minute. We need to talk with you."

Ainsley held up her index finger as she walked outside and turned the corner.

"He following you?" Jake asked.

"I think so."

"Run to your car and get out of there right now. Don't go out on East Ave. Exit the back way. Turn right, it'll be easier to lose them."

Her Prius was still in the turnaround driveway for the emergency room. She got in and took off, but, just as she'd put it into drive, Dillard was at the sliding door flashing a badge and yelling at her.

"He's telling me to stop."

"Don't Ainsley, floor it."

She took off, but Dillard tried to open her locked passenger door as it was passing him. He even knocked on her window. She didn't stop. Her ferocious little hybrid car was quietly zooming out of the driveway. Since Simon had the keys, Dillard wasn't able to just jump in their car and follow. He went back inside to get his partner.

"Go up a few streets and turn left," Jake said.

"You said to turn right."

"You're not out of the parking lot yet?"

"No, I'm at the stop."

"No time for stop signs. Go. Turn right, and then turn left."

"Where'm I going?"

"I don't know. Just want to get you away from them. Make some random turns. I'll get you out through Lower Town. Those guys'll never find you."

"They're probably following my phone. Probably how they found me in the first place."

"No. Your boss was following your phone. He'd never in a million years give the government the ability to follow the phone. Not without a fight. Freedom of the press and all that nonsense."

"Probably right. He does hate the government interfering with the press."

"They all do. Unless of course they're in bed with the politicians that need to manipulate the press, but these guys are FBI. Press hates the feebs. They following you?"

"Can't tell. I don't see any cars moving. I'm on some residential street."

"All right, go east," Jake said.

"Which way's that?"

"The same direction you took when you turned right. Forget Lower Town. Go east for a while, the exact opposite direction they'd expect you to go. Then go south. Make your way to Lincoln and then out to Davidson Road. No. It's Robinson Road. Take that west and cross Transit. It turns into Lockport Road, right after Johnson Country Store. Got that?"

"Yeah. I think."

"They following you?"

"No."

"Good," he paused for a moment, "Ainsley, I've got something to tell you."

"Okay." She was hoping he was going to tell her that he'd like to take her out to dinner after this was all done. He was still quiet. "What is it?"

"I found Skylar. I've got her, but she's knocked out. There's no bruises on her face. I think she's been drugged."

"My God," Ainsley said. The date would have to wait.

"Yeah, and I don't know what to do with her. I can't take her to Cash's. That's where they kidnapped her. I can't take her to a hospital for the same reason I couldn't take the other girl."

"Her name is Luce."

"Loose?"

"I think like Lucy."

"Okay. That's good. She talk to you?"

"Yeah."

"Can you help me again?"

"Yes," Ainsley said, "anything you need. But I doubt I can get away with taking her to the Lockport Hospital though. Not with Goon One and Goon Two."

"I was thinking the same thing."

Ainsley was driving normally through Lockport, drawing as little attention to herself as possible. She crossed East Avenue and then took a left on South. Still going east.

"How bad is Skylar?" She asked.

"She's out and bad. I hear her groan here and there, but she's out. She needs medical attention."

"I'll take her to Amherst then. Where do you want to meet?"

"Cash's."

"I thought that wasn't a good spot."

"It's fine, as long as I'm there. No one's gonna touch us."

"What about Simon and Dillard?"

"Those morons wouldn't dare try to ambush me on home turf. They might seem tough, but they're more afraid of me than you think."

"You're not full of yourself."

"Don't need to be. Those guys are out-of-shape feds who've been sitting on their butts getting fat for the last decade. Their hands are probably soft as a baby's bottom."

"You're funny, Jake Charm."

"Not even trying to be. Look, those two guys aren't following you right now because they're trying to check Luce out of the hospital. Once they have her, they'll have a chip to play. And that's what they see her as. If you'd stayed, you'd be the chip. Guarantee it."

"Are you telling me that I just delivered that poor young girl from one set of kidnappers to another?"

"Yeah, I guess. But don't worry. They won't hurt Luce."

"What if they rape her?"

"Probably not their style. She'll be fine. You, on the other hand, might not have been."

"What's the difference?"

"That's a big question that doesn't have a pretty answer."

"I don't need a pretty answer, Jake. I'm all ears. Give it to me straight."

"You're not a young girl barely clinging to consciousness after getting repeatedly gang raped by who knows how many nasty Mexican banditos loaded up with third-world diseases. They might want to make her disappear because she's a symbol of their failure at running the government with policies that have invited the worst attributes of the third world to take up residence in our once great nation, but they wouldn't rape her."

"You telling me they'd rape me."

"Maybe. I wouldn't put it past them. You'd just end up dead anyway."

"What? But I'm with the press. Don't they think that would make for a bad story on the FBI."

Jake laughed. "Don't be naïve, Ainsley. You're assuming that, once they got me, you'd be free to go. Uhn-uh. Once I was dead, you'd be too. They'd probably throw us in the same grave."

"Why me?"

"You know too much. You think stories this big remain uncovered by accident? No loose strings."

"No, I guess."

"Of course not. There are factions in the government that will go to any length to cover up what's really going on. That's what Simon and Dillard are. They're fixers."

"You said they weren't a part of the government."

"Officially, they're not, but that don't mean they aren't really just another part of the government. Once a spy, always a spy. License to kill never expires, as long as you know how to make the evidence disappear. Those guys know what they're doing, even though they're morons. And if it comes down to taking care of the cops who threaten them, a dead cop's just as easy to hide as anyone."

Ainsley was quiet.

"Ainsley, you there?"

"Yeah, just got to thinking about what I've gotten myself into. You warned me, I guess."

"Don't sweat it. I'll keep you safe. They only way they take you down is if they take me down. It's just two of them right now. They want to take me down, they'll need a hundred-man army. They don't have that yet."

"I guess."

"Listen. The story is worth it all, and I promise to make sure you get out of this. I'm at Cash's. I gotta get Skylar in there. Where are you?"

"I'm on Davidson, heading south."

"Good. When you get to Lincoln, take a right, and then take a left. Head south until you get to Robinson and take a right. That's Lockport Road. You'll be here in twenty. I gotta go. Keep an eye on your six. Make sure they're not following you. You see them, call me. See you soon." Click. Maybe he was not one for goodbyes.

Ainsley Reed was earning the story of her life, and she finally understood why the people that defy danger to get the big story are so respected. She was earning her chops. She had some pride in that but worried she might have bitten off more than she could chew. Then she thought it weird that she envisioned herself as a dog – bitten off more than she could chew. She wasn't a dog, and she was sure she'd win Jake's heart at the end. At least she hoped there'd still be a heart to win.

Chapter 22

As soon as Jake dropped me off, I grabbed a sandwich from the fridge. One of those delicious ones Skylar had made the day before. Bread was a bit hardened on the outside and soggy on the inside, but it hit the spot. I'd finished it even before I got to the attic.

I moved the bed in the far corner and made sure not to leave hand and footprints in the dust. Like an obsessive compulsive, I swept under the bed. I grabbed my work computer and five one-hundred-dollar bills off one of my stacks. I left my brother's stacks alone. If they ever discover I'm not Cash, that's evidence, maybe even evidence that would keep me out of jail. Granted, I didn't know why he had stacks of cash hidden in the floorboards, but that's the kind of thing that creates the reasonable doubt that keeps me out of jail. After replacing the bed, I moved the other bed to sweep up the dust. Didn't want to leave any clues that would point an investigator at the one bed over the other. Then again, an attic that isn't dusty *is* a clue.

I went downstairs, grabbed another sandwich, sat on the couch and turned on the TV. I was hoping to catch a news snippet on the big Pendleton murder case. Nothing though. Just a homemaker marathon, the kind that keeps mothers happy and calm in the last hour or two before their children get home from school. Skylar was having my brother's baby. I was about to be a father. Unless she was lying. Unless we never find her again. But Jake was probably right when he said they wouldn't kill her until they got what they wanted. *Maybe he's full of crap too though. Who knows? Cash, help me out. I need you, brother.*

I turned off my brother's router first. I don't think my computer would automatically hook up, but I couldn't be sure I hadn't logged on in the past from my brother's house. The last thing I want to do is hook up to the internet using the computer of a murder victim. Computer forensics guys would be all over that.

I fired up the Curt Cutler business computer and entered the password that no one else would know – my brother's birthday. Just joking. That would be my birthday too. I'm not that stupid. The password was actually "JohnDareadeer3000." It's what we used to call my Uncle John's truck. He had four custom-made metal bars across the front of his truck that he used to hunt deer. He was too lazy to sit out in the woods like everyone else. He did his hunting on the side of the road. He'd hit 'em, call his DEC buddy to get a tag, gut 'em and throw 'em in the back. He'd get more meat than ninety percent of the hunters out there. Used to throw parties with barbecued pulled rump roast. Delicious. He died of a heart attack when I was a teen. Too much deer meat, I guess. He was a big man. Cheers to you Uncle John, may you develop a liking and a patience for hunting in the Great Beyond. You've got time.

Once fired up, the first thing I did was turn the network tools off, so the computer would no longer even tried to connect to the internet without being asked. I had files on all of the Board of Directors. Resumes, contact info and notes on each – kids' and grandkids' names, where they'd vacation, favorite foods, activities, groups they belonged to, anything that would help facilitate small talk. Always a good idea to know about the people upon whom you depend for getting what you want done at work. People love it when you take an interest in them. It's much easier to get their votes after you've let them tell you about the latest T-ball story of their grandson Jimmy who just got back from a week in Florida with his parents who took him to Disney World *and* Universal. A man becomes putty in your hand once you've taken an interest in the stories about his grandson. Women are even easier. They love talking. That's not sexist. It's true.

Who should I talk to first? I had seven board members. Three were against the merger, and four were for it. I hadn't made up my mind yet. I had other responsibilities to worry about, like running the bank. To me, the whole thing was a bunch of extra work with only the mere insinuation that it might be worth it in the form of a raise, as long as the new larger reconstituted board didn't decide to replace me. Of course, they wouldn't because most of the board members would be ours, but these seven board members were already at each other's throats over the merger. How could I think taking sides would assure me those whose side I didn't take wouldn't be out for my blood? So, I stayed away from it the best I could. I sided with no one, but I had to hear each of them backbiting the others, once they were in my office and alone with me.

The three women were all against the merger, while the four men were for it. Was it a sex thing? Were the men willing to take more risk than the women? Or was it nationality? Mitzy Bertuzzi and Holly Scalisi were definitely Italian, and they were married to Italians. I didn't know what Jo Jo Dozier was though. I don't know what kind of name Dozier is. Jo Jo looked Italian though. Lord knows she had the mustache. I shouldn't have written that. She's a wonderful lady, with five adorable grandchildren and a husband who is an upstanding member of our community.

Why would Italians be against the merger?

Now, I don't think any of them had ties to the mob, but in the end, chances were, their church did. Catholic mobsters like to buy indulgences, and the Catholic Church likes to sell them. Whether we like it or not, there is a marketplace, and money talks. But no, that wasn't why these fine ladies opposed the merger. I mean technically, the merger would actually help the Italian mob. It would shut down the money laundering scheme the Mexicans had with the Indians running the First Iroquois Trust. That is, if I'm right about that. But the whole bank would go up in smoke once the feds discovered all the stuff going on. So no, it would have nothing to do with helping the Italian mob maintain market share over the Mexicans trying to bump them out.

Now, the four men were all for the merger. Daren Vanburen and Gill Murdock are German Protestants. Both are Lutheran. Rich Olaski and Stanley Bartowski are both Polish Catholics. They go to the same church as Mitzy, in fact. The one up on Tonawanda Creek. Holly goes to the small one in Lockport. Why in the world would the German and Polish guys want to buy the bank owned by the Indians and used by the Indians to fund grander and grander adventures on tax-free property?

I mean, this was the subject not one of the board members ever brought up with me. What if the First Iroquois Trust was giving loans to people using property owned by the Indian reservation as collateral? That was the big concern I'd always had, but I didn't bring it up with any of them. I wanted them to bring it up. I wanted them to take responsibility for the possibility that we'd discover that as soon as we started doing our due diligence before the actual merger. I mean, that was the thing. These guys seemed to have no idea that no merger was ever going to take place without due diligence. In order for that to happen, First Iroquois had to open up their books, and none of those guys wanted anything to do with that. This was as hostile as the cowboys wiping out the Indian lands back in the day.

This was actually the first time I'd put any thought into this. Any actual hard thought, anyway. I was just kind of hoping that it would all blow over once the board realized it wasn't a good idea. I knew it was a bad idea and couldn't see why anyone else didn't. What good could come from initiating a hostile takeover of a bank run by Indians with money from the casinos? I mean, who would think getting in bed with criminals makes good business sense? Not that all Indians are criminals or that all casinos are run by criminals,, but the whole casino racket is loaded with them. Of course, they like to call themselves "good businessmen."

Whatever happened to the promise that letting the Indians run the casinos would help the poor people on the reservation? Just another unfulfilled promise to get the votes of bought-and-paid-for politicians. Oh, we'll alleviate our liberal white guilt by letting the connected Indians run a casino racket and pretend it makes the plight of the people on the reservations better. Delusions of grandeur in exchange for political favors for the tribal leaders in charge of making sure the rest of the reservation remains self-oppressed. Like the public school system in the big cities – the ones that get almost twice as much money per student as the better-performing ones in the suburban and rural areas. The money never gets to the students. Same with the casino racket. The money never gets to the little Indian on the reservation. They just stay oppressed in a state where they can't own land because all the land is owned by the reservation. They therefore can't get a loan to build a house on the reservation land because the bank couldn't foreclose upon them and repossess the house that stands upon land that can only be owned by the reservation. So, they live in trailers, huts and makeshift hovels.

Truth was, the best thing an Indian could do was get off the reservation. If they want to accumulate wealth, they have to own property. First plank of the Communist Manifesto is to eliminate all private property. It's not an accident that the first plank of the Indian reservation model is to eliminate all private property. Those with the delusions of grandeur can cling all they want to the idealistic revisionist concept that all Indians are equal and therefore, helping to enrich the tribe makes them all more equal because they're all richer. Only a crackhead believes that nonsense. The chief and the friends of the chief make the money, take the money, and keep the money. Everybody else obediently remains on the reservation with the smug satisfaction that, by doing so, they're screwing the white man by being exempt from paying his taxes. Little do they realize, by doing so, they end up making so little money they wouldn't be paying taxes in the first place.

Ah, whatever. Anger and resentment are the stuff that socialists use to keep people in line. The people stay poor, and the socialists in control of their well-being are clever enough to convince them that they're poor because of all the oppressors. In reality though, it's the socialists in control of their well-being that are the oppressors. On the reservations, it's the chief and his buddies that are the socialists in control, and when the people aren't getting anywhere near their fair share of the booty that results from the special favors, the little socialist system has failed and broken down – all due to the fact that the love of money is the root of all evil. The casino is nothing more than a wealth redistribution system that facilitates the transfer of money from those who hate their money to those who love it.

Gamblers can do all the praying to whatever god they want, but it's nothing more than a numbers game. They may get lucky here and there, maybe even at the whim of the guy on the other side of the camera who's in control of the Pavlovian quarter distribution machine, but the house always wins. Most people are way too undisciplined to walk away when they should. So, the money leaves the wallets of those who hate their money and goes to those whose love of money is the root of the evil that inspires them to oppress their own people. But hey, if you got that white-liberal guilt, you think everything is peachy, as long as you never look at the real consequences of your efforts to assuage your white-liberal guilt by any means necessary. It's not like you'll ever be allowed to drive back on the Indian reservation.

As a bank CEO, I wouldn't get caught dead actually saying any of this though. Out would come the knives. Not allowed to think like a regular human and keep that kind of job. That's why I never said anything. I wanted them to come to their own conclusions, but not a one of them ever once mentioned that this was most likely why the people running the First Iroquois Trust didn't want anything to do with this takeover. But I wasn't a CEO anymore. I was officially allowed to think what I really thought without having to worry about losing my job. Yeah, I was not ignoring the irony in the fact that the Mexicans wanted to take over my brother's bar from me.

So, what was the reason Daren, Rich, Stanley and Gill wanted to take over the Indian Bank? They couldn't all be that stupid. Maybe naïve was a better word. Where did they get off sitting on a bank board with such poor business intuition?

Then it hit me. They never wanted to take over the bank at all. They just wanted to get the books open. If they could prove that the only other bank in Pendleton was involved in criminal enterprises and violating the trust of non-connected bank customers by making risky and illegal loans with their money, they could put the Indian bank out of business.

Why the men and not the women? Why did the women want to avoid this risky venture, while the men were out to conquer? I didn't know. But this was the only thing that would make sense. Why hadn't I thought of this before?

Assuming that's right, who in the heck would want to kill me and my wife over this? Why go for the CEO and not the board members? Other than the principals at the Indian bank, who would benefit if the merger were called off and opening the bank books didn't happen? What if the principals at the Indian bank didn't benefit now that the murders had occurred? Don't the murders ensure the books get opened in the investigation? Maybe this would make it even more public than if they'd gotten opened by our board and the truth never saw the light of the day. The public never gets to know about why a merger failed to take place if the merger dies before it ever becomes public information. People in the know tend to walk away and shut up. They don't normally brag about failure or want to get caught snitching on criminals with guns and a lot to lose.

So, the big question was, who benefits the most when the information about the wrongdoing of the Indian bank becomes public? The answer would have to be the enemy of whomever really, really wants the wrongdoing kept a secret. Those wanting to keep the secret were the casino guys, the Mexicans running girls and drugs, and whoever gets paid off to look the other way. That's actually a big list. If I was right about the killings being the reason the Indian bank's books get opened, the killer was their enemy.

I wrote down the numbers and addresses of every board member. Didn't have a printer. I needed internet access to get the drivers to Cash's printer, and I didn't have the password to get onto his computer. I thought about leaving my computer out, but then I remembered they might be serving me with a warrant at any moment. Surprised they hadn't yet. They'd want to know why I had my dead brother's computer, so I went upstairs, moved the bed and stashed it with the cash. Just to be safe.

After replacing the floorboards, I pulled them back up and decided to put the computer under the cash. I don't know why that made it any better, but I did it on a whim. I kept my two stacks separate and then removed Cash's one by one. There were many thousands of dollars there. Under the cash, Cash left me an envelope. It was

164

sealed, and on the top was written, "To my Brother Curt." *It's about time Cash. A message from the grave.*

I wasn't ready for the message yet. Nor did I have time to stop and read it, so I put it in my left inside jacket pocket with the Glock Jake gave me. Honestly, my real fear is that he'd be admitting to having an affair with my wife, and I just didn't want to see anything about that. I slipped the computer under the floorboards that weren't lifted. Maybe they'd find the cash but not the computer. Then I put the cash back, just as it had been.

It was still cold. I had the .38 from the safe and the Glock Jake gave me weighing down my coat, but I wasn't going to be unarmed. Not with all this going on. I really wanted to call Jake to find out if he'd found Skylar, but I knew that would be a bad idea. The cops would be looking for any sort of collusion between us.

Not wanting to sit around my house where I might be served a search warrant that I wouldn't have time for, I left the house. Figured I'd find a place to park and try and contact the board members. Ideally, I'd meet them in person, but I didn't have time to do all that running. I wanted to open the bar. I decided to call some of the members on my way to Stanley Bartowski's farm. He had a big farm on Meahl Road, which was just north of Lockport Road near Aiken.

On the way, I called Jo Jo Dozier. No answer, and I wasn't about to leave a message. Same with Holly Scalisi and Mitzy Bertuzzi. No answer.

I called Daren Vanburen's law office in Lockport, but his receptionist told me he was in court. When asked if she could take a message, I told her no and that I'd call him on his cell. Defensively, she quickly reminded me he was in court and couldn't be contacted.

"Lockport courthouse? I'll go and visit him then."

"No, no you can't. I'm not sure if it is that courthouse."

"Which one?" I asked.

"I'm not authorized to tell you that, sir."

"How legalistic of you," I said. "What *are* you authorized to tell me?"

"I can take your name and have him call you when he's available."

"When might that be?" I remained as polite as possible, but I could tell she was hiding something.

"I don't know. Can I have your name?"

"No ma'am. I'll just call him on his cell phone, thank you."

"Wait, wait, no, no." She was stressed.

"Is there something wrong, ma'am?"

"Um, yes, maybe."

"What's wrong?"

"I don't quite know, but I don't even know you." She sounded like she was almost crying.

"Ma'am, my name is Cash Cutler. My brother..."

"Oh, I'm sorry about your brother."

"You knew my brother?"

"Yes, a little. He was always nice when I've spoken with him in the past."

"Did you speak with him often?" I figured I'd get her impression of me.

"No, only when he called for Mr. Vanburen. But he was always nice." I tried to be.

"Ma'am, I'm trying to figure out who killed my brother and his wife. I would really like to speak with Daren. Can you make that happen?"

"They say you and your friend did it."

"*They* don't know anything. I had nothing to do with this. I promise you."

"That's what I thought too. Just so you know. I mean, how could you kill your twin brother and the woman you were having..." She went quiet.

"I wasn't having an affair with my brother's wife."

"Oh, well, I didn't..."

"Don't worry about it," I saved her from discomfort. "Listen, I really need to speak with Daren. It could be a matter of life and death."

"I haven't heard from him."

"He's not in court?"

"No, he didn't come in, he hasn't called, he isn't answering my calls, his wife either. I don't know where he is." She started weeping.

"It's all right ma'am. You're Sally, right?" I shouldn't have said that. Shouldn't have even admitted I knew her name.

166

"Yeah, how'd you know?"

"It's, uh, written here, on the forms I'm looking at."

"Your brother's forms?"

"Yes. I'm just trying to find out why my brother was killed. Figured I'd speak with the board members of my brother's bank."

"Of course," she said. She'd composed herself.

"Sally, I'm sure he's fine. He probably took his wife out of town for a few days. Could you please have him call me if you hear from him?"

"Absolutely. I've got your number here on the caller ID. Sorry for your loss."

"Thank you, Sally."

I pulled into Stanley Bartowski's farm just as I'd hung up. Farmers are a big part of Pendleton Savings and Loan's business. Farming is big business period, and debt is very often used to finance the purchase of equipment, animals, buildings and farm supplies. Stanley Bartowski was just about as connected to all the local farmers as anyone could be. He was older and had grandchildren, but he still worked with the vigor of a twenty-year-old. Even though he was nearly thirty years older than me, I wouldn't want to mess with him. He grew up in a time when disagreements were still settled with fists, instead of lawyers and nuisance suits.

As I was walking towards his white pole barn with the front doors open enough to get out a combine, he lifted his head from behind the left rear wheel of the old New Holland tractor that was facing away from me. He was wearing grease-covered blue denim overalls and holding a foot-and-a-half long crescent wrench. He moved his long white bangs to the side of his face and squinted at me to make sure his eyes weren't deceiving him. Once convinced, he set down the crescent wrench and lifted a .357 off the tractor's foot rail. He let it hang to his side as I walked nearer.

"You don't need that, Mr. Bartowski. I come in peace."

"You look just like your brother." The gun stayed at his side.

"Heard that before."

"I'm sorry about Curt and Callie."

"Me too."

"What can I do for you?"

"Not sure. Why's it you're the only board member I can get a hold of?"

"The others are smarter than me, maybe. Don't have a farm to run."

"What's with the gun?"

"Just 'cause I ain't smart, don't mean I'm suicidal. If they're willing to kill Curt and Callie, what makes me think I'm not next?"

"You think I did it?"

"I know you didn't," he paused. "But if you think I did it, you're getting ready to pull the gun in your jacket on me."

I put my hands in the air to set him at ease. I was five feet from him by then. "Nah, that's not why I'm here. I want to know about the merger."

"You know about that?"

"'Fraid I do," I said. "I'd offer to shake your hand, but the whole reason for shaking hands is to prove you don't have a gun in your hand." I directed my smile at his .357.

He put it in his left hand, wiped his right hand on his overalls and took my hand. His giant calloused hand just swallowed mine with a squeeze of epic strength. He put the gun next to the crescent wrench and grabbed the rag to wipe down his hands. "Let's go to my office. Don't know how many ears are listening."

We walked from the pole barn over to a regular barn, but not a barn with all the cows. They were all in the back barns. The Bartowski Dairy farm had hundreds and hundreds of Holsteins. His office was covered with straw, saw dust, grease stains, cans of oil, tractor fluids, tractor parts, broken pitchforks waiting for a new handle and ancient farm tools that had been replaced. He had a big desk and cabinet space along two walls behind the desk and along the far wall. They were all covered with papers, envelopes and spreadsheets. He used the old carbon-copy spread sheets with yellow, green and pink sheets, each taking a copy of the numbers. There was a computer, but it wasn't used much. He was too old-school to mess with that kind of thing.

"Have a seat." He pointed at the two chairs facing his desk. Both were covered with dirty overalls and a jacket. I put the jacket on the other chair and sat down. He closed the door and sat at his desk.

"You know you're not supposed to know about the merger. Isn't public knowledge." He was right to the point.

"Yeah, I know. Curt was my twin though. Tells me everything. Did, anyway."

"All right. Why do you think he didn't like the deal?"

"You think that's why he was killed?"

"No, no one liked the deal."

"Why'd you guys support it? Why'd you support it?" I'm not sure I was supposed to know that.

"Was the right thing to do," he said.

"What do you mean?"

"That bank is a criminal enterprise. They're making loans that are illegal and wrong. On top of that, they're bringing in the dollars of people you and I know, with their super high interest rates. Aside from taking business from PS&L, farmers I know are putting money with them. When it all implodes, what do you think happens to all that money?"

"It's insured, isn't it?"

"I don't think so. I haven't seen even a single FDIC sticker at that bank. Believe me, I checked. The bank isn't a real bank. It's a scam, and it's taking people for a ride."

"How do they get away with that? Aren't there rules to prevent that stuff?"

"Sure, but the rules of our government have no control over what happens on Indian sovereign land. Other than murder and a few other things, I suppose."

"This is kind of what I expected, but I didn't want to believe this is what could happen in this day and age."

"Believe it," he said.

"Guess I'll have to. Why the merger and not just tell people the truth?"

"You need proof. Can't just go around calling businesses a scam without proof. You get sued and lose friends. You think the farmers around here want me... I sit on the board of the Indian bank's competition. Do you think these farmers want *me* to tell them they've been scammed? – That their money's in danger? It'd cause a run on the bank, and some would lose everything. Then they'd blame me."

"Makes sense," I said. He was right, but I had to make like I hadn't ever thought about any of this before because I was *not* the CEO of a bank.

"So, we've been trying to get their books open with the merger. That's all. If we did, we'd be able to report all the wrongdoing to the appropriate authorities and put making restitution in their hands. At that point, the principals behind the bank, the casino guys, would be legally obligated to make restitution or lose their gaming licenses. That was the plan anyway. Didn't work though."

"What do you mean?"

"Your brother's dead. The merger's called off. Our board's directors are hiding. Mitzy, Holly and Jo Jo never wanted anything to do with this. I get that, but the

169

rest of us thought we had the obligation to do what it took. They've all left town. So has Daren. I told them all to take off. I don't know what Rich and Gill are doing though. No one's taking calls. I'd be gone too, but I have a farm to run. Listen to me. I'm talking to you as if you were Curt."

"Happens all the time. Don't you have anyone to man the farm while you're on vacation?"

"What's vacation?" He looked at me as if I were from Mars. "This farm's run by my kids and their kids. A few neighbor kids help out. I don't hire the illegals. Thank God for that. Wouldn't want anything whatsoever to do with that Garcia lady. They're all cartel. By the way, that's another problem with that Indian bank."

"What is?"

"They're laundering money for the cartel. The Mexicans are running drugs and workers, and the money's being laundered at that bank. I don't know everything, but that's what's happening. I'm sure of it."

"You think the Indians or the Mexicans killed my brother?"

"No. It kills the merger, but it doesn't take away the scrutiny. They'll probably get more scrutiny once the media gets wind of the merger."

"Aren't they protected? You know, politically?"

"Of course, but, until you get your hands on them books, no one knows who's getting paid off. We have ideas, but we can't prove any of them. Keep an eye on Bennett Glazebrook though. His wife works with the governor. If he has anything to hide, he'll do whatever it takes to keep it hidden."

"Can I ask you something personal, Mr. Bartowski? It's personal to me, I suppose."

"Maybe."

"Did Curt know the real reason you were trying to go forward with the merger? Did you tell him it wasn't about the merger but getting those books open?"

"No, son. We couldn't let your brother in on that. We, as a board, met in secret. Had to, to protect PS&L. As CEO, your brother wouldn't be able to approve such a cockamamie plan. The ladies on the board didn't either. More worried about their families, and I get that. Basically, Curt couldn't support this plan because it would violate his obligation to do what's best for the bank. He didn't know about it, and we made sure he didn't know about it. That doesn't mean he didn't figure it out though. Your brother wasn't a dumb guy." I must not have been as smart as he thought, because I didn't figure it out until they'd already killed me. Nothing like that realization to make me feel small.

170

"Think that might be why they killed him? 'Cause he figured it out?"

"Depends on who 'they' is, and no. I think if he figured it out, he'd be knocking on our doors demanding answers. He wasn't. He was just running the bank and doing what he could to quell the infighting of the board members. But his efforts there were useless because he didn't know why we were really fighting."

"What about the ladies, you said they're all against it. Might they have told him what it was really about? You know, to get him to stop your plan?"

"I've Thought about that prospect too, and I can't come up with a single reason they'd tell Curt on us. You start talking about the same illegal things none of those ladies wanted to be caught talking about, eventually it gets out that you're the one talking about it, meaning you're the one that needs shutting up. Seems to me, they'd be better off following through with our plan than to go on blabbing about the plan with their name at the top of the blabbing memo. Too dangerous for them. They wouldn't have told him. They didn't want anything to do with what we were up to. Too afraid of who's behind the Indian bank. I'd pretty much guarantee that all those ladies would quit the board before telling anyone what we were up to."

That's what I needed. "Thanks so much, Mr. Bartowski. Is there any way you can get me in touch with any of the other board members?"

"No." He was definitive. "Leave them be. I told you all you need to know. They got families to protect right now. Let this thing blow over."

"Blow over? They're trying to set me up for my brother's murder. I need to figure out who did this before they lock me up."

"I know, but you won't go down for this. Lyman and I went to school together. Known him fer... since we were kids. It comes down to it, I'll make sure he gets pointed in the right direction. For now, though, leave the rest of the board members be. You got what it takes to figure it out." He stood up to tell me it was time to leave.

"Thanks. I'll let you get back to work then." I stood up and walked through the door he was holding for me.

"I hear you're working with Jake Chambliss. Tell him hi. I knew his father. You guys will be just fine."

"Hope you're right. Thanks for having my back."

"*Jake* has your back. I've got his. Be good."

Chapter 23

Jake pulled up next to Cash's barn, went inside and grabbed the house key that sat on the windowsill above the workbench to the left. The dusty old key had been kept there since they were in high school. After moving the truck around the curve to in front of the porch, he carried Skylar into the house. He held her in his left arm as he opened the door with his right. The horror of carrying the dead boy Ali, in much the same manner, fought its way into his consciousness. His dream from the night before was still haunting him.

Skylar was groaning and starting to wake. Going from the heat to the freezing snow might've had something to do with it, like a bucket of ice-cold water to the face. He was tempted to set her in the snow drift but didn't have the heart to do it.

After shaking the snow off his boots, he set her on the couch in the living room, unzipped her coat and put the blanket over her. He sat in the chair and put his head back.

He hadn't slept well the night before. The Pastor Gabriel nightmare nagged him into staying awake once he'd woken out of it. He didn't want to finish it. A good night's sleep is a luxury for those without demons. He wanted to stop thinking about it all together, but this moment of rest and relaxation made it hard. Why *that* memory? Why was he having it now? What's the moral of the story? There was none. At the end, he walked away and never returned. He failed at his mission to protect Pastor Gabriel, and little Ali was killed for his interest in what Pastor Gabriel was preaching. How does that help? He went on to find another place where people needed him, just like he'd done numerous times before and numerous times after. At that moment though, his friends from childhood needed him. Walking away was not an option. While not yet failed, this mission was growing by the minute.

Just a moment of rest, he promised himself, but the moment turned into thirty. Like he feared, the nightmare swooped right in. It would not be denied.

He was walking out of the mosque where he had just laid waste to the ten or so Muslim men who'd put out the assassination calls. His hands and face were covered with blood. Theirs, of course. The fury had subsided, but the self-hatred was kicking in. He needed to grab his pack, change his shirt and get the heck out of the villages. It was time to move on. He took off his shirt and found a dry spot on the back to wipe the blood off his face and out of his eyes.

He felt as though he'd learned nothing from Pastor Gabriel. The pastor would always tell him that vengeance belonged to God. The pastor knew about the cauldron of fury that resided in Jake and was trying to teach Jake to control it and tame it. Jake felt it was working until then. The government made him a killing machine, and he hated himself for it. The same government that now wanted him dead. It had a habit of killing anything it couldn't control.

As he was wiping off the dust-covered blood from his chest and belly, a woman in a black burka came at him screaming in a mixture of Swahili and Arabic. She was hysterical and hard to understand, but she had a young village boy to interpret.

"I don't understand," Jake told her.

The young boy, probably a few years older and a half foot taller than Ali, said, "She's Ali's mom."

"Does she know what happened to him?" Jake asked.

"Yes."

"Tell her I'm really sorry for her loss. I wish I could have gotten there sooner. I tried to save him."

After talking with the hysterical woman, the boy said, "Her husband was in the mosque. You killed her husband."

That moment, Jake's self-hatred was strong enough to get him to pull the trigger of a gun strategically pointed into his brain. He wanted to disappear, and suicide was the only thing he could think of. How do you apologize for killing the husband of a woman who'd just lost her son? Sorry wouldn't be good enough.

"You mean her husband was attacking the men that killed her son? And I just killed him?"

The boy spoke again to the angry mother, listened to her hysterical response and said, "No. Her husband had ordered it."

"Ordered what?"

"Ali to be killed."

"You sure? Check again."

He did. "Yes," the boy said, "Ali was a blasphemer. He had to die. It's Allah's will."

Jake felt like he was in a hell where everything that's good is evil and everything that's evil is good. "What about Pastor Gabriel? Did he deserve to be beheaded? Did his wife deserve to be raped and murdered? Did the other folks deserve to be killed?"

The boy directed the questions at the mother, listened to her diatribe and said, "Yes. He was a tool of Satan, and his wife was a harlot of Satan. If the others were with these people, yes, death is what they deserve."

Jake looked at them in disbelief, but he could see nothing of the woman but the dark sections of her eyes. "If I understand you correctly, hopefully I'm not, I should kill you too. But I'm done killing for today. Here's the blood of your husband." He threw his soiled shirt at her burka-ed face. It stuck for a half second and then fell to the ground. Jake turned his back, walked to his pack, put on another green shirt, slung it over his shoulders and walked out of the village to the path along the lake, hoping to get out before the military guys came. They rarely rushed to the Muslim sections, and he wasn't going to hide from them. He was going to leave via foot right out in the open. The lake still glittered by the lanterns of the fishermen...

Jake's dream was interrupted by Skylar's gagging. He jumped off the chair. His face was damp with sweat. Skylar was puking over the side of the couch. What a mess. Jake ran to the downstairs' bathroom to grab the wastebasket for her. He then got a roll of paper towels from the kitchen.

"Can you sit up?"

After spraying another stream of liquid into the wastebasket and then a few dry heaves, Skylar moved her feet to the floor.

"Careful with the blanket," Jake said. It was about a foot from the puke splatter on the floor. Jake was scraping the chunks with paper towels and throwing the dirty ones into her basket she held under her chin that was dripping with saliva. She didn't even have the energy to care. Jake used a fresh paper towel to wipe her chin.

Skylar spoke her first word and sounded like a sick and feverish child in bed fighting the flu. "Thanks."

"How are you feeling? I have someone coming to take you to the hospital."

She shook her head, "No, I don't want..." She dry heaved again into the basket.

"You want some water?"

She nodded her head as she hung it over the basket. Jake found a glass and poured some water while Skylar got control of the dry heaves. As he handed it to her, he asked, "You sure you don't want to go to the hospital?"

"Yeah," She took the glass and drank as if she'd been walking through the desert for days.

"Slow down."

"I have to go to the bathroom."

"Can you walk?"

"Yeah, maybe, I don't know..." She puked up the water.

She set the basket up against the front arm of the couch to her right, tossed the blanket to the side and took off her jacket with help from Jake. She was wet with sweat. Jake helped her stand up and held her by the arm and shoulder as she walked her way to the bathroom. When they were halfway there, there was a knock at the door. Jake leaned back in order to get a view of the door.

"I'm gonna yell."

"Go ahead," she said.

Jake hollered toward the door. "Who is it?"

"It's Ainsley."

"Hang on a second."

"Okay."

"Yelling hurts," Skylar informed him.

"Your head?"

"My whole body."

"Sorry."

She got to the bathroom and she used the counter to steady herself as she made her way to the toilet. He closed the door for her privacy and went to let in Ainsley.

"How is she?"

"She's in the bathroom."

"She's awake and moving?"

"Yes."

"That's great news."

"Yeah. She puked. I was in the middle of cleaning it up." Jake went back to the mess in front of the couch. "Come in. Take off your coat."

Ainsley set it on a chair around the dining room table as she slowly made her way to the living room, observing everything as if she were an investigative reporter. Jake took the full wastebasket to the kitchen and emptied it out into the big garbage can. The mass of towels and puke slid out slowly. He put the wastebasket in the sink and let the faucet run water into it while he searched for some sort of cleaning spray under the sink.

He found something that didn't have bleach. After emptying the basket of the water and drying it out, he brought it over to the couch and sprayed the wet spot and scrubbed it with clean paper towels.

Ainsley stood at the border between the living room and dining room seemingly fascinated by a home that hadn't been updated in decades. It was a time capsule of Cash and Curt's childhood.

Jake said, "It's been like this since we were kids. New TV, but just about everything else is the same."

"Wow," she said, "that TV's like fifteen years old."

"Yeah, new. It's awesome. You should see my house. Looks just like it did when I left. Check out those plastic TV trays over there. The corners are all gone or bent, but those things are from the '60s." They were whitish fiberglass splattered with random splotches of grey paint and glitter.

"Unbelievable," she said while shaking her head in awe. "Where's Cash?"

"Recon." Jake put the last of the dirty paper towels in the recently cleaned basket and took it to the kitchen.

"What?"

"He's getting information."

"For what?"

"You writing a book?"

"Maybe."

"At least you're honest."

"So, for what?"

"He's trying to figure out why someone might've wanted to kill his brother."

"Yeah Sherlock, I figured that. What's he looking for? Where's he looking?"

"Not sure."

"Looking for plausible deniability, I see."

"Always," Jake declared.

"At least *you're* honest."

"So, we got that out of the way. We're both honest."

The door to the bathroom slid open loudly because the doorframe had shifted as the house had settled over time. Skylar came out walking with small steps. Her eyes were red, and she was breathing through her mouth with a glaze of disbelief on her face.

"How you feeling?" Jake asked with compassion in his purposely softened voice.

"Awful. Just need to sit down."

"This is Ainsley."

"I've seen you before," Skylar said.

"On the news," Jake filled in the blank.

"That's right. You're the one who told everyone Cash was having an affair with his brother's wife. Nice to meet you."

"I guess I'm probably lucky you're in the state you're in," Ainsley said, "Sorry about that. Boss made me say it."

"It's true. You *are* lucky I feel like crap." She plopped herself onto the couch.

"What happened to you?" Ainsley asked.

Skylar looked to Jake with disbelief. Without saying a word, Jake could tell she wanted to know who this lady was and why the heck she was in Cash's house. "Ainsley's all right. You can talk to her," Jake assured her.

"I don't know what happened. I can't remember much. I was about to open the door, some car pulled in, and I just can't remember anything after that."

"I found you in the trunk of a car. Do you remember that?"

"Not a bit," Skylar said while shaking her head.

"You sure you don't want to go to the hospital and get yourself checked out?" Jake asked her.

"Who's gonna take me?"

"Ainsley will."

"No thanks. I'm done taking rides with people I don't know. Can I get a piece of bread?"

"Sure can." Jake went and found her some. "You don't think this'll make you throw up again?"

"I don't care. I just want something in my stomach. I'll make the basket this time. Thanks for cleaning up my mess."

"Don't worry about it."

"Well," Ainsley bobbed her head side to side a few of times, luring Jake's eye from Skylar, "if I'm not needed, then I think I'm going to get back to work."

"Hold up," Jake said, "you want to have some fun?"

Ainsley gyrated her body a couple of times like a giddy schoolgirl, "I'm listening. Whatcha got in mind?"

"My buddy Tyler needs a date tonight."

"A date?" She looked deflated.

"At the bar," Jake said. "The Mexicans forcing Cash to sell the bar are coming by midnight to make him an offer they say he shouldn't refuse. Tyler Graveline, the local cop, he used to play football with me and Cash, he's gonna be there in plain clothes. I figure he could use some company, you know, maybe not look so out of place."

"Will you be there?"

"No. I can't be seen with Cash. But I'll be there in case the whole thing goes sideways."

"What whole thing?"

"With the Mexicans. When Cash says no."

Skylar lifted her head off the back of the couch with a burst of energy. "Cash is turning them down?"

Jake looked back at her. "He has to. I'll tell you about it in a minute."

Ainsley said, "What happens if it goes sideways? As you called it."

"Fireworks. But don't worry, you'll have a gun." Jake pulled an extra Glock out of his jacket and handed it to her. "Tyler has a gun, Cash is packing, and I'll be there just in case."

She looked at the gun with her eyes in awe. "I don't know how to shoot. I can't carry that."

"It's easy. Here's the safety, take it off, pull this back like this, point and shoot. And sure, you can carry it. Just don't tell Tyler you have it though. It might make him like you more, but he'll have to arrest you. It's our secret."

"I don't know," she said, looking for a way out.

"This is how you empty the chamber." He took the shell out, put it back in the magazine and then put the magazine back in. "You don't want it, no big deal, but I'd put in your purse, just in case. Be at the bar by ten. Cash will introduce you to Tyler. You might like him."

"What if I get shot?"

"Shoot back. Don't stop until you're empty."

She shook her head in disbelief. "Simple as that for you?"

"Simple as that," Jake said. "Hopefully you won't get shot, and you might just be witness to a big story. Think about it like that."

"But what if I get shot?"

"It'll hurt. A lot. But Tyler'll protect you. It's his nature."

"You're crazy, Jake."

"I hear it so often, I'm starting to believe it."

"You should." Ainsley opened her purse and put the gun under her wallet before zipping it back up. "I'll get out of your hair now. I hope you feel better, Skylar. If you need me for a ride, Jake knows how to get a hold of me."

Skylar had her head resting on the back of the couch again, after eating some bread. "See you. I won't need a ride." Her voice was quiet enough that Ainsley couldn't hear how she said the last part of that. But Jake heard. Cat fight, he thought, not tonight.

At the door, the smiling Ainsley said, "See you, Jake Charm," as she looked him up and down and paused her process of leaving.

"Probably not tonight, though. I'll be out of sight."

"You know what I mean."

"Yeah, see you, Ainsley Reed. See you."

Chapter 24

I drove straight from the Bartowski Farm to the Sanborn Library. I needed some internet access, and I found Cash's library card in his wallet. Sanborn's a little town just northwest of Pendleton. They put me on one of their six computers without hesitation. All were empty. No homeless people looking for a place to watch porn in public in Sanborn. They'd get shot.

First, I pulled up the state government's site for political campaign contribution reporting. I entered Bennett Glazebrook's name. Sure enough, as Tyler said, the guy was getting huge donations. I printed them out. The big ones all came from different people with the same address. It was the address of Shapiro, Berkowitz and Steinman, Attorneys at Law. On several days in the last two years, he'd get four to eight contributions for the maximum, all from people with the law firm's address. That doesn't raise red flags? If a red flag goes up and no one important bothers to see it, does it really signify anything? Why does an appointed attorney with a wife in the governor's office need campaign contributions?

I plugged Glazebrook's name into the search engine and came up with a bunch of stories in the Buffalo News. He'd formed an exploratory committee to consider a run for Congress in Erie County. *Who does that? He needs an exploratory committee? It's not like he's running for president.*

There must be a conflict of interest with his appointment and his ability to run a political campaign. It looked like a way to run for office and collect contributions without actually committing to it. Maybe. Election law wasn't my specialty, and I didn't have time to research it. Didn't even care that much.

I plugged in Shapiro, Berkowitz and Steinman, Attorneys at Law. In addition to discovering they're also known as SBS, Attorneys at Law, I discovered they had a habit of representing "undocumented workers." That's what you and I would call illegal aliens committing crimes and avoiding deportation with lawyers on the taxpayers' dime. There was even a story how they'd received a twenty-five-million-dollar government grant for doing pro-bono work for illegal aliens. Is it really pro-bono when the government's paying you more than you'd even charge to begin with? Nothing made sense anymore. The whole government was turned into an ATM for anyone doing whatever it takes to replace Americans with non-Americans using the money stolen from the Americans getting replaced. Meanwhile, Jake was being hunted down for having attempted to protect Americans from the same illegal aliens that had come to kill us. By killing Jake, the government was hoping to bury the fact that an illegal immigrant, who happened to be a radical Muslim, was also in on the Oklahoma City Bombing, thus destroying the myth that Tim McVeigh was a racist white supremacist right-winger. What kind of white supremacist willingly works with brown-skinned Muslims? – That's the question the government wanted no one to ask themselves. Misplaced governmental priorities would seem to be the understatement of the century.

There were also a couple of stories about them defending various people working at a night club on the Boulevard called Club Entrance. Club Entrance was a big nightclub with food, a dance floor with club kids dressed to the nines selling drug samples to people on the dance floor, a small jazz club loaded with heroin addicts, a live music stage for hippies and a never-ending line out the door. It attracted hipsters from the two counties, Canada and beyond.

So, I plugged Club Entrance into the search engine. There were several stories about Italian-named guys getting busted for drug sales at the club and then getting off without jail time, all with representation from SBS, Attorneys at Law. Could it really be that easy? A firm on the government's payroll for protecting illegal alien criminals also seemed to have an incredible knack for keeping mob guys out of jail?

Just as Tyler said, the stories about them getting off all occurred within days of Bennett Glazebrook getting multiple donations from people with the address of the law firm. It sounded so unbelievable that I had to see it myself. How do criminals get so overconfident that they make it this easy? They might as well just tattoo the words "Guilty Criminal" across their forehead.

Next question that needed to be answered: who is Glazebrook running against? I couldn't find anyone from the other party named yet, but it appeared Glazebrook was planning to primary Congressman Porter Nichols. What? He didn't have a shot.

Could Glazebrook really be that stupid? Sure, Nichols was just as corrupt as anyone, probably more so, but he'd been Congressman for at least a decade and a half. He was a trust fund kid living off the fortune left to him by his dead father who ran a bunch of the now-abandoned steel mills in Buffalo and Lackawanna. Glazebrook might have thought he was untouchable, but Porter Nichols was – no one ever finds the bodies buried in the old abandoned and dilapidated steel mills littering the once great manufacturing areas of Buffalo because no one's brave enough to even look. Some secrets stay secret. That, or the bodies get thrown into a pool of molten metal to disappear forever. No one knows for sure, but everyone knows not to cross the Nichols family – that's not a secret.

I printed out duplicate copies of all the information, including the stories with the dates that matched the contributions, and then found a list of addresses of the plants once owned by Nicholed Steel, Inc. That's what they called it. It was a play on their

181

family name that someone must have thought was clever. I'm not suggesting I was brave enough to go and look for the bodies. Just figured it might come in handy.

The computer then printed out my printer-fee receipt. I put the copies of the huge printout in two slim paper bags that the library provided. Before I left, I spoke with the librarian. She was a slim and proper-long-skirt-wearing lady with her greying hair pulled back and held by a big plastic clip. In the '80s, they'd call the clip a banana clip, but someone eventually said that was racist like everything is, so now they're just clips. Her oft-repeated manufactured smile brought out the wrinkles around her mouth.

"Ma'am, they might come in here to find out what I was looking at. Can you keep of copy of my printouts behind the desk in case anyone asks?"

"Who's they?" she asked with a puzzled look to replace her fake smile.

"My name is Cash Cutler. Someone killed my brother, and they're trying to frame me. I'm sure you've seen it on the TV."

"I'm sure I haven't," she begged to differ in her haughty manner. "I haven't had a TV in the house for over twenty years." Maybe that's why she was still wearing a banana clip.

"Not a problem." I wrote my name on the brown paper bag covering the papers. "Can you just keep this behind your desk in case someone asks?"

"I don't really feel comfortable doing that. It's an invasion of your privacy, and we don't want residents of Sanborn to think we'd, in any way, compromise their privacy."

"I get that. But it's not an invasion of privacy if I'm asking you to share this information."

"Maybe not, but," she was about to beg to differ again, "someone might get the wrong idea..."

I cut her off. "Listen, I'll sign this saying I'd like you to share it with any law enforcement official who asks." I wrote out that sentence and signed it on the cover of the paper bag.

"That might work, but why would anyone ask about this?"

"Because I used my credit card to pay for the printing. If they're following my financial transactions, they're going to come here."

"Well, I'm not sure I want to be involved in this," she said in a snooty sort of stand-offish way.

"Ma'am, you're not. But someone killed my brother and is trying to make me look guilty for it. I didn't kill my brother or his wife. I'm just trying to prove my innocence."

"Well, I don't know how this is going to help. Scaring me half to death doesn't make your case any better."

"I'm not trying to scare you at all. I'm just trying to leave a bread crumb in case they kill me too."

"You think they want to kill you?"

"I don't know. Wouldn't surprise me though."

"Well, I don't want this information then. They might want to kill me too."

She had a point. I thought a moment without words. "You're right. I'm going to go. Forget this whole conversation. Thanks for your help."

On my way out, I dropped the packet into the outdoor book return. I don't know why I did it, but in case I didn't make it, I wanted someone to know where I was looking. Once I dropped it though, I couldn't get over the feeling that I was going to regret it. I thought about going back in and grabbing it from the book return, but I also thought second-guessing myself might be a bad idea. I sat there in my truck for at least a full minute swimming through a sewer of indecision. No one should swim in the sewer. I said a quick prayer and left. That was my final decision.

***

I wanted to get this information to the police immediately and give them a chance to look in the right place. Tyler had already pointed me in the right direction, but I needed Mr. Beck on my side too. I drove to the Pendleton Police Department. If the two feds were there, I wasn't going to stop, but since I only saw one cop car, I did.

I knocked on the inner door of the Pendleton Police Station, but no one answered. So, I walked in to be greeted by a terrible smell attracting my eyes left. Chief Beck had been shot in the forehead. His slouching body was sitting at his desk in his office in front of a bloody mess on the wall behind him. My Smith and Wesson, the one I'd turned in that morning, was sitting on his desk right next to the empty evidence bags.

I was back to swimming in the sewer of indecision. If I took the gun and left, I'd be the number one suspect because the gun they'd checked into evidence was gone. If I left it and pretended I was never there, there'd be a chance someone might figure out they were trying to frame me. Question was, who did this? Was it the same person or people that killed my brother, or was it the feds? Had Chief Beck discovered they were retired and confronted them? Or what about the Mexicans? Were they that stupid?

What about the video tapes? Without touching anything, I peered around the desk at the computer screen. It was split into four quadrants, and each was a blank blue screen with the red words, "No signal." My only hope was that there were backups,

183

perhaps even offsite. But then again, it was good if there was no proof I'd even been there. I had to find Tyler.

I got out of there with my copy of the packet of breadcrumbs and drove home – no one to leave them with. I needed to shower and get over to work. I wasn't going to make it by four, but people would understand. Tyler would catch up to me at the bar, but only after he'd seen Mr. Beck. I had to hope I could get to him first. Then again, I decided to act as if I'd never known. I couldn't be sure Tyler'd stay on our side after finding Mr. Beck.

Chapter 25

I saw Jake's new Dodge Ram truck when I pulled in to my house. It gave me some relief.

Even more relief when I saw Skylar on the couch. "My gosh," I said as I was kicking the snow off my boots, "he found you. You're a sight for sore eyes."

She smiled at me, even though it looked tough to do. Then she used her arms to cover her face and said, "No, don't look at me. I'm gross."

"No, you look wonderful."

"Oh, quit it."

"What happened?"

"They must have drugged me. Jake found me in a trunk."

"Whose trunk?"

"The Mexicans that came to see you this morning."

"Really?" So much for being good beeeseneesmen. "Where's Jake?"

"Hey Cash," he said as he walked out of the bathroom drying his hands on his shirt, "right here."

"They killed Mr. Beck," I said.

"Who did?"

"I don't know. The feds, the Mexicans, I don't know. They used my gun."

"How do you know?"

"It was on his desk, right next to the evidence bag. They left it pointed right at him."

"Did you grab it?"

"No, I left it and got out of there without touching anything. You think I should have taken it?"

"Uh, I don't know. Question is, do we tell Tyler about this before you're at the bar? If he finds it, he's going to have to arrest you right away. Won't have a choice. But if we tell him, he still might not have a choice. Gotta think about this one."

"I need a shower."

"Go get one."

Skylar piped up, "What is wrong with you guys? A man is dead, and all you can think about is strategy?"

I didn't have an answer for her. I saw her point but couldn't give her an answer. I looked to Jake, and he took a shot. "It's mission focus."

"What?" she asked as if he were crazy.

"Put yourself in Cash's shoes. Someone is trying to frame him for murders, and the closer he gets to proving it, the more people that are dying. If he loses focus, his mission will fail."

"What's his mission?"

"Obvious. To prove his innocence before he's locked up or dead, and to keep people he cares about from getting killed and kidnapped."

She didn't say anything, but she rested her head back and started to cry.

I came down off the lower steps and sat next to her. "I'm sorry, baby. It's been a crazy day." I put my arm around her and pulled her in close. "We'll get through this."

"How can you say that? I was kidnapped, and they drugged me. That can't be good for the baby."

I hadn't even thought about that. I hugged her harder. "We'll get through this. I promise."

"Is that all you've got?"

It was. I looked at her as if I were perplexed anyway. Pursed my lips for good measure. It's the kind of moment when a woman leaves you with nothing to say so you're forced to better sympathize with her own sense of helplessness. When nothing I could say would help, I was left helpless too.

"Jake says you're not going to sell the bar. I thought we'd talked about this." First, she made me helpless and then threw that at me. She was good.

"That was before they kidnapped you," *and offered me half the original deal.*

186

"Cash, they're just going to kidnap me again, or kill you, or kill me or kill Jake, maybe all of us. Can't we just get that money and go, leave, get out of here and never come back? Please...please, Cash."

I wanted to ask her if this was about her mother, but I didn't have the heart to do that. Even though she should have figured out by now that I'd known about that situation, she really wanted me to sell it. She was completely ignoring the fact that I'd be a wanted man. Who would want to go through life always having to look over your shoulder for whoever's coming for you? Jake already lived like that. Was she willing to live with me like that, or was she just looking out for her own interest in this whole thing? When was she going to realize this was a little bigger than just saving her mother? I had to keep it together. She was in pain, and I didn't want to make it worse. It *was* her mother after all.

"Skylar, I can't sell it to these criminals. Not after what they did to you."

"Yeah, but what about my mother?"

I didn't even flinch. "Jake's got that."

"Got what?"

"He's breaking your mother out tonight. We just had to get you to a safe place before we did that."

"Seriously?" She looked at Jake.

"Yep. I know where she's at, and I'm going to get her before those guys who kidnapped you get to the bar. Take away their lucky chip."

"What about me?"

"Haven't figured that out yet," Jake said. "You were originally going with Ainsley, but that didn't happen."

"She was spreading rumors about Cash cheating on me. I wasn't going anywhere with that lying tramp."

Jake looked at me with pursed lips and raised eyebrows to shrug it off as my problem. "Have any other ideas?"

"Can't I just stay here?" she pleaded.

"No," Jake said.

"Why not? No one's going to bother me. It's you guys they want."

"And that's why they'll bother you. Just like they did today."

187

"I'm just not feeling well. I don't want to go anywhere. I just want to sit here and do nothing."

"I get that," Jake said, "and I'm sympathetic, but, if I don't get you someplace safe before I leave, once I'm gone, they'll be back. And I'll promise you this, they won't be sympathetic at all. They won't care that you don't feel well. They'll take you anyway. Do you have any friends or family you can stay with?"

"No, I don't want any of them to see me right now."

"Get over that, this is life or death." Jake stressed the word "death."

"I don't want to talk about this with anyone. I don't want them to see me like this, and I don't want to have to answer the questions."

"Oh," Jake said. Good enough.

I stood there on the steps feeling kind of impotent. Helpless is a better word. There wasn't a thing I wanted to say. Jake was handling her, and as much as she wanted stay at the house, I wanted to say nothing. Anything I would say would just piss her off because I was losing my patience. However, I didn't want her to know that. She was the one who had been kidnapped and drugged. I didn't want to sound insensitive to that, but I did have my own problems. I was going to work, knowing I was going to be visited by some representatives of the cartel to make sure I gave up my bar. I was stressed about it. At the same time, I couldn't pretend she wasn't stressed. Her mother was probably in even more danger now that she'd been saved.

"Jake, what about a motel?" I asked.

He thought with his lips pulled back for what seemed like fifteen seconds, at which point his lips transformed into a pucker to the left. "That might work. What do you think, Skylar? You could lay in bed with no one bothering you."

"Okay," she said, "but I want to change out of these nasty clothes first."

"No time," Jake said, "I'm taking you now. Then I'm going after your mother. You can change there. Cash has to shower and get the bar open."

"You're doing it in the middle of the day?"

"That's when they'll least expect it."

"You really are crazy. Would you get my bag? It's in our room, Cash." *Our room? It's not even mine, in reality. What's her game? We already know about her mother.*

I ran up the steps, two at a time, and grabbed her bag, brought it down and handed it to Jake. She stood up with the blanket around her shoulders and flung her arms around me. The blanket fell to the floor. She burrowed her head into my neck and kissed me. She tasted like toothpaste, mouthwash and puke. Thank God she didn't put her

188

tongue in my mouth. "Be careful, Cash," she whispered. "I really do love you." She emphasized both the word "really" and the word "you," making her statement harder to interpret than if she'd just emphasized only one of those words. I no longer knew what to think about her. Women????

I thought about going full Han Solo and saying, "I know," but I mumbled nonsense so I could sound cryptic. If I said "I love you" back, she might think me full of crap if she'd already known I wasn't really Cash. And if I blew it off unexpectedly because Cash might normally return her love, she might end up thinking I wasn't Cash.

It didn't work. She stepped back, looked up at me and said, "What'd you just say?" At least she had a smile on her face.

I nudged my head in Jake's direction twice to indicate I wasn't comfortable talking like that in front of Jake, gave her a smile and two winks of my right eye, finished off with a pleading smile and a couple more mumbles.

That worked. She smiled back, moved in close, grabbed my balls and whispered, "I can't wait to see you later."

She picked the blanket off the floor, put it around her shoulders and said, "See you later."

Jake held the door as she walked out into the blizzardy conditions with her blanket cape.

I got a shower and went to work.

Chapter 26

Herman Nighthorse sat at his desk on the thirteenth floor of the Longhouse Casino. His was supposed to be an easy job – head of security with a lot of kickbacks. Beat the heck out of living on the reservation and taking care of his wife Cindy "Who Drinks Too Much" Nighthorse and his useless drug-addled sons who'd be sent to jail the second they stepped foot off the reservation, for crimes he'd had the power to make the white man ignore for just the right-sized political contribution – but only as long as they stayed on the reservation. This was supposed to be a sixty-hour-a-week job, but, if he'd had his way, he'd work around the clock and live in his hotel room all seven nights a week, rather than just three or four. He hated his family and loved his job.

That is, until the Mexicans came in with all sorts of new ideas about how to increase profits. He didn't have anything to do with any of it, not originally. He just wanted to make a living. He had no interest in increasing profits. The chiefs and their wild-eyed powwow boys, however, saw dollar signs, and they liked it even better that the Cartel was offering to cover some of the costs for the security. That meant they'd have their Cartel assassins working alongside Nighthorse's men. Awesome – Mexican Cartel thugs are the easiest and the humblest, most law-abiding guys to work with ever. And they love taking orders from a college-educated Indian who just wants to do his job and doesn't care about higher profits, none of which ever seem to show up in his paycheck. Nevertheless, he knew he'd be in charge of taking some of the blame when all these Cartel schemes went up in smoke. As much as he'd like to walk away, the thought of spending more time with his drunk wife and useless sons made him stay.

It wasn't like the chiefs would even let him walk away. He knew too much. They had their regular sweat-lodge meetings in a private sauna just off the private locker room next to the racquetball courts in the basement. Somehow, that was the old Indian way or some nonsense. While never invited himself, every time they'd go into the private meeting, it was Nighthorse who did the sweating. It always meant more responsibilities and obligations to make sure the Mexicans make the casino more money without drawing too much attention. Attention had to be so limited that the casino's political connections would all feel completely comfortable and insulated in every way from any blowback whatsoever. Talk about stress.

On top of that, because Nighthorse had the college education, he was the one in charge of talking with the politicos. That's what they told him anyway. He figured it was because they all wanted plausible deniability, come the day it all went to hell. Let college boy take the fall. They weren't concerned at all that Nighthorse would be abandoning his drunk wife and kids if he were shipped off to jail in order to keep the casino in business. Knowing Nighthorse, they figured he'd actually rather go to jail than spend more time with his family, but that was beside the point.

Nighthorse learned to hate his job, even though it was once the greatest job he could ever have imagined.

His phone rang, breaking the silence driving his thoughts into dark territories and paralyzing his ability to even figure out what to do next. "Nighthorse," he answered as if he actually believed he were still in control.

"Herman?"

"Yes."

"It's Bennett Glazebrook." Just the person Nighthorse did *not* want to talk to. One of the many. Glazebrook was the U.S. Attorney for Western New York. His wife was in the governor's office, and he was the political fixer extraordinaire. He was the guy that made it all happen. The guy that brought in the Mexicans and turned the chiefs into money-hungry animals willing to do anything to make the casino even more profitable than it already was. Nighthorse will be happy to be the fall guy, they assured themselves. They must not have put much thought into that, considering how little Nighthorse had to protect, other than a family he despised.

"Hi Bennett. What can I do for you?" Not the question he really wanted an answer to, just the social etiquette.

"Herman, what the hell are you guys doing?"

"What do you mean?" Nighthorse asked with a faux innocence. Everybody wants a little plausible deniability.

"Who the hell told you to kill Curt Cutler and his wife? They're gonna make us open up the books at the bank."

"Cutler's bank?" Nighthorse had no idea what he was getting at. He knew who Curt Cutler was because of the news but nothing about the potential bank merger.

"No. Our bank. First Iroquois."

"You're Indian now?" *These comfortable white guys.*

"No. But that bank doesn't exist without my facilitation." The political fixer beat his chest like the indispensable genius he must have imagined himself to be.

"Maybe so, but what does that have to do with the Cutler killings?"

191

"You really don't know, do you?"

"No, sir. I'm in charge of security here. That's it."

"Yeah, well, we know that's a lie. Look Herman, Cutler's bank was trying to buy our bank."

"That would be bad," Nighthorse said. He was smart enough to know that.

"Damn right it'd be bad. That's why we've been refusing to consider the bid."

"Okay."

"Okay what? Still not seeing it, are you?"

"No." If this prick was taping the conversation, Nighthorse was going to come out smelling like a still-in-the-plastic-shrink-wrapped virgin peace pipe – clean.

"Now that you killed Curt Cutler, if they don't send his brother up the river for it, the investigators are going to look into why he was killed. When they discover it was to prevent the merger, the feds are gonna to come in and look at the books. There'll be nothing I can do."

"Look, Bennett," Nighthorse said, "it sounds like you've got a problem over there, but I had nothing whatsoever to do with killing the Cutlers. Nothing."

"What about those damn Mexicans?"

"*Your* damn Mexicans. You have more control over what they do than I do." If this conversation was to be used as evidence, Glazebrook was going to have to cut some of it, making it look even more suspicious.

"You still have the girl's mother, right?"

"Yes, and we almost had the girl too, thanks to your Mexican friends," Nighthorse added. "I had nothing to do with that either. I told them to take her back."

"What are you talking about?"

"Your dumb Mexicans thought it would be smart to kidnap the girl after some friend of hers killed about seven of my men this morning. They left her in the trunk. In the parking lot. Morons. The guy comes back, shoots up the place and takes the girl. He shot up my Caddy. I am not happy about this at all. My windows are shattered, and my seats are all shot to hell."

"Who told them to do that? What the hell is going on over there?"

"Now you understand my plight. I've been telling you for months that these Mexicans are bad news. I don't control them. Can't. Not even allowed to. I get tough, they talk to their bosses, and their bosses send someone to pay me a little visit. But you don't know anything about that, do you?"

"No. Who knows about all these dead guys? What'd you do with the bodies?"

"We took care of them, and the police have no idea. Don't worry about it."

"Good. Let's keep it that way," Glazebrook said. "The guy that did all that is friends of the Cutler boys, and he used to date Cutler's dead wife. He's some rogue Special Forces guy the feds have been looking for, for like two decades. He's been a ghost for years, but then all of a sudden, he shows up. Outta nowhere. They've got a shoot-to-kill order on the guy."

"How do you know who did it if you're just now finding out it happened?" Nighthorse knew there was no reason to trust Glazebrook.

"Don't worry about that. It's my job to know these things. They've got a shoot-to-kill order on the guy."

"What? You saying, he shows up again, I'm supposed to call the cops and have 'em come and shoot him?"

"No. You're supposed to shoot him until he's dead. Make sure he's dead. Then I'll figure out a way to blame him for the Cutler murders. Help take some heat off the bank."

"What about his brother and the girl?"

"Let me worry about them. This guy's killing everybody it seems. We need to put a stop to him."

"Yeah, but what about the casino? Doesn't play well in the news if our casino's in the business of killing unwelcomed visitors."

"Don't worry about that. Let me worry about that. First and foremost, we need to protect the bank from an audit."

"What's that got to do with people like me? All the other people that work here too? You know, the people with jobs?"

"Screw them for now. If the bank goes down, it all goes down. Those people will all be without a job. Them and many more."

"Told you those Mexicans were no good. What's so special about the bank?"

"Listen Herman, some secrets need to stay secret. Gotta go. Just make sure you take care of that girl's mother. She's the key right now. You'll get some relief from the Mexicans if we can get them that bar."

"Wait a second. What's so special about that bar they want?"

"They want to set up a huge strip club or something. It's right down the street from the bank where they do all their business. It's a heck of a lot cheaper and less dangerous than trying to smuggle all those drug dollars back into Mexico. That simple. They get the strip club, they're out of the casino, and we still get our share through the bank. No more Mexicans for you to worry about. That's why this works."

"Yeah, like they'd ever get a strip club in Pendleton. They'll never get the zoning for it."

"That's where I come in. Every decision maker in Pendleton has some secret they want to protect. If they wanted to open up a brothel, I'd make it happen. I'm the U.S. Attorney. At least this way, the decision makers can argue they didn't rezone any new land as commercial, and this land is one of the few places where there's already a liquor license. That's the deal."

"Simple as that, huh."

"Yeah, simple as that."

"Does the bar owner know all this?"

"Most of it. Doesn't know about the girl's mother though. Or the strip club, but the girl's in on it. Either way, he's been fighting us tooth and nail. Doesn't want to sell."

"That why you killed his brother?" Nighthorse thought he might catch Bennett in a lie.

"I told you, Herman, I had nothing to do with those murders. That's the last thing we'd do. It doesn't make a bit of sense for us. Far as I can tell, it was the guy that shot your men that did it. Keep the woman safe. Gotta go."

Nighthorse felt pretty confident that Glazebrook was not taping that conversation. No one would voluntarily be that self-incriminating. Unless he had feds on the line with him. Nighthorse actually wished he'd had the conversation taped. The silence was back, and the paralysis was creeping in at the speed of sound.

***

Five minutes of silence were interrupted when the two Mexican kidnappers, Carlos and Diego, barged in without knocking. They weren't even in their tuxedos. Jeans and a jacket?

"Hola, jefecito. Ees done," Carlos claimed. They called Nighthorse "jefecito" because it meant "little boss." They always wanted to remind him he was not the actual boss.

"What's done?" Nighthorse asked without wanting to know what these morons had done this time.

"Thee woomin. She went-for-a sweeem. She sleeps wit da feeshes. Thass how you say, right, jefecito? She sleeps wit da feeshes." He had a big old proud smirk on his face for his buddy's benefit. Then Diego had one too.

Nighthorse looked at them with the disbelief of a devout atheist in the middle of a prayer circle. His cheeks lifted involuntarily as he squinted in hopes of seeing more clearly. "What did you guys do?"

"She gone. No problemo."

"Who... who told you to do it?"

"El Jefe." That was their boss. Nighthorse was only the little boss, jefecito. The real boss was El Jefe. Nighthorse didn't really know who El Jefe was. Didn't even know if the guy was in the U.S. or still back in Mexico. It was really tough sometimes to be responsible for the actions of workers who aren't really loyal to you. But the law doesn't see it that way.

"Why? Don't you need her to get the bar?"

"No, jefecito,"--always belittling--"too hot. El Jefe doesn't want the bar anymore. Told us to get rid of the evidence."

"What evidence?"

"All of it."

"Translate for me."

"Allllll.... ovvvvvv... it." Carlos cracked another smug smile at his quiet buddy Diego.

The phone rang.

Nighthorse picked it up while giving the Mexicans a gesture to keep quiet. "Nighthorse."

"He's here." It was Balozi, the African. Nighthorse liked to put the big intimidating African at the front door where the people convert their cash into chips. He was from the jungle or something. Totally intimidating. That's why Nighthorse hired him. He was loyal too.

"Chambliss?" Nighthorse knew who Chambliss was, but he didn't let Glazebrook know that.

"Yes."

195

Nighthorse cursed and took a closer look at the black and white security screens on the three computer monitors that curved around his keyboard. He clicked on the lobby screen where Jake Chambliss was buying chips. It went full screen on his center monitor. Chambliss was in a sweatshirt and baggy pants with pockets on the legs, both weighted down in certain spots. Guns and ammo, of course. "What's he doing?"

"Getting chips," Balozi said.

"He armed?"

"Heavily. You want me to take him?"

"No. Watch him. Don't do anything to him on the floor. Wait 'til he goes to the bathroom or starts wandering."

"Want me to put some guys on him?"

"No. I've got some."

"Not the Mexicans." From firsthand experience, Balozi knew what trouble Carlos and Diego were. Nighthorse could see Balozi shaking his head and rolling his eyes in disbelief.

"No. Forget it. I'll watch him. Make sure Vinnie has the service elevator stuck at the top. Lock it down." That was the back elevator to the thirteenth floor.

When Nighthorse put down the phone and looked back up at the cartel stooges in front of him, Carlos asked, "Da gringo's here?"

"Yeah."

"You want we take care of him? Take heem fer a sweem?"

"No," Nighthorse demanded with all the impotent command he could inject into his voice, "you stay the hell the away from him." Swearing would hopefully help.

"You gettin' nervous, jefecito? We got deess."

"No, you stay out of the way, and save your energy for getting the bar tonight."

"We told you, we're not getting the bar. That deal's done. El jefe says no más."

"What are your orders then?"

Carlos looked at Diego in disbelief. "El jefecito wants to know what our orders are." They smiled at each other as a way to further belittle Nighthorse.

"What did he tell you maricons to do?" Nighthorse was pretty sure that was the Spanish word for faggots.

Carlos looked at Nighthorse with a raised eyebrow before relenting. He said, "Kill them all, burn the bar down and make sure no one gets out. Make gringo there," he pointed at the security screen, "write a note about how he still loves his high school chica and had to kill Cash when he found out Cash killed his chica. Then of course gringo couldn't go on living and had to put a bullet in his head. Case closed. Terminado."

"Everyone sleeps wit da feeshes," the quiet Diego added, and both stooges laughed, before adding, "as your Italian amigos say."

"Yeah, well, how you gonna do that if you kill the gringo now? How's he gonna start a fire tonight if he's already dead?"

"Good one, jefecito. We weren't really gonna kill heem. We just wanted to get heem and keep heem until later. That way our plan works. Just didn't think you needed to know all dat. We was just looking out for you. We like you, jefecito." He nodded at the computer screen. "What's the gringo doin' now?"

"Playing blackjack."

"Bring him up here, jefecito. We'll show him a blackjack."

"No. He's not the kind of person that goes anywhere he doesn't want to. Right now, he's peaceful. Let's see if we can't keep it that way. You guys get out of here. Don't let him see you. Go out the back way." Nighthorse pointed to the door behind his desk. It led into the locked office that opened up on the thirteenth floor where they kept the help. It was the only way onto that part of the floor, other than the elevator that was being held at the top so as to prevent Jake Chambliss from getting back to his friend's mother. The rest of the thirteenth floor was used for executive offices. They'd built a wall in the hallway to separate the two sections of the floor.

Carlos said, "No. We need the gringo. We should take him."

"The gringo will be there, you morons. He's already planning on it. Let us end this situation peacefully. You guys just get out of here safely. He sees you, you're dead. Nothing I can do about it. I'll send Balozi to back you up tonight. You're gonna need it."

"You sure, jefe?" *Not jefecito?*

"Yeah. Just get out of here. Let me take care of this."

"Hasta luego."

"Yeah, hasta luego." *Sh*theads.*

The Mexicans left through the door into the other side of the thirteenth floor.

Nighthorse was alone in the silence again, other than the low volume on the security camera watching Jake Chambliss play blackjack. There was noise in the room, but Jake played quietly. Every time he'd make a decision though, he'd look at the camera and

197

acknowledge it. He was communicating with Nighthorse. He'd blink, he'd point to his chips, or he'd shrug his shoulders with a smile at the camera when he'd just lost a hand. It was if he wanted whoever was watching to know that their time was running out because his pile of chips was getting smaller. Nighthorse wanted to turn it off, but he couldn't. He had to know what was going to happen next. Balozi could be seen on another camera. He was twenty feet away, standing at a post.

Then the peacefulness ended. Jake pulled his phone out of his sweatshirt. While he could see the negative reaction on Chambliss' face to the news he'd just received, Nighthorse wasn't able to hear what was said. After Jake hung up and put the phone away, he put all of his chips forward. Wasn't more than a few hundred dollars, but it was all of them. Dealer had twenty-one, and there was no longer any reason for Chambliss to be at the table.

He got up and headed towards the bathroom.

Nighthorse called Balozi.

"Got him," Balozi said, "I've got two guys on the john."

"Be discreet."

"They know."

Nighthorse watched him walk through four cameras to get to the bathroom, at which point he switched to the camera on the doorway. His two men were on either side. Jake nodded to them as he walked in. A couple of seconds later, the two men followed him in. Twenty seconds later, a young college kid with a University of Buffalo hat and a chubby man in a striped sweater exited quickly. They must have been told to leave by the two security guards.

Nighthorse had beads of sweat running down either side of his ribcage. He lowered his arms to make his shirt soak them up.

Thirty seconds later, Jake Chambliss exited. He was drying his hand on his pants. He found the camera and winked at Nighthorse, smiled and jolted his head in the direction of the bathroom, at which point he made a sad face for the camera. He actually used his two index fingers to lower the edges of his lips to form a frown.

Nighthorse watched him make his way to the elevators. When he got in, Nighthorse was able to watch him from the overhead camera. Chambliss pushed the button for the thirteenth floor, looked up at the light where the camera was and smiled. He pulled a Glock out of his pants pocket, chambered a bullet, pointed it at the camera with the little twist of a gangster and put it in the pouch pocket on his sweatshirt.

Nighthorse cursed, pulled his top drawer open, grabbed his gun and locked the door to his office.

"Balozi. Balozi. You hear me?"

He was getting static through the receiver, but he made out something that sounded like "elevator."

Chambliss got out and noticed another elevator on its way up. It was Balozi's.

"Balozi, he's waiting for you. Can you hear me?" All he heard was static.

Luckily, thought Nighthorse, Balozi was a big guy, much bigger than Chambliss. That mattered for about two seconds. Chambliss grabbed the fire extinguisher out of its glass case on the wall. The second Balozi stepped out of the elevator, he was on the ground. Chambliss jammed his knee into Balozi's back, pulled back his arms, almost out of their sockets, and zip tied them. He dragged Balozi over to the nearest doorknob and then zip tied the zip-tied hands to the doorknob. Balozi was laying on his stomach with his arms cranked up backwards and attached to the doorknob. It looked uncomfortable. His weight was pulling them out of their sockets. He didn't notice though because Jake had knocked him out cold.

Being unwilling to go out and shoot the guy, Nighthorse considered following after the Mexican stooges. He knew Chambliss had a gun in his sweatshirt and didn't think himself nearly skilled enough to go up against this guy.

He felt his impotence turning to cowardice, but what did he care? This wasn't his fight. He was only left to fight it. Maybe he'll look around and go away. He hoped. That's all Nighthorse had.

Hope wasn't a plan, though. Jake Chambliss came around the corner and found the wall in the hallway right outside Nighthorse's office and started pounding on it with the fire extinguisher. Nighthorse watched him on the camera. Three hits, he was already through the wall. It was just wallboard. He tore away the big pieces and stepped through. The jig was up.

Nighthorse heard gunfire. Some far, some near and then none. There were no cameras on the other side of the wall. He should have followed the Mexicans. He was sure of it. That was the only way to avoid the cameras making a record of his cowardice, and it was too late.

Chapter 27

Jake didn't have the heart to kill the African. He'd seen his kind before and knew he was from Africa. His dark skin wasn't diluted with the blood of the slave master, and he didn't have the stink of entitlement. Nor did Jake sense the African hated him because of the color of Jake's skin. Playing wide receiver in high school, Jake often felt that black defenders would go after him with a chip on their shoulders because Jake wasn't a black wide receiver. It wasn't his fault though that Starpoint didn't have enough black kids for a football team. He played before many minorities had even moved there. There were a few, but they were mostly adopted. Either way, Jake didn't kill him. The guy was just here to make a buck in the New World.

Jake had figured out the architecture on his way over. The thirteenth floor wasn't as large as the base of the hotel. There's no way in the world that any construction company would build a hotel with only one access point to the thirteenth floor. That meant changes must have been made after construction. The elevators to the hotel floors were on the opposite side of the hotel than the one he'd been in earlier. The service elevator was on the right, and the guest elevators were on the left. The only way they were able to close off the area where Skylar's mom was would have been to build a wall between the guest elevators and the rooms for the slaves. Jake was sure of it, and, after disabling the African, Jake walked around the corner near the elevators.

Sure enough, there was a wall there. He was just holding out hope it wasn't reinforced. One smash of the fire extinguisher, and he was sure it wasn't. Just some cheap wallboard, probably put there by the illegal-alien migrants looking for truck-bed rides to day jobs outside the Home Depot every morning. Slap some wallboard on some two-by-fours and cover the mess with gaudy wallpaper, and voilà! Pay off the inspectors not to notice, and there you go – cheap labor building the residences for the even cheaper labor.

Once he'd smashed through the piece of wallboard on the other side of the wall, the guards stationed there shot at him a few times. Luckily, he'd expected it and stood to the side from where he was smashing. Once his hole was about a foot and a half big, he took two random shots to distract the guards and then looked and aimed before taking his two kill shots.

Lucy, the slave-desk dispatcher, wasn't there. Jake made the holes bigger and climbed through as the two guards were turning the rug red with their bleeding heads. Walking up to the residential wing to his left, he ducked his head around the corner to make sure it was clear. It was. He then looked around Lucy's desk to make sure no one was under it or behind it. The photo of Lucy and her kids had fallen flat on the desk. Lucy had a pretty smile while holding her young children lit up with smiles filled with oblivion. He smashed the glass with her stapler and drew a little Hitler mustache on Lucy's face. Since she wasn't there to get his message in person, he'd leave her one for later. One thing Jake had learned in his decades on the run through some of the worst places on earth, sometimes monsters have no idea they're monsters until they see themselves through the eyes of others.

To Lucy, it might be just a job, but her duty as a human was to tell the police. She failed. He wouldn't have killed her for it, but a little mustache on a photo would suffice. She should be thankful she could buy another photo because he didn't kill her, and hopefully she'd get the real picture and repent.

Jake checked the service elevator. It was held open by a piece of wood. Must have been put there by the dead guards before they volunteered to eat bullets. Jake doubted there'd be a bonus in their paychecks, but hey, at least Jake was creating job openings.

With the elevator clear, the only place a hostile could come from was through the hole in the wall or from the rooms in the residence wing. Or the room next to the wall. Jake checked the knob. It was locked. Just as he'd figured. That there though was probably another access point, probably through the office that opens on the other side of the wall. So, in addition to putting up wallboard and wallpaper, the illegal-alien day laborers had to know how to hang a door. At least they had talents.

Jake was ready to go and get Skylar's mom Shelly and Samantha the prostitute, but he knew he had to clear the office first. He could see they weren't coming through the hole in the wall yet, but he had to know what was in that office.

He kicked the door in. The trim on the doorway was metal, but the door was only wood. The doorknob gave way as it ripped out of the cheap door. It clung to the door with shattered wood sinews. The office was dark, so he turned on the light. It was filled with copying machines and computers. Sure enough, the door to the other side was on the wall to his right. He kicked it in. This one was nowhere near as strong as the first. A wooden frame on a makeshift door frame held up by wallboard. The whole frame came out of the wall. The day laborers barely even connected the door frame to the wall frame. What a joke. No wonder America was falling apart.

The Indian guy who escorted Skylar's mom earlier that morning was standing on the other side of the room holding a gun in a shaky hand. "I don't want to kill you."

"I don't want you to kill me either," Jake said as he knocked the door frame holding the locked door to the floor.

"But I will," the Indian lifted his gun up as if he meant business.

"Well, put the gun down and we'll talk. Give you to the count of three. One…"

Before Jake got to two, Jake picked up the closest computer monitor and threw it as hard as he could at the Indian. It didn't go farther than the cords would let it though. Nonetheless, the Indian was so distracted by the fact he'd just gotten his desk straightened out he didn't see Jake had already taken his gun and had the Indian's arm cranked upwards to the point of no more mobility.

"How 'bout you sit down."

The Indian wasn't begging for his life yet, so Jake knew there was more fun to be had. He led him over to his chair and sat him down without giving up control of his right hand. While no longer putting pressure on the elbow, Jake held him by the middle finger with his left hand around the guy's wrist. Any pressure on the finger, and the guy would be on the floor crying like a baby. Once the guy was in the chair, without giving up control of the finger, Jake fished some zip ties out of his pouch. First, he tied the hand with the controlled finger to the armrest, and then he did the other.

Unfortunately for the Indian, Jake was in the mood for getting information. Jake put another zip tie around the Indian's neck. He pulled it just enough so that the Indian would feel pressure.

"You gonna choke me with a zip tie?"

"If you don't tell me what I want to know," Jake said, "Every time I think you're lying, I'll tighten it one click. Why am I here?"

"I-I don't know."

Jake tightened it. "Sorry, that was two clicks. Why am I here?"

"I really don't know."

"You keep getting clicks for the easy stuff, you ain't gonna live through the hard questions. I'll let this one slide. Start telling me the truth."

"It was the Mexicans."

"What was?"

"Who killed Shelly. That's what they told me. I had nothing to do with it?"

"They killed Shelly? Why?"

"Said their boss told them to."

202

"I thought you were their boss."

"No. Their Mexican boss."

"Why'd they kill her?"

"I don't know."

"I'll try and make it only one click. Oh crap, two again. Sorry."

"This hurts."

"It's supposed to," Jake reminded him. "You're telling me Shelly is dead?"

"I think so. Can't verify it." Nighthorse tried to cough, but his face started reddening with blood flow. "This hurts."

"Keep lying then. You won't feel a thing soon. Who are you protecting?"

"Just my job. I will give you everything you need to know," Nighthorse pleaded.

"Then go."

"It's Glazebrook you want."

"Bennett Glazebrook?"

"Yes, he's behind it all. He's the one that brought the Mexicans in."

"For what?"

"Extra money streams."

"What extra money streams?"

"The drugs and the women. The loan sharking. All of it."

"You're telling me the Indians had nothing to do with this?" Jake went to tighten the zip tie.

"No. That's not what I'm saying."

"What are you saying?"

"The Mexicans talked the chiefs into it. I had nothing to do with the meetings. Once it started though, it wasn't going to be stopped."

"Anyone try to stop it?"

"Well," he paused, and Jake tightened it one click. "I tried, but no one cared. I was just the head of security. They gave me a raise and told me to shut up."

203

"So, you did."

"Or they were going to make me."

"Who killed the Cutlers?"

"No one knows."

"No one knows, or no one's saying?"

"It's getting hard to breathe."

Jake said, "Good, hurry up and say what you're gonna say then. Who do you think did it?"

"Honestly," he paused.

"No, I want you to lie to me, yeah honestly, who?"

"I think Glazebrook's enemies did. Glazebrook said that the killings are making it all fall apart. I don't think he did it."

"Why not the Mexicans? They're trying to buy the bar."

"Deal's off. That's why they killed Shelly."

"What do you mean?"

"They're going to blow up the bar, kill the other Cutler kid and then kill you, and get you blamed for the killings. Something about how you couldn't live knowing that one of the Cutlers was married to your high school sweetie. That's what they said."

"Who said that?"

"The two Mexicans that kidnapped Shelly's daughter."

"Where are they?"

"They left. I told them to get out of here before you saw them."

"Why? Why did you tell them that?" Jake tightened the zip tie.

"Because you'd kill them and that would be bad for business. I need this job."

"That's all you care about? This job? You hear people are going to be killed, and you're protecting your job?"

"I don't know what I was thinking. I just want this to end."

"Of course, you do." Jake put his gun up to the guy's head. "Any last thoughts?"

"Oh, come on. You said I couldn't lie to you. I'm telling you the truth. Please let me live. I told you what you needed."

Jake squinched his face to look like he was thinking. "I don't know. You just admitted to aiding and abetting the murders of untold numbers of people to save your job. How can I let you live?"

"I'll be a witness when it comes to saving you guys from jail if you stop the Mexicans."

"How do I know that? Aren't you going to be more interested in hiding your sex slaves and debt slaves and all the murders you helped to hide?"

"No, no, I'll come clean. Just let me live. I'll tell them everything they need to know."

"What about the slaves?"

"Take them. I won't stop you. I won't stop them. I don't care."

"Hold on." Jake called Cash to tell them what was up but just got a voice mail. "Jake, the Mexicans are going to blow up the bar and kill you. Get everyone out." He then called Ainsley and got voicemail again. "Ainsley, the Mexicans are going to blow up the bar and kill Cash. Don't go anywhere near the bar. Call the bar and warn Cash. I can't get him on his cell. Call the bar and get him out of there." He then called Samantha.

"Hey, baby. You coming to save me?"

"Yes."

"How 'bout a little fun first. I just got out of the shower."

"Shh and listen. Go knock on Shelly's door."

"You're serious. What's going on?" The act stopped.

"Go do it."

"Okay, hold on." He heard her door open and a moment later she knocked. "I'm knocking."

"Knock again." She did.

"No answer."

"Okay, I'll be there in a minute."

Jake told Nighthorse to stay still. "Scream and I'll kill you." He walked out of his office door and through the hole in the wall he'd put there before. The African was still tied to the door. Surprisingly, there weren't any guards to come to Nighthorse's rescue.

205

Must have gotten the message or been completely oblivious as to what was going on. In the servants' hallway, he saw Samantha at the end of the hall still in front of the door.

Jake told her to stand aside. He kicked the door twice before it opened. No one was there. "Come on, let's go. Knock on those doors. He pointed to the ones on the other side of the hall as he started knocking on the doors on Shelly's side. By the time they'd made their way to the other end of the hall, some had come out to see what all the commotion was. Many weren't even in, probably working.

Samantha said, "We can go. We're free, let's go."

Most of them just went back into their rooms. Must have thought her crazy. One woman, probably another prostitute said, "What are you talking about, Samantha?"

"This guy's here to save us."

"You're crazy, girl," and she went back into her room.

"I told you, cowboy. You don't just walk away from this job. They'll kill us and our families. I shouldn't be talking to you either, not unless you're taking me on a date."

"No time for dates, kid. Let's go."

"I can't. They'll kill my family. I'm not joking," she pleaded.

"You stay here, they're going to kill *you*." He bent down and put her over his shoulder.

He entered Nighthorse's office through the two doors he'd kicked in earlier and set Samantha on the desk. "Don't move."

"Okay, cowboy." At least she had the sense to listen.

He searched the desk for scissors and found them in the drawer. In the process, he found the guy's name on his desk. "Mr. Nighthorse, I'm going to let you live under one condition."

"Anything."

"You testify against everyone involved, and you leave Samantha's family and all of these slaves' families alone. You got it?" Nighthorse nodded. "You do anything different, and I will kill you personally, but I will do it over a matter of days. I will give you more pain than the Mexicans could even imagine giving you. Forget the Mexicans. I'm much better trained."

"Okay. Anything. I promise." With that, Jake cut the zip tie around Nighthorse's neck. Nighthorse's neck was bleeding where he slipped the scissors in.

"Let's go."

"Sure thing."

Samantha followed him through the kicked-in doors and to the servants' elevator. He kicked the piece of wood out and hit the button for the first floor.

"Where are we going?" Samantha asked.

"Not sure. I'm going to stash you someplace safe."

At the first floor, there were two guards watching the elevator. Jake dusted them the second the door opened. They walked down the loading dock steps and got into his neighbor's Caprice Classic. It was cold. Jake found a red and black woolen blanket on the back seat and gave it to Samantha. He'd left his jacket in the truck but no time for that now. Wait a minute. He had to get the guns.

"We have to make a quick stop."

He drove around the front to where he'd parked the truck, got out, grabbed his jacket and the two ARs. He put the guns in the back over the front seat back, jumped into the car and tossed his jacket onto Samantha's lap. He took off quickly, hoping no one was following.

"Ow, what you got in this thing?"

"Guns. You want one?"

"You think I'd look hot with a gun?"

"Sure."

"Then yes."

"You won't need it."

"How do you know?"

"I just do."

"Cause I'm already hot?"

"No."

"What's with you, cowboy? You don't like girls?" She reached over and fidgeted with his junk. Blood flowed there immediately.

"Don't," he said as he moved her hand back to her side of the car without taking his eyes off the road.

"Why, 'cause you liked it? I think you did. I felt it move."

"You were moving it."

207

"That's not what I mean. You saved me. Don't you want a reward?"

"No."

"Violate the cowboy code or something?"

"I'm not a cowboy."

"You sure don't like the Indians much."

"Don't make me a cowboy."

As he was nearing the Grand Island bridge, Jake called Cash again.

"You calling your girlfriend?" Samantha asked.

"Don't have one." It went to voicemail again.

"Then what's wrong with me?"

"Nothing." He dialed Ainsley again.

She veered over to look at his phone. "Is Ainsley your girlfriend?"

"Could be." It went to voicemail as well.

"You mean she might be, or you want her to be?"

"Something like that."

"Like what, Jake? What is it you're not telling me?"

"A lot."

"Okay, I guess." Samantha leaned over and kissed him on the cheek. "Thank you."

"That my reward?"

"Yes."

"Well then, thank you back."

"You're welcome," she said and put her head back and pulled the blanket up to her neck. The heat was kicking on, but nothing like the comfort of a blanket when you can't get any from a man.

Up to this point, Jake was set to drop her off with Skylar but then remembered that Samantha probably knew about Shelly and couldn't risk what Skylar might do if she were to find out about her dead mother.

"Are you stashing me someplace?"

"No time. You're coming with me."

"Now we're getting someplace. Where we going?"

"It's not like that. I'm going to stop the Mexicans from killing my buddy and Shelly's daughter."

"Can I have a gun then?"

"Yes. You know how to use it?"

"Heck yeah, cowboy. My uncle used to take me shooting when I was a little girl."

"Why not your dad?"

"Didn't have one."

"Oh."

"Why else you think I'm a sex worker? Think I *didn't* have daddy issues?"

"No."

"So, you think I have daddy issues?"

"No, that's not what I meant. I didn't even think about it."

"I'm just kidding, Jake. I'm sure I have daddy issues. Don't even know the guy. Just don't keep thinking I'm unworthy of love."

"Never did. If that's what I thought, I'd have left you back there to be killed."

"That's what I love about you, cowboy. You don't even have the ability to lie to me. Me, everything I do is lying. It's my whole job. Lie, make money."

"Not anymore. You're unemployed."

"For now, it seems, but I'll be right back there. Just the way things go in my life. You know your life is crap when going to fight Mexicans at the O.K. Corral is an exciting vacation. And the sad thing is, no matter what I say to you, I can't get you to want me. What is wrong with you, Samantha?" She smacked her head up against the window and started to weep.

Jake felt bad for her. The real Samantha was bubbling up through all the lies, personas, masks and costumes, and she couldn't keep herself suppressed. "Let me ask you something."

"Shoot."

"Why were you working as a sex slave?"

209

"The only way to pay down my debt. I could've cleaned like Shelly, but the economics didn't work out. I'd be cleaning for the rest of my life and still have more debt than I had when they first gave me the ultimatum. It was the only way to pay it down. That's how they structured the deal, whether I liked it or not."

"Were you a prostitute before?"

"No. Never. I was a sex slave. They didn't give me a choice that made sense. Sex slave or always a slave."

"That's terrible." Jake drove on through the quiet. They were nearing Pendleton on Lockport Road.

As they crossed Shawnee, Samantha asked in her real voice, uninspired by her need to deceive for money, "Do you despise me, Jake? Is there any way a man like you could love a woman like me?"

"No, I don't despise you. Not a bit. I can't speak for all men like me. Who am I to say?"

"I mean you, then. Is there any way *you* could ever love *me*?"

"That's a big question, Samantha, filled with variables you have no idea about. If I ever fell in love with you, it wouldn't be fair to you. If that happens, you should run. I mean it. You have no idea what my life is like. None. You'd hate it."

"How do you know?"

"What do you know about me?" He asked the question while looking down at her with a furrowed brow.

"I know," she thought, "I know you've been like a ghost for years. That's what they call you. A ghost. I know you came back to either kill your once true love and her husband or to avenge her murder. I'm not sure which, but I think it's to avenge her murder. That's so romantic. I'm telling you, it is. I know you didn't kill her like they say on the TV."

"Well," he stopped her, "you're already wrong. I didn't kill her, and I didn't come back to avenge her murder. I came back because she begged me to come back. Said her husband and his brother were in trouble. They were my friends too, always have been. I was here before the murders. So, don't trust everything you hear on the TV."

"You still love her, don't you?"

"Yes."

"You never stopped, did you?"

"No."

210

"That's so sad," she said. "So romantic, but sad. You know, it's my job to make men's fantasies come true. It's what I do, but you, you just gave me a fantasy better than anything I've ever been asked to fulfill. It makes me want to cry for you. Have you ever loved another woman?"

"No."

"See, there you go. That's the kind of fantasy every woman has. That some guy out there pines away for her so much he'd be willing to come to her need on a whim and give her everything she needed."

"Callie's dead. That's no fantasy."

"You know what I mean."

"Yeah, maybe."

"Well, I will speak for all women, period. We are all suffering that you won't bother to fall in love with any one of us because of the love you have for that one girl. God rest her soul."

"Thanks," he said, as he was trying to keep back the tear popping its head into his eye. She hit a nerve.

She leaned over and kissed him on the cheek again. "No. Thank you."

Chapter 28

Jake pulled into Cash's driveway.

"Where are we?"

"Getting supplies. Gotta get you some clothes. It's going to be cold. Follow me."

He opened the door with the key he found in the barn earlier. No one was home. He took Samantha upstairs where he found some clothes in Cash's room that might fit her. He made her put three layers on. Then he found her a winter jacket that was a little big for her, but it would keep her warm.

He sat down on the bed to pull a pair of Cash's overalls over his clothes for another layer of warmth. While he was sitting there, she sat next to him and said, "Think about this, Jake. We are about to maybe go and get killed by the cartel. Is there any chance you'll give me a minute to show you how I feel about you?"

"I don't think that's a good idea, Samantha. We've got to get to the bar."

"Just a second." She wasn't taking no for an answer. She climbed on his lap in order to make it harder for him to stop her. And then she kissed him on the lips in the most sensual way he'd ever been kissed in his life. He stood up, but she was clinging to his neck with her arms like she'd never let go. Then she wrapped her legs around his back. Just then, Ainsley's Prius pulled into the driveway below. He could see it in the driveway looking around Samantha's face.

"Someone's here," he said.

She lowered her legs and took her weight off Jake before turning to look out the window. Ainsley got out of the car in front of the garage and looked up to see both of them looking through the window. At that point, Samantha grabbed Jake's junk again and said, "I knew you weren't gay."

"Didn't say I was. Let's get down there."

"Hold on. You can't go down there like that." Samantha wiped the lipstick off his face. "Go ahead, I'll be right down, gotta fix my face now. I won't ruin it with your girlfriend. I know you like her."

Jake smirked and walked down the stairs. Ainsley was in the dining room by the time he'd gotten to the living room. "I got your message. Who's that?"

"No one. Did you get ahold of Cash? Get him out of there?"

"Yes and no. He said he ain't letting them blow up his bar. I told him what you said, but he wouldn't listen."

"Figured. I gotta go."

Samantha came down and punched Jake in the arm. "I'm no one, Jake?"

"Ainsley, this is…"

"Samantha. I worked with Skylar's mom."

Ainsley went white, and her mouth hung open with nothing to say.

"Oh, it's not what it looks like, Ainsley," Samantha helped her. "He was just getting me some clothes to keep me warm before we kick some cartel ass."

"She's going with us?" Ainsley said in surprise.

"Yeah, with me. She knows how to shoot." Jake would have liked to leave her, but he didn't think it was fair to Ainsley. He didn't know what she was capable of, and he knew she saw Ainsley as someone she thought he liked. As well, she was an asset. She knew all about the operations at the casino, and, if he needed her as a witness, it was best to keep her close and not let her get in the wind.

"Aren't I going too? You taught me how to shoot."

"No, Ainsley. You ain't ready for still targets, let alone moving human ones."

"You don't want Samantha to stay with me?"

"No, she's my backup."

"You still want me to meet Tyler at the bar?"

Jake thought about that one. He looked up, didn't find an answer, looked at Samantha and then back at Ainsley. "I don't think so. You should stay here until we get back."

"You're not welching on the story, are you, Jake Charm?"

"Of course not. I just don't know if I want you in that bar, now that I know they're planning on blowing it up." Jake exhaled big.

Ainsley saw that as her moment. "What do you mean you used to work with Skylar's mom?"

Jake exhaled again while looking at Samantha who said, "I meant Jake got me out of there. I'm no longer a slave to the Indians."

"Oh, good. Where's Skylar's mom?" She looked to Jake for the answer.

He shook his head and became the bearer of bad news. "They killed her."

"Who did?"

"The Mexicans that kidnapped Skylar."

"My God," Ainsley said, "Are you sure?"

"No, but I believe it's true. No body though, not yet. Said she went for swim over the Falls."

"Should I call it in? Does Skylar know?"

"No, and no. Skylar can't know yet, and we can't have authorities looking for a body either. The casino catches wind they're about to get raided, who knows what they'll do to the rest of the slaves."

"Why didn't they come with you?"

"Too afraid of what would happen if they did. You're a thorough questioner, Ainsley. It's like you're a reporter or something."

She gave a half-hearted smirk and sighed. "Why're you so calm, Jake?"

"I'm not. I'm seething with rage."

Samantha responded to the claim by looking Jake up and down and punching him again in her love tap way. "He's just way too cool to show it."

"Huh," Ainsley offered.

Jake ended the interrogation. "We're going to take the four-wheeler to the bar and wait out back. You wait here. If anyone comes, go to the attic. The barracks. Lock the door, don't stand in front of it. They'll shoot you. If anyone you don't know knocks it down, shoot until they're dead. Text me if anyone comes to the house. If I think it's good, I'll call and have you come sit with Tyler, but I first want to get a lay of the land. I have no idea what we're up against. You still have that gun I gave you, right?"

"Yes."

214

"Good. Keep the doors locked."

In the barn, after a walk through the tundra when they got the ARs out of the Caprice Classic, Samantha said, "You know, Jake, you really are way too cool. You think we can finish that kiss that was rudely interrupted by your girlfriend?"

"After the mission." He started the four-wheeler with the full choke. He put the guns in the toolbox on the back rack.

"Seriously?"

"Seriously what?" He'd forgotten what she was talking about.

"You'll seriously let me finish the kiss after the mission?"

"Sure. If that's what keeps you focused enough to get us both out of this alive. You got it."

"What about Ainsley?"

"I have the same problem with Ainsley I have with you, or any other woman, for that matter. My life doesn't allow me to love anyone." He opened the barn door and pulled out. She walked out, slid the door shut and got on the back.

"Except Callie?"

"Exactly."

"No wonder Ainsley wants your story so bad."

The four-wheeler wasn't warm enough and it almost stalled before puttering off in fits and starts.

"This thing broken?" she asked.

"No, just cold. Don't have time to warm it up though."

She slipped her hands around his ribs and into his hand-warming pockets. Slipped them right in between his body and the gun resting on her knuckles.

Chapter 29

Ainsley watched from the dining-room window as Samantha put her hands into Jake's pockets. The wind and snow stopped blowing long enough for her to see it. It was darkening outside, but they were under the overhead barn light. How she wished that was her.

What's he see in her? Ainsley wondered, *Sure, she's beautiful but come on. She's probably a prostitute. And because of that I'm supposed to wait here? Yeah, that's not gonna happen.*

Ainsley waited until they were gone and got back into her Prius. She drove to The Trough and parked in front, hoping Jake wouldn't see her. She entered through the front door and took a seat at the front of the bar. Cash was talking with someone on the other side of the horseshoe-shaped bar. She took a look around. The place was mostly empty, but there were a few people taking up space at the tables. She didn't find the guy she thought she was supposed to meet. No cop-sized guy was sitting alone. It was 9:30. He was supposed to be there by 10.

When Cash turned around to check the bar, he saw Ainsley and threw a damp white towel over his shoulders. "Can I get you anything?"

"A Coke, please."

He leaned in like he couldn't hear her. "Are you sure you want to be here?"

"Yes, Jake and Samantha are outside."

"Samantha?"

"Girl he met at the casino. Used to work with Skylar's mom."

"Did he get *her?*"

"No," she shook her head and came right out with it, "he thinks they killed her."

Cash went pale. "Skylar know?"

"No. He said not to tell her yet."

He nodded his head while contemplating what to do next and filling a glass with Coke from his beverage dispenser.

He leaned in again and whispered, "I think I'm gonna be arrested tonight. I want to give you something that no one can know about. I can't let them get it."

"What is it?"

"A letter to my dead brother I wrote a couple of weeks ago, before I knew he'd be dead. Get it to Jake, and please don't read it. If I'm put away, Jake'll know what to do."

"Why they arresting you?" Always inquisitive.

"They killed Mr. Beck, and I think they're framing me for it."

"Chief Beck?" Cash nodded. "Who killed him?"

"I don't know. Think it was the feds after Jake. If they get him too, hang onto this letter."

Cash grabbed the letter from under the bar and slid it across the bar to her. She put it in her purse. Slid it under the gun. She was no longer sure she'd be alive to write this story.

Chapter 30

Early in that evening, Chief Deputy Tyler Graveline stopped off at the office to check in, do his write up and lock up before he'd go home and get ready for a little undercover and off-the-books work at The Trough. Chief Beck's car was in the lot, and he'd hopefully get to compare some notes on the developing Cutler murders case.

That hope was strangled in the crib though. Chief Beck was dead.

Chief Deputy Graveline immediately pulled his gun and cleared the office. No one was there with him. He then looked outside and did a perimeter check to make sure no one was casing the place and waiting for him. While it was dark, he saw nothing.

Back inside, careful not to touch anything, he searched for clues. The main one was obvious. Cash's Smith and Wesson sitting on the desk, not in the evidence bag. It didn't seem like anything Cash would do, but protocol made him the number one suspect.

Careful not to disturb the crime scene, Tyler went behind the chief's chair and looked at the moving screen saver on the computer. He nudged the mouse with a knuckle. The computer was set to security camera mode, and the four screens were all blue with "No Signal" messages. He immediately suspected the feds. There was a difference between what protocol suggests Tyler was supposed to conclude and what his gut told him.

He walked over to the holding cell, directly across the room from the chief's desk. Earlier that day, he used white duct tape to attach a hunting trail-cam to the soap dispenser sitting above the sink. He used the white tape to cover up the camo on the camera as best he could to make it hard to notice. After Jake and Cash talked him out of taking Jake in and then discovering the two feds weren't on active duty, he concluded he needed an insurance policy. Tyler trusted his gut, first and foremost.

He pulled the flash card, plugged it into his computer and hit play.

The video showed Chief Beck at his desk for a while, doing some paperwork, answering a call. Other than a bar from the jail cell down the middle of his face, it was situated perfectly. Tyler watched it in fast forward until two others entered. He hit play. It was Simon and Dillard, just like he figured. With no sound, he couldn't tell what they were saying, but he watched them have a conversation with the chief for a bit.

After a while, the chief looked agitated. He showed them some paperwork on his desk. Tyler thought they must have taken it, remembering there was no paperwork on the desk. Then Simon left the screen, walking back towards Tyler's desk. The chief wasn't paying attention.

Simon came back a moment later with the evidence bag in his left hand and Cash's gun in his gloved right hand. He shot as soon as he lifted it. Chief Beck slumped.

They went right to work erasing the security footage and disconnecting the camera system. While they looked like they'd hit their prime before the invention of the computer, they moved like pros. Knew exactly what they were doing. Then they rifled through the paperwork and walked out with a bunch of files. The camera focused on Chief Beck's still body for about five seconds, and the motion-detecting camera stopped filming.

A second later, it clicked on again. This time Cash came in and stood in disbelief for a moment before considering what to do. Tyler could see he was about to take the gun, knowing it would come back on him. Cash then looked at the security screens and doubtlessly saw exactly what Tyler'd just seen. He left the gun, just as he should have. Good man, Cash, thought Tyler.

Chief Deputy Tyler copied the footage onto his hard drive and then from the hard drive to two flash drives. Then he put the original flash card back into the trail-cam just in case someone were to come and disturb the crime scene.

On his way out, he said a prayer for Chief Beck and begged his boss for forgiveness, knowing there was no time to call the murder in. Granted, he'd already solved it, but still… he was up against rogue feds, whose apparent disregard for the rule of law knew no bounds. On top of that, that these guys were floating above the law like this meant there were bigger people making sure they could. That's why he made sure there were four copies of the evidence. Wasn't even sure four was enough.

He turned out the lights and locked the door, including the dead bolt that was rarely used. He knew for sure he was violating protocol, but he also knew the Mexicans would be meeting with Cash soon. Big problems in a small town.

Chapter 31

As it neared ten o'clock, I was getting antsy. While I knew Jake had my back, I didn't know what to expect from Tyler. He'd have to arrest me. No other way around it, but I was counting on his understanding the gravity of the situation enough to hold off. Why would he force me to leave the bar, knowing the Mexicans would be coming shortly thereafter? I was the key to taking down the Mexicans. No way he'd want the Cartel owning the main Pendleton bar. No one wanted that. Except maybe Skylar.

A moment after seeing some car lights move past the front window before leaving the parking lot, Skylar walked into the bar. Of all the women in all the gin joints in all the world, she was the last one I wanted walking into mine. Sure, I kind of liked her, but I needed her emotions at that moment like I needed the hole in the head the Mexicans had planned for me.

"Skylar. How are you, baby?"

"Better, Cash. A whole lot better now that I'm with you. God, I missed you." I didn't know what to think at this point. Was she in character, or did she really like me? "Hi, Ainsley. That's your name, right?"

"Yes, hi Skylar. You feeling better?"

"I just needed some sleep and a couple of Bloody Marys. I feel a lot better now."

"Good," Ainsley said.

Skylar put her attention on me. "Can I talk with you in the back?"

"Sure." I came out from behind the bar and led her to the kitchen just as Pacho came out and declared the kitchen closed.

"Thanks, Pacho. Have a good night."

"You too, Cash. Good luck tonight." He crossed himself and winked.

I winked back, and he left out the back door.

Once we were in the kitchen, Skylar threw her arms around me and weighed me down with a hug. She held me tight for a good twenty seconds, whether I wanted it or not. Then she whispered something in my ear that made me sweat and freeze. "I love you Curt, more than I ever pretended to love Cash. I really do. It's not an act. Not even about my mom. If we get through this, I want to stay with you. Just want you to know it."

"Wow," is the only thing I knew how to say. I kissed her gently, and she turned it passionate, the kind of kissing that's the preamble to the things you do in privacy. I heard the bells on the front door and tried to get her to stop.

She looked up at me and asked, "Something wrong?"

"No. No. Just that someone's here," and I looked down the front of me. I was not in the proper state for public display. I smiled all innocently, and she smiled back at me as she grabbed my balls.

"Save it for later," she said.

"Right now, I got to get rid of it. Walk it off."

"You're funny, Curt."

"Shh. Don't say that name."

"Sorry. Want me to see who it is?"

"Sure. I'll be good in a bit."

I did a little adjusting while I walked around and then followed her out. It was Tyler Graveline. Perfect timing.

I heard Skylar say, "Can I get you anything?" as she walked behind the bar.

"I'll have a Labatt's"

"Coming right up." She pulled the beer from the fridge, popped the top like a natural and served the bottle with a napkin.

I came out and sat across from Tyler at the table, as she returned to the back of the bar. He was dressed in civilian clothes. Wore a pair of jeans and a sweater, and he donned a Starpoint Spartans Football cap on his head.

"Nice hat, Tyler."

He responded with a nod and no smile and said, "I see you know about Chief Beck."

"How'd you know?" I wasn't about to lie to him and pretend I was completely unaware. Had too much respect for him.

221

"I planted a trail-cam in the holding cell." A weight lifted off me like you wouldn't believe.

"Who did it?"

"The feds."

"Knew it was them. Those bastards. I'm really sorry about your loss, Tyler."

"I know. But you've got your own problems right now. I get it. But I may have to arrest you to throw them off the scent. Here, take this and put it in a safe spot though."

He handed me a flash drive. "The footage?"

"Yeah. I've got multiple copies. We're going to try and take these bastards down."

"Try? You've got the proof. What's with try?"

"Listen, Cash. These guys are protected by some seriously powerful people. It's just not that simple."

"Never is. What about Jake? They're gonna try and kill him. Anything you can do to stop them?"

"I hope so. I'm with you guys, but if I have to arrest you, just play along. I don't know how this is all going to go down."

"By the way," I said, "Jake found out the Mexicans are pulling out of the deal. Word is, they're going to kill us, make it look like Jake did it and blow the bar up. I'm not sure in what order."

"Why are we here then? What are you doing, Cash?"

"Jake's outside with some sharp-shooting sidekick. Unless they come here with some RPGs, they're not doing anything. We're just going to find out what they're up to."

He pointed to Ainsley. "Isn't that the news reporter?"

"Yeah, she has a crush on Jake. Also wants his story on John Doe Number Two. She's good. A little crazy to be here, but anything for the story, I guess."

"I guess everything's a little easier, knowing Jake's got your back."

"Always was," I agreed.

"That's for sure."

"How about I have Ainsley sit over here with you. That was our plan anyway."

"Sure. Not a problem."

"Keep an eye on the front window."

"Already am," he said as if it was the first time I'd ever met him.

"Oh, well, you're in civilian clothes. Must have forgotten you're a cop."

"Heh," he smiled.

I let Ainsley know she could go and sit with Tyler and got back behind the bar with Skylar, who was talking with the Bobby Owens, the guy I'd been talking with before. Bobby was getting ready to leave but not before another round of condolences.

"Thanks Bobby, drive safe."

"Why? Half the police force is in this bar. Hi Tyler," he spoke loud enough to be heard across the bar.

"Have a good one, Bobby. And listen to the barkeep. Drive safe."

He left through the back door, and the remaining customers also started to make their way out soon after. The kitchen was closed, and it was a somber night at The Trough. No one felt the need to be there and miss all the nothing that seemed to be going on. All the better because none of them needed to know what was really going on.

Chapter 32

Jake and Samantha parked the four-wheeler behind the bushes on the east side of the path into the fields out behind the bar. He was posted with the AR over his right shoulder. He adjusted the other AR sling to fit around Samantha's smaller shoulder. He wanted her posted behind the bushes on the other side of the path where she could get extra cover behind the metal dumpster that sat in front of the bushes, but she kept talking. Rather than make so much noise, he had her stand behind the bush he was on. She couldn't see anything, but it didn't matter. Even with all her yakking, he was focused enough to see and hear everything.

Of course, he saw Ainsley pull in. Wasn't happy about that but didn't really expect anything different. He saw Tyler come and was happy he didn't see him arrest Cash. Saw Pacho leave and then a few others.

"Game time," he whispered.

"They on their way?" she asked.

"More likely now than when there were so many people in the bar."

"Think it'll just be the two of them, or are we going to have to…"

"I don't know."

"Ready for anything? Like that," she said, "just like a cowboy."

"Always."

The curvy-looking Monte Carlo's lights turned their way as it pulled into the parking lot. Jake moved to his left to get behind the bushes. It drove to the rear parking lot and turned to park close the door. Three car doors opened. The black guy Jake tied to the doorknob earlier got out of the back and walked around to the other rear door. He let out a woman. Jake was pretty sure it was Shelly. Great news. Nighthorse was a liar.

"Is that Shelly?" Samantha asked.

"Shh. Think so."

"That's Balozi. The African," she said. "He's head of security."

"We've met."

"And he's still alive?"

"Yeah. Balozi work for the Indians or the Mexicans?"

"Don't know."

"Huh."

A couple of minutes later Jake got a text message from Cash: "They want you to come in while we do the deal."

Jake whispered to Samantha, "I'm going in. You stay here. If there's trouble, get yourself out of here. You know how to drive this thing?" He put it in neutral to make sure it would start.

"How you know I won't just leave and take this thing?"

"The least of my concerns right now. If that's what you want to do, go for it."

"I don't." She reached up and kissed him. "Careful."

He took off his gloves and trudged through the snow with his gun pointed down.

Chapter 33

Tyler yelled over to me at the bar. "We've got company, Cash. A grey sedan."

"That's them. Show time," I said. I was nervous. "Hey Skylar, why don't you and Ainsley hang out in the kitchen?"

"Not a chance," she said, "these bastards kidnapped me."

"I'll stay too," Ainsley said, not as excitedly though.

"Suit yourselves, but play it cool," I said.

Carlos and Diego entered first and stomped the snow off their boots and wiped it off their jeans. Shelly and a big black guy followed.

"Mom, oh my God, Mom."

"Hi Skylar." She shook her head quickly and put a finger to her lips – the universal hand signal for, "Be quiet and shut up."

"Surprise, Cash," Carlos said with a smile. "Why don't you have your buddy out there in the bushes come in? We like to see who we're doing business with." He pointed his gun at Shelly's head.

"Do it, Cash." Skylar nudged me with the back of her hand under the bar.

I sent a text to Jake.

Carlos held position with his gun on Shelly until Jake opened the door a few minutes later.

"Take his gun." Carlos was the boss.

Jake placed it in Balozi's outstretched hand, who was standing to his left.

"Your coat too. Easy."

Jake slid out of his coat, handed it to Balozi and proceeded to take off his sweatshirt too.

He set the sweatshirt, probably with a gun in the handwarmer pocket, on the chair to his right. Always thinking ahead.

"Check him."

While Balozi was patting him down, he smacked Jake in the balls. Jake bent forward and gasped a bit. We might get the impression Jake's a superman sometimes, but apparently his balls aren't made of steel. "That's for earlier," Balozi said in his native accent. I heard a quiet sympathy gasp come from Ainsley behind me, but I made no acknowledgement.

"Fair enough," Jake said, with a smirk for my benefit.

Jake was standing still wearing my padded overalls hanging down in the front. He had on a grey muscle shirt. Nothing better for hand to hand I figured, except the overalls would be hindering. While Balozi was patting down his legs, I noticed him look at the burn marks on Jake's wrists. First the left wrist and then the right. He deliberately focused on each. Balozi took his time. "He's clean."

"Take a seat at the bar."

Jake complied. "I'll have a Molson Canadian."

Skylar got him one.

Balozi took over for Carlos holding the gun to Shelly's head. Carlos locked the rear door, and Diego locked the front door. As Carlos walked back towards the bar, he said, "You two, why don't you join us at the bar." Ainsley looked to Tyler who nodded, and they joined us.

As Carlos sidled up to the bottom of the U-shaped section of the bar between the front bar and the back bar, he said, "I'll have what he's having," pointing to Jake. Skylar got him a bottle of Molson. She was way cooler than I imagined she could be, especially after the kidnapping.

"I know we're a bit early, but I figured," Carlos paused to take a slow five-gulp taste, "we'd have time to discuss the new terms of the deal."

"I thought the deal was off," I said, not sure if I should have.

"I thought so too, but lucky for the lady here, I got in touch with our bosses before I took her for a swim. Which is good for all of us. Cheers to that." He was the only one who lifted his drink.

He looked around for a response but got none.

"Not in a festive mood, I see." Carlos took another swallow of beer. "Our deal with the Indians is done, they got too many troubles now, but the bosses still want dis bar. Your lucky day."

227

"What are the terms?"

"Knew you'd ask. They aren't as good, not with all the recent troubles, but still fair. For the bar and land, one seventy-five. Shelly is free and clear of her debts to us, and you all get to walk." He circled his pointed finger around the room and then brought it to the document in front of his face. "Just sign here. The money's outside. Oh, and you get to keep all the other money you already have." Everyone looked at me as if I were holding out on them. "That's more than fair," he concluded.

"And if I say no?"

"You all die."

Skylar smacked me again and whispered, "Quit it, Cash."

"Do as your woman pleases, Cash." Up to that point, his English was surprisingly good.

"It's 'do what pleases your woman.' You didn't say it right," I corrected him.

"Oh, lo siento, sorry. Do what pleases your woman. Whatever, eess good advice," he suddenly seemed to remember to make like he doesn't speak English well. Must have thought it gave him street cred.

"Better. Let me get this straight, you think you can kill us all before we kill you?"

"Eess just business. Don't take it personal. Our guns are out. You have a pea shooter under the bar. She," pointing to Ainsley, "might have a gun in that heavy bag. The cop's is under a sweater, probably buttoned in. You and your unarmed friend over there go first, then the cop, then the three women. Eess easy." He continued with poor English to sound intimidating.

"That easy, huh?"

"If wrong, my replacements come later and finish the job. Eess just business."

"How are you going to get away with this though? Don't you think that me selling the bar, right after my brother's been murdered, might make it look a little suspicious for you?"

"Not my problem. I'm just doing what I'm told. The rest is just details. Someone else's details. I'm offering you the deal of a lifetime. Besides, you need the money for the lawyers. Won't look bad. Just say you needed the money."

"Deal of a lifetime, huh? And we all just walk out of here unharmed?"

"Sí. Unarmed and unharmed." He smiled at his own cleverness.

228

"All right, let me see the paperwork." I had too many women there to worry about. I wasn't going to start a shootout. Didn't even think the sale would be valid anyway, not after all the investigations about to hit.

Carlos put a folder of papers on the bar. "Sign anywhere it's got the stickers."

"Are there documents for Shelly's debt?"

"It's on top. Sign and have her sign. It's all explained. S'what dey say, anyway. Just sign. Diego," Carlos called for his attention before he threw him the car keys, "get the briefcase in the trunk."

To me, it looked pretty official. All drawn up by actual lawyers. I'm not sure about how legal the form freeing a slave is, but I signed her form anyway, set it aside and skimmed through the rest of the documents. Just about everything necessary, but I wasn't supposed to be a banker. I was just a barkeep trying to sell a bar and letting money people take care of the details. There's no way I was going to look through these documents with the eyes of a banker. Too many guns and not enough time. As long as the document looked normal and boilerplate, I signed.

Before I finished though, Diego returned, and he had his hands up. A petite young girl bundled up in honor of the frozen tundra followed. In her right hand, she was holding one of Jake's ARs. In her left hand, she held the briefcase.

Just when I thought I was done, another variable. One of Jake's angels.

Samantha looked at Jake with a smile and said, "Hi Jake. Hi Shelly. I'm thinking we should change the terms of the deal."

Shelly shook her head but was too afraid to say anything. Jake was in the ready-to-strike-any-nanosecond mode but wasn't sure who to strike. The big black guy slowly made his way over towards Carlos, who had his gun pointed at Samantha.

"Easy, Balozi," Samantha said, as if they were old friends.

Without making Samantha flinch, Balozi grabbed Carlos' gun and smacked him over the head with it. He didn't go to the floor but bent over and grabbed a stool with his one hand while his other was attempting to keep the blood in his head.

Jake took that as his cue. In the blink of an eye, Diego was on the ground and Samantha'd been disarmed. Balozi had his hands up, and Jake delivered the money in the briefcase to the bar.

Jake ordered Balozi to sit at the bar with Carlos. Tyler had his gun on both of them, and Jake backed off towards the kitchen a bit to be out of Tyler's shooting path.

Ainsley stuck her head back above the bar but forgot her gun. Amateurs.

229

Jake broke the silence. "Hold your fire everyone. Let's figure this out. You. I take it your name's Balozi. Did I pronounce it right?"

"Close'nuff."

"Are you and Samantha working together?"

"Not anymore. I doubt either of us will be employed at the casino again."

"You know what I mean. Answer the question." Jake lifted his persuader up and down a couple of times.

"No."

"Then why? Why are you here, and why'd you hit Carlos? Hold up. Cash, why are you selling the bar? Thought it wasn't gonna happen."

"Changed my mind. I'll tell you later. I want to sell it and walk away tonight."

"Okay. Back to you. Balozi. Why are you here, and why'd you take out Carlos? I know you're not with the Mexicans."

Balozi looked straight into Jake's eyes. None of the looking downward in order to lie nonsense that most criminals employ to hide the shame of being caught. He was straight up. "When they untied me earlier, they asked if I'd like a little revenge on the guy who did this. I said sure. They were going to pay me to back them up. That's all. Mexican money's just as green as the Indians'. You're not well-liked at the casino anyway. Thought I'd be doing my bosses a favor."

"So, why'd you turn on Carlos when Samantha came in?" She looked interested in the answer to that question too. "You got a thing for her?" Jake blinked with a nod and a smile at the guy.

"No," said Balozi, "I saw my tribe's markings on your wrists. Other tribes' too. You and I are not enemies. Can't be."

"Nice. What luck. My name's Jake Chambliss. What's your tribe?"

"Assa."

"Really?" Jake sounded blown away. "How'd you end up in America? That's a small tribe. And, you know..." Jake sounded like he could say something but didn't want to offend him.

"Missionaries."

"They turned you?" Jake was even more surprised.

Balozi put his head down in thought. "Some yes, but I'm still..."

"I get it."

Balozi then said, "How did you make peace with my tribe?"

"Missionaries."

"Noooo."

"I know what you mean. They didn't like the missionaries much, but I helped take out a warlord for them. It was one of those deals. Didn't use witchcraft, but I did make him disappear."

Balozi smiled with a small laugh. "Thank you."

"You're welcome."

"You are my friend then."

"And you are mine," Jake said. "So, let's finish this up then. Carlos, you still want to buy the bar?" Jake was the gun-wielding three-ring party host.

Carlos wiped the blood off his hand onto his jeans and grabbed a few napkins. "We want her back," he pointed to Samantha.

She piped up, "No way. Don't do this to me Jake, please. Don't send me back."

"No," Jake said. "What does it matter? You're done with the Indians. Said it yourself. She's no concern of yours."

"She had a gun on Diego, and she almost ruined the deal. No deal without her."

"Then the deal's off," Jake spoke for me whether I liked it or not.

Skylar smacked me again, but I agreed with Jake. "Yeah, deal's off." I grabbed the folder of paperwork and brought it under the bar. I grabbed the lighter we have for smokers and candles and worked my way over to the sink.

Jake stopped me. "Hold on, Cash. What if I sweetened the deal for you, Carlos? If you free her and let bygones be bygones, I won't kill you. I've spared you twice now. This will be a third time. It's a win-win. You live, and your bosses aren't killing you for failing. Seems like a good deal." Jake pointed the gun right at Carlos' head. "I'm splitting soon anyway. What's a couple more dead security guards to me?"

"Take the deal, Carlos," the quiet Diego was awake enough to mumble.

Carlos looked like he wasn't new to having a gun pointed at his head as he pretended to be giving it some thought. "Okay."

"Okay then," I said. Skylar rubbed my thigh and let her fingernails dig in a little. She was happy.

I continued signing the papers. With Tyler's gun on the bar and with Carlos and Diego unarmed, Jake took the time to question Samantha about what the heck she was thinking. I heard her say she did it for Jake. She was just so grateful to him for saving her. She was just trying to help. Said if she wanted to keep the money, she just would have taken their car. I couldn't argue with that. She was probably right. She could have just popped Diego right there and taken off. He had the keys.

Just as I was telling Carlos that my lawyers would be checking the documents the next day and that I'd be getting my stuff out before they'd get the keys, Dillard and Simon burst through the back door with their guns on Jake.

"You're coming with us, Jake Chambliss. Drop it."

As Jake was lowering his weapon, Chief Deputy Tyler Graveline said, "Hold on. Cash Cutler and Jake Chambliss, you are under arrest for the murder of Chief Lyman Beck. Sorry, guys. These gentlemen have a more important issue to deal with."

"You can have Cutler. We don't care about him. We're taking Chambliss though. He's ours."

"Should I call your bosses in DC?"

"Sure. The number's on our card," Dillard pulled a card out and moved to hand it to Tyler.

"That's all right. I've got the home office number on my phone. Do you think I don't know what they're going to say? Do you think that doesn't give me reason enough to arrest you too, for impersonating federal officers?"

"You're going to arrest *us*? You lost your mind, boy?" Dillard pretended to be offended.

Jake lifted his gun in Dillard's direction. "Seems to me, you guys are the ones outgunned here."

"I oughta pop you right here, Chambliss."

"You'll be dead before he hits the ground, Dillard." Tyler was holding his ground. "I have a dead chief at the station, and these guys are spending the night in the holding cells. Run along, gentlemen. This is my jurisdiction."

Dillard reluctantly acquiesced. "We'll be back tomorrow afternoon with all the paperwork we'll need to take him off your hands. Make sure he goes nowhere."

"Whatever," Tyler said, "they'll be there."

Simon and Dillard backed their way out the door, unwilling to take their eyes off Jake and his persuader.

The room remained quiet until the car had officially left the front parking lot. Tyler watched from the window. Skylar was quietly encouraging me to run instead of getting arrested. I shook my head and whispered, "Don't worry." But I could tell she was.

Thank God for Carlos and Diego. Carlos interrupted Skylar's attempt to keep me free. "Eess time for us to go too. I need the paperwork though. You can have copies, but I can't leave the money without the signed paperwork, and, if I don't leave the money, the deal never happened. Gotta be deess way. Our people will contact your people and supply them copies." He continued with his fake accent. Strangest thing, but I didn't mention it.

"Okay," I said, "you can keep the money if you want though, you know, until I give you the keys."

"Like I said, my boss say I gotta leave the money. Don't come back with half-done deal. It must be done."

"Keys too?"

"No, we don't need keys. Just going to change the locks anyway. But you need to get your stuff out tonight."

"I might have a problem with that," I said, looking at Tyler.

"Not my problem. Eess just business."

"Okay, whatever. I'll figure it out." Other than the paperwork, none of this seemed legit, but I went with it anyway. I ripped my copies out of the paperwork that had carbon copies and had Shelly sign her document. Again, I wondered, how was that legal? It didn't say anything about the slavery, but it did say her debt to some LLC was taken care of with the completion of sale of The Trough to another LLC. Probably figured it would never see the light of a court room, seeing as Shelly was sure to just keep her mouth shut, for whatever reason they gave her. They may not seem like they're good businessmen, but they sure do have enough confidence in their being able to get it done though.

I gave him the folder of paperwork. He skimmed through it as if he were a secretly-educated lawyer, closed it up and proclaimed, "Looks good. Congratulations Cash Cutler, you are no longer the part owner of this bar."

I was hoping no one would notice his mention of my part-ownership. That was explained in my brother's letter to me, and I did not want to get into that at this moment.

As Carlos and Diego were leaving without Balozi, who wasn't hoping to get ride with them, Skylar alleviated my worry about that.

"Why are you arresting Cash? And Jake? They didn't kill the chief," she demanded of Tyler.

"I know they didn't," Tyler tried to comfort her.

"How?"

I told her quietly, "I got this. Don't worry about it."

Ainsley then kicked in, "Wait a minute. Chief Beck is really dead?"

"Yes ma'am," Tyler said, "I found him earlier."

"You didn't call this in?"

"To who, the police? I *am* the police."

"Good point. What about the body?" she followed up.

"He's still there. I couldn't let that get out, not knowing what was supposed to go down tonight."

"What about tomorrow? You just going to hand Jake over?"

"No. Tomorrow, I'll have those fake agents arrested for murdering Chief Beck and impersonating federal agents."

"How can you prove they did it?"

"Are you speaking as Jake's friend or as a reporter?"

"Both," Ainsley said.

"Then, I have no comment at this time," Tyler reverted to speaking as the chief deputy. I tried to calm Ainsley by touching her arm on the bar with my supposed barkeep's hand of calm. She just pulled away and went at Tyler from another direction.

"Oh, come on," she pleaded, "You can't arrest these guys and leave us hanging."

"I'm not arresting them. I just told those guys I would so they wouldn't take Jake. I know they want to kill him. I've got this."

"Wait a minute, Tyler," I said, "What if we give the footage to Ainsley? She could make these guys go away."

"Thought about it. No."

"You've got security footage of them?" Ainsley said. "What?"

234

Tyler finished, "No, I don't want them gone yet. I want to arrest them tomorrow when they come to the station."

"What if they come with more feds?" Jake asked. "You'll need backup. They're not alone, and they won't hesitate to kill you. I promise you. The cover up is that important. They're not just protecting a few agents. This goes up to the former head of the FBI and President Clinton himself. These aren't people you want to mess with. Trust me, Tyler. I'm just looking out for you. And don't worry about them leaving too soon. As long as I'm breathing, they'll be on my tail."

Tyler took this all in, nodding occasionally as Jake was speaking. "Then I've got my work cut out for me."

"You'll need our help," Jake said, pointing to me and then to Balozi with a questioning nod.

"Yes," Balozi said, "I'm with you, friend."

"That's three of us. Plus, you, that's four. May not be enough but makes your odds better."

"You can't be anywhere near there, Jake. None of you should. I have to call this in, and I'll have some officers from Lockport back me up. If you're there, it will just complicate everything. I can't have civilians doing this, especially a civilian with a conflict of interest. Besides, you need to clean this bar out tonight."

"That's nothing," I said, "just some old Starpoint jerseys and clean out the safe. I'm with Jake. I don't think you should do this alone either."

"Look, you can't be a part of arresting these guys," Tyler protested.

"And you assume you'll be able to arrest them," Jake said. "That's crazy. These guys will kill you. I promise that. They'll kill you and anyone with you. Those Lockport cops are going in by the book and they'll be slaughtered. You have no idea what you're up against."

"My hands are tied, Jake. I have to play this by the book."

"Then they'll kill you." Jake held his head low.

"A risk I have to take. You guys are already suspects in the other murders. How do you think it'll look if you get caught helping me take the feds off the table? The only reason you guys are free is that no one can figure which one of you did it."

"I see your point," I said. "What if we stay hidden and work as back up?"

"No, just stay away. And Ainsley, you cannot, whatsoever, report that you know about the death of Chief Beck. You cannot say a word. If the media show up, those guys will never come by. They know what they did."

Ainsley begged to differ. "As a reporter, I have an obligation to…"

Jake interrupted, "You can't."

"Okay, Jake."

"Wow," Tyler said, "if I had a dime for every time a reporter did that for me, I'd be broke." He smiled at Ainsley. "Thank you. You'll get the exclusive, and I'll give you the footage to boot. I just need to keep this quiet until we have Simon and Dillard in custody. I've gotta go. A lot to do before tomorrow. Just stay away. That's an order." He left through the front door.

I went into the kitchen, grabbed an empty lettuce box, taped up the bottom and filled it with the money and documents in the safe. I then took a few jerseys out of their glass cases and put them on top of the things from the safe. Lastly, I took a bunch of old photos off the walls. Just a few old photos of my parents and a few big moments of the restaurant and a couple of Cash in the bar. The box was a little top heavy but more than manageable. I noticed Samantha still sitting over by the door. She'd been quiet the whole time.

"You all right?" I asked her.

"I guess. I just don't know what I'm going to do now." She said it in a way only I could hear.

I didn't either. "I get it." I didn't really. "While I'll have a full house tonight, you can crash there. With us." I didn't actually think she was in cahoots with Balozi, and Jake was sure Balozi was on his side. I had to go with Jake's gut on that.

"Thanks." But her doubts were embedded in the sadness with which she spoke the thanks. She must not have been sure I'd be the one that could make that call.

Jake noticed it too. "Yeah Samantha, you can stay with us at Cash's tonight."

Ainsley heard that. "You're sleeping at Cash's tonight?" Samantha got sad again.

"I doubt I'll be sleeping much, Ainsley." Jake paused, realizing he might have given her and Samantha, who immediately brightened up, the wrong impression. "We have to prepare for tomorrow." Samantha darkened. Her face worked like one of those '70s hippie mood rings.

"Tomorrow?" Ainsley asked, pretending not to notice Samantha.

"We need to back Tyler up."

"He was adamant. Stay away. You can't go there." Ainsley was so worried about his safety, she was inadvertently talking him into having time to spend with the newly invited Samantha. So sweet.

"*You* need to stay away Ainsley," Jake said. "He just doesn't know what he's up against. He'll thank us later. If we're not needed, which is doubtful, he won't even know we were there. But, if I'm right, and I'm sure I am, he's going to need us."

"Do you want to crash at my place too, Ainsley?" I offered to even up the playing field.

"No, I can't. I have to be at work tomorrow. Brief the cap."

"Hold up," Jake said, "you can't yet. You can't let him know what you know, not 'til this is done."

"I don't have a choice, Jake. I have to tell him something."

"Not yet. Crash with us and call in sick or something."

"Cap knows I'm not sick. He'll never go for it."

"You've got the story of a lifetime coming. Just hang on. Go off the grid for a morning. That's all I ask."

"I don't know, Jake."

"He'll forgive you."

"Maybe. But I'm going home. I need to start getting some of this down on paper. There's so much."

"Don't let your boss know anything yet. Just promise me."

"I promise you, Jake."

"Thanks."

"Yeah. I'm gonna go." She left through the front door and Jake followed her to her car.

"All right then, let's get out of here," I said.

As I was leaving, I patted the doorframe and said, "Bye, Trough...for now at least." Then I shut the door.

We piled into my car. Balozi in the front seat, Skylar, Shelly and Samantha in the back. As we moved towards the front parking lot, I rolled down the window to talk with Jake. "You squishing in?"

"No, I'll take the four-wheeler. Can you let me back in to get my stuff?" I gave him the key.

"Lock it up when you're done."

Samantha got out and said, "I'll ride with Jake."

At that moment, I realized I'd stupidly left the letter with Ainsley. Oh man. I mean seriously, what was I thinking?

Chapter 34

After leaving the bar, Agents Bob Dillard and Sam Simon drove east toward Five Corners in Pendleton. After driving nearly a mile Dillard said, "Turn around here."

Simon turned the lights out and turned around to park on the snow just shy of the ditch and the foot-wide snow-covered gravel shoulder of the small-town road. They were halfway parked on the west-bound lane.

"You sure this is good enough cover?" Simon questioned.

"Yeah, it's fine. She'll be going the other way anyway."

It wasn't a stake out like the old days. It was just a strategic retreat and strategizing. They would have lost at the bar, and now they had to find the weak link. They waited.

"Here she comes." It was Ainsley's Prius. "Get down."

The Prius was quiet, but they still heard the slush on the road get parted by her tiny tires, the sound of a wave splashing on the shore. Simon looked back to make sure she was alone.

"The tiny sheep strays from the herd."

After letting her pass, they turned around and only turned their lights back on once she'd turned the corner.

"Look's like Jake's spending his last night on earth with the whore and not the reporter."

"Ah," Dillard grumbled, "they're both whores. One wants money, the other wants the story."

"Heh. What do you want to do with this one?"

"Follow her. We'll get her at her place, make sure we have everything she has on Jake Chambliss."

"We gonna kill her there?"

239

"Now, why would we do that? We need her to get Jake. Once we have Jake, we'll kill her then."

"So, she's our paperwork. Saves a lot of writer's cramp."

"Yeah, it does. And don't even think about trying to sleep with her, Sam. She's not for you."

"You don't know that. She might like a little Vitamin S, especially since she's never gonna get with Jake."

"Shut up, Sam. Keep it in your pants."

"I'm just joking with you. I know you won't let me sleep with her unless she invites me to her bed. But don't be surprised if she does."

"Same ole' Sam. Somethings never change. It's good to be back with you. This is fun."

"Yep, just like old times."

Chapter 35

The lights were on in the house when I pulled in. Jake and Samantha had beaten us, taking the back trails.

Samantha was on the couch scanning for news stories. Jake was digging through the fridge.

Shelly was tired and couldn't stop yawning, so I told Skylar to set her up in one of the guest rooms. I set the box of bar stuff on the table and the briefcase next to it.

"Goodnight, Shelly," Samantha said as Shelly walked through the living room.

"Goodnight, sweetie. I just want to say, I'm glad you made it out."

"Thanks, Shelly. I'm glad you're out of there too. Get some sleep."

"Oh, I don't have much choice in the matter. I'll be sleeping before my head hits the pillow." Skylar led her upstairs.

Balozi took a seat at the dining room table. "You hungry?" I asked him.

Jake responded, "I'm making food for everyone." He had a pot of water boiling and a pan of sauce warming up. "We're gonna carb up for tomorrow." Nothing like a good old spaghetti dinner before the game. Reminding me of the old all-you-can-eat fundraising carb-up pasta dinners in high school, he knew exactly what I was thinking. He winked at me to tell me I was welcome for the memory.

"I'll be back," I said. I grabbed the briefcase and the lettuce box. Walking past the room where Skylar and Shelly were talking, I leaped up the stairs to the barracks. I closed the door and locked it, hoping to be quicker than Skylar would be with her mom. They did hopefully seem to be in some sort of mother-daughter heart-to-heart. If not though, I knew she'd head right up here if I wasn't quick.

I moved the bed and lifted the boards. The stacks of cash had taken most of the room, so I had to move a few of them to slide the briefcase back under the boards that weren't lifted. I put the important stuff from the box in there as well. This reminded me of the letter I needed to get back from Ainsley. I sure hoped she didn't read it, but it was opened. The fact that she's a reporter made my hopes null and void in my head.

241

How was I going to explain the meaning of the letter and why I gave it to *her*, of all people?

Honestly, she was the only option I had at that moment. Tyler was a cop trying to rule us out as suspects. I didn't know if I'd be getting killed. I considered that evidence in case I did get arrested. Couldn't risk losing it in the bar that might blow up. Was hoping she'd be out of there before the cartel guys had arrived. Didn't quite know yet that Skylar knew who I was, and I didn't have the luxury of walking out to the bushes and giving away Jake's position. Who knew who was watching us? Giving it to Ainsley was the last worst option I had. I had to count on her adoration of Jake to keep it a secret. Samantha wasn't making that easy. She and Ainsley were kind of alike in that matter. Neither hesitated in going after what they wanted. Too bad they wanted the same person. Trouble ahead.

As I was moving the bed back into place, the doorknob rattled, and a knock followed. Skylar.

"Whatcha doing, Cash?"

"Just tidying up."

I let her in.

"Why'd you lock the door?"

"Didn't know I had. Old habits never die, I guess."

"Gotta lock the door to the barracks, huh?"

"Not a barracks if just about anyone can get in here. Right?"

"I'm in here."

"You're not just anyone though. You're a damsel. In distress." She sat on my brother's old bed, the one that doesn't cover the stash of money. The box was on the other bed.

"Hmm. That mean you thought about what I said earlier?" She patted her hand on bed next to her.

"Not deeply, no," I said. "Didn't have a lot of time to be thinking."

"Yeah, I get that. Come sit."

I neared her but didn't sit yet. "Let me ask you something, Skylar..."

"Of course."

"What if I say no? I'm not saying that's what I'm saying. I just want to know where you're at."

242

"I don't know. Haven't thought about it. But I like you."

"How do you know? You barely even know me."

"Not true. I've known you through your brother, and, the secret's out, I've always liked you better. I could see you weren't happy with Callie, and I always figured that's because your brother was sleeping with her. He denied it to me, but admitted he had in the past. I could see you were miserable though. Callie... I'm not going to say that."

"Good, don't. Did you ever love my brother?"

"No. Not really. No. I had a job, and I think he knew it. I think he sensed it and was just letting me do what I needed. That, and I knew what he was doing. If he broke up with me, he knew I knew too much. It wasn't real. He was always too busy trying to outwit himself to hide what he was doing while regretting he'd ever gotten into this mess. Me, I was just an afterthought. That, or he resented me for pushing him into it."

"You pushed him into it?"

"A little. It was my job. Get close to him and talk him into taking the deal when the deal came."

"That's kind of bad."

"I know. I feel terrible, but it was the only way to save my mother. Please forgive me."

"I get it. But how do you know what you feel for me is real?"

"Woman's intuition, I guess. There's more to you. That's why I let you know I knew who you were. I don't want lies and secrets between us."

"I appreciate that. But how do I know you'll be there if this all ever gets sorted out? I mean, I don't even know if we're going to live through tomorrow, and who knows what's coming after that? I'm still a suspect in my brother's murder."

"I know, and I know you didn't do it. It will get sorted out. And tomorrow, you've got Jake. He ain't gonna let anything happen to you. Speaking of Jake, holy cow. What's he going to do? Samantha and Ainsley both like him. What's up with that?"

"I don't know what he's thinking about them two. Haven't had a chance to ask. But I like your confidence."

"By the way, did you know Cash had sold half the bar already? I changed the subject quickly tonight, but did you know about that?"

"No, not 'til I read his letter earlier."

"What letter? Can I see it?"

"No, I gave it to Ainsley."

"To Ainsley? You crazy? She'll blow your cover."

"Nah, she won't. Likes Jake too much, and I'll just tell her I was getting rid of a letter I'd written to my brother in case I didn't make it. She already knows that Cash was in trouble and that's why Jake came back."

"Might work. Don't you think she'll wonder why you didn't just destroy it like you were going to destroy the bar documents?"

"A small problem on top a slew of big ones. I can't worry about that right now."

I moved over to the bed where she was sitting and took a seat next to her. She threw her arms around me and just held me.

"I get it," she whispered and kissed me on the cheek.

"We should head downstairs."

I turned the light out when we left. *What should I do, Cash?*

Chapter 36

Sam Simon and Bob Dillard drove by Ainsley's house, just as she'd shut the front door. He turned around in the parking lot of the pizza joint and parked on the same side of the road as Ainsley's house.

"We going in now, or you want to wait?"

Dillard said, "Let her get settled. Living room light's still on."

After thirty minutes, the light was still on.

"All right, let's go. Too frickin' cold out here," Dillard declared.

They couldn't see anything through the shade of the window. A neighbor's dog started to bark, but he was indoors. Dillard picked the lock with some tools he'd pulled from his glove compartment. As quietly as possible, he opened the door and walked in. Simon followed.

Ainsley was in her baby blue pajamas holding a gun. "Get out of here."

"No ma'am," Dillard said, "we're here for your protection." He had his hands up, but Simon's gun was pointed at Ainsley to even the odds.

"I don't need your protection. Wouldn't want it if I did. Please go."

"As I'm sure you can understand, we can't yet. We need to apprehend our fugitive, and we need your help."

"I'm not helping you get Jake."

"Put the gun down and we'll talk. You can't go shooting FBI agents."

"You're not agents. I know the truth."

"You know the lies of a charming fugitive. There's not a thing he says you can believe. Jake will say anything to avoid justice. Please put the gun down, and we'll talk. We're civilized people."

"You're lying."

"No, we can prove it."

"How?"

"Put the gun down." Dillard moved in and took the gun from her shaking hand and slapped her with his right hand. "Sit down." He pushed her into the couch. Simon kept his gun pointed at her.

"What do you want with me?"

"You're going to help us apprehend a wanted fugitive. That's it."

"You going to kill me?"

"Why would we do that?"

"Because I know too much?"

"Do you?"

"No."

"What do you know? Do you know he's wanted for treason? Do you know he is wanted for aiding and abetting a terrorist? Do you know he went AWOL?"

"No, I didn't know any of that."

"Then you don't know too much, do you? We don't have to kill you. We just need your help."

"Why do you think I'll help you?"

"Because, as a public servant and journalist, you have no other goal than to seek the truth. Jake Chambliss is a bad man. That's the truth. You do want justice, right?"

"How do I know you aren't the bad men?"

"We are FBI agents. We're sworn to protect and serve. That's why."

"But what about what Tyler said, that…"

"Don't worry about what Jake's buddy said. He and Jake go way back. You can't trust a thing that guy says either. Why else would he be stuck in a podunk little town handing out speeding tickets and saving cats from trees? We're the real deal, ma'am. Ask your boss if he thinks you should help us. Call him."

"All right, give me my phone." She pointed to it on her coffee table.

"Ah, there it is," Dillard picked it up and lit it up by pushing a button, apparently to see what time it was. He looked at the call history and put it in his pocket. "It's too late to call him now. You can call him tomorrow. For now, get some sleep. We're crashing here to keep you safe. In the meantime, where is all the stuff you have on the Cutlers and Jake?"

"At my office. Why?"

"What about on this computer?" He pointed to her opened laptop on her desk next to her TV. Dillard told Simon, "Check that first."

Simon looked at the most recently opened files, all of which had to do with the Cutlers, and one had to do with Jake Chambliss. He skimmed through them.

"Looks like she's writing an exposé filled with Jake Chambliss' lies."

"See ma'am, it's our job to make sure none of those lies see the light of day. Close it and set it over there." Dillard pointed to the doorway.

"Of course, it is," Ainsley sneered.

Dillard said, "Check the rest of the house."

Simon proceeded to look through the kitchen, the drawers, cupboards, the fridge and any place where something might be hidden. Then he made his way to her bedroom. Checked her drawers, the mattress, under the bed, the closet, boxes in the closet. Then he looked through the bathroom, where he spent more time examining the panties she'd dropped to the floor than the medicine cabinet or the vanity. After smelling them, he returned her panties where he found them by the tub. Nothing.

Dillard went through her purse while she watched. He set it down.

"Don't take this personal. National security requires we do this."

Ainsley scoffed, "Chinese national security, maybe. What happened to a free press?"

"Nothing, but national security takes precedence. Without security, there is no free press."

Simon came back. "I didn't find anything."

"Put her to bed."

Simon demanded, "Follow me."

He led her to her bedroom, which he'd left a mess. He put a cuff on her hand and attached it to her bed frame. "Get some sleep. Tomorrow's a new day."

Simon and Dillard each took an end of the couch to get some sleep.

As Dillard was nodding off, Ainsley's phone rang. He pulled it out of his pocket. It said AJ was calling. He hit ignore and put it back in his pocket. Must be a boyfriend he thought. What about her thing for Jake? Nah, whatever.

His eyes closed again heavily.

Chapter 37

When Skylar and I had come back downstairs, Jake was serving spaghetti with some meatballs he'd fried up in the pan. Samantha had found her way from the couch to the dining room table, where she was keeping Balozi company. Balozi wasn't very talkative.

I couldn't really figure him out. I just trusted Jake on that. Seemed like an African thing, a little too esoteric for my understanding. He didn't hesitate to eat though. Jake gave him a helping twice as large as he gave the less-than-half-his-size Samantha. She didn't hesitate either. Midnight hunger will not be denied.

He served me up large, Skylar a smaller portion, fixed himself a nice-sized plate, and then joined us at the table. I got up and grabbed some bread and butter. It wasn't the most sophisticated sauce and meatballs, but who had time for some Sunday sauce? We needed to eat and plan.

"You still have your dad's thirty-aught-six?" Jake asked me.

"Upstairs."

"Sighted?"

"Yep. Good to go. I have tons of ammo too."

"I always liked that gun."

"He did too."

"I'm going to use that gun." He took a bite and chewed a bit. "You guys good with the ARs?" He pointed to them leaning up against the cupboard corner near where the door opens.

"Fine with me," I said.

"Balozi?"

"That will be fine."

"I'm going to post up in the hedge row just to the north of the police station. Gives me a view of the parking lot and the door."

"Where should we be?" I asked.

"What do you think, Cash? You know the area better than I do."

"Honestly, I think we should all be in that hedge row, maybe separated. There's no other doors to the station, so, I don't see much point in being around back. If we're needed, might as well be close to *where* we're needed."

"What I think too, but I wanted your input. I'll stand up front. Balozi, you back about fifteen feet, and Cash, you back another fifteen feet. Don't think we should be too close. Three targets are better than one. There's some big trees there, right?"

"Big enough to blend in."

"You have any white camo?"

"Maybe someplace," I said, "one coat. I have a bunch of green camo coats, though."

"All right," Jake said, "you wear the white, and Balozi and I will wear the green camos. Face paints?"

"Yes."

"Find them too."

"Are you going to kill those guys?" I asked.

"No. Can't. That's murder one. I take them out, more will come, and I'll never get justice. I don't even want to shoot them. That's attempted murder."

"I thought they were fake."

"No, they're real. Real agents anyway. Just not active. Off the books, but still agents of the government. You guys can't kill them either. Only shoot them if they're about to kill you, and that will only happen if they've already killed me. Don't give up your position unless I'm already dead. Let me handle this. You got that?"

"Yes," I said.

"Balozi?"

"Got it."

After swallowing, he continued. "I mean it. This is my battle. You don't need to be a part of this. You're just my backup. Only reason you might need to shoot is if I'm dead, and they're about to kill Tyler. If that's the case, do what you think. If you can save

250

Tyler, do it. But if Tyler and I are both dead, get out of there and make sure they don't know you were there. Otherwise, they'll come for you too. No revenge. Just let it be. I'm serious about this. If I'm dead, so be it. I don't need vengeance." He took another bite.

I nodded.

"We need to dress warm. We're going in early."

"What time?"

"7:30. Tyler won't be there before that. Remember, my only goal is to get them in those cells. Tyler can handle it from there, and we can then figure out who killed Curt and Callie."

"By the way," I said, "I think I've got something. You ain't gonna like it though."

"Why? What is it?"

"Not quite sure, but I think it might have something to do with the enemy of U.S. Attorney Bennett Glazebrook."

"What enemy?"

"He's planning on running a primary against Congressman Porter Nichols."

"Oh," Jake said.

"I've got a folder's worth of paperwork on how Glazebrook, whose wife works with the governor, has been making money off the drug trade in Buffalo to Niagara Falls. It's obvious. I just followed the money. He's dirty in a big way, and the only reason to kill Curt was to open up the books that prove he's guilty. Who benefits? Porter Nichols."

"Is Nichols dirty too?"

"Well, he *is* in government."

"Good point. So, you want to kick a killer hornets' nest?"

"Or go to jail for a murder I didn't commit," I said sarcastically.

"Then we'll kick it hard and bring a flame thrower," Jake said. "No other leads? You sure about this?"

"Not absolutely sure, but I can't get anything else. I spoke to one of the board members, and he pointed me in the direction. Tyler did too. All the other board members are in hiding."

"What board members?" Skylar asked.

251

"The board for my brother's bank. Said they were only trying to acquire the Iroquois bank in order to get a look at their books. It's running money for the casinos but also the for the cartel running the drugs and prostitutes."

Samantha looked up. "Sex slaves, you mean. I was a sex slave. I didn't grow up hoping to be a prostitute. Trust me."

"Yes. I didn't mean anything bad."

"I know," she said, "just want you to understand what you're up against. They're not just a bunch of beeesinessmen." She tilted her head left, right, left and right while rolling her eyes as she imitated Carlos. "They're monsters. I was a sex slave. Not some girl who likes getting raped by creeps."

"I know," I said.

"Are you sure you know?" She seemed like she was trying to warn me off.

Jake interrupted. "What about your family, Samantha? Are they safe?"

"I think so. My mom's out of the country right now. She's all I have left."

"You've spoken with her?"

"Yes. She wanted to come back, but I told her not to. Told her to watch her back though."

"Can they figure out where she is?"

"No. She's not even from here. Has a different name in a different state. I doubt they'll go after her. Probably don't even know who she is."

"What were you so worried about?" Jake asked.

"I wasn't worried about her. I was really worried about me. I was just explaining why the others wouldn't come. Most of them have family right here, and they are in fear. Really though, I doubt those people are still at the hotel. I'm sure they've been cleared out by now. If the Mexicans aren't working with the Indians, the Indians are going to hide the evidence."

"You think they'll kill them?" Skylar asked nervously.

Balozi answered, "No. The Indians aren't like the Mexicans. They want to be good businessmen, you know, better than the Mexicans at least. I was there before the Mexicans came, and they weren't breaking the law much. Not too violent either."

"I wasn't there that long," Samantha said, "but I don't think the Indians are anything like the Mexicans. I agree. Doubt they'll kill them. They have bigger problems to deal with."

Skylar broke in. "Not to change the subject, but I want to. Balozi and Jake, what is it between you? Balozi goes from wanting to kill you to your best friend in the snap of a finger. What's that all about?"

Balozi answered, "I saw my tribe's markings on his wrist. I also saw the markings of other tribes. Those markings make him a friend of my tribe and a friend of other tribes. If I killed him, all of those tribes would be my enemy, including my own. That bond is much more sacred than the one I had with Carlos and Diego or with the casino. I made a choice."

"Wow," Skylar said in awe. "What about you Jake? What made you change?"

"It was just like he said. Those tribes gave me these markings as a thank you and for protection out in the world. By marking me, they were warning all my enemies, that, to be my enemy, that made them enemies of the tribes as well. That sound about right, Balozi?"

"Yes, about right." He nodded and smiled at Jake.

We finished eating, and Jake started clearing the table.

"Stop, Jake," Skylar said, "I'll get that. Go get some sleep."

Samantha got up to help as well.

"Are you going to sleep, Jake?" I asked it because he said he wasn't planning on going to sleep earlier.

"I don't know. A lot to think about. I'll probably just watch a little TV on the couch."

"I've got a room for you, Balozi, right through that door there." I pointed to the downstairs bedroom to the left of the stairway and bathroom.

"Thank you. I will try to get some sleep."

"I'm going to go get our supplies ready," I said. I walked up the stairs.

I brought their camos, a wooden box full of ammo and the thirty-aught-six down and put them on the dining room table, which had already been cleaned. I leaned the gun against the cupboard with the others. Jake was on the couch, Balozi was in the other room, and Skylar and Samantha were doing the dishes. I could hear them giggling like sisters.

"I'm going to go get some shut-eye. See you in the morning," I said.

"I'll be right up, Cash. Almost done." She was so real and natural, I no longer knew if Skylar and I were acting or if this was my life from then on. No time to figure it out though. More pressing issues.

253

I set the clothes I was going to wear on the hamper next to my bed, got undressed and climbed in bed. It had to be one of the most tiring days of my life. I was just about asleep in a matter of minutes when the door opened, latched shut and clicked locked. A few seconds later, a naked Skylar was climbing up on me and making it impossible for me to get back to sleep. Not a word was said.

Chapter 38

Jake was staring at the TV but not paying attention at all to the infomercial that was playing. Fearing the drama of a nightmare and wondering which one he was about to have, he was in no hurry to fall asleep, but he was tired enough to know he eventually would. He tried to focus on his visualization techniques. He was visualizing the mission, while at the same time trying to keep his fury under control. He didn't want to kill the agents but knew he might. Breathe and visualize, breathe in, breathe out...

Skylar broke his focus when she kissed him on the forehead. "Good luck tomorrow, Jake. Please take care of my Cash."

He looked up at her and nodded. A slight smile.

"Thanks. Get some sleep," Skylar said as she walked up the stairs.

Samantha grabbed his attention as she came into the living room from the kitchen. She was really beautiful, even after a crazy day's events and without all her makeup. She was no longer the plastic princess but a real woman, wiping her wet hands on the T-shirt she'd changed into after they'd gotten home. It was so oversized, it must have been Cash's.

"We're all alone," she said with a growing smile.

Jake sat up a bit, trying to figure out how everyone had just left him alone with her without even offering her a place to sleep. *What are you doing to me, Cash-Curt?*

Jake looked around for show. "I guess you're right."

"Were you sleeping, Jake Charm?"

"No, just thinking about tomorrow."

"Don't think about that right now. Tomorrow can wait."

"You know I can't stop. I'm just thinking about what I have to do and how I'm going to do it."

"Yeah, I know," Samantha said, as she climbed onto his lap, much like she had before.

"What are you doing?"

"Thanking you for dinner. It was delicious."

"This isn't necessary."

She kissed him on the lips while moving his hands to her butt. She was wearing tight black leggings. He just left them there still, and then she grabbed the back of his neck and kissed him as passionately as she had earlier.

"I can't do this," Jake said.

"You promised."

"Promised what?"

"That you'd let me finish the kiss if we made it out alive. Guess what, Jake Charm, I'm cashing in on your promise."

"Oh, right."

She resumed kissing him. He kissed her back a little and then stopped. It was the nicest kiss he'd ever had, and he so wanted to give in. But he couldn't.

Samantha pulled back and said, "Maybe you *are* gay."

"No. I just can't, Samantha. It's not right."

"What's not right?"

"None of it, Samantha. I'm not in love with you."

"Well, I'm not in love with you either, baby. Doesn't mean I can get you out of my mind. That's more than enough, isn't it?"

"No, Samantha. It shouldn't be. Have you ever been in love? I mean, really in love with a person?"

"Yeah, sure, a few times. When I was younger."

"Do you have those feelings for me?"

"I don't know. Probably more, for you." She stole a kiss.

"Yeah, that's just because I'm the one that got you out of there. If that hadn't happened. If I was just a cowboy, like you used to call me, calling you up, as you'd told me to do, would you have these feelings for me?"

"Not at all. You'd just be another guy."

"Exactly. But now I'm not just another guy. I did something for you, and you feel like you owe me."

"No, that's not it, Jake. I like you. You've done nothing but treat me like a human. No one else does."

"But they should, and you know what, now that you're out of there, they will. You just need to let them. Don't let them treat you any other way. Take your time with people. They're not all going to dehumanize you."

"But I don't have time with you. After tomorrow, you might be gone."

"Don't say that. It's bad luck."

"I don't mean it like that," she said apologetically. "I mean, you said yourself, you'll have to leave."

"And that's true. If I do this with you now and then leave, won't I just be doing exactly what everyone else has done? It's not fair to you, and that's the last thing I want to do to you. I like you, Samantha, but it's not right to love you and leave you. That's what I mean when I say it's not right. I don't know where I'll be in two days, let alone next week. I'm on the run."

"Let me go with you. I'll be your back up, like tonight."

"You can't. You don't want that kind of life, trust me."

"I find it hard to trust anyone who says trust me, and how do you know? Look where I just came from, Jake. Anything's better than that."

"Yeah, maybe, but…"

"Maybe you'll let me go?" she asked flirtingly.

"No, maybe it's better than what you've been living, but…"

"Listen, Jake. I've got nothing. I don't have a place to live, I don't have a job, I have no money. I have nothing. And for all I know, I'm on the run too. Who knows what the Mexicans will do? They wanted to kill me tonight. Sure, they'd have waited until they were bored of raping me, but they were going to kill me. You know…"

"I know. These are good points. Let me think about it." Jake kissed her on the head and picked her up under her arms and set her to the side.

"So that's it?" she said, somewhat offended.

"I have to focus on the morning. Otherwise, I might end up dead. You don't want that, do you?"

257

"'Course not. I was just hoping to give you something to remember me by. Something that might make you come back, you know, if you don't take me with you."

"I get it. I just can't accept it. You're fragile right now, and you just need to get your life back in order."

"You sound like a social worker."

"Don't mean to, I've just helped enough people out of bad situations to know they don't always have the ability to make good decisions right off. You first need to understand that life isn't anything like what you've just been through."

"Jake?"

"Yeah?"

"If I wasn't in love with you five minutes ago, I think I am now. You're not just another pretty face."

Jake laughed a little. "I know. There's a lot to me."

"You're not too conceited, are you?"

"No. If I was, I'd just love you and leave you. Not feel a thing."

"All right," she said with a beaming smile that was lipstick free, "let's try that. If you can actually do that, I won't go with you when you leave."

"Sounds like a good deal."

"I don't think you *can* do it," she said with her own confidence.

"Now who's conceited? You're probably right though. We'll just have to wonder."

She grabbed a pillow from the other end of the couch and hit him in the chest. "You are so aggravating."

"That's not the worst of my problems."

"Probably not," she said, "so you win, for now."

"Thanks, Samantha."

"Just focus. Do what you have to, so you don't get killed tomorrow. Mind if I lay next to you and go to sleep?"

"No, that's fine."

He laid his head against the low couch back, and she nuzzled into his chest with her arm across his abs. He considered it a good compromise and went back to focusing and visualizing. She fell asleep.

He carefully grabbed the remote, so as not to disturb her. He surfed a little but found nothing that would take his mind off the mission ahead.

Chapter 39

Junior-high Jake was playing hockey on the field ice out behind Hebelers, the ATV and motorcycle dealer, with a bunch of older kids. The makeshift hockey rink was only good in the perfect winter weather. Cold and not super snowy. There was a shovel plow to clear the ice if it got too covered, and there were two nets to get a full rink going.

During those perfect weekends, if you wanted to play hockey, you just showed up. Cash and Curt met Jake there, and they figured out how to get some playing time with the high school kids. Sure, they were smaller, but they were drinking milk. Going up against the guys who are bigger, faster and stronger was always a good way to get better.

Jake and Curt were on Jimmy Owens' team, and Cash was on Tim McVeigh's team. Tim wasn't a super strong kid, but he knew how to skate and play hockey. He was tall and skinny, but even though he wasn't built like the football guys, he had leverage over Jake, who still had a bunch of growth spurts to hit. Jimmy's little sister Wendy was over on the other piece of ice figure skating with Callie. Jake liked Callie and was very conscious of his performance that day. Nothing like victory on the ice to impress the girl he liked.

If he played well, and she noticed, that would be good. If he got crushed, hopefully she wouldn't notice. He knew she knew he liked her, but he was still too shy to say it out loud. Today was his day. He didn't know why, but today was his day.

Problem was, Tim McVeigh was beating Jake on the ice like a rented mule. He'd already stolen the puck from Jake three times and outskated him to the net every time. Went one goal for three opportunities. Jake couldn't keep his eyes off Callie and Wendy. Why weren't they looking over?

So, he decided to go for it. Instead of getting beat, he was going to take Tim out. Make a little excitement. She was sure to wonder what all the noise was about and look over to see Jake beating the upperclassman.

Tim was skating at Jake, and Jake, pretending to go for the puck, jabbed his stick between Tim's legs, missing the puck, and then skated to the right. His stick swept Tim's legs and took him to the ice. Sure, it was tripping, and everyone on the ice knew it was on purpose. Callie wasn't looking.

Jake pretended to apologize to Tim who hit the ice hard, but no one thought it was over. Tim took a penalty shot and scored. Those were neighborhood-ice rules. Undisputed penalties got you a free shot. That way no one had to watch a clock for two-minutes to run a penalty box.

They continued to play, and Tim just kept beating Jake, who eventually called a time out to take a leak. Because the ladies were out there, he actually walked in the snow with his skates over to the trees to do his business. A couple of other guys took the time to do the same thing as well.

Jake dropped his stick in the snow behind him, put his gloves in his pockets, undid three layers of pants and thermals, and got the job done. As he was peeing, he heard some foot thuds behind him. And then boom, he got pushed in the back hard. His head went back, while his body moved forward. He was still in his skates, and that didn't make staying on his feet any easier. He hit the snow hard and peed all over his leg accidentally.

This was the one time he didn't want Callie to be looking, but everyone was. He zipped up his pants while on the ground, turned around to look up and find the tall and lanky Tim McVeigh laughing at him. "That's for the trip."

Now, thing was, Tim McVeigh was not a bully. He was laughing, but it was more of a laughing with Jake than at him. But Jake had no way to decipher that. He was way too concerned about what Callie would think of what he did next.

Tim, with a smile on his face, leaned over and grabbed Jake's unwashed hand to help him up. Jake took it and used the help to get to his feet, but as soon as he was up, Jake lunged at and punched the unprepared Tim in the face as hard as he could.

Tim spun a hundred and eighty and bent over with his hands cupping his face. His nose was gushing with blood. He put a handful of snow to his face, but it just turned red and melted. The nose wanted to bleed. Fight was over.

Jake looked himself over to see if there was any pee on his pants. If there was, it couldn't be deciphered from the snow-caused wetness without a sensitive nose in the near vicinity, but that didn't take away the shame Jake felt after being knocked into the same snow he'd just turned yellow.

After being pushed down, a fury ignited immediately, and that's why he hit Tim. If you'd asked him why, he would've had no answer. To answer that question required some sort of premeditation. There was none. He went from zero to the speed of sound in a flash of lightning. Not even Einsteinian thoughts occur that fast.

People noticed. He heard one of the older kids say, "Where the hell did that kid come from?" And a few other things too insignificant to remember. It was just crowd chatter.

261

He was nearly a foot shorter than Tim, a whole bunch lighter, and three or four grades younger.

Unable to even know where this ferocity came from and not even able to understand it, Jake held his head down. He tilted his eyes upward to keep an eye on what was coming but hid his face. What emotion do you show at a time like this? He didn't know, so he hid his face and walked past Tim without even acknowledging him. He almost apologized, but he didn't – a point that haunts him to this day. Probably the reason he's had this dream so often.

Everything had stopped, the game and the girl skaters. Surely most of them were hoping to see a fight, but, at the same time, it ended so quickly and without any braggadocious fanfare. Okay, that happened. We still playing?

Tim was holding his nose in a fresh handful of snow, trying to hold his head back a bit so the blood would stop flowing. He was done for the day. He eventually sat in the snow, with blood flowing over his lips and down to his chin, took off his hockey skates, slammed them into the snow and replaced them with his boots. When he got up, he didn't even say goodbye to anyone. Just turned and walked through the field alone using his stick as a cane. He walked north east towards Main Road and Campbell Boulevard, where he lived.

Jake walked over past the girl's ice. Callie and Wendy were standing there with puzzled looks.

"Why'd you hit him so hard, Jake Chambliss?" That was the first thing Callie'd said to him in the nearly two weeks that had passed since someone told her Jake Chambliss liked her and made everything weird. He wasn't yet known as Jake Charm. Still just Jake Chambliss, and she used his last name to emphasize her disgust. He felt it burn.

He wanted to feel like Jake Champ, but the scorn in Callie's voice made that impossible. He was just Jake Chambliss, and Callie was the girl who didn't impress easily. Sure, there was no premeditation in what he did, but what was he going to say?

"Hi Callie." He lifted his hand for a quick wave and quickly brought it down while he posed his lips and cheeks for a juvenile's facial claim of innocence. "I don't know."

"You don't know? You probably broke his nose, Jake. Why?" She said his name in a scolding manner.

"I don't know. It just happened."

"Oh my gosh, Jake. You didn't have to do that."

Jake didn't have anything to say that would help deal with the shame he felt. Also, the sorrow about ruining any chance he might have had with Callie. He couldn't even imagine telling her the only answer he could come up with: "I don't know that I *did* do it. It was like I was taken over by my anger and controlled by instinct…" He didn't really know how to say anything like that without having to be worried about being called Psycho Jake for the rest of his life. So, he said nothing. He was more afraid of himself than Tim McVeigh was, and Tim walked away after one punch.

Jake took Tim's lead and went in a different direction. Instead of suffering with Callie's seemingly incessant shaming, he switched his skates for his boots, tied the skate laces together and threw them over his back like Tim had done just a few minutes earlier.

Walking through the choppy field towards the road with the ever-silencing crowd chatter of those he'd left behind, Jake saw a lot of snowy white with tunnel vision. Tears welling up in his eyes blurred his peripheral vision, but he just kept walking…

***

Jake Chambliss woke up in a sweat. While he had repeatedly relived this moment of his life in his dreams over and over, it was never one of the violent nightmares he considered to be in his top ten least favorite. However, it was the oldest recurring dream he couldn't stop having.

It normally left him wondering, what if he'd never punched Tim McVeigh? Would Tim have become such a stellar soldier? Was that why he was dragged into the whole Oklahoma City bombing scheme? Was this the moment that Tim decided to never get bullied again? Whenever Jake put himself in Tim's hockey skates, he could never imagine what it would be like to get his face blasted by a kid who was four years younger. It violated every code of conduct for the youth of America.

But this night wasn't normal. Instead, his first thoughts on the night he woke up in Cash's living room were: *Who is this laying on me?* and *What did I do?*

It was Samantha, and he calmly remembered he did not violate his own code of conduct. As he stood up, he helped shift Samantha to the other arm of the couch.

She startled though and woke up. "Hey, you all right? You're covered in sweat." She rubbed his belly. "It's barely four in the morning. Go back to sleep."

"No, can't, gotta go. They've got her."

"Got who? Who's got her?"

"Dillard and Simon. They've got Ainsley." He got up and took off his wet shirt and put on some thermals Cash had left him.

"What are you talking about? Ainsley went home. Remember? Last night?"

"No. I called her, and she didn't answer. Didn't think much of it at the time, but…"

"She was probably sleeping," Samantha tried to reassure him.

"No, she'd have been writing. Wanted to get it on paper. She told me that. Said she'd be up until five, probably. Had too much to get down before she forgot it."

"She's fine."

"I gotta go. Tell Cash and Balozi to post up out there if I don't get back in time. But I'll be back. Remind him not to call me. If he needs to talk to me, let him use your phone. I'll answer if I can."

"Will you answer if I call?"

"Don't. Only in emergencies. I need as much radio silence as possible."

He tied his boots tight, put on a hat, grabbed his keys from his inner pants, checked his Glock, grabbed a few boxes of ammo from Cash's big box on the table, pocketed them and then grabbed one of the ARs. This wasn't a sniper situation. He didn't need the bolt-action rifle. He needed a semi-automatic persuader with human-sawing capabilities.

He was ready to walk out the door when Samantha ran over to try once more and stop him. "Jake, hold on a sec. How do you know they have her?"

"Because that's exactly what I would do."

"What?"

"After they left, they waited for her to leave and followed her home. They knew they weren't going to get official paperwork to get me in custody. That was a bluff. They need a chip. Ainsley's their chip."

"Why, 'cause you like Ainsley?"

"It's not like that. If they had you, I'd do whatever I could to save you too."

"I'm just messing with you. You're lucky I have morning breath right now because I want to kiss you big-time, Jake." That didn't stop her from throwing her arms around him and hugging him. He let her, hoping she'd stop soon so he could go. She whispered, "Be safe, Jake Charm," into his ear and finally released him.

"Okay, gotta go."

Chapter 40

Sam Simon woke up on Ainsley Reed's couch to Bob Dillard's incessantly loud snoring. Just like old times. One thing Sam knew, Dillard wasn't going to wake up. He'd learned to sleep through just about anything back in the war, and Simon learned that, if you want to get any sleep in the room with Dillard, you need to fall asleep first and don't bother waking up.

Simon was awake. Kicking Dillard did no good. Never did. The man was a snorer.

Sam got up, walked into the kitchen and poured himself a glass of water. Then he giggled at himself for thinking he should wipe the prints off the glass. What for? He's with the FBI. Once a fed, always a fed. While he knew he wasn't supposed to feel it, he felt above the law. Why would anyone go and find a fed's prints and think something untoward? Then he giggled at the use of the word untoward in his head. Where's he come up with this stuff? – he wondered, as he admired the good flavor of the Buffalo tap water. Impressive.

While he stood there, he couldn't believe it. He and his partner Dillard were about to get retired for real. They had their pension going and all that, but there were still a few loose ends they were obligated to tie up. They all had to do with Jake Chambliss. The more he thought about it, Sam couldn't believe he was this close.

He didn't really know who was ultimately pulling the strings on their off-the-book mission to take down Chambliss, but he had his suspicions. While neither he nor Dillard were confident they'd find out in the end, they did stand to get a final payoff as soon as Chambliss was dead. Of course, Ainsley had to die too. Who knew how much she knew?

Simon always figured it was their old boss Larry Potts. They helped him cover up Ruby Ridge and Waco, but ultimately, Potts was demoted from his promotion to deputy director of the FBI under Louis Freeh when more of the truth came out. Nonetheless, their coverup of the Oklahoma City bombing operation was still working. Just one or two loose ends. The other might be John Doe Number Two, but he and Dillard weren't given that task.

Their original job was only to retrieve John Doe Number Two from Chambliss and that other guy they killed. He couldn't remember his name. Remembered the smell and the dismantling of the face, but nothing more. In fact, he'd always contended that the mess they made with the first guy is the reason they didn't fully end up killing Chambliss. They missed the brain and the heart. What a mistake. The higherups chewed them out for days. Still do on occasion.

Nonetheless, Simon and Dillard weren't expendable. Covering up the government's involvement in the OKC bombing needed as few people in the know as possible. Waco and Ruby Ridge were puny in comparison. First, someone changed the mission on the sheep-dipped patsy Tim McVeigh. What a sucker. Some thought it was to get the biggest emotional charge of blowing up a building with daycare full of dead children at the end. The first target didn't have the children to kill.

That wasn't even it though. The documents for the investigation into the Clinton Administration had been moved to the Murrah Building only a few weeks earlier. These documents also included files on the JFK assassination and on the George H. W. Bush administration. Imagine if the country actually knew what its own government had been up to. Imagine if the world knew that Bush and Clinton had a cozy relationship involving the running of guns and drugs through Arkansas while Clinton was governor and Bush was president. Sure, they have ideas and conspiracy theories on it, but it's all tin foil hat stuff. Were it not for patriots like Simon and Dillard, America might no longer be incorporated. The truth they helped hide might have shattered the union more than it would have been shattered had the South won the Civil War.

Sam's reflections on his own greatness and that of Dillard's to boot had him yearning for a beer. Sure, his doctor said he shouldn't drink anymore, but this was a time for celebration. He looked in Ainsley's fridge. Bingo. He grabbed a bottle of Molson Golden and drank it like it was about to turn warm. First beer he'd had in months. Then he grabbed another. Took his time with this one.

He knew what he wanted to do, but he needed to build up the courage. He knew Dillard wouldn't approve, but, what the hell? They were just going to kill her as soon as they had Chambliss. Dillard wouldn't rat him out. He'd just be happy to get this whole thing done with.

Sure, they're retired, but they were required to spend their days monitoring every intelligence agency they had access to. Jake Chambliss was a wanted man. Most in the government had no idea the real reason. It was just aiding and abetting a terrorist and a few other boilerplate charges they'd made up a long time ago. For the last several years, he was pretty sure they were all wasting their time and that Chambliss was already dead. He was a total ghost.

Then this federal attorney from Western New York called. How the frick did this guy know about all this? He said, "I think I know how to get Jake Chambliss."

266

Sam Simon's first question was, "Who is Jake Chambliss?" Thought it had to be some sort of entrapment thing. This stuff was so top secret that even the guys with top level security clearance weren't allowed to know about it.

It took Simon and Dillard a full day of discussions before they were willing to meet with the guy. First and foremost, they needed to verify that what this attorney had was real.

His name was Bennett Glazebrook. What a blue-blood name. Neither Simon nor Dillard ever put much stock into what the governmental blue bloods were saying or doing. All of them were up to their eyeballs in corruption and always needing a new coverup. Glazebrook swore up and down though that this woman Callie Cutler, Chambliss' old high school girlfriend, had reached out and called for him. Begged him to come home. She was supposedly the only one who could ever get him back in the States. Simon had to consider this guy's intel after that though. He knew who Callie was and came to the same conclusion. After a day of verifying his intel, they determined he was telling the truth.

Simon wasn't ready to do what he wanted to do though. He finished his second beer in a few large gulps and popped the top on a third. Was he really sure he wanted to do this? All this thinking about how he'd gotten to this point made him second-guess himself.

This Glazebrook guy was full of himself. He thought he was untouchable. His plan was to have the Cutlers killed, thinking that this would somehow get blamed on Congressman Porter Nichols, whom Glazebrook was hoping to defeat in a primary the next year. He'd been monitoring the phones of the Cutlers when the plea for Jake to come home came, and he did his research. This guy was connected, way more than most. He wanted Simon and Dillard to take them out, but Simon and Dillard assured him that they only wanted Jake. In the old days, back when they were active agents, Simon and Dillard wouldn't think twice about it, but now they didn't want their hands dirty. That hope wasn't rewarded. They had to take out the chief when he confronted them about their lack of credentials and tried to arrest them. As if they were going to get this close to full retirement, just to be arrested by some little podunk copper.

Sam was becoming angry. That was one of the reasons his doctor made him stop drinking. He wasn't a social drinker. Alcohol had already ruined two marriages and many relationships over the years, but he wanted to celebrate. He finished the third beer, noticed that Dillard was still cutting logs and opened a fourth. He swore this was the last one.

He was sure the other Cutler kid or Chambliss would get blamed for killing the chief, but it still made him angry. Why couldn't this be a clean op? Kill Jake and be done with it?

They were heroes to the Republic, whatever that meant. They were the reason this country was still intact. Why shouldn't he get a little bonus? He'd finally overcome his sense of what he could get away with and what he couldn't. He could get away with it. He was convinced, and he downed the fourth beer and set it next to the other three and the empty glass of water.

First, he used the john and left the seat up. Then he crept into Ainsley's room. She still had the gag in her mouth, but she looked at him with wild eyes of fear. This was going to be fun.

"If you scream or make any noise, I'll kill you." He set his gun on a table by the door she couldn't reach. Then, he pulled her pajama bottoms off her butt. Was a bit infatuated with her black panties. A littler lacier than the ones he found in the bathroom. Started salivating. With that, he undid his pants and dropped them to his knees. He hadn't taken his shoes off, so his pants would have to stay on.

She made some muffled noise.

"Shut up."

She didn't. She was struggling to stay on her side.

Chapter 41

Just as Sam Simon was about to drop his undershorts, he took a gunstock to the back of the head. It put him in a daze, as he fell onto Ainsley's partially stripped body. He rolled off her legs and onto his back to see his attacker. Jake Chambliss was out from behind the door taking a photo of him with a phone. He immediately tried to get up, but the room was still spinning.

He tried again, but Jake met his rising face with a fist. That didn't stop the room from spinning, so Simon rolled to the floor at the foot of the bed. On his knees and hands, he tried to stand up. Jake kicked him in the ribs and grabbed him by the back of his shirt to pull him to his feet where he elbowed him in the back of the head, knocking him toward the far wall. Jake then drove him into the wall, dragged his face across the window molding and then smashed Simon's face through the inner pane of glass. Jake rubbed Sam's bleeding forehead along the lower shards of the broken window and then pulled him up and stepped to the left to take a look at his facial rearrangement work with the pride of a plastic surgeon.

As he stepped back, he heard a gunshot come from the doorway. The bullet went through Simon. Jake leapt at Dillard, standing in the doorway and looking at his bleeding friend with eyes wild with regret. He knocked the gun from Dillard's hand, grabbed a fistful of his shaggy hair and smashed his head into the doorway. That wasn't enough, so he smashed him a couple more times, kneed him in the balls and dragged him into the bathroom where he smashed his head on the ceramic sink and then put it in the unflushed toilet where he held it while Dillard struggled to get a sturdy grip on the rim of the toilet. Eventually he did and pushed himself up enough to get his head out of the toilet. So, Jake rammed his head into the back of the toilet a few times, but it wasn't very effective. Just something to do.

Jake backed off to consider his next lesson of pain. Simon grabbed him around the neck and started choking him, giving Dillard a chance to get to his feet. Jake lifted his feet and kicked Dillard into the sink as hard as he could. That sent Simon back into the kitchen, holding Jake's neck as hard as he could. Simon hit the ground, and Jake came down on top of him. Simon's grip loosened enough for Jake to lift himself out of the head lock and get a look at his bloody face. Then he saw the bullet hole in Simon's left side. He put his finger in it, and Simon screamed in excruciating pain. Anticipating Dillard's recovery, Jake stood up, boot-stomped Simon in the face, and grabbed one of the empty beer bottles. He smashed the bottom of the bottle off on the edge of the counter and went looking for Dillard, who walked right into the jagged bottle as he rushed into the kitchen. Jake twisted the bottle with his right hand and used his left hand to open the freezer door, which he quickly dented with Dillard's bloody face. He thought about grabbing his Glock, but he'd promised himself he wouldn't kill them.

Simon, with his pants still around his ankles, unable to double over and pull them up with a bullet in his side, was trying to pull himself up by climbing Dillard's pants. Jake kicked his bullet hole and then his face got another close-up of the bottom of his boot. Simon was back writhing in pain on the floor where he belonged.

Jake used the time to dent the freezer door some more with Dillard's head. Once bored of that, he closed the door, but it wouldn't seal. "You ruined her fridge," he said, as he drove Dillard into the living room doorway face first. "Now you got blood all over her wall." He smashed Dillard's head again, and then looked at Simon. He knocked the wind out of Simon with a quick boot to the belly around where the bullet was lodged. Simon was mostly out of it, so Jake threw Dillard into a chair at the small white table in the kitchen across from the fridge.

He pulled out his Glock and held it on Dillard. Simon wasn't moving much. "I'm thirsty." He looked in the fridge and grabbed one of the beers Simon hadn't taken. Without taking the gun off Dillard or his finger off the trigger, he pried the top off with the slide of his Glock.

He took a large swig and said, "So talk."

"About what?"

"What are you doing here?"

"Why ask questions you know the answer to?"

"Did you kill the Cutlers?"

"No."

"Who did?"

"Don't know."

"Were you there?"

"Yes."

"Why?"

"Waiting for you."

"Who you working for?"

"The government."

"Gonna play that card."

"Not a card. That's who I work for."

"Who do you really work for?"

"The government."

"Who wanted the Cutlers dead?"

"Don't know."

Jake kicked Simon in the bullet hole. Simon yelled, while Jake continued questioning, "Quit giving me nonsense. Who wanted them dead?"

"Still don't know."

He kicked Simon again. "I got all night. I don't think he does though. Start talking. Who brought you here?"

"You did."

"How?"

"Callie got a message to you. We followed that."

"Who told you?"

"The government. You're a wanted man, Jake. There's no statute of limitations on treason."

"Why'd they kill Curt and Callie?"

"Who?" Dillard asked as Jake kicked Simon again. "I don't know."

"Yes, you do," Jake said as he kicked Simon again. "He needs help ya know."

"So, do I," Dillard claimed.

"Tell me what I want to know, and I'll call you an ambulance."

"As if that's gonna happen," Dillard said.

"I don't want to kill you."

"Then turn yourself over to us."

"Funny. They teach you that at Quantico?" He kicked Simon again, but Simon wasn't yelling as much. Just burped up some blood. "Your friend's not looking good."

"The worse we look, the worse it's gonna be when they catch you."

271

"Who?"

"The government. Are you not listening?"

"What did you do with John Doe Number Two?"

"Who's that?"

"I'm getting tired of kicking your buddy. He doesn't have much left. Answer the question."

"I don't understand the question."

Jake stepped back into the hallway to check on Ainsley. She was still cuffed and gagged while she looked at Jake. Jake saw Dillard's gun on the floor and then saw another on the table just inside the door. He pulled the thermals under his coat through the sleeve and picked it up without letting his skin touch it. He put his own gun in his pocket.

Dillard ran at him from across the kitchen, and Jake shot him in the thigh and then the shoulder. Dillard fell to the ground.

"Get up. Just a couple of flesh wounds." Jake grabbed him by the good shoulder and threw him back in the chair. "Looks like Sam shot you after you shot him. Huh."

"You're not gonna get away with this, you moron," Dillard said.

"Away with what? To me, it looks like a love triangle gone wrong. A couple of rogue agents kill each other over who gets to rape the newsgirl first."

"Heh," Dillard spit and sighed.

"That all you got? Who killed the Cutlers?"

"I don't know."

"Why were you talking with Ainsley's boss?"

"Don't know what you're talking about."

"I'd kick your buddy, but it looks like he's dead. If you were me, two dead rogue agents isn't any worse than one, right?"

"I'm already dead."

Jake said, "Really?" He walked over to Dillard and grabbed the shoulder with the bullet and hit him on the side his head with Simon's gun as Dillard cowered under the only arm he could lift. "Not dead yet."

Jake hit him again, but a little harder, knocking him out.

"Don't go anywhere."

Chapter 42

With his hand covered in his thermal sleeve, Jake went through Dillard's pockets, found his keys and set them on the table. In his inside sport-jacket pocket, he found some cards. One was a business card. Bennett Glazebrook, U.S. Attorney for the Western District of New York. "Huh," he sighed to himself. He pulled out his phone, took a photo of it and put it back where he found it. He grabbed the handcuff key with his shirt-covered fingers and carried them into Ainsley's room. He unlocked her cuffs and took off her gag.

"Thank God, Jake," she said as she was pulling up her pajamas.

"Thanks God," he said as he looked to the ceiling with a smile.

"You're a sight for sore eyes."

"Yeah, well, we've gotta go. Gunshots get reported. Get some shoes."

Jake found her coat and put it on over her pajamas as she was tying her shoes. He moved to the front of the house to look out the window behind the shades. Then he set Simon's gun next to fridge on the floor, cuffed Dillard's bad arm to one of Simon's dead arms and set Dillard's gun on the counter, far enough away that the wounded Dillard wouldn't be able to get at it were he to wake up. At least not without dragging Simon's dead body across the floor with a bullet in his shoulder and another in his thigh.

Ainsley stepped around Simon's bloody body and made her way to the living room where she waited for Jake. He looked again through the window and saw nothing. "Let's go."

"Wait. He's got my phone."

Jake found it in Dillard's pocket and gave it to her.

He walked right to his car, which he parked behind Simon and Dillard's car. He heard the dog barking again. She followed but ran back to her car.

"This way," Jake said.

"I gotta get something."

He pulled his car up in front of her driveway, where she was holding her laptop under a big file of papers she'd grabbed from her car. She jumped in, and he was moving before the door had even closed. It was still snowing, and his wheels spun in the snow.

"Where we going?" she asked.

"I don't know."

"We going to Cash's?"

"Not a good idea. Not yet."

"Are you hurt?"

"More than most of the time."

"You're covered in blood."

"It's not mine."

"Yeah, but it's still gross."

"Better than being dead."

"How did you know to come?"

"Had a dream."

"You dreamt that I was kidnapped by those jerks?"

"No. It was the dream about the time I punched Tim McVeigh in the face."

"What does that have to do with this?"

"Nothing."

"Well then, how did you know about me after that random dream?"

"I have that dream when I'm overlooking the obvious. Not always random."

"What do you mean?" She tried not to sound like she thought he was crazy.

"The obvious. If I were Dillard and Simon, and I knew I wasn't going to be getting the promised paperwork to take custody of me, the fugitive, what would I do? I'd follow Ainsley home and use her to get Jake. The obvious. I don't know how I missed it."

"All that because you punched Tim McVeigh."

"No. It's what else happened. And didn't happen. Hard to explain."

"You can tell me," Ainsley said in her innocent, girlish, story-getting newsgirl voice. Jake liked that voice. Even though he knew he shouldn't trust it, he did.

275

"Because I didn't apologize after busting up his nose, even though I was so much younger and smaller than him. I embarrassed him and showed no remorse. It bothers me to this day."

"Why? He was a mass murderer."

"No, he wasn't. Not then. He was just a kid we used to play hockey with. He hadn't killed anyone."

"Okay. So, what if you had apologized?"

"I don't know. Maybe he wouldn't have become such a great soldier and become the bomber. I don't know. It's just something I regret. He was bullying me, and I put him down hard. It was embarrassing. That's all. Should've just taken it, but I didn't. I stepped out of line. The kind of thing that makes someone want to train and get revenge or something. I don't know."

"You can't take that on yourself. He didn't become a mass murderer because of you."

"Thanks. Maybe that moment will stop haunting me. I'll let you know."

"Sarcasm, huh."

"It's been a long day."

"It has, hasn't it? I can't believe it's still going. You figure out where we're headed?"

"I was waiting for you to tell me."

"Me? I almost got raped by that pig back there."

"No, you didn't. I was right there the whole time, and you knew it."

"Yeah, but it was scary. I thought those guys were going to kill me."

"They were."

"What do you mean?"

"After they got me, they had to kill you. You're a loose end."

"My God."

"Yeah, exactly."

"Are they dead?"

"Mostly."

276

"What do you mean by that?"

"If they get help soon, maybe not. Otherwise, yes. Hopefully, your neighbors are all sound sleepers."

"I have to go into work this morning."

"You can't," Jake stated firmly. "Not until we know you're safe."

"When will that be?"

"I don't know. After we know they're gone, and we figure out who killed the Cutlers."

"You don't think they did?"

"No. That was the only thing Dillard wasn't lying about."

"How do you know?"

"Trained to know," he said as he turned north onto Campbell Boulevard, heading back towards Pendleton.

"You mean you can tell if the person you're torturing is telling the truth? What kind of fascist nonsense is that?"

"Is that what they taught you in J-school?"

"Don't need to go to journalism school to know torture doesn't work. Everybody knows that."

"You're so cute," he said as he turned to smile at her.

"What's that mean? And, well, thanks."

"First off, what I did back there wasn't torture. That was just a little tuning. I didn't have time to torture them. Second off, yes, there is a difference in the way someone tells the truth and a lie. Dillard was obvious. Wasn't even trying to hide his lies, but it was also easy to tell when he was telling the truth. That one time."

"Have you ever tortured anyone?"

"Depends on whose definition of torture we're using," he began. "If you're asking if I've used various methods of pain delivery to persuade enemy combatants into giving me information I want, then yes. But if you're asking if I've doled out pain purely for the fun of it, then not very often."

"That's terrible, Jake. How can you be so nonchalant about torture?"

"So says the girl who didn't get raped tonight."

277

Ainsley went silent and looked forward. Kind of looked like she was holding back tears. Jake knew he might have been too harsh. Never mind the "might have." *Huh,* he thought, *the Tim McVeigh dream really has its moments.* Ainsley's silence was as close to Callie's scorn as anything he'd ever experienced. Must have meant he liked her. *Oh, crap.*

"Ainsley?" She let her name hang in the finally warming air in the car. Didn't even budge at his calling her. "Ainsley?"

"Yeah, Jake?" She said his name as if she were still mad at him.

"I'm sorry." She let that hang in the air. "I'm not good at human relationships."

"So, I'm a human, Jake, and we're in a relationship? Thanks."

"That's not what I meant. I spend a lot of time alone. That's what I meant. I'm not in tuned with human emotions. I scout for trouble, I isolate it and I eliminate it. That's what I'm good at. Sensitivity isn't normally a part of the equation. And right now, I'm still in that mission mode. Trouble is not yet eliminated. You are not one hundred percent safe."

"I get it. And that's actually fascinating." She turned to look at him from a different perspective, "So, because you didn't apologize to Tim McVeigh, you are learning from that and apologizing to me? Are you worried that I'll become the next Oklahoma City Bomber?"

Jake laughed as best he could. "You're funny, Ainsley. No, you're not Tim McVeigh. Although, you did remind me of Callie a bit earlier"

"Callie Cutler?"

"Yes. She was in the dream too."

"This is an important dream, huh? What'd she do?"

"I can't believe I'm talking about this with you," he said. "I've never spoken of this dream to anyone."

"Just a deep dark secret inside the mysterious Jake Charm?"

"Don't mock. I've been telling you things like I've never told anyone, and I'm only endangering your life even more. Are you sure you want the answers to these questions?"

"Yeah, I do, Jake." She lifted her left hand off her computer in her lap and touched his shoulder. "You're like no one I've ever met, and I'm sorry you thought I was mocking you. You can tell me. How did I remind you of Callie Cutler?"

"She saw me hit Tim and acted like she despised me for it, and I liked her. Granted, she didn't see him first push me in the yellow snow while I was peeing."

278

"So, the future mass murderer was bullying *you*, the underclassman?"

"No, he was just getting me back for tripping him on the ice. I was trying to impress Callie. She didn't see that either. Just saw me punch Tim, and then she was cold to me."

"Well, how did you end up with her as your girlfriend then?"

"I don't know. Didn't happen right away. Only after all the talk around school happened. All the Jake-Chambliss-beat-up-an-upperclassman stuff, but Tim McVeigh deserved it for pushing me while I was peeing, dot-dot-dot."

"Dot-dot-dot, huh. Are you saying you like me, Jake?"

"No. I'm saying you made me feel like Callie made me feel in the dream I had right before I came to my senses and figured you needed my help." They crossed the bridge over Tonawanda Creek that separated Erie County from Niagara County.

"That's so romantic, buddy."

"I told you, I'm not good…"

"At human relationships. I'll get you a puppy."

"Thanks," he smiled at her. "By the way, though, isn't there some kind of journalists' code that says you can't be romantic with someone whose story you're writing?"

"Probably, but the closer I get to your story, the closer I seem to be to getting killed. At this rate, I may not live long enough to tell it. Besides, what about your other girlfriend, what's her name?"

"Who, Samantha?"

"Yeah, Samantha. What's that story?"

"No story. She's just going through that phase that comes after you've been saved from being a sex slave, you have nothing, and you cling to the only person who's been nice to you in as long as you can remember."

"That's all it is? That's a lot."

"Yeah, probably. But she'll get through it. I told her what it is. She just doesn't believe me yet."

"You told her what you just told me about her?"

"Not in the same words."

"You really *don't* have the ability to have human relationships, do you? That's so insensitive."

"Well, I also explained that it wouldn't be fair of me to have relations with her because I'm surely going to have to leave."

"What do you mean? You're not staying?"

"I won't be able to, Ainsley. As long as the government is trying to kill me, I will be on the run."

"For the rest of your life? My God."

"Mine too."

"What?"

"My God too."

"Oh." She smiled at him and touched his arm again.

"What if I get this story out, and the world knows?"

"It won't matter. They probably won't even let you do the story. I'll give it to you, but they'll just paint you as a tinfoil-hat crazy person, if you're not careful. Nah, they'll do it anyway."

"How do you know?"

"Just the way they do things. You know the CIA came up with the term 'conspiracy theory,' right?"

"No."

"Yes. They did that to discredit anyone who spoke about theories as to why they killed JFK."

"Not possible. You think they *did* kill him? I thought that was just conspiracy theory stuff."

Jake laughed at what she'd just said. "See what I mean? I actually wouldn't be surprised if they did though, especially after *all I've* seen them do."

"You talking about McVeigh?"

"That's a small part of a big conspiracy. It's so big, I don't even know if I want to believe it. I wish I couldn't actually. I wish life could go back to when I was blissfully ignorant. Just do what you're told and don't ask questions. Those were the days."

"Where we going?"

"You haven't figured that out yet, Ainsley?"

"No. I'm just along for ride."

"That's it?"

"You want me along for more?"

"Sometimes."

"Wow, human relationships. You flirting with me?"

"Is that flirting?"

"I'm not sure. What's in your heart, Jake?"

"Very little I'm allowed to acknowledge."

"That's so sad."

"Yeah, I know. I'm a victim."

"I'm serious, Jake."

"I don't doubt it. Let's drive by Cash's and see if we can get away with talking to him for now. I don't want to call him. He's not supposed to be cavorting with a fugitive."

"You're still a fugitive?"

"Until I'm caught, dead, or pardoned."

"So, no human relationships."

"Something like that."

Chapter 43

When the alarm rang, I tried not to wake Skylar, but she woke and tried to keep me in bed with her arms and some morning groans. At least she wasn't snoring all night. I wriggled out, and she fell back asleep pretty quickly.

Got dressed and went downstairs. Samantha was curled up in an afghan on the couch. I figured Jake was in the bathroom or the kitchen, only to discover I figured wrong. I knocked on the door where Balozi was sleeping. He told me to come in.

He was sitting on the bed with his hands on his thighs, fully dressed, maybe deep in thought but ready to go.

"Have you seen Jake?"

"No, I just woke," he said.

I nudged Samantha awake.

"Jake?" she asked, without looking.

"No, it's Cash. You know where Jake is?"

"He went to save the reporter girl."

"Ainsley?"

"Yeah, if that's her name."

"What happened?"

"I don't know. He just woke up and said he had to go save her. Said the federal guys had her."

"Is he coming back?"

"Said he was." She rolled over and went back to sleep with a smile on her face.

I walked back into Balozi's room.

"You want some cereal?"

"Sure," Balozi said.

I poured a couple of bowls and ate mine standing up while watching the driveway through the dining room window. It needed to be plowed, but I wasn't going to get to it that morning. I noticed Jake took an AR and left the box of ammo open. This could mean trouble. Brilliant observation, huh?

I saw the Caprice Jake was driving slow down before turning into the barn-side driveway. He and Ainsley came in the house, Ainsley carrying a laptop and some papers. Jake's blood-covered face was so serious that Ainsley smiling hello at me seemed odd.

"What's up?"

"They had her," Jake said.

"The feds?"

"Yep."

"They still alive?"

"Don't know, didn't wait for the coroner to arrive."

"Smart. So, this morning's off?"

"No point in meeting someone who isn't showing up. We need to talk with Tyler though. Probably best that you go. Might have to arrest me."

"He wouldn't arrest you."

"Yeah, I don't know. By the way, it's the U.S. attorney. Found his card in Dillard's pocket."

"What's the U.S. attorney?"

"I think he's who had your brother and Callie killed. He's the one that got Dillard and Simon on my trail. Or at least ratted Callie out for contacting me."

"Did you keep his card?"

"No. Took a picture but left it there for the cops. That's why we need to talk with Tyler."

"I can just call him, have him come over."

"I don't know. You tell him I'm here, he might come with other cops. I don't know where I stand if the cops found the feds already."

"You call him. I have his number right here."

Jake thought about it, moving his lips and cheeks the way he does when he's mulling things over. Ainsley watched with nothing she was willing to offer.

"All right. What's the number?"

Jake punched it in and waited for Tyler to answer.

"Graveline." I could hear him through Jake's phone.

"Tyler, it's Jake."

"What's up, Jake? Little busy here with Chief Beck."

"Sorry about that, Tyler. Dillard and Simon aren't coming today."

"How you know that?"

"They kidnapped and almost raped Ainsley Reed."

"And how do you know that?"

"She's with me now."

"What about the agents?"

"I left them at Ainsley's place and got her out of there before they raped her."

"You're serious?"

"Yeah, Tyler. I left them there. Dillard had Bennett Glazebrook's card in his coat. It's still there. Inner right pocket."

"Glazebrook, huh? Knew it."

"I figured I'd tell you about it before the locals got on the scene, assuming they haven't already."

"Thanks, Jake. We already have an APB on these guys for the chief's murder, but who knows how that's gonna fly? I've got Lockport detectives going through the station right now. An APB on feds probably won't last long, especially with Glazebrook as attorney."

"Does he have authority over the police?"

"Probably not, but with him, who knows? His wife's in the governor's office. He can do no wrong. The guy has his fingers in everything. I'm telling you, he's up to his eyeballs..."

"Yeah, Cash showed me. He did the research you suggested. I'll have Ainsley give you her address."

284

"Okay, lemme grab a pen."

Jake handed the phone to Ainsley.

"Hi Officer," Ainsley said before giving him her address and handing the phone back to Jake.

"What should I do, Tyler?" Jake asked.

"Lay low for now. Let me check the status on these guys. In the meantime, don't make a move on Glazebrook. Let me handle that."

"You got it. Let me know what you hear on the feds. Thanks."

"Yeah, thanks Jake. Talk to you soon."

A little after 8:00am, Ainsley's phone rang. She went white and her eyes grew wide as she was trying to figure out whether she should answer it. "It's my boss." She held her shush finger to her lips before she answered, "Yeah, Cap?"

"Where the $%@^ are you, Reed?" The whole neighborhood could hear him through the phone.

"On my way. Stuck in traffic. Be there soon."

"Get in here now, Reed. If you're not here in a Buffalo-New-York minute, you're fired." He hung up.

Ainsley looked at Jake for an answer. He was her ride. Her car was still back at her house.

Jake saw her need and must have understood without her even saying a world, "Let's go. I'll give you a ride to work."

"What about my car?"

"It's evidence. Can't touch it."

"Can I just borrow someone's car?"

Skylar offered hers.

"No," Jake said, "I'm going with her. It's too dangerous." I saw Samantha's mood-ring face turn glum, but she knew to stay quiet. Jake was directing the whole thing. We were all just his little helpers. I was fine accepting the position. He knew what decisions to make, and I didn't bother second-guessing them.

"Let's go," he said, looking at Ainsley.

"I'm in my pajamas, Jake." Jake apparently wasn't one to sweat the small details.

"Uuuuummm..." He verbalized his cheek and lip dance with a simultaneous eyebrow wave that went from one side of his face to the other and then back.

Skylar piped up. "I've got clothes she can wear. Come on, Ainsley." They ran upstairs.

Chapter 44

Skylar's clothes were pretty comfortable. Much more comfortable than the normal business clothes Ainsley was used to wearing. This was just going to have to be a casual day.

She couldn't help feeling the excitement of being driven around by an innocent fugitive, wanted by corrupt government officials who wanted to kill him to hide their secrets. As well, she viewed herself as the spokesman that would tell his story and clear him of the false charges.

She looked at him driving her through barely plowed side roads. While she was incredibly thankful for saving her, as much as she was thankful, she wanted to be the one to save *him*. Sad thing was, she knew he thought it impossible, and even still, didn't hesitate to risk his life to save her and keep her safe. The more she thought about him, the more she liked him.

Aside from his casual treatment of torture, he was the greatest man she'd ever been even able to consider. Definitely not the pompous lawyers, political clingers-on and financial guys in expensive suits that regularly crossed her path with a wink of an eye meant to direct her attention to their wads of cash at the bar. The standard pickup ritual of the player with too much self-regard, all derived from his apparent ability to build a wad of cash for a night at the bar. In his eyes, a woman's dream guy is one with enough money to keep her drinking for free until she was too drunk to say "no" the moment he started taking off her clothes.

Sure, it might be said that Jake has a high self-regard, but she thought that might be a simple mistaking of confidence for arrogance. Arrogance was nothing more than feigned confidence with nothing to back it up. Jake could back it up. More than confidence, he had competence. Even sexier. She felt herself blushing and was glad his eyes were on the road.

"When we get to the office, you want to come in and give me your story?"

"That might be the perfect cover story as to why I'm there, but I need to wait until I know the story on Dillard and Simon. Tyler hasn't called me. Until then, I will wait outside. Let you smooth things over with your boss."

"That's gonna be hell."

"Nah, just smile at him and nod. He's all show. Just pretend you respect him and let him blow off steam."

"I do respect him. He's a brilliant guy. Just a little curmudgeonly at times."

"Even easier then. Just respect him and let him yell at you with a smile. After a while, if the smile doesn't disappear, he'll give up and figure you're onto something big and leave you alone."

"That how it works?"

"Yep."

"You act like life is so simple and everything's easy to figure out," She stated her observation.

"Life isn't complex. Everyone needs something. Men just want to be respected. Some deserve it, and some don't. You say he does. It's simple. Respect him, and he will let you be. Right now, he's mad because he thinks you aren't respecting him. He told you to leave the Cutler story alone. All right, never mind. This might be less than simple."

Ainsley smiled at the admission. "Less than simple? Is that like complex?"

"Yeah, okay. Complex. Your life is complex. Congratulations. And sorry about that."

"Sorry about what?" Ainsley asked.

"Having to live a complex life. It must suck."

"My life sucks? Compared to yours, Jake? You are wanted for a crime you didn't commit, and..."

"Yeah. That's simple. *You* have all sorts of weird people with weird motivations to deal with. I know what the motivations of the people who want to kill me are. That's simple."

"You're crazy, Jake."

"Nah, just like things simple, is all."

Ainsley couldn't help herself. She reached over and kissed him on the cheek. "Is that simple enough for you?"

"Yeah."

"Because if you want complex, I can give you that too." She didn't even know what she was talking about, just playing with words.

"Nah, simple is good. It's great."

She blushed again and turned her head to the right so he wouldn't see it.

The car remained quiet until they neared North French Road. Jake broke the silence. "You want to drive by your house?"

"You think we should?"

"Can't hurt. We drive close, and if we see a bunch of cop cars, we turn on a side street before we get there."

"Okay. You make the call."

As they neared her house, there were no cop cars. They drove right past it. Dillard and Simon's car was gone, but her car was in the driveway. He turned around at the pizza joint and parked where he'd parked the night before. He scanned the neighborhood. Seeing nothing out of place, he asked, "You want to go in?"

"Umm," she thought out loud, "not without you. Just too nervous."

"Let's go in."

The whole place was clean. Dillard and Simon were gone, the beer bottles were gone, there was no blood, the room that was a mess was tidied up, the fridge door was pounded back into shape enough to be sealed, and aside from it being somewhat dented, there was no sign of what had happened just several hours ago.

"Jake, am I crazy?"

"Not unless I'm crazy, and I'm not, so no. Let's get out of here."

Ainsley walked to her car, but before she even clicked the key fob Jake yelled, "Don't touch the car!"

"What? Why?"

"Let me see your keys."

She surrendered them.

"Stand over there, by my car."

"What's going on, Jake?"

"I don't know. Too many footprints around your car. Stand over there."

He got on his knees in the snow where he'd already seen the snow moved under the driver's door. He saw the bomb in the wheel well next to the front tire. Rather than touch it, he said, "Let's go."

"What is it?"

"A bomb. Life's simple. They were going to kill you with a bomb."

She went white again, "My God. What if I'd unlocked the door?"

"I don't know. Might not have gone off until you started it. Probably that. Let's go."

He pulled away, and just as they were about to turn onto Campbell Boulevard, they saw some cops coming from the west. Two cop cars turned onto Ainsley's road. Jake turned left.

"Looks like we left just in time."

Jake called Tyler.

"What's up, Jake?"

"Tyler, we just went through Ainsley's house. It's cleaned and scrubbed. Dillard and Simon are gone. All signs of the struggle are missing. Wait, I'm not sure about the window in the bedroom. Didn't check that. The fridge door is still a bit bent, but not as bad as it was. But this is really important. Call those cops that are heading there right now. There is a bomb next to the Prius' front tire. Maybe there's one in the house too. I don't know. They need bomb squad before they go in there."

"Got it." Line went dead. Tyler didn't wait to find out if Jake had more to say.

"Let's get you to work."

Ainsley took a deep breath, not sure that was the smartest thing to do, but she followed Jake's lead. "Okay, I guess."

"Hey, call Samantha." Jake was in traffic and apparently didn't want to be on the phone while driving.

"Why?"

"I need to talk with Cash and can't call his phone with my phone."

"Oh." She hit Samantha's number.

"Hey baby," Samantha answered through a smile Ainsley could see through the phone."

"Hi Samantha, this is Ainsley…"

"What do *you* want?"

"Jake needs to talk with Cash."

"Oh. Cash, it's Jake."

"Hey Jake," Cash answered.

"No, it's Ainsley…"

Jake grabbed the phone from her. "Cash, Simon and Dillard are gone, the house is clean, and there was a bomb under Ainsley's car. Watch your house. If the feds show up, let me know immediately."

"Simon and Dillard?"

"No, it won't be them. It'll be the guys who cleaned up their mess. They might be legit too, so be careful. Don't get into a fight with them. If they do show up, call me, put it on mute and leave the line open so I can hear what's what. I'm taking Ainsley to work now."

"Okay, got it. Be careful."

"Yep." Click.

Chapter 45

Ainsley directed Jake through downtown Buffalo to her station.

"Park in there," Ainsley said, pointing to the fenced-in lot to the right of the building.

Jake drove past the lot and went around the block.

"Where you going?"

"Just seeing who's here."

"See anything?"

"Yeah. Feds are here. You sure you want to go in?"

"I don't know. What do you think?"

Jake used air to fill his cheeks and squeezed his eyes as if he were trying to see better. "You might get arrested or taken to interrogation. Maybe even then used to get me."

"Well, I don't want that," she said.

"Yeah, well, your boss may be luring you into custody."

"Why would he do that?"

"He probably doesn't have a choice."

"Oh. I'll call him." She dialed.

"Where the hell are you? You need to be here right now," Cap said without as much anger as earlier.

"Cap, are there feds there waiting for me?"

"What are you talking about, Ainsley? Why would I know about that, Ainsley?"

"Thanks, Cap. Be there soon." Click.

"Let's get out of here," she said.

"Why? What's up?" Jake said.

"Cap wasn't yelling as much as normal. Only used the word hell, and he called me Ainsley twice. He never calls me Ainsley. He calls me Reed so much I didn't even know if he still knew my first name. That and he answered a question I didn't ask."

"Wow. You got all that? Nice boss."

"Hey, he told me what I needed to know, basically said, 'Get the hell away from here.'"

"Okay. That's cool."

"Yeah, he's not a bad guy. Just grumpy and stressed all the time. That's all."

"Okay, then." Jake changed the subject. "What do you say we figure out who killed the Cutlers?"

"Thought you said Tyler told you to leave Glazebrook alone."

"We will. Let's go talk with Porter Nichols."

"The congressman?"

"Yeah, I hear he's in town for a fundraiser tonight. Heard it on the news last night," Jake said.

"We going to the fundraiser?"

"Yeah, sure, why not? Can you get tickets?"

She typed on her phone. "I'm on their website."

"Get two, you'll be my date."

"Your date? Woo. I barely even know you, good sir."

"My pretend date, then. How much?"

"Twelve hundred. Two thousand for a private audience."

"Get those then. We need a private audience."

"I don't have four thousand dollars, Jake."

"Cash does. He'll pay you back."

"Are you sure?"

"Let me see my phone." He redialed Samantha's number. "Samantha, I need Cash... Cash, Ainsley and I need four thousand dollars to go to a Porter Nichols fundraiser. Can you cover it?"

"Yeah, anything. Everything good?"

"The feds are waiting for Ainsley back at her office. Her boss tipped her off, so that's where we won't be. Figured I'd go and talk with the congressman. See what he can do about Glazebrook."

"Good idea. Can I pay her in cash?"

"Yeah. Talk with you soon." Click.

Ainsley entered her credit card number to get the tickets. "They texted me the code we give them at the door tonight."

"We're in. We are highfalutin now."

Without premeditation or pre-calculation, Ainsley slipped her hand under Jake's arm and laid her head against him. "If this is what it feels like to be highfalutin, I like it." Then she realized what she'd done. "Oh, sorry."

"You're forgiven. If you're going to be my pretend date Miss Ainsley Reed, that's the kind of stuff you'll have to get good at."

"Oh, Jake Charm, if that's the case, let me return my head to the comfort of your arm."

"Of course, my dear. Just watch the PDA. We blue bloods can only tolerate the smallest level of scandal before we must gossip like birds. Wouldn't want gossip about us."

"Of course not. Birds gossip?"

"I don't know really, but they yak a lot, and no one knows what they're talking about. So, maybe it's gossip."

"If they were to gossip about us, what would they say?"

"I don't know. Maybe we should give them something worthy of their gossip though."

"I like the sound of that, my pretend date. What ever should we do?"

"Let's go get some clothes to wear, right off the rack," he said.

"Well, that's not scandalous, Jake. What gives?"

"Then we'll get a hotel room near the fundraiser."

"Now you're talking."

Jake started feeling like he was taking it too far though. He wanted to get into it, but he knew he couldn't. "Yeah, and before we get ready, I can give you the story I promised."

"Of course," she said with slumping excitement, "the story. Perfect day to do it. It's snowing."

Then Jake changed the subject, "That doesn't mean you shouldn't help me brush up on my human relationship skills."

"Seriously, Jake?"

"Yeah. I don't want to go in there cold tonight. I need your help."

"Great. Because I actually have some ideas that might help you out."

"Awesome, I look forward to it."

Speaking in code.

Chapter 46

"Who was that?" Skylar asked me as I flipped my phone shut.

"The coroner's office. Said the bodies will be ready by Friday or Monday. So, I can prepare to have the funeral. Wow. Not something I wanted to think about."

"Are you having a single funeral or two?"

"I don't know. I haven't even heard from Callie's family. Doubt they're in a hurry to talk with me, considering I'm still a suspect."

Samantha came over from the couch. "I think you should call them and suggest a single funeral. If you call them before they call you, they won't consider you a suspect. But, if you wait, it might make it seem like you have something to hide."

"Sounds like good advice. Thanks, Samantha. I'll call them now." I wanted to put it off, but what she said might have some truth, so I decided to make the call right then.

I walked up stairs, hoping to have a little privacy. Skylar followed. So much for privacy. I sat on my bed and looked into the nightstand drawer to appear as though I were looking for Callie's parents' number, but I knew it by heart. It's been the same number since we were kids. Skylar walked past the room to check on her mom.

I took a deep breath and dialed. "Mrs. Olmstead?"

"Yes?"

"This is Cash."

"Oh, hello Cash. How are you doing?"

"Terrible, ma'am."

"So are we. I'm so sorry, son."

"Me too. I would have called earlier, but I've been so busy."

"Everything all right?"

"No, not at all. Just trying to figure out who killed my brother and sister-in-law."

"Why don't you leave that to the police?"

"Because they seem to think it was me or Jake. They're crazy."

"You sure it wasn't Jake? I mean he disappeared and then came back all of a sudden out of nowhere. He always had a thing for Callie."

"It wasn't Jake. He came back because Callie reached out to him begging him to come back to help Curt and me."

"What's going… or what *was* going on with you two?"

"It's a long story, and I promise to tell you once this is all figured out. I'm calling though because the coroner called and said the bodies would be ready for a funeral for early next week. I was hoping to have a single funeral for both of them and wanted to run it by you."

"That's a wonderful idea. Of course. And Cash, we can take care of it if you'd like. You sound like you've got a lot on your plate."

"Mrs. Olmstead, you are a life saver. I'll help financially, but if you can deal with the funeral home and whatnot, that would be amazing."

"Of course, Cash."

"Thank you so much. I should go though. I have to meet with Tyler Graveline."

"Okay. Please tell Jake I said hello and tell him to make sure he comes by to see us before he leaves. Please. I do miss that boy." Not even Mrs. Olmstead expected him to stay.

"Will do, Mrs. Olmstead. Talk with you soon." Click.

Skylar sat down beside me halfway through the conversation. "How's your mother-in-law?"

"Not much better than I am,," I said.

Chapter 46

Jake and Ainsley found a motel a few miles from the fundraiser that would accept cash. Jake knew he shouldn't have let her buy the tickets with a credit card, but he was actually hoping they *would* use it to track them down. Regarding the formal clothes and toiletries, there wasn't any other choice. Neither of them had that kind of cash on hand. Nonetheless, there was no way he would allow them to use a credit history to find out where they were staying. Therefore, they could only stay at a place that didn't require a credit card – not the easiest place to find.

Jake scanned the TV stations for any pertinent news while Ainsley was in the shower. He was looking forward to a shower as well.

She walked out of the bathroom with her wet red hair pulled back, wearing some baggy grey sweatpants and white T-shirt from the packet he bought for himself. He could see her black bra through the white shirt. She was barefoot and strutting. Smelled good too. Heck of a lot better than he smelled.

"You clean up nice. Look at you."

"Why thank you, sir. I'm really looking forward to giving you your lesson on human relationships, so get thee to the shower quick, man."

"Here, I thought you just wanted my story. What kind of journalist are you?"

"Go take a shower and find out, my pretend date. One that might make you wish this date was real. Wink wink." She laughed through a smile at him.

"How do you know I don't?"

Jake couldn't help himself. If he could erase all the troubles and just dedicate all his time to her, he would. He wanted to, so badly, but couldn't.

He came out of the shower a little while later, also dressed in a pair of cheap grey sweatpants and a T-shirt from the same pack. He smelled a lot better.

"Now it's time for me to look at you," Ainsley greeted him. She had her notebooks and digital recorder ready to hear his story.

"Am I supposed to take notes on my lesson?"

She smiled. "I doubt you'll need to take notes. Doubt you even need the lesson."

"Oh, but I might," Jake said.

"Yeah well, just so you know, it's only for the pretend date. Because we're kind of like undercover."

"Of course," he said. "What do I do?"

She reached over to the radio alarm clock, found a station with a slow-dance song, stood up and put her arms around his neck. "Put your hands on my hips." He did. "Now sway to the music."

"This is easy. I think I'll be all right tonight."

"Yeah, you'll be fine. All the women on the dance floor will be dying to be me tonight because, look at you."

"Oh, stop. Look at you, the guys are all going to be wishing they weren't married when they see you."

"Oh, that's good. You have the small talk down."

"What if, to throw someone off our scent, I need to kiss you?" Jake threw that out there.

"That's a tough one. If you really have to do that, okay, but remember, it's a major violation of journalistic integrity. It'd best be pretend. Otherwise, my boss will throw the whole story out."

"He's probably gonna anyway. No way he's going to believe this story."

While the boss seemed like a mean old SOB, Jake was kind of happy the boss was getting him out of this situation. The boss was saving him from acting on his own desires. At the same time though, he was wishing this whole situation were different. Unlike Samantha, Ainsley wasn't trying to make him violate his code, and, as well, she had a code of her own. Much to admire.

"You better *not* be right. Let's get the story inked."

For the rest of the morning and most of the afternoon, he told her everything. Everything he knew about Tim McVeigh, what happened with Simon and Dillard, his numerous run-ins with them over the years, and even much of what he'd done during those years. She never found a stopping point, and always had a follow-up question. Except when they ordered a pizza delivery. Paid in cash again.

When pressing him on how it was so unbelievable that some people in the government were covering this up for whatever reasons, he made some points that convinced her he was onto something: "In a country that takes decades to put anyone to death, why was Tim McVeigh put to death only six years after the bombing? Consider that the documents, which were destroyed in the Murrah building, would have implicated the first President Bush as having run guns and drugs through Arkansas with then-Governor Clinton. Then, it was the son of the president who would have been implicated who put McVeigh to death – George W. Bush. It was the first federal prisoner put to death in since the Nazi spies of World War II. Why didn't they keep him alive to find out who was above him? Of course, there were people above him because not even Terry Nichols would talk, meaning he was protecting his son and wife or family or whomever they said would be killed if he talked. Even after being offered a deal, he refused to name names. If those in the government weren't the ones they were protecting, or weren't the ones protecting those they were protecting, why did the government refuse to let more than a select few pre-approved people interview them before McVeigh was killed? If the government really wanted the story uncovered, wouldn't they let others get in there and try to get information? Why, when, in 2005, Terry Nichols admitted that there was indeed a John Doe Number Two and that he saw McVeigh working with other Iraqis, did the government not pursue the truth further? If Terry Nichols was unemployed, who paid for his trips to the Philippines to get training to make ammonium nitrate fertilizer bombs? Did Tim McVeigh learn to make ANFO bombs in the military? – No, the U.S. military doesn't use ANFO bombs. That's a type of bomb used by Islamic radicals. What if, as asserted, Terry Nichols did meet with Ramzi Yousef there? Didn't Ramzi Yousef try to blow up the World Trade Center in 1993? Is it true, as has been asserted, that bin Laden was there as well? Why, when the Muslim guy named by the Oklahoma City local reporter as John Doe Number Two, did the government not investigate him? Why did they let him sue her? And after he lost a civil suit for libel, why didn't the government investigate him? He lost the suit. Why was he allowed to work in food service at Logan Airport on September 11, 2001, if he was rumored to be John Doe Number Two? How'd he pass the background check, or did they have no background checks whatsoever before 9/11? Wasn't it theorized that those in food service were responsible for getting the box cutters on the planes? Where did he go after 9/11? Why did 9/11 happen exactly three months after Tim McVeigh was put to death on June 11, 2001? Might it simply be because nine is an upside-down six and those in charge of blowing up the WTC were into numerology, or might this all be just a random thing? They said Tim McVeigh was a white supremacist, and the Clinton government used this as a way to clamp down on right-wing militias and conservative talk show hosts who were the main critics of President Clinton. If they didn't cover up the fact that he was in cahoots with brown-skinned Muslims, how does that make him a white supremacist? I'm not trying to make McVeigh seem sympathetic, but how does working with people who aren't white to blow up a government building and killing 168 men, women, and children make it scream 'white supremacist?' In his letters from the jail cell, he actually regretted having killed women and children in Iraq with the government bombs. He resented that the government called them "collateral damage." Does sympathizing with dead Muslims make him sound like a white supremacist? Or does it indicate there were other motives? No matter how you look at it, the truth they're covering up destroys the whole lie they've created. Many others know this. I'm just the only one that would testify under oath that I had John Doe Number Two in custody. That's why they need me dead. So, no one ever asks me to testify."

Ainsley could only ask, "Why'd they do it, and how'd they get away with it?"

Jake said, "Ask Merrick Garland. He's the guy that convinced the prosecutors at the DOJ to get rid of any evidence that might suggest this wasn't the act of white supremacists. I'm not sympathetic to white supremacists, but that's not what the bombing was about. And there would never be justice for those who died if the DOJ refused to go after those who were actually behind it, but that's exactly what happened. It was Merrick Garland. He's the one that talked them into hiding the evidence so they could paint a picture of middle America as a seething hot bed of white supremacists. The government was still looking for a reason to have ordered the shooting of Randy Weaver's young son in the back and his wife in the face while she held their little baby in her arms at Ruby Ridge, and then for purposely liquidating the little children at the Waco compound. White Supremacism. Whatever. Tim McVeigh was a left-wing simp who did his duty and then blamed it on the supposed heartache he had over all the Iraqi women and children he was forced to kill by the government he later bombed, you know, because white supremacists are famous for having huge regrets after killing brown people. You'll remember the government didn't use that letter of heartache in its case or do much to publicize it. It's all crap. And think about this. If Terry Nichols were a white supremacist, would he really marry Marife Torres from the Philippines? Are we to believe that marrying a non-white immigrant mail-order bride is the secret dream of every white supremacist? 'Hey white brothers, look what I got in the mail. White power. She's gonna have my children, and while they may not be white, I'm gonna love them anyway. So much so that I'll never tell anyone who made us blow up the Murrah Building.' The story doesn't add up because it's all nonsense."

Ainsley ended the conversation with nothing to say. She couldn't believe it, but she was a believer. She had no doubt Jake was telling the truth.

Chapter 48

"Graveline."

"Tyler, it's Cash. I need to get a suit for my brother's funeral. Can you get me into the house?"

"Umm, you need this today?"

"Yeah, as soon as possible." I tried to express my dire need.

"All right, look. I can't let you in there yet. Still a crime scene. Wouldn't look good. But I have to go get some lunch in a bit. I can stop over and grab a suit. Any particular one? Shirt and tie too?"

"Yes, get the black checkered suit, a white shirt and a...maybe a tie that goes with the suit. I have to get it to Callie's mom, who's taking care of the funeral."

"No problem, Cash."

"Thanks, Tyler. I owe you big."

"Don't sweat it. Gotta go."

If Jake and Ainsley were going out on the town that night, so were Skylar and me. That wasn't really my motivation. I just wanted to back Jake up, for one, but I also knew he'd never let me come if I told him. I needed a suit, and my brother's small collection was a bit too moth-eaten and from the '90s. He didn't like wearing suits. I wore one every day. Like I said, we were different.

I ordered the tickets online with the bar's credit card. Give them as little information as possible. Cost me another $2,400. I didn't get the backstage passes to meet the congressman. Figured Jake had that taken care of. Like I said, just wanted to be there in case he needed me and see where this investigation was going. Jake never really told me why he was going to see the congressman if we thought it was Glazebrook calling the shots.

Skylar and I left my house full of people I didn't know in order to get her some clothes from her apartment. Her mom must have kept things under control because the house was still intact when we got back.

Coming to the conclusion that Jake didn't need him anymore that day, Balozi had me drive him to the casino so he could get his car, go home, get changed and then scope out the situation at the casino. He was already late for work but then decided to actually go in. He hadn't been fired, and maybe there was something he could do to figure out how to handle all those remaining on the thirteenth floor against their will, if that's where they still were. Either that or find out what happened to them for the police.

I asked Samantha if there was any place she wanted me to take her. She had no place to go, and Shelly, being completely sympathetic, said that Samantha should stay with her until things got sorted out. She kind of told me that in no uncertain terms, and I wasn't about to challenge her. Shelly had apparently grown fond of Samantha while they were in captivity. Found that out later.

Standing in front of my mirror in my suit again, I looked just like Curt Cutler. Go figure. Skylar noticed too. She walked in saying, "Oooh, Cash, you look just like your brother." She pinched my butt passing behind me, backed up to the toilet, lifted her lacy black dress, dropped her panties and peed. In my three days as Cash Cutler, Skylar had gotten more comfortable with me than my deceased wife ever had.

Chapter 49

Jake drove around the city block the hotel was on before they entered the fundraiser.

"What are you looking for?"

"I'll know it when I see it."

He drove around three times, looking left, looking right and looking up. Ainsley watched and noted his method. He was more than just checking out the parking options. There were two parking garages and some spots on one of the smaller side streets behind the hotel. That's where they parked and walked through the whipping wind funneling through the side street to the front of the building.

The hotel was an historic hotel located in the middle of downtown Buffalo. It wasn't one of the sprawling modern hotels under sun-lighted atriums surrounded by a vast network of hallways. After the metal detectors for the exclusive event with VIPs, there was a rounded stairway to the left and one to the right. Both were covered in gaudy hotel rug designs and led to the same second-floor landing. At the reception table outside the event on the landing, name tags were offered. While Jake was using the code on Ainsley's cell phone to get their tickets, Ainsley wrote "Jane Eyre" on one name tag and "Edward Rochester" on another. She waited until they were free from the table to put Jake's name tag on him.

"I don't want a name tag."

"It's not your name. See, mine says Jane Eyre. Don't worry, I'm not suggesting anything by the use of the names."

"Don't worry back. If you *were* suggesting anything, I wouldn't know what it was. Recognize the names from some book but can't tell you a thing about it."

"No surprise. It was a girly book, Jake. Most boys hate the boring thing."

"Why did they make us read it then?"

"To give girls something they're better at than boys."

"Miss Jane Eyre, why I never. Did you just cash in your feminist card?"

"Of course, Edward. With you by my side, there's no need for feminism. Feminism's for women who can't get a man like you. Or a man, period."

"Spoken like a true American girl. I like it, Reed."

Ainsley punched him in the side with a smile on her face as they entered the bustling ballroom set up like it was a wedding. The attendees were all dressed to the nines, drinking, laughing, guffawing and celebrating their better standing away from the hoi polloi.

"I hate these things," Ainsley said.

"You go to a lot of them?"

"No, only to cover them for the news here and there. Never really a part of it. Just an observer."

"Kind of tells you everything you need to know about why our country's a mess, huh? People like this have no clue."

"Probably." Ainsley was looking at it through his eyes. "What do you want to do, Mr. Rochester?"

"Well, there doesn't seem to be a dance floor, so my human relationships lesson seems to have been in vain. Might as well get a drink and wait in line to meet the congressman."

"Okay, I'll have a white wine, my good sir."

Jake ordered a Killian's Red for himself and a chardonnay for Ainsley. They joined the others outside the back room where all the deals were happening before the congressman would be late to give a speech and thank everyone for their support, simply because he had to make so many deals. Sell your soul, sell your soul, sell your soul, sell your soul... politics in America.

By the time Jake was able to shake the slimy congressman's hand, Nichols had shaken so many hands that Jake said, "I see your palm's been greased," as he wiped his hand on his suit pants.

Congressman Porter Nichols looked at him with his eyes crossed. "Thank you for supporting me, Mr. Rochester. And Miss Eyre." But he pronounced it "Iyer." Nichols really was a boy.

"We're not here to support you. We're here to help you," Jake said.

"If I had a dollar every time someone told me that, I'd be rich."

"You are rich, sir," Ainsley said.

Jake took over before they got the boot. "Sir, Bennett Glazebrook is trying to frame you for the murders of Curt and Callie Cutler."

He shook his head like he was hearing the ravings of a lunatic. "What are you saying?" He whistled and put his hand in the air. Three bodyguards surrounded them.

"Hold up," Ainsley said, "I'm Ainsley Reed, local news. He's telling the truth." It was her news-story signoff that caught his attention.

"Oh, I recognize you." He called off his dogs who stood at bay, still salivating. "But who's this guy?"

"Sir, may we speak with you in private? What you are about to discover isn't appropriate in this crowded room."

"You're serious."

"As a lightning strike," Ainsley said. Jake saw her succeeding, so he let her lead the way.

"But who is this guy?" He pointed to Jake.

"We should discuss this in private. Bring your bodyguards if you feel more comfortable."

He looked at her for a few seconds trying to read her face. "All right, you two, let's go." He pointed to two of his bodyguards and led the four of us into a room off the back reception area and shut the door.

He took a seat behind the desk in the back of the room and had us sit in two of the four chairs situated in front of the desk. One of his bodyguards stood by the door, and the other stood by the desk.

"So, start from the top, Miss Ainsley Reed, Local News."

Jake started, but Nichols cut him off.

"No, I want to hear it from her. I don't know you."

"All right, sir. As you know, Glazebrook refuses to prosecute major drug crimes, in exchange for donations to his campaign fund, and gets away with it because his wife works in the governor's office."

"I can't say I know that..."

"But you do, sir. Because you know he's running against you and you did your due diligence. If you haven't figured it out yet, you need to hire better people. It's obvious to anyone with a brain."

"Okay, go on."

"Well, the dealers supporting his campaign are both mafia and cartel. The cartel guys are working with the casino, and they're laundering money through the Indian bank in Pendleton. Curt Cutler and his wife were murdered a few days ago. You heard about that, right?"

"I heard something. Nothing that had to do with me."

"Of course not. The news doesn't put the pieces together for you. Curt Cutler was the president of the Pendleton Savings and Loan, and they were trying to acquire the Indian bank."

"Why would they want to do that?"

"Exactly, they wouldn't. They just wanted to get the books opened to prove that the bank was in violation of every banking law America has."

"Well, what does that matter? It's on Indian sovereign land. We have no jurisdiction."

"Maybe that *is* the problem. But when murders happen, you better believe we have jurisdiction. One. And two, Bennett Glazebrook's up to his eyeballs in this. He had the bank president and his wife murdered to throw them off the scent in hopes you'd be held responsible for the murders, thus making it easier for him to take you down."

"That's a mighty story. Do you have any proof?"

"Yes. We have numerous campaign contributions from known drug kingpins that correlate with the release of lower ranked dealers. We have two dead Cutlers, the board of directors, the head of security at the Grand Island casino, a dead Pendleton police chief, and Glazebrook's associates killing him on video. We have it on video. They tried to rape me..."

Nichols' phone rang. He cut her off with an apology and an "I've got a take this."

He listened to the caller for a few seconds. "That's weird, we were just talking about him. Any reason he'd be *here*?... No, bring him to me in the conference room right now. Thanks." Click.

His attention was back on Ainsley. "Who tried to rape you?"

"Glazebrook's associates."

"That's terrible. How'd you escape?"

"Jake beat the crap out of them, and that's when we discovered the Glazebrook connection, even though we suspected already."

"You a tough guy, Jake?"

307

Ainsley answered, "He's the toughest I've ever met."

"Maybe I should hire you." He smiled. "Listen," and Ainsley was afraid her time was up, "I just got word Bennett Glazebrook came to support me tonight. Perhaps he's reconsidered his run against me, and your story's nothing but B.S."

"It's not, sir. Let's talk with him."

"Oh, he's coming. And we will. Listen, I agree with you, he's a dirtbag. Always has been. But your story is a little short on substance. Let's just see what he has to say. He'll be here shortly."

Ainsley felt a chill.

Chapter 50

Skylar and I looked good. When I saw the metal detectors, I was happy I'd left my gun in the car. I kind of figured they wouldn't let me carry a gun but was glad to see there was indeed no chance I'd get in with one.

We made our way up the stairs and through the check in. Neither of us saw the use for name tags. Wanted to remain as anonymous as possible.

That didn't work. As soon as we'd walked in, I heard my name and responded instinctually.

"Curt Cutler?"

It was a bank president from Niagara Falls I knew. I looked at him and pretended I had no recollection of him. "Jim Verbose, from Niagara Falls," he said.

"I'm not Curt Cutler."

"You look just like someone I know."

"I'm his twin brother."

"Oh my God, you look just like him," he slurred. He'd been drinking too much and was a little louder than a respectable man should be in public. "Hey, look," he yelled at anyone in the vicinity of his loud voice, "it's Curt Cutler's twin brother. He looks just like him."

In a matter of seconds, there were about twelve people around me, many of which I knew. One of them whispered into Jim's ear, and Jim went white. "Oh my God, I'm sorry to hear about your brother. We just flew in from Tampa this morning. I had no idea."

"Don't sweat it, sir. Curt and I have been getting mixed up all our lives." I shook his hand, and we walked away before he started asking me questions I didn't care to answer.

We went to the bar and saw Jake and Ainsley waiting in line at a reception area.

"Should we talk to him?" Skylar said.

"No. I don't want him to worry about me right now. We'll just follow them."

We got our drinks and sat at a half-empty table of people who knew each other and didn't look like they needed new friends. We kept to ourselves with just enough view of Jake and Ainsley.

After a while, they were speaking with the congressman and were eventually invited back into another room. We had just enough view of the door to that room to feel comfortable holding this position.

Shortly after that, Bennett Glazebrook entered the room with a slew of his men. The whole place looked aghast. They all knew Glazebrook was funding up for a primary against Nichols and couldn't believe the guy would show his face. Intra-party politics gets dirty in primary season, especially when one local heavy is trying to take out a bigger one.

Glazebrook stood athwart his posse as his eyes scanned the room. When they landed on Skylar and me, he nodded with a wink. No surprise in his eyes, nothing. He was looking for me, found me, and acknowledged me. He must have been monitoring my credit cards. No other way he'd have such a reaction. But he was still scanning when some other large gentlemen walked across the floor to interrupt his hunt. At first, he was blocked by Glazebrook's men, but then they let him in. Spoke a few words, Glazebrook nodded and followed him with his own muscle close behind. They walked past our table, and he turned to me and winked again. They were led right to the door where Jake and Ainsley were meeting with the congressman. The door opened, and only Glazebrook entered.

"Should we join them?" Skylar asked.

"No. Let this play out. They don't need to know we're here."

"Glazebrook already does."

"That's the last thing on his mind, I'm thinking. He's going into the lion's den and doesn't even know it."

Chapter 51

The door finally opened and let in a loud crowd chatter, punctuated with a, "You guys can stay out here." The security guard at the door only let in Bennett Glazebrook.

He walked in with a smile on his face that turned downward as his eyebrows rose upon seeing Jake and Ainsley.

Congressman Nichols said, "Have a seat, Bennett."

He looked again and said, "I'd rather stand."

"No, I insist."

Glazebrook took a chair next to Ainsley. Ainsley got up and took the chair on the other side of Jake. The congressman smiled.

Nichols sat forward in his chair behind the desk. "Well, now that we're all situated, Bennett, what's this I hear about you trying to pin the Cutler murders on my campaign? Don't think you have the chops to beat me in a primary?"

"I don't know what you're talking about, Porter."

"Well, Ainsley Reed, Local News, has convincingly shown me that, when Cutler's bank was about to uncover your well-known get-out-of-jail-for-campaign-contributions scheme, you had the Cutlers killed and set out to frame my campaign."

Glazebrook shook his head in denial and said, "I don't even know where this is coming from. It's pure nonsense. Why are you listening to some local news reporter and a fugitive wanted for numerous murders?"

"So, you *do* know these folks, Bennett?"

"I've seen her on the news, and this other guy, well, he's probably the one who committed the murders you're talking about. This is just nuts. I came here to tell you I'm not getting into the primary."

"Interesting. What made you change your mind?"

"I did an exploratory and discovered the people like you."

"That's flattering, but, if what these folks say is true, isn't that exactly what you *would* do? Quit the race and hope to buy my backing when they come to put you in jail?"

At this point, Glazebrook pleaded, "Porter, you and I go back, what, thirty years? You know me. I didn't kill the Cutlers, and I'm sure as hell not trying to frame the campaign I came to support."

The congressman guffawed before saying more. "I never said you killed the Cutlers. Why would I think you'd do the wet work yourself? You're a snake. Always were…"

"Porter, I didn't have them killed either. How would Curt Cutler's death benefit me?"

"It halts the bank acquisition of the bank used by the drug dealers that keep you in business with dirty campaign donations."

"What are you talking about? Every contribution I've ever gotten is reported and legal. I'm not hiding anything. Have nothing to hide."

"Then why did you have the Cutlers killed?"

"I…" he stopped and looked at Jake and Ainsley, "I had nothing to do with those murders." He added another "Nothing," for emphasis.

Porter Nichols looked at him and said, "I believe you, Bennett. Listen. I have to give a speech here, and you and I will hash this out. My guys will escort you to my private residence, and I will meet you there after the speech. This is not the place for the conversation we need to have." At that point he spoke to his bodyguard next to him, "Buddy. Have Frank and Bill escort Bennett."

"Wait a minute, Congressman, I want to hear your speech."

"Not tonight. It's just the same ole, same ole. You go with Frank and Bill. Afterwards, we'll bring you back to your people. But tonight, you and I will have some things to talk about." Buddy took Glazebrook out the door behind the desk, so as to avoid Glazebrook's people. Porter Nichols then turned his attention to Jake and Ainsley. "Don't worry about Glazebrook. He'll call his people on the way to our meeting, and everything will be fine. To you though, I'm thankful that you've brought this to my attention. I'm sorry for your loss, but I will take care of this. As well, thank you for your support this evening. Please stay around for my speech."

"You said it's just the same ole stuff," Jake said.

"It is, but I've had a lot of practice giving the speech. It's riveting," and with that he smiled and winked.

312

"Yeah, I think we'll try to beat the rush out of here. You do know he's full of crap, right?" Ainsley needed to be sure.

"Of course, I do," the congressman said. "This isn't the first I've heard of this either. Bennett didn't come here because he thought he was on the verge of getting away with it. He came looking for mercy. Saw his plan unraveling as soon as he realized no one's been arrested for the murders. Let me handle this. Go back to your lives and forget you ever heard of Bennett Glazebrook. But I must go."

Congressman Porter Nichols leaned over the desk to shake their hands and then sent Jake and Ainsley back into the crowd that was building in anticipation of his speech.

They brushed their way through security and the cocktailed crowd just outside the inner meeting space. The crowd lightened up a lot once they'd gotten to the ballroom. They weaved their way right to the hallway, down the stairs, into the cold, past the valet, down the side street with the wind at their backs, around the corner and then to the Caprice Classic.

Ainsley was quiet while Jake was on a mission to get away from the fundraiser. She had her guesses why but figured she'd wait until they got into the car. Even though it was cold, he walked up on the sidewalk to open Ainsley's door for her, and, as he was inserting the key, he heard some running steps. His gun was in the car.

Before he'd gotten it opened, a formally dressed bearded man had Ainsley in a choke hold with a gun to her head. His mustached partner had his gun pointed at Jake. Both guns had silencers.

"You know that silencers are illegal, and isn't it a little cold for a mugging, boys?" Jake asked. "I think I hear your mom calling. Better hurry on."

"Shut up, Chambliss, and let's go." The talking beard with his hand across Ainsley's neck started backing away, while the other guy used his mustache to indicate they'd be walking down the street away from the hotel.

"If you wanted to go on a double date with us, you should've just called. The guns weren't necessary," Jake said.

"I said shut up." They were all walking at the speed of the guy pulling Ainsley along, when they heard the drunken cackle of a girl laughing at what her date must have said. He laughed as well, as they headed towards Jake and the men they were with.

Jake recognized Cash's laugh and loudly said, "Oh, shoot, I forgot my gun. Let me go back to my car and get it."

Chapter 52

I heard Jake's smart-aleck verbal diversion and took the cue. I almost shot my gun into the street but remembered there was a lot of security in the vicinity. Instead, I yelled, "Freeze. You're surrounded." Skylar ducked behind the nearest car. I hid my body behind the trunk of the same car but held my head and gun up over the side of the trunk to see what I was looking at.

While the guy holding the gun on Jake was looking for me, Jake slammed the guy holding Ainsley before stripping him of his gun. The other guy couldn't decide where he should focus. He couldn't see who was behind him, and Jake had already put his buddy in the snow. With Jake in control, I stepped out with my gun pointed at him. "Drop it," I commanded. Felt like a cop.

He took a couple of shots in my direction. I could barely hear them. He was not a sharpshooter. The shooting stopped when Jake put the other guy's gun to his head. He slowly bent over to set his gun in the snow on the sidewalk and backed away. Jake picked it up, wiped the snow off as best he could and slipped it in his pocket without taking his own gun off the newly disarmed. I could see this as I got closer, Skylar following me.

As soon as I was close enough for the henchman to see my face, he went white and he shook his head in disbelief. "I thought you were dead." A man, faced with the man he thought he'd recently killed, will sometimes be relieved of his mental faculties. That was this guy's problem. If it seems too easy, I agree, but that's how it happened. The dude just admitted he tried to kill me. What an idiot.

I quickly responded, "I only pretended to be dead. You're a terrible shot."

"No, not possible. I shot you point blank, three times."

That's all Jake needed to hear. Lights out for the dummy. One swift butt of the gun to his skull, and his body collapsed like the World Trade Center into the snow. I wanted to kick him for good measure but didn't. I didn't even get to tell him I was Curt's twin before he was out. While Jake and I were figuring out what to do, Ainsley was fiddling with something she'd pulled from her pocket. She pressed play, listened to exactly what the guy just admitted to, and looked at Jake and Cash with a big old sparkly-eyed smile. "I got it." It was her digital recorder.

314

"The confession?" Jake asked excitedly. I found out later that she taped the whole conversation with Nichols and Glazebrook too.

She just nodded without breaking her smile or taking her eyes off Jake.

"Way to go, Reed. Oh, that's beautiful, and it's decided, Cash. We take these guys to Tyler. Cutler murders solved."

"What about Glazebrook?" I asked.

"Don't worry about it," Jake said. "The cops will figure out whoever these guys are connected to by following the money, the phone history, whatever. They'll figure that all out. Without getting your fingerprints on them or touching any of the buttons, secure their phones, and we'll put these guys in my trunk. Caprice Classic – it's extra big."

Ainsley pulled the car up. Jake and I lifted the facial haired ne'er-do-wells into the trunk after zip-tying their hands and feet. Closed the trunk, and they were secured.

"I'll call Tyler now," I thought out loud.

"No. Wait until we're across the county line. If he figures out we're in Buffalo, he'll make us hand them over to the Buffalo PD. Not a good idea. Too close to Glazebrook. Tyler'd go by the book. Don't give him the option. This is Tyler's collar."

"Makes sense," I said.

"Where are you parked?"

"In a parking garage, that way."

"Jump in. We'll take you there."

Jake followed us out of Buffalo. When we got across the Tonawanda Creek Bridge, I called Tyler. It went to voice mail. I hung up and called again, but, as it was dialing, he called back. "Just as I think I can take my shoes off and relax a minute, you're calling me. What's up, Cash?"

"We got the guys who killed Curt and Callie."

"What? Where?"

"At Porter Nichols' fundraiser. They followed Jake and Ainsley out, and we took them out."

"Well, I'm not supposed to say it because it's not your job, but nice job. How do you know they're the ones?"

"They confessed. Ainsley got it on tape."

"You kidding me?"

315

"No, seriously. We have a verbal admission, their guns, and their cell phones. Meet us at the station. You can book 'em, Danno."

"Let me get some clothes on. Be over in thirteen minutes."

"Hey, while I have you, anything on the feds?"

I could hear him moving around his house while on the phone. "No, nothing. They are gone without a trace. Ainsley's place was cleaned by professionals. They dismantled the bomb though. BPD has her car. Still checking it out."

"Imagine that. See you in twelve." Click.

We'd been waiting for about five minutes when Tyler rolled up in his black and white. He was in full uniform, but his first words upon seeing us gathered around the Carprice were, "I feel underdressed. Look at you guys. That the suit you're burying your brother in?"

"Yeah," I said, "and the one I was wearing when I got his killers."

Tyler nodded with a slight smile.

He opened the doors to the station, while we opened the trunk to let the two murderers out. I cut their leg ties, and we helped them out. Both were fully awake and quiet. It was pretty obvious they knew they were done. Tyler put cuffs on their wrists just to be safe and guided them into the station and to the cells. They each got their own cell. Tyler cut the trail cam from the soap dispenser before uncuffing the bearded guy. Jake and I waited inside the doorway as backup.

Once in the cells, Ainsley and Skylar joined us in the warmth. Skylar brought in the guns and cellphones. She'd wrapped them in a scarf and unwrapped them on Tyler's desk. Ainsley showed him her digital recorder. "I need most of these files, but I can download the admission on your computer."

Tyler looked at her and said, "You sure I can't enter it all into evidence?"

"Yes. I'm sure you can't. I have the biggest story of my career on this. You can't have it."

"Okay. Just don't erase it. But, yeah, let me get you on this computer."

He typed in his password before she downloaded the file onto his desktop and played it just to make sure she'd given him the right one.

"That's pretty damning," Tyler said. "Good job."

Jake said, "That's Ainsley Reed, Local News."

"That's my new name, I guess," she said.

316

Must have been an inside joke because I didn't get why they were smiling like goofballs.

Jake and Ainsley went back to Buffalo to check out of their motel and get Ainsley situated to write her story. Tyler stayed at the office and did paperwork, while waiting for the two murderers to be picked up and taken to the jail. Skylar and I went home to go to bed. We were exhausted.

Chapter 53

In the coming days, it became more and more apparent how corrupt the whole system was. With the Cutler murders solved, the casino and the Indian bank got off scot-free. No one was willing to look into it because, guess what, "We have no jurisdiction over Native American sovereignty." The murders were connected to men working for Bennett Glazebrook, but Bennett Glazebrook had disappeared. Porter Nichols was just as astonished as everyone else. He admitted he was supposed to have a meeting with Glazebrook after his fundraiser, but apparently Glazebrook didn't show. While it's assumed by the public that he just ran from justice and is probably in some country without an extradition agreement with the United States, we all think he was disappeared at one of Porter Nichols' steel plants. It's one of those situations where, if you're going to shoot the king, you better shoot to kill. Glazebrook was shooting blanks.

While the Grand Island police investigated our claims, they found no proof of slavery or anything we spoke about. Balozi continued to work for them, but he could come up with no proof whatsoever. Nighthorse disappeared. Can't be a witness if they can't find you. Carlos and Diego were found executed in their Monte Carlo parked in a Niagara Falls alleyway in the factory district. No videos and no suspects.

My attorneys were never given any paperwork regarding the sale of The Trough, so I kept it, opened it, and gave Samantha a job after Shelly made me an argument I couldn't refuse. I have no complaints about her.

Samantha and Shelly moved into Skylar's apartment, and Skylar talked me into letting her move in with me. She works at the bar when she can. Pacho's happy to back as well. Forget Taco Tuesdays, he's serving tacos every day. They're still delicious. Funny how a little Starpoint bar has the best Mexican food in three counties.

Ainsley had such a great first-hand scoop on the solving of the Cutler murders, as they call them, she had to get permission from her boss to get interviewed by other local TV and radio stations. She was all over the airwaves for a little while. Unfortunately, some seemed to escape justice. As we learned from Glazebrook though, if you have connections, you'll get away with murder.

I still have the suitcase full of the cash they paid me stashed in the barracks. I'm not as confidant as Pacho that someone isn't going to come to collect it at some point.

Pacho thinks that money was Glazebrook's. He'd heard that, after the cartel changed their minds, Glazebrook talked Carlos and Diego into buying it for him. He planned on buying the other half later. Or being partners with the cartel. The shell corp that bought the first half of the bar sold it back to me for a dollar and disappeared. Without Glazebrook in their pocket, they seemed to retreat from the area for a while. Unlike I suspected, Pacho wasn't with the cartel, but he still had his sources. He was just a guy who liked to cook.

The Indian bank representatives took care of all the paperwork and picked up the dollar at the bar personally. They didn't allow me to ask questions, but my attorneys were convinced it was legit. While the bank wasn't closed and investigated, word got out about it being shady. A lot of local farm business returned to my old bank. High interest rates come with risks. But hey, as long as there are casinos, there's money to be laundered. The Indian bank lived on.

As promised, Jake disappeared. I tried to talk him out of it but was talking to deaf ears. Ainsley tried even harder. She still calls me once in a while wanting to know if I'd heard from Jake Charm. She has some way of getting a hold of him, but he made her promise she'd only use it in an emergency. So, she's afraid to use it. Doesn't want to lose her last connection to him. I'm still waiting to read the story of her career.

Chapter 54

Ainsley was a bit broken hearted after Jake said goodbye. While she didn't believe it was goodbye forever, she was hoping to be the one person who'd be able to get his name cleared, so he could come back home. In her ever-dwindling free time while being constantly interviewed about her ordeal in the Cutler murder case, she wrote the story of Jake Chambliss. It wasn't small enough to be a local news story, but she did do a quick synopsis in hopes of talking Cap into letting her whet people's appetites for her larger story, whether it was for the local newspaper or a book, which she easily thought she could write.

She gave him the synopsis of the big story right before she left work one night. She was walking on eggshells the next morning coming into the station. Sam the weather geek was there to greet her.

"Hey Ainsley, now that your warrior is gone, maybe I'll take you out some night."

"In your dreams, Sam."

"Not ready, huh? I'll check back with you tomorrow."

"Won't matter, Sam."

"Rrrraaaooowww," he imitated a tiger taking a swipe at her with his hand.

"Persistence normally pays, Sam, but not this time."

"You don't know that, girl. I predict sunny skies are right around the corner."

"Well, then maybe."

"Really?"

"No."

She set her stuff on her desk and opened her laptop. She'd already decided to wait until Cap came to her, not wanting to pressure him on the story. She knew he was going to resist it. Just had a feeling.

As soon as she'd gotten to her email folder, she heard the call she was expecting. "Reed, get in here." Moment of truth.

She took the seat in front of his desk, keeping her head up like she'd given him the story of a lifetime.

"What is this #$%@, Reed? Where'd you dig this wacko up?"

"Wacko? He's the main reason we solved the Cutler murders."

"After I told you to stay away."

"Yeah, but Cap, there's still a story there."

"Yeah, sure."

"Cap, how do you explain Glazebrook's disappearance, the dead cartel guys…"

"No, none of that matters. It's all a dead end. The murders are solved. I'm talking about this."

"You don't care about all the other people behind the coverup?"

"What coverup? No crime, no coverup. The cops have nothing and are done with the case. That means you are too. Forget it."

"What about the Jake Chambliss story?"

"It's nonsense, Reed. Nonsense. We can't report this. It's bat#%@ crazy. Sheep-dipped, working for the CIA. FBI covering up a Middle East connection, blah blah blah."

"It's not nonsense. I'm telling you, it's real."

"Oh yeah, then where is Jake Chambliss? Is he here to confirm this story?"

"Well, no, he had to…"

"Yeah, avoid the rogue FBI agents. Where are they?"

"They were in your office, right here, the day before the Cutler murders. You know they exist."

"Yeah, well, where are they? You've got nothing here. I need proof. You can't just make these accusations and think there won't be blow back." He held up his 4am morning talking points and asked, "You know where these come from, right?" Ainsley nodded. "These come from the CIA. You think I can make this accusation and not get shut down. They'll take our license. You're crazy, Reed."

"Cap, there needs to be an investigation. There never will be unless people hear the story."

"And they never will hear it unless there's proof. You come in here with more crap like this, Reed, and I'll have to put you on morning-drive detail." To reporters, that's like parking-ticket duty.

"Cap, they almost raped me."

"I'm sorry about that, but they didn't, and you don't even have proof they were there."

"So, you believe me?"

"It doesn't matter what I believe. Without proof, there's no story. Now get out of here before I put you on the morning drive."

On her way back to her desk, she finally realized why Jake said it was going to be impossible to clear his name. Under her breath, though, she promised him she wasn't done. She immediately looked up the reporter from Oklahoma City whom Jake told her about and sent her a message. Then she ordered her book. Jake highly recommended it.

Untamed Fury Book 2 – The Unfinished Business

Chapter 1

Here are the first chapters of the upcoming *Untamed Fury Book 2 – The Unfinished Business*. When things don't quite make sense at the finish, it's because we haven't yet reached the END.

My twin brother and my wife were killed about six months ago. The mourning didn't start until after I'd been cleared of suspicion.

Unfortunately, the survivor's guilt is worse than the mourning.

It should have been me that was killed. Not my brother. My brother Cash and I were in the middle of our annual life-switch game. Ever since we were kids, for a day or two a year, we'd switch lives. We had a five-dollar bet that the other would be the first to get caught. Five bucks doesn't sound like much, but when we were kids, that was like bar of gold.

Neither of us ever got caught, so the money never changed hands. Actually though, Cash was caught back in high school. He was the quarterback with the golden arm. Jake Chambliss and I were his go-to receivers. Turns out, when we switched lives and I had to play quarterback, Jake figured it out. He went to Cash and promised not to tell if he always received more of the throws than I did.

That probably cost me an opportunity to play in college, but I got over it. By the time Jake admitted his clever method of getting the extra passes, it was the day after Cash and my wife Callie were murdered. Though it was less an admission and more of an "I got you sucker," life had just given us a whole bunch of more important things to worry about. Other than Jake, only Skylar, the hot young girlfriend my brother Cash left for me, and maybe my dead wife Callie ever figured it out. My dead brother Cash and I were good at playing each other, and now I play Cash all day every day, because, as far as the world is concerned, it was Curt Cutler that died with his wife Callie Cutler that night.

Imagine that. Six months have passed since the murders, and I'm still with my dead brother's girlfriend Skylar Meade. I'll admit it, at times she's great. Better than my wife. The last several years with my wife Callie were miserable. Found out later though, might have been because she was having an affair with her old boyfriend Cash, my twin brother. But I'm not totally sure. The only two who'd know for sure on that died that fateful night. That's one of the things I don't like to think about. I'd prefer to think they were still just friends.

Sure, he told Skylar about the affair, but he had reason to lie to her at times, and it might have just been misinformation. Again, not something I like to think about much.

There were a number of other things I didn't like to think about too. I just can't help it though, and that was the main cause of the stress between Skylar and me. Less than a month after the murders, Skylar had a miscarriage, and the baby of my brother died. My little nephew that I was ready to raise as my son died. I didn't know what to think about that. I'm sure it had to do with all the stress – sure of it. He might have been all that was left of my brother though, and he was gone. Every day of my life is just a little sadder because of his loss.

Skylar wanted to move on. She wanted to forget about all the things that led to the murders and what happened afterwards. Repression's a great defense mechanism when used properly. I couldn't do it without drinking though. Maybe Skylar is stronger that way than I am. I don't know. I did want to forget as much as I could, but there was a briefcase full of cash and several stacks of cash sitting up in the secret compartment under the floorboards of the bedroom in the attic that Cash and I shared when we were kids. Without my nagging questions answered, I didn't dare spend that cash. Nor did I feel comfortable that someone wouldn't come knocking on my door at some point looking for it. It was an incessant fear that lurked in the background of my every thought.

It was especially bad that Jake Chambliss left right after we'd solved the murders and brought the killers to justice – most of them at least. He's been on the run since 1995, when he was left for dead by some rogue FBI agents who took his capture and killed his partner. After the Oklahoma City Bombing, he and his partner captured John Doe Number Two, called it in and waited. The agents, in charge of covering up the Islamic connection so the Clinton administration could blame the right wingers by conflating them with the supposedly burgeoning white supremacist movement, came, killed Jake's partner, shot Jake in the head and chest and saved John Doe Number Two from being brought to justice.

Might sound crazy and all, but it's not. The same rogue FBI agents chased him down when he came home at Callie's request to help Cash and me. We were in trouble, Callie knew it and figured out how to get a message to Jake. Nonetheless, the rogue FBI agents in charge of tying up loose ends intercepted the message and came to Pendleton in hopes of intercepting Jake.

Didn't happen though. Jake outsmarted them and beat the living crap out of them when he found one of them trying to rape Ainsley Reed. He might have killed them, but by the time the police were on the scene, the whole house had been scrubbed clean and repaired. They were gone without a trace. Surely, they had help, but whether either agent Dillard of Simon died, we did not know. As they'd left Jake for dead in 1995, he left them for dead in 2011. The only difference though, Jake didn't want to kill them. Killing a federal agent would get him the death penalty. He only wanted to clear his name, even though he was sure it never would be.

Ainsley Reed begged to differ though. She liked Jake so much, she'd dedicated her spare time of the last six months to clearing his name. While it might be selfish in that she was hoping for a future with Jake if he were ever free to come home, it definitely also had to do with her idealistic desire for justice. Ainsley Reed is a local reporter who developed such a strong bond with Jake that he told her his story. Most of it anyway. It's a big story, and they didn't have enough time for it all. Her boss refused to let it see the light of day though. Like a vampire in church, it was too hot. Didn't matter to her. Even though he told her over and over to stay the #$#% away, she wrote a whole book about Jake and was trying to get it published.

I was rooting for her success. I wanted Jake back too. I had no idea where he was. Word around the campfire was, Ainsley knew how to get in touch with him if there ever were an emergency. The emergency must not have come yet because I still hadn't seen Jake since he'd left. He even left before the funeral. By the way, Callie, my dead wife, was his high school sweetheart and only girl he ever loved. Their breakup hit him so hard, he joined the military and didn't return for twenty years. He skipped the funeral anyway.

And that was how it was. I was living the life of my dead brother because I was too afraid to admit we were in the middle of our stupid life-switch game. Coming clean would have made it much harder to clear our names. While we eventually did, how would I come back and admit I was actually Curt Cutler, the one who was supposed to be murdered along with my wife? Never figured that one out. There'd be too much shame. I'd spend the rest of my life having people look at me as the one who escaped the death I left for my brother and my wife.

On top of that, my old bank might find grounds to sue me for potentially having allowed my brother Cash to work at the bank – not only was he unqualified but it would be a huge violation of privacy in regard to the bank's customers. While I never did that, the bank had no way of knowing for sure. That might cause me legal trouble.

Furthermore, if the people in charge of killing my brother wanted revenge, why in the world wouldn't they seek it on the guy whom they wanted dead but then turned around and foiled their plans? Just some things to be concerned about.

Not wanting to go to jail, not wanting to live the life of shame and not wanting to be killed added up to enough reason not to admit I was really Curt. I became Cash.

But there's still the survivor's guilt. How can I live with myself, knowing that if I'd only listened to my brother, who didn't want to play this year for his own reasons, I'd have been the one who'd gotten to be killed? It's loony, I know, but as soon as I think about how glad I am that it wasn't me who was killed, I get crushed with the weight of the guilt over my brother's death. And rightly so. It should have been me. Really, it should have been me.

Skylar disagrees though. She likes me more. At least she did early on. I was no longer so sure. I'd been drinking a lot – Skylar said, "too much." While objectively that may be true, I didn't agree. I was enjoying it. A permanent vacation from life, and when I was drinking, I wasn't thinking. As Curt, I was the CEO of the Pendleton Savings and Loan. That was stressful as heck.

It was doubly stressful because my board of directors wanted to acquire the shady First Iroquois Trust, which is the bank run by the Indians that run the casinos and the reservations. While everyone, in the know, knew they were up to no good, the only reason for the acquisition was to get the books open so they could expose the corruption. It involved money laundering, a Mexican cartel, drug money, money from sex slaves, sex-slave trafficking, borrowing money to build on land owned by the Indian reservation and on and on.

They got off, of course. The US government claims no jurisdiction over tribal assets and that kind of nonsense. But the truth came out enough that a lot of the local farmers did eventually bring their accounts back to PS and L after realizing that the higher interest rates the Indians were giving on deposits came with the risks associated with illegal loans and a vast syndicate of crime.

Skylar didn't like that I drank so much, unless she was drinking too, but I was enjoying it. I was no longer under the stress of running a bank. I had money from my old job that came to me as one of the contingent beneficiaries of the estate of myself and my wife. While nice, it was also another financial motivation they would have thrown at me if I was being tried for killing my brother and wife. It would have been like getting away with divorce without having to give up all my stuff, except Callie's sister did get some of the money too. While I didn't begrudge her anything, I had no choice but to remain as Cash. *At least that's what I keep telling myself Cash, so I can sleep at night.*

That's another thing. Even though he's dead, I still have the same ongoing internal conversation with my brother that he and I have been having all our lives. We were so close in life, it's like his thoughts are imprinted in the part of my brain that supplies his voice. I don't know if that's scientific or not, but that's what it's like. In the world he's dead but not in my head. It's part of the reason I can't entertain the idea that he was having an affair with my wife. What would happen to our conversation if I were convinced that they were more than friends and confidants? I didn't want him to go quiet in my head. He's my twin brother.

Being Cash, I wasn't as stressed running a bar, and I always had someone to drink with. At first, drinking was tricky though. I had to make sure I didn't say anything that would make someone realize I wasn't Cash Cutler. I had to nod my way through a lot of conversations about things in Cash's life I wasn't there for, but it eventually got easy and natural. For all intents and purposes, I became Cash, and no one, other than Skylar, bothered to question why I was drinking so much. I had just lost my brother and sister-in-law. Drinking was the natural way dealing with grief – especially to those who frequent bars. New job, new peers, new life and new rules.

Skylar knew better though. I think she still liked me more than my brother, but she liked me more when I wasn't drinking or hung over. At the same time though, I was never really sure she actually *did* love me. She admitted she didn't love Cash when he was alive. She was originally only there to get him to sell the bar to the Mexicans so she could get her mother freed from the Indian casino where her mother was working as a house-cleaning slave to pay off her gambling debts to the Mexican loan sharks staked with the Indian casino's money.

We did save Skylar's mom Shelly, we technically sold the bar, but then we found we didn't sell it to the Mexicans. We actually sold it to the US Attorney for Western New York, who disappeared after it was discovered he ordered the deaths of my brother and my wife.

So, that's another thing I couldn't figure out. Why did the Mexicans sell back the half of the bar that Cash, my brother, had already sold to them? Why did the Mexicans walk away without coming for the money that Cash had stashed? He'd been talked into laundering money through one of their shell corps, but they were laundering so much money, he couldn't even declare the cash he was making at the bar as income. It was just too much income. No auditor would believe the bar had that large an increase in income. This was all in the letter he left for me under the stacks of cash in the attic. He was freaked out and felt like he was in way over his head.

In the letter he explained the Mexicans thought they could get away with it because they planned on turning it into a strip club so they could launder even more money – for this, they were employing the US Attorney Bennet Glazebrook. With his wife in the governor's office, he had enough dirt on just about anyone in Western New York to get the zoning for a strip club anywhere. But he disappeared, so it seems he wrote a check he couldn't cash.

Either way, the whole situation had me freaked out too. When I filed the taxes for the last year though, it was all taken care of through the shell corp, and they overpaid. I ended up getting a refund. Again, that was another concern. Why haven't those people come back for the money? Like a Pavlovian dog, thinking about it always made me want another beer. Think about it later.

Trying to explain that to Skylar only earned me a roll of the eyes. But then again, maybe I was testing her too. Maybe I just wanted to know if she'd still liked me when I was down and out. I wasn't down and out though. I was enjoying myself. Living the life of Cash, always the favorite. The boy with the golden arm. Bottom line, when I wasn't thinking, I was enjoying life more than I had in years. She had a different opinion. I *did* want to know if she'd fight for me though.

Chapter 2

The Cap was still punishing Ainsley Reed for her persistence on this go-nowhere story about some AWOL soldier claiming to having been framed for treason, something to do with the Oklahoma City Bombing. She hadn't been demoted to traffic detail yet, but he was always threatening.

Instead of fighting back, Ainsley was just taking his small feel-good assignments and doing her work like a good little soldier. In her spare time, she'd written the story of Jake Chambliss. While it might read as a classic tale of war and intrigue, it was 100% true, as far as she knew. She'd been investigating relentlessly.

That's why she got into journalism, to be an investigative reporter. Not to glad hand and smile at the locals during feel-good six o'clock news stories. But whatever. She'd set aside her passion for hard-hitting journalism to keep her job while she secretly worked on the story of her career.

Sure, she couldn't get Jake Chambliss out of her mind, but he was innocent, and this story upended everything we'd ever heard about how Tim McVeigh and Terry Nichols took down a federal building to kill children and get revenge for government overreach at Waco and Ruby Ridge. It was much bigger and darker than she could ever have imagined before meeting Jake Chambliss. Jake Charm, as they used to call him.

It was July, and that meant the Italian Fest on Buffalo's historic Hertel Avenue. It was here, in 1973, when four guys put together six thousand dollars to make "Mexican sandwiches" at what would later be called the first Mighty Taco. As legend was told, they had the North Buffalo Italian ladies come in and ask what they were. They'd tell them they were Mexican sandwiches. The ladies would politely thank them and leave. It wasn't until the late-night college crowd discovered the most delicious Mexican fast food ever invented that the Mighty One would take off. In 1973, few in Buffalo knew what a taco was, but the restaurant still thrives to this day, with locations all over Western New York.

Ainsley honestly didn't like Mighty Taco too much. She considered it better than Taco Bell, but she didn't like fast food enough to frequent the beloved spicy taco joint of Buffalo. She just knew the story because the Cap made her cover it recently. Yay, tell the story of a famous Buffalo taco joint and pretend it compared to the Anchor Bar's feat of being the first place to fry chicken wings and cover them with hot sauce and melted butter. In her eyes, that was world changing. Feeding drunk college and high school kids spicy tacos wasn't, even though she knew Jake and Cash had a whole different opinion. They considered Mighty Taco to be the Mighty ONE.

For this moment in July, the blocked streets in the Hertel Avenue district were for celebrating the Italian Culture.

"Oh, here honey," an old Italian lady moved in with a napkin to wipe a bit of sauce off Ainsley's face. Ainsley had just tried one of her homemade meatballs, and the lady didn't want her sauce to make Ainsley look like a slob on TV. The camera guy got it all.

With her red hair glistening in the sunlight, Ainsley thanked her with a beaming smile and said, "That was delicious," while shrugging her shoulders and shaking her head in disbelief and amazement that someone could make something so spectacular. She then named the restaurant, as the camera man panned out to show Ainsley in a lightly colored sundress holding a microphone. Using the microphone to direct the camera to take a look at all the nearby food booths, she said, "It's all delicious." The sun was on her fair skin. "The 2011 Italian Festival will be going until Sunday evening. Come out to Hertel Avenue and enjoy all the old world has to offer us. Admission is five dollars, children and seniors get in free. You won't regret it. I'm Ainsley Reed, Local News."

Cut.

Ainsley's smile disappeared the second the camera light went out.

Her camera guy Bill asked, "What's wrong with you lately?"

She thought about telling him the truth but didn't, "I'm hot. It's hot out here. I just want a drink and get back to the studio. Get this thing edited."

"So, you can work on your other story?"

Ainsley just gave him a stressed look and shook her head to tell him to drop it. Her battles with Cap weren't a secret by any means.

Bill didn't take the hint, "Well how's that going?" He was sympathetic to her plight and was eager to get his eyes on her story. But she held it tight and refused to talk much about it with anyone. Didn't know who she could trust and definitely knew she couldn't trust everyone around the office. The news business is cutthroat, especially for those who want to move up.

But she gave him a little anyway, "It's with my editor."

"Soon then?"

"I don't know. It's taking forever. Forget I mentioned it."

"Ok," Bill left it at that.

"Let's get back to the studio."

Bill took the footage to editing, while Ainsley went directly to her office. Happy to see Cap's door closed, she didn't have to hear about her next punishing assignment. Her voicemail was flashing, and she couldn't wait to find out if it were Nancy, her editor. The lady hadn't returned her call for three days, and it was Friday. She wanted an update before the weekend. Needed to know what to do. What was the next step?

Unfortunately, it was some computer voice calling about extending her warranty for her Prius. She'd gotten rid of the thing after someone had planted a bomb under the driver's side of the car. She was sure it was the FBI guys in charge of killing Jake, but the police didn't care to find out the truth. The police were told about the bomb that Jake found, got rid of it, held her car as evidence so long she had to buy a new one, and then finally gave it back to her so she could sell it. Ridiculous. She didn't want to drive it again anyway. Nor did she want to move back into the house where those agents kidnapped her and tried to rape her. She moved a little more north. Closer to Jake's hometown, but not too much farther from work. She was afraid she'd be cut out of the good news stories if she had to drive too far to get into Buffalo every time an emergency story required her to be on the scene. So, she moved to Campbell Boulevard, just north of her old street.

While she didn't think for a second those FBI agents couldn't find her if they needed to, she just didn't want to make it super easy. New car and new house. And with a ground-breaking book about to hit the streets, hopefully a new Ainsley.

But her editor wasn't calling her back. She'd hoped it was because she was out of town for a funeral or something, but that made Ainsley feel terrible. What kind of person hopes someone's relatives died so they had a good excuse not to call? Didn't change the fact Ainsley feared it was the editor's way of telling her this story is crap, it's going nowhere, and they said I couldn't publish it. She knew she was playing with fire and stepping on toes belonging to the big feet used to doing the stepping. But it was right.

She called Nancy again. The office number went right to voicemail, and so did her cell phone. She didn't leave a message.

Instead, she got a headache, took some Advil, put her head down and cried. Alone in her office, she thought she might get away with it.

On cue though, Sam the weatherman barged into her door. She wasn't sure, but when she lifted her face after wiping the tears, she thought she saw him hanging his tongue out like a dog. He *was* a dog, but, with his face for radio, it was all aspirational. That didn't curb his ambition and enthusiasm for harassing the fairer sex. Ainsley was just one of many who was forced to tolerate his incessant comments and insinuations, all in his own fantasyland belief it was getting him nearer to bedding women way out of his league. In his mind, he was Rico Suave, but he still had the scrawny body of a boy who'd suffered growth spurts without puberty.

"Hey Ainsley, awe, what's wrong?"

"Nothing Sam. What's up?"

"Your editor called?"

"She did? When?"

"No, not really. I was just trying to pick you up. You look sad. Do you need a little Vitamin Sam to fix your day?"

"Yeah, you know what, let's do it," Ainsley said, "when can you get out of here? We'll do it at my place."

"Really," his face lost that boyish goofiness and looked puzzled. Had the dog actually caught the car he was chasing?

"Yeah, we'll get a bottle of tequila and see where it takes us."

"I don't like tequila. Makes me puke. How about wine coolers or Zima?"

"You're such a girl Sam. Tequila or nothing. Man up."

"Alright, when do you want to do this?"

"Right now, Sam. I want your body *right* now. Let's go."

The puzzlement betrayed his bravado, "You're joking with me, right?"

"Of course, I am Sam. People'd see us and think I was dating someone who hadn't even reached puberty. Get out of here."

"That's low, even for you Ainsley Reed. I came in here with nothing but good intentions, and this is how you treat me. Look, I've reached puberty. I'll show you." He started to unbuckle his pants.

"Ewe, get out of here Sam."

"Well, just so you know, the offer still stands. Vitamin Sam cures all."

Ainsley stood up behind her desk with a look of disgust and rage before Sam weaseled his way out of her office.

She called Nancy's numbers again with the same results as earlier. Then she called Nancy's main office. The lady at the desk admitted they hadn't heard from her in two days. Thought it was personal business.

She couldn't take it any longer. After sticking her head out her door to check on Cap's door, she packed her things and left. For the most part, her day was done, and if anyone called her, she could say she had something to do. Really though, she just wanted to go home and take a bubble bath.

Unfortunately, the call to get her on a scene pronto came just as she'd pulled into her driveway to discover her front door had been kicked in.

She grabbed the Glock that Jake had given her back in January. It was kept under her seat in her new Honda CRV. She held it under her hands as she approached her house. As she opened the door, she lifted the gun as if she were a cop clearing a potential crime scene. Granted, she didn't have a permit for it, but after what she went through, she'd concluded it's better to ask forgiveness than die before getting permission. And there probably wasn't any way for her to register a gun stolen from a dead and disappeared casino security guard.

She entered her foyer and walked back to the kitchen. It looked normal. Her office was a different story. Her desk was a mess, and the stack of files on top of it was gone. It was the files and research she'd done on the Jake Chambliss and Oklahoma City Bombing story. Sure, it was all in her computer, but these were her files. On her desk was a note. They'd left it right where she'd place her laptop to write. "Leave it alone." That's all it said. What it lacked in eloquence, it made up for in brevity.

She checked the rest of the house. Nothing was noticeably amiss, so she left after securing the door as best she could. She had to get to some address in Williamsville. Some sort of news emergency, the gist of which she missed because of all the curse words that adorned it – Cap.

The address came in a text message, along with a couple more curse words.

Chapter 3

I'd been up for a little while. Still had a headache from the night before. A couple of old buddies stayed until about 4:30 drinking with me at the bar. Last call was 2 on a weeknight, but that didn't mean the afterparty had to end. Right?

Skylar was quiet on the couch doing a crossword or something in her book with the TV on. I'd eaten a roll and washed some aspirin down with a beer as I went up for a shower. Pacho the kitchen boy and Samantha were opening The Trough. I told Samantha I'd be in around 6:30 or 7.

While I was eating the dinner Skylar had made me, we were watching the 6 o'clock news. Ever since we'd met Ainsley a while back, we kind of made it a habit to watch her channel. See what she was up to. Didn't hear much from her, but we were fairly sure we would at some point.

She was reporting live from a murder scene. It was a circus, as all the local news organizations were waiting for the police to give up some of the details. Word so far was that the body had been there for a couple of days. Her home was only checked after a missing person notification had been filed.

"She looks stressed out," Skylar said.

"You're right," I admitted. The professional newsgirl look was gone, and instead, she looked like she was just getting dragged by her nose through the day by a grim reaper not allowed to release her soul until the strike of midnight. She looked like she blamed the unnamed victim for ruining her evening. That's cold. We couldn't take our eyes off her.

They went to another news story before cutting back to Ainsley. The camera was on Ainsley with the front porch of a nice house in Williamsville behind her. Police officers were on the porch, and they were trying to get the press away so they could remove the body and get on with their investigation. First though, the main cop had to release some details.

Ainsley spoke to the audience, "Officer Whitman is about to release the details to what has been described as a grisly murder scene. Here's Officer Whitman."

The camera focused in on his face as he spoke into a bouquet of microphones. He looked sober and confused by all the unwanted commotion behind him – other police officers and crime-scene investigators trying to take their positions and get their jobs done.

To quiet the questioning press in front of him, he used his lifted hands asking for a moment to make his statement. "Earlier today, a wellness check was made after a missing person's report. Investigators have found this missing person's body, but until the next of kin has been notified, the name of the victim will not be released. For now, I need you all to move back and give our investigators room to work."

Ainsley cut in when the officer walked away from the mics. "There you have it. A missing person was found dead. Hold on one second, I've just gotten word," Ainsley looked at her phone for additional information, "Oh my God, NO, Oh my God. She looked back at the camera with tears in her eyes. I am not sure if my sources are correct and will have to verify before I release this information." She used her head to tell the cameraman to stop filming. He just kept filming her teary face. She nodded her head again, but he was still taping, "This is Ainsley News, Local Reed. Ainsley Reed, Local News." She nodded her head with a look of disgust, "Cut. Cut Bill."

The news flashed to another story.

"Holy cow Cash," Skylar said, "she almost lost it on live TV."

"Huh," I sighed. I didn't have anything else I could say. I'd just seen her act like I'd been feeling a lot lately. Made me want another beer. I knew there was more to it and wasn't looking forward to finding out what.

I finished up, kissed Skylar and told her I'd wake her up when I got home.

"Great," she said. She didn't pretend to be sincere.

Chapter 4

I got into work about 6:35. There were some occupied tables and only two people at the bar. It was early.

A slick looking Italian guy, in a suit with the tie still tight at the top button and way overdressed for Pendleton, was chatting up Samantha at the front of the bar. Joe Popp, a regular, was watching the news on the TV above the liquor shelves.

Samantha was a sex slave that Jake saved from the casino six months earlier. She was close with Skylar's mom who talked me into giving her a job. It's worked out great though. She's drop-dead gorgeous, brings in a lot of guys and does her job without complaints. She's the dream employee.

After checking with Pacho in the kitchen, I took my spot behind the bar. Joe immediately told me that our friend Ainsley from the news lost it at a crime scene on the local news.

"I saw it," I said.

"What's that all about?"

"I have no idea Joe. Wondered that myself?"

"You gonna call her and make sure she's alright?"

"Doubt it. She'll reach out if she needs us. Until then, I figure we ought to give her space."

"She's your friend though, isn't she?"

"In a different time and circumstance, maybe. But there's a lot of things all of us would like to just get past."

"Yeah, sorry about that Cash. I didn't mean to pry."

"Don't sweat it Joe. Here, have another." I popped the top of another Labatt's for him.

I turned around and saw a pause in Samantha's conversation with slick dark and handsome. "Hi Sam."

"Hi cutie." She pinched my ribs hello.

Joe called me in with his finger once Sam had gotten back with the customer. "What's going on with you and Sam?" He asked as if he'd just seen something he shouldn't have.

"Nothing Joe. I'm still with Skylar. Sam's just being flirty. Gets her bigger tips."

"Oh, too bad. She's pretty."

"No Joe, not too bad. Skylar's beautiful too."

"Yeah, well, you know."

"No, I don't know Joe. Drink your beer and think nothing of it."

"Ok, sorry Cash. It's the beer talking."

"Don't sweat it."

Pacho called order up. Samantha slung her towel over her shoulder and excused herself from her conversation to go get it. I stopped her, "Don't worry. I got it."

I took two taco platters from the kitchen to a table and asked them if they needed more drinks. Instead, they had me get them some of the special hot sauce and jalapeños. I delivered them, and as I was going back behind the bar again, Skylar walked in through the back door.

"Hey baby, what's up?"

"Nothing," she said, "it's Friday night, and I want to be with my man. I'm drinking with *you* tonight."

"Sounds good," I said. And it did. Misery loves company, and that would mean I wouldn't have to feel shame if I came home all drunk. Having her by my side was less stressful.

She took a seat at the bar and asked me for a Molson Canadian. I reached down below to pull it out of the fridge, and as I was coming up with her beer, she went white. She picked up a menu and covered her face with it. Nothing more obvious than the old cover-your-face-with-a-menu-to-stay-inconspicuous.

"What is it?"

"Nothing. I'll tell you later. I have to go." Then she reached across the bar as if to kiss me goodnight but whispered into my ear. "Make sure Samantha doesn't go home

337

with that guy. Protect her at all costs. I'll tell you everything later. Right now, I've got to get out of here."

"Ok. Love you."

"Love you too." She got up and left through the door she came in.

Well, that didn't work. I was thinking we were in for a good night of drinking and merriment. Instead, she left me with the job of protecting Samantha from slick, dark and gruesome.

As I started drinking the Molson Skylar didn't stay to drink, Joe asked me, "What's that all about."

"No idea. I'll find out later."

"Women," Joe said.

"Yep," I agreed.

Joe had a wife back home, but I only knew her from his stories. He didn't bring her to the bar. So, rather than worrying about all my problems, I sat and talked with Joe for a while. Really, I was just listening to him. He had a lot to say and listening to him meant I didn't have to answer any of his prying questions.

It remained a slow night. At a little after 8:00, I popped the top on my third Molson Canadian. They were going down nicely. Promised myself I'd slow down though. I knew Skylar would be loaded for bear about this Italian guy. The way that conversation was going, Samantha was looking at a big tip, probably wrapped around the guy's business card. She never gives her phone number to guys at the bar. She doesn't like stalkers. Knowing where she came from, I didn't blame her.

Either way, she knew how to earn her tips when a guy who wasn't a regular took an interest in her. She had a talent. Come to think of it though, I hadn't seen or heard about her dating anyone since she'd been freed from the casino. Maybe she was holding out for Jake. Maybe she just had a trust issue with men. I imagined it was both of those things, but probably a little more of the latter. She and Skylar do the girl-talk thing often, but I'm rarely privy to that. You'd think they were sisters sometimes, the way they get along. Doesn't hurt that it was Skylar's mom who took Samantha under her wing and was letting her share her apartment.

Shelly was nice too. Living with her daughter, I'd gotten to know her well. She completely erased that image I had of her initially, that of an indebted gambling addict. Sure, she was addicted to gambling but she's learned her lesson, undoubtedly. She never went to the casinos anymore. Believe me, the casinos have been terrible for a lot of people around here. Ever since they started allowing the Indians to run the casinos, lives and families have been destroyed. Little old women blowing their social security checks in one or two nights on a regular basis. Say all you want about the gambling scolds, but what they say is true. Gambling can ruin anyone without self-control. If you're going to ruin your life, do it in a bar – at least you'll still have money to eat.

In any case, after being denied at least five times that I heard, our Italian gentleman decided to look for greener pastures. He did leave his card and a promise that he'd come back and bug her again if she didn't call him.

As soon as the door had shut behind him, she looked at me with some wide eyes and a smile divided by the crisp hundred-dollar bill she held in front of her nose. Then she said, "Stalker Gino thinks he can buy me for a hundred dollars. What a loser."

She threw his card in the garbage.

"Maybe that's why Skylar didn't like him."

"Skylar knows him?"

"I guess," I said, "that's why she left so quickly. Saw him, said she had to leave and that I had to make sure you don't buy whatever he's selling."

"No problem there. He's just a player."

"At least he gave us hundred bucks," I said pretending I was going to be sharing in her fortune.

"What do you mean we Kemosabe?"

"Oh, that's not part of the communal tip jar?"

"Heck no boss man. I'm the one that had to put up with him."

"I know, I'm just messing with you. Good job by the way. He probably undertipped you, what with all that flirting you had to do."

"Yeah, right, I'll mention that when he comes back."

"You think he's coming back?" I asked in disbelief.

"Of course, he will. Probably twice in the next week. He's not used to being turned down and doesn't like it. You'll see. Turning him down made him want me more. More tips coming."

"Good for you, I guess, but Skylar does *not* like that guy."

"I look forward to hearing why," Samantha said as she shrugged and started wiping the front bar where Gino had been sitting.

While she wasn't looking, I grabbed the card out of the garbage and put it in my pocket to show Skylar later.

339

The back door opened, and to my surprise, Ainsley Reed walked in. She looked flustered to begin with, but then she stopped the moment she and Samantha made eye contact.

"What's she doing her?" Samantha asked me.

"I don't know," I said quietly so only she could hear and then raised my voice to make it across the bar, "What's up Ainsley? Long time no see."

"Thank God you're here Cash."

"Does this have anything to do with what made you freeze on the TV tonight?"

"Oh, you saw that?" She shook it off and continued, "That was embarrassing, but to answer your question, yes."

"What is it.?"

"The person murdered at that house was my editor, and I think she was murdered because of my book on Jake."

"My gosh, that's terrible. Why do you think that?"

"Right before I went over there, I found my front door kicked in, and they stole my files on Jake. They left me this note."

She pulled a piece of paper from her purse and brought it over to the bar. It said, "Leave it alone." I read it out loud.

"Can I get a beer?" Ainsley asked, "Labatt's?"

Samantha pulled one from the fridge, popped the top and set it in front of her on a napkin. Professional. I was thankful.

"Thanks Samantha. I'm glad to see you're well."

"Thanks." Samantha backed away so I could talk with her.

"Have you called the police?"

"No. As soon as I could get away from work, I came here. Here, I've got something for you." She pulled a flash drive out of her purse. "This is a copy of my book and some of my files. Can you keep this in your safe?"

"Sure thing." I took it and put it in my pocket.

"Please don't lose that."

"Of course not. Can I read it?"

340

"Absolutely. Just keep it safe in case they get everything." After a pause she asked, "What if they don't stop?"

"Does Jake know about this?"

"No, she said."

"You heard from Jake?" Samantha might have backed away, but she was listening to the conversation.

"Not a word since he left."

"Well," I stepped back in, "Don't you think this is something he should know about?"

"Yeah, I don't know, maybe. I don't want to get him in trouble. If those guys are back, that's just what they'd want. Right?"

"Yeah, maybe, but don't you think Jake should make that decision?" That was me wanting Jake to be here for this. I didn't know if I were going to able to handle this without him, and I sure as heck knew Ainsley would need my help.

"Again, maybe, but what if this is what gets him killed? I don't want to bring him home to be put in the hands of those monsters."

"How do you know it's them?"

"Who else would do this? It's either them or John Doe Number Two, and I doubt that guy knows anything of what I've been up to."

"Probably right."

"Where are you staying tonight?"

"Home, I imagine. Why?"

"Well, you have no front door. You can't stay there."

"I can't just leave my home open either."

"Ok. I'll go and fix it up for you."

"Replace the door?"

"Not tonight, no. But we can probably rig it up, so it won't open. Then maybe you should stay at my house tonight. Skylar would love it."

She smiled at me, "You living with Skylar now?"

"Ever since... the troubles."

"That's good."

"Yeah, it has been. Thanks. Let me call her."

"Skylar."

"Hey Cash. Gino leave yet?"

"Yes."

"You want me to come over now?"

"Yes, but I need you to help Sam with the bar. Ainsley's here."

"Really?"

"Yes, bad things are happening. Someone broke into her house. I'm going over there to fix her door. She's staying with us tonight."

"We still going to drink tonight?"

"You know what, yeah. Hey Ainsley, Skylar wants to drink tonight. You in?"

She thought for a second, "I could use that. Sounds good."

"Then it's settled. I'm bringing Ainsley home now. Get some tools and some wood."

"See you soon baby," Skylar said.

"When I get back. You'll be at the bar, remember."

"That's when I mean. Won't take you long to fix her door."

'Shouldn't. See you soon."

Click.

"Let's go fix your door Ainsley."

Made in the USA
Middletown, DE
30 April 2021

38119534R00190